RAVE REVIEWS FOR DEBRA DIER!

"An exciting and action-packed adventure. . . . Once again, Debra Dier proves that she is a sparkling jewel in the romantic adventure world of books."

—*Affaire de Coeur* on *Deceptions & Dreams*

"Deceptions and Dreams is tightly plotted with plenty of well-developed characters. . . . Ms. Dier's writing is skillful and sure, painting with words a story filled with passion, adventure, and emotion."

—*Rendezvous*

"Captivating from beginning to end . . . a stunningly beautiful and evocative love story brimming with action, adventure, and a touch of fantasy. Steamy and lush as the Amazon jungle, *A Quest of Dreams* will grab your heart and won't let go."

—Kathleen Morgan, author of *Firestar*

"A steamy romantic romp with just the right touch of fantasy. A treat for Debra Dier fans!"

—Bobbi Smith, author of *Half-Breed's Lady*
on *A Quest of Dreams*

THE CRITICS LOVE DEBRA DIER!

Ms. Dier, with deft turn of phrase and insight into human nature, wrings an emotionally charged tale from her characters which engages both the interest and empathy of her readers!"

—*The Literary Times* on *Saint's Temptation*

"Debra Dier will keep you turning the pages in this entertaining, fast-paced tale . . . it both charms and delights with a little mystery, passion and even a bit of humor."

—*Romantic Times* on *Devil's Honor*

"The talented Ms. Dier captures the English/Scottish animosity to perfection and weaves an exhilarating tale that will touch your heart and fire the emotions. Great reading!"

—*Rendezvous* on *MacLaren's Bride*

Lord Savage is "exhilarating and fascinating!"

—*Affaire de Coeur*

"Debra Dier pens a delightfully original romance. *Scoundrel* is an enchanting book to treasure."

—*Romantic Times*

A MIRACLE

The question fluttered through the haze in her mind. "You know me. You've always known me," she whispered, her own words surprising her with the truth they held. She felt she had known this man since the beginning of time and beyond.

He slid his tongue down her neck. She quivered in response, her entire body coming alive beneath his touch. "What are you doing here, Julia?"

"Holding you," she whispered, sliding her fingers through his thick hair. She hadn't realized just how much she had longed to have her arms around him, until this moment. "I can't believe I'm really holding you."

He tightened his arms around her, holding her close against the solid strength of his body. A sigh fluttered past her lips as he opened his mouth against the curve of her neck and shoulder. "What brought you here?"

"A miracle," she whispered.

Other *Leisure* and *Love Spell* books by Debra Dier:
SAINT'S TEMPTATION
DEVIL'S HONOR
MacLAREN'S BRIDE
LORD SAVAGE
SCOUNDREL
THE SORCERER'S LADY
DECEPTIONS & DREAMS
A QUEST OF DREAMS
SHADOW OF THE STORM
SURRENDER THE DREAM

BEYOND Forever

DEBRA DIER

LEISURE BOOKS NEW YORK CITY

A LEISURE BOOK®

November 1999

Published by

Dorchester Publishing Co., Inc.
276 Fifth Avenue
New York, NY 10001

ISBN 0-8439-4623-7

Printed in the United States of America.

For my mother who helped make this book possible with hours of baby play. And for the friends and family who gave Sarah her first parties: Jan, Joyce, and Patty; Carol, Bill, and Ellen; Georgia, Junie, Linda, and Mary Kay. Thanks for helping to celebrate the arrival of our darling Sarah.

BEYOND
Forever

Chapter One

Our birth is but a sleep and a forgetting:
The Soul that rises with us, our life's Star,
Hath had elsewhere its setting,
And cometh from afar:
Not in entire forgetfulness,
And not in utter nakedness,
But trailing clouds of glory do we come . . .
—William Wordsworth

You're the one, Julia.

The masculine whisper rippled through Julia Fairfield, tingling her skin as though she'd been touched by a warm breath. She glanced over her shoulder, her heart hammering. From the edge of the cliff where she sat the ground sloped down to a wide expanse of open field before reaching a dark stretch of woodlands. To the west the rugged slopes of Ben Cuimhne rose like a great beast awakening in the moonlight. No one was in sight. Nothing stood near, except an ancient oak stationed like a lone sentinel on the edge of the cliffs.

"Jet lag," she whispered, shaking her head. She stood and stretched, easing the tension from her shoulders.

Mist swirled in from the sea, climbing the rocky cliffs until it curled around her feet like an affectionate feline. Filmy strands of mist entwined the branches of an oak, silken veils abandoned to the breeze. In the distance to the northeast, gray stones rose, forming a rugged structure at the edge of the cliffs. Countless spires, turrets, and towers reached upward toward the full face of the moon. Mist swirled in from the sea, curling around the base of the castle, severing its ties to earth.

Dunmore Castle didn't merely look like something from another century. It looked as though it came from another world, where magic ruled the realm. The story of Brigadoon came to mind. Julia could easily believe Dunmore appeared for only one day every hundred years. So why did it seem so familiar?

Although she had accompanied her grandmother on trips to visit her friend Helen Bainbridge in the past, they had always stayed at Helen's estate in Devonshire. This year Helen had invited Julia and her grandmother and niece to spend the summer with her at Dunmore. From the first moment Julia had seen the castle this afternoon, she hadn't been able to shake an odd sense of déjà vu.

She frowned, taking note of how far she had walked from the castle. The mist had already started swirling over the path she had taken along the clifftop. Even though the path was rough, littered with stones and clumps of grass, the hike had been lovely—moonlight glinting on the rippling dark waves, cool air kissed with salt brushing her face—a treat from the summer heat of Illinois. The hike was exactly what she had needed to ease the tension in limbs that had spent too much time confined in an airplane, a train, a taxi, and, finally, a boat. Getting to the Isle of Mist off the coast of Scotland had required nearly every form of transportation available to man.

She hadn't really intended to stay on the cliff quite this long. Her gaze plunged two hundred feet to the shoreline, where rugged masses of rock peeked through a shifting field of vapor. The clash of water pounding the rocks carried on the mist, bringing the sound of the waves so close that they seemed to crash against her.

Her throat tightened when she thought of the hike back. More than once she had nearly tripped on a clump of grass, and that was when she could see the ground below her feet. She should have paid closer attention to the incoming fog.

"You can't go back that way. It's too treacherous."

Julia nearly choked on her breath. She pivoted in the direction of that deep, masculine voice. At first she thought her mind was playing tricks with her again. No one was there. Moonlight shimmered on the mist, a glimmering column piercing the filmy veil. Then the gossamer strands swirled, as though caught in a slow exhalation of breath. Moonlight shifted with the mist, a shimmering spotlight on a darkened stage. Pale vapor parted, filmy curtains drawing away as a man materialized from the mist.

Julia stared transfixed, unable to move in spite of a small voice shouting in her brain *Run!* She was not a child. She was not frightened, she told herself, though the gooseflesh rising on her arms disputed that fact.

He moved closer, the moonlight revealing his features. Dark hair deeper than the richest coffee fell in undisciplined waves to the white fabric covering his broad shoulders. Eyes as dark and endless as a midnight sky regarded her with a hint of mischief, a blatantly male look that kicked her blood into a mad dash through her veins. He wasn't merely handsome. The word was far too simple for the complexity of his appeal.

Arrogance sculpted the high blades of his cheekbones, the slim straight line of his nose, the full curve of his lips. The intriguing arrogance of a man who shaped his own world. The mist glowed around him, as if radiating the power of this man. A soft scent of leather and sandalwood teased her senses as he paused before her, so close she could have touched his cheek. She didn't, even though she wanted so very much to touch him. She certainly did not go around caressing the faces of strangers. Still, she couldn't shake the feeling that she knew this man. She felt that truth reach deep into her soul. Yet reason told her that she had never in her life met him before.

"You'll get yourself killed if you're not careful."

His words were colored with a deep Scottish burr. Not so thick and slurred that she had trouble understanding, as she had with several people at the train station, but a soft lilt that could make a recitation of the telephone directory as fascinating as Shakespeare. Recollection nibbled at the corner of her mind, like a distant, half-remembered memory trying to work its way out of the shadows. Why did he seem so familiar?

He tilted his head, thick dark brows lifting over his stunning eyes. "Did you fall, lass? Bump your head?"

It was then that she realized she was staring. With her mouth open. She snapped her mouth closed, then realized she needed to reply. "No. I'm fine. Perfectly fine."

He frowned. "You'll be perfectly dead if you keep running about like a goose without a head. One misstep and you'll be explaining to St. Pete why he should be allowing hen-witted females to be entering the pearly gates."

Julia stiffened. "Hen-witted females?"

"Aye. That's fair enough, considering where you're standing."

He grinned, and she nearly forgot her anger. Nearly. "I didn't realize the fog was coming in."

"At this time of night the cliff walk isn't safe. Even without the fog."

"I needed to stretch my legs. I didn't realize the fog would be coming in. I was just thinking I might . . ." She paused, angry at her own ridiculous need to explain herself to this arrogant stranger. He might be one of the most attractive men she had ever met, but she didn't need to explain her behavior to this man, to any man, hadn't needed to for a very long time. "This really isn't any of your concern."

He shrugged, white cloth crinkling over broad shoulders. "Appears as though it is. Someone has to make sure you don't get yourself killed."

"I can take care of myself." Julia pivoted and started back the way she had come, only to halt a few feet away, when the path disappeared beneath a carpet of mist. Filmy strands of vapor curled around her knees and stretched out toward the ocean, the crashing waves hidden now beneath a blanket of fog drenched in moonlight.

"Does your stubborn streak often get you into trouble?"

Julia could hear the roguish, all too self-assured grin in his deep baritone. She closed her eyes and counted to ten before turning to face the rogue. He stood leaning his shoulder against the oak, twirling a sprig of clover in his fingers, mist curling around his close-fitting knee-high black boots. She shouldn't have noticed the way his black breeches molded the powerful lines of his legs, but she did. The breeze ruffled the sleeves of his white shirt. The garment looked like something out of an old movie, a shirt Errol Flynn might have worn while playing a dashing pirate—loose-fitting, falling open at the neck, revealing a dark wedge of skin and hair. Once again a slow simmer started low in her belly and spiraled outward, heating every inch of her skin. "Does your arrogance often get you into arguments?"

He laughed, a dark rumble that tempted her own lips into a smile. "There's a path through the woodlands that leads right to the front drive of Dunmore. If you can manage to admit you need some help, I'll see you home."

She glanced toward the thick stand of trees spreading out from the border of the field. Fingers of fog were already spreading outward across the clover. Her chances of finding her way through that small forest without him were slim at best. She could risk spending a cold and damp, thoroughly miserable night lost in the woods, or follow this inexplicably familiar stranger.

Without waiting for her reply, he turned and headed toward the woods. "Come along. If we hurry, we can get you back to Dunmore before the island is lost to the mist."

She stared at his broad back, good sense warring with

her desire to show the rogue she could do fine without him. Apparently he thought she would just go trailing after him, like some grateful puppy. From the looks of him, she suspected that more than a few women trailed after this man. The sound of waves crashing against the rocks below shivered through her.

He paused and turned back to fix her in a steady gaze. "If you're frightened to be alone with me . . ."

She stiffened. "I'm not frightened of you."

"I'm glad of that. I promise I'll see you back to Dunmore safe and sound, Miss Fairfield."

"How did you know my name?"

"The Isle of Mist isn't a big place. The whole village of Dunmore knows that three Americans arrived late this afternoon to spend the summer with Mrs. Bainbridge at Dunmore."

"So, you're from the village." Had he been hiking all the way out here? The village was a good ten miles from Dunmore, on the far side of the mountain.

"As much as I would enjoy continuing this delightful conversation, I think it best if we get started. I for one don't plan to be sleeping in the woods tonight." He turned and strolled down a gentle slope leading to a wide field that skirted the woodlands, leaving Julia with a choice.

She cast one last glance along the foggy cliffs, then hurried to catch up with her arrogant guide. She fell into step beside him, matching his long-limbed stride. He didn't spare her a glance. Using her own five-feet-seven-and-a-quarter inches as a guide, she judged he was a couple of inches over six feet tall. Not extraordinarily tall. Still, he gave subtle subtext to the simple word *commanding*. "If the cliff walk is so dangerous at this hour, what were you doing on it?"

He cast her a grin. "I saw you and thought someone needed to rescue you."

Julia shoved a damp lock of hair back from her face. She didn't need a mirror to know the thick, shoulder-length strands were curling into a frizzy mess. It shouldn't bother her to know she looked dreadful, but it did. The fact that she cared added more fuel to her anger. "I really didn't intend to walk back along the cliffs in the fog."

His dark brows slid upward. "Didn't you?"

"I was going to head off in this direction, before you showed up and made me so angry that I couldn't see straight."

Moonlight caught the mischief in his dark eyes. "Is that what I did? And here I thought I was only offering to help keep you safe."

In spite of her anger, and her humiliation at being caught in such a foolish and possibly dangerous situation, she managed a smile. "I assure you, I'm quite capable of taking care of . . ." Her words ended in a gasp as she tripped over a stone hidden beneath the swirling carpet of mist. Even with her hiking boots, her toes stung from the impact. She caught herself before she fell, staggering a step before gaining control of her balance.

He stood a few feet in front of her, grinning. "Be careful. The field is littered with stones."

She shot him a sarcastic smile, gritting her teeth against the sting in her battered toes. "Thank you for telling me."

He inclined his head in a small bow. "At your service, milady."

She fell in behind him, deciding it was safer to use

him as a guide across the minefield than try to walk beside him. The scent of crushed clover drifted on the mist swirling around them. The pale vapor glimmered in the moonlight, lending an odd preternatural glow to everything it touched, including the man walking ahead of her.

Larger than life. It was a term often attributed to fictional characters, but in his case it fit. He was tall and broad shouldered, each movement filled with a patently male brand of confidence, the kind that led men into battle and women into reckless choices. He moved at a steady pace, as though he knew where every stone lay hidden. She suspected he would be just as sure of himself in a boardroom on Madison Avenue as he would in a field in Scotland.

Who was he? In spite of her best efforts to ignore her curiosity, she wanted to know all about him. What did he do for a living on this small island? Where did he live? Was he married? She silently chastised herself for heading down that path. She didn't care if he was married.

He certainly wasn't the type of man she wanted in her life. He was the type of man who could control a woman. She would end up trying to be everything he wanted and failing. She would not contemplate that path. No sir, she would not. She had taken a few steps down that path before. She would never do it again. Now if she could just gain control of the foolish racing of her heart, she would be just fine.

Still, she couldn't control her erratic pulse any more than she could quell the wayward flutter in her stomach. She stared at him, fascinated by the shift of muscles beneath cloth. He didn't seem to mind the cool, damp air that made her glad she had worn her navy windbreaker this evening. Still, she suspected he was the type of male who would never admit his susceptibility to something as mundane as the weather.

There was something about him, something aside from the obvious male magnetism and her unfortunate female response. For some reason she could not banish the strange sensation of familiarity. Why did she feel as though she knew him? She was certain she had never met him before. She would not have forgotten him. She shook her head. No doubt she had spent far too many late nights watching the exploits of a tall, dark, and devastating Scotsman on television.

They hiked for more than a mile in silence across the field before turning into the woodlands. Wood chips muffled their footsteps here. The path had been carved out of the wilderness by the Dunmore gardeners. Moonlight filtered through the leaves overhead, illuminating their way.

"Do you often hike on Dunmore property?" she asked, resuming a place beside him.

"Aye. It brings me peace to walk the land."

Moonlight pierced the darkness, a shimmering column of silver spilling over his face. The wistful look in his eyes made her wonder why this place should be so special to him. Perhaps he was one of the servants. It wasn't unusual for the servants of large estates to have worked on the same one for generations. Still, there was something regal in his carriage, an overwhelming air of command that made her doubt that he had ever served anyone. "It's a long way from the village. Did you drive?"

"No. I didn't." He grinned in a way that made her

think he was enjoying a private joke. At her expense. "Tell me, why is it there are no gentlemen accompanying three ladies from America?"

Was this his subtle way of finding out if she was married? She tried to crush the sudden surge of excitement gripping her vitals. "My grandfather died several years ago, and my niece lost her parents five years ago." On the same night and in the same accident that had taken Julia's parents.

"Have you become your niece's guardian?"

Julia drew in a deep breath, tasting the faint salty spice of the mist. "Yes."

"And you aren't married?"

She kept her gaze on the path, hoping to hide her expression. He was curious about her, that's all. There certainly was no reason to believe he had any interest in her. "No. I'm not."

"You manage to take care of your niece and your grandmother without any man to help you?"

She looked up into the endless beauty of his dark eyes. "We manage quite well without a man."

"I see." He grinned at her. "Independent."

"Yes." Very independent, she assured herself. At least she tried to be. She had been taking care of herself, Lauren, and Angela for five years, without any help from anyone. They stepped from the woods onto the wide expanse of the front lawn of Dunmore Castle. Mist swirled around them as they walked toward the huge manse.

He paused on the gravel drive leading to the house. Light poured from several windows on the ground floor, providing golden beacons in the gathering mist. "As I promised. Safe and sound."

She glanced up at him, searching for something terribly sophisticated and cutting to say. She settled for, "Thank you, Mr. . . ." She hesitated, realizing she didn't even know his name.

"MacKinnon. Gavin MacKinnon."

The name swirled through her memory. "Thank you, Mr. MacKinnon."

"It was my pleasure." He smiled, a warm and generous curve of sensual lips. She finally understood how someone's knees could go weak. Hers suddenly felt like overcooked spaghetti. "Good night, Julia."

The soft whisper of her name did something altogether wicked to her vitals. She stood on the drive, watching him, wanting to deny an attraction that played like Chopin through her veins. The fog swirled around him, until mist and man seemed to dissolve one into the other. She blinked at the trick of the moonlight. She stared at the place where he had disappeared trying to shake off the odd sense of loss coiling around her. For some strange reason she wanted to run after him.

"Easy," she whispered as she headed for the house. She might be guilty of being shamefully romantic—the two unpublished manuscripts sitting under her bed at home were testament to that affliction. Her fellow English professors at Chamberlain College would shudder in horror if they ever discovered that their colleague hoped one day to see her romance novels in print. Still, she had only been reckless once in her relationships with the opposite sex. It was a lesson she would never forget.

Gravel crunched beneath her boots. What did she know of Gavin MacKinnon? Nothing. True, he could send her heart racing. And yes, she had never in her life felt such an instant connection to another person. But she might never see him again. She squeezed her hands into tight balls, hating the sudden sinking feeling that gripped her stomach.

She certainly would not go running around the island looking for him. That would be careless. Reckless. She was not reckless. She examined all sides of an issue before voting. She read consumer magazines, checked out Web sites, did her research before making major purchases. She was not going to jump into anything. She glanced over her shoulder at the place where he had disappeared. Where did he live? What would be the best way to find him again? She fought a completely insane impulse to run into the mist, searching for him.

She turned and marched up the wide stone steps. She was behaving with all the hormonal angst of a fifteen-year-old with her first infatuation. This just wasn't normal. Not for her. Although she appreciated male beauty, she certainly would not allow a handsome face and splendid body to sway her intellect.

She had never been one of those women who flitted from one relationship to the next. Although she had been an outgoing little girl, school had altered her. It had started in third grade, when she was the tallest child in her class. Children could be cruel to anyone who stuck out from the crowd, and she stuck out like the Jolly Green Giant. By the time she reached high school she had taken refuge with the other outcasts, the kids who were too smart and too nerdy to be cool. Her mother had been fond of saying, "Julia you're too pretty and too smart. If you were dumb and pretty the boys would be brave enough to ask you out. But smart and pretty, now that combination will take a truly brave young man. Don't worry. One day you'll find him."

She managed to reach her second year of grad school

without ever having a serious relationship. While her social life had remained stunted, her inner life had flourished. Romance novels were her escape from reality, her promise of a happy ending. She had penned her first story when she was a junior in college. And then she had met Nathan.

Nathan Riley had plowed his way through the tangle of defenses she had built up over the years. After three months of dating he had decided they would get married. And she hadn't disagreed with him. Deep in her heart she knew she didn't love him, but Nathan was the stereotype of every woman's dream—handsome, wealthy, head of his class in law school, and destined for greatness. How could she possibly think of not accepting his offer of marriage? Still, she hadn't been able to quell the doubts, the queasy feeling that had gripped her stomach far too often, the sense she was selling herself short, living a dream of his fashioning, not her own. But each time she pulled away from Nathan, he found a way to draw her back into his sphere of control.

Nathan had been so certain of what he wanted from life. He kept a list and checked off each item as he managed to acquire it. He had penciled Julia in as his wife. Apparently she had fit his criteria perfectly—a female he could twist and shape until she fit his ideal. Nathan immediately started the process of molding her into his image of the perfect wife. When she looked back on it, she was amazed that she had ever fallen for his brand of male dominance. Of course, Nathan had been a master of manipulation, and she had been so damn vulnerable. She would never allow herself that kind of vulnerability again.

Fortunately her parents had recognized what was

happening to their daughter. With their emotional support, Julia had regained her wits before she made a horrible mistake. But none of them had realized that saving Julia would cause so much tragedy. She only wished to God she had never planned that wedding in the first place.

Still, in spite of it all, she remained hopeful. One of these days she would meet the man destiny meant for her. She knew it. This time she wouldn't think of settling for anything less than a love so complete she could never in her life imagine being with another man. She owed it to the memory of her parents to wait for the right man. She owed it to herself.

The soft thump of the front door closing behind her echoed through the huge entry hall. Her feet crossed alternating squares of black and white marble as she traversed the hall. She stripped off her jacket and hung it in a closet that had been built behind one of the wall panels before she headed for the drawing room, where she had left her grandmother and Helen. She had tucked Lauren into bed shortly before she took her solitary walk.

The scent of lemon oil drifted from the polished mahogany wainscoting where artificial flames flickered behind crystal and brass wall sconces. Julia halted in the middle of the hall, an odd sensation seizing her. She suddenly felt unsure of herself, as though she were wandering around in a half-remembered dream, as though she had something important to do but couldn't remember what.

In some distant, hazy part of her brain, she became aware of subtle changes around her. The candles glowing against polished wood no longer flickered with the predictable pulse of electric current, but with the dancing red-gold flame of fire trapped behind crystal. She stared at the wide mahogany staircase that rose from one end of the hall, her heart pounding. She felt disconnected, as though she stood outside of her body watching the world from a distance.

Through the haze fogging her mind a figure took shape at the base of the stairs, a lovely woman with dark hair and a warm, welcoming smile. *It's so good to see you again.* The image vanished as quickly as it had appeared. Julia remained fixed in the hall, until the clang of a tall case clock sounded the hour. She jumped at the soft burnished sound of the chimes. Chills scattered across her arms.

She had never been here before today. Why did it all seem so familiar? Why was she having glimpses of memories she could not possibly have made? She suddenly didn't want to be alone.

Chapter Two

They that love beyond the world cannot be separated by it.
Death cannot kill what never dies.

—William Penn

Julia hurried down the corridor leading to the green drawing room. She found Angela and Helen where she had left them hours earlier. Here emerald silk damask draped the long diamond-shaped panes of the windows, shutting out the moonlight. Figured mint-green silk wall coverings flowed from the high plastered ceiling to the polished mahogany wainscoting.

The ladies sat on a camelback sofa in front of a large mahogany framed fireplace. Helen and Angela were still chatting in the all-consuming way of close friends who haven't seen each other face to face for several years. The friendship between Helen and Angela had started when they were children at boarding school and had continued for more than sixty years.

After greeting the ladies, Julia served herself hot chocolate from a tea cart that stood beside the sofa and sank into a wing-back armchair near the hearth. Even though it was early June, she was grateful for the log burning in the fireplace. She felt cold from more than the damp chill of evening.

"Angela was just telling me that you have finished another one of your manuscripts," Helen said. "I would love to read them."

Julia crinkled her nose. Gram was always touting Julia's stories. It was a pity she didn't have as much confidence in them as her grandmother did. "They really aren't good enough for public consumption."

Behind the oval lenses of her black-rimmed glasses, the corners of Helen's blue eyes crinkled with her warm smile. She never bothered with coloring her hair. She wore the curly gray and brown mass twisted up in a bun. At seventy-four, she still walked three miles every morning, and often rode one of the Thoroughbreds she raised. She not only sat on the board of directors for the bank her great-great-grandfather had started, she also contributed articles to the National Historical Society's magazine, and worked with several charities. Short and slim, she had a preference for slacks, like the gray tweeds she was wearing, and a supply of energy that could put a ten-year-old to shame. "I would wager it's common for writers to doubt the merit of their work."

"I keep telling her that she has to mail her manuscripts off to a publisher." Angela nibbled a chocolate cookie. At one time the honey-blond shade of her hair had been as natural as Julia's. Now a stylist kept the shoulder-length waves perfectly tinted. Angela had no intention of allowing the years to win without a fight. Although she insisted she was five foot five, she was closer to five foot three in her stocking feet. With a rounded figure that betrayed her passion for sweets and pastries, she looked even shorter. "I think her books would make wonderful movies."

"Thank you, Gram. But they just aren't good enough. Not yet."

Angela shook her head. "All you need is confidence."

"You know, Julia, I think you might find some wonderful inspiration here at Dunmore."

"I hope so." English literature and history had always fascinated Julia. The architecture of Dunmore alone would keep her interested for weeks. Fortunately, Helen shared Julia's love of history. She had given them a quick tour of this wing soon after they'd arrived that afternoon, but Julia was looking forward to weeks of exploration.

"Tomorrow, if you like, we can start with the library," Helen said. "I think you'll find some of the journals interesting. It's a wonderful way to touch the lives of people who have lived in another time."

"I would enjoy that." Still, there was a man of this time Julia would like to know first. An image of Gavin MacKinnon blossomed in her mind, bringing a tingling excitement. Would Helen know him? "I met a man on the cliff walk this evening."

"The cliff walk?" Helen settled her cup on her saucer. "I didn't realize you had taken the cliff walk. I should have warned you that it can become quite dangerous if the fog rolls in. And it usually does roll in."

"Thank heavens you didn't get stranded in it," Angela said.

"I did. But Mr. MacKinnon brought me home through the woods. Otherwise I might still be wandering in the fog."

"I'm terribly sorry," Helen said. "I should have warned you."

Julia smiled. "It's all right. I'm fine."

"Did you say his name was MacKinnon?" Helen asked.

"Yes." Julia sipped her hot chocolate, trying to appear calm when she wanted to ask a hundred questions. "Gavin MacKinnon. I thought you might know him."

"Gavin MacKinnon?" Helen lifted her brows, her expression revealing her surprise. "How odd."

"Odd?" Julia smoothed the pad of her thumb over the handle of her cup. "In what way?"

"MacKinnon was the family name of the first earl. He built Dunmore in 1372. The MacKinnons lived here until the early part of the nineteenth century. The family bloodline ended with the death of the seventh earl." Helen set her cup and saucer on the tea cart. "And, unless I have my history muddled, his name was Gavin."

Julia frowned. "There must be another family on the island by that surname."

"Not that I'm aware of." Helen sat back, pursing her lips. "I suppose he could be from a different branch of the MacKinnon family. Perhaps he is here doing some research on the family name."

"Perhaps. Still, I don't think he was a tourist. He knew his way around Dunmore. And he said he often liked to walk the grounds."

Helen tapped her forefinger against her chin. "Now that is odd. I'm surprised I have never come across this man. Or perhaps I have and just never noticed him."

Julia shook her head. "Mr. MacKinnon is not a man to go unnoticed. If you saw him, you would remember him."

"Attractive?" Angela asked.

Julia grinned. "If you like that tall, dark, and devastating look."

Angela's blue eyes glittered with humor. "He made an impression, I can see."

"I suppose he did." Julia sipped her hot chocolate, the steam brushing her upper lip, the sweet, milky taste flooding her tongue. "For some reason, Gavin MacKinnon seemed familiar to me. Although I'm certain I have never met him before."

"You felt that way about Dunmore," Helen said.

"I know." Julia stood and set her cup and saucer on the tea cart. "I can't seem to shake the feeling that I've been here before. Everything seems so familiar. As though I were walking through a half-remembered dream."

Angela brushed a crumb of chocolate from her chin. "If your grandfather were here, Henry would say you had been at Dunmore before, in another life."

"Another life?" Julia rubbed the stiff muscles at the back of her neck. "You mean to say Grandfather believed in reincarnation?"

"Oh, your grandfather had a great many theories on life." Although it had been more than fifty years since she had lived in England, Angela had never lost the English in her accent or in her humor. "He also believed colonists from Atlantis lived in the Bermuda Triangle."

Julia grinned. "You mean you don't?"

Angela lifted her carefully sculpted brows. "It would explain a great many odd occurrences."

Julia wasn't ready to blame reincarnation for the odd feelings she had about Dunmore. "I prefer to think jet lag is the problem."

"It isn't so odd, the concept of reincarnation." Helen

rubbed her hand over her knee absently. "What are we but souls wandering about, contained for a brief space of time in a corporeal body? I have to say I honestly believe it is possible that the Almighty sends us back to earth for more than one chance at life. I know the first time I met Frederick . . ." She hesitated, looking at Julia. "Frederick was my fiancé. He died in the war."

"Gram told me about him." Gram had also said it was a shame her dear friend had never married. According to her grandmother, a legion of young men had tried to coax Helen to the altar. But she had chosen instead to live with memories.

"The first time I met Frederick, I felt I knew him. I know it sounds very Eastern of me, but I honestly believe we were soul mates. We had loved in another lifetime, perhaps a hundred lifetimes." Helen smiled, her eyes soft with memories. "And I believe we shall meet again. And love again."

Angela propped her elbow on the arm of the sofa and rested her chin on her hand. "It's a comforting thought."

"Soul mates." The concept appealed to Julia's innate sense of romance. All of her life, she had believed there was one man destiny meant for her. Still, with each passing year she wondered if fate had managed to mess things up in her case. What if something had happened to her mate? What if he had stepped out in front of a bus, or settled for marriage with the wrong woman? When should she just give up hope?

Soon after the case clock in the hall chimed eleven, Julia bid both ladies good night and headed for her bed-chamber. Unlike her grandmother, she had not been able to take a nap soon after arriving that afternoon. The time difference and exhaustion of a day of travel were piling up on her.

According to Helen, this wing had been added in the late eighteenth century. Though the exterior was built to complement the ancient gray stones of the original fourteenth-century castle, the interior was designed for luxury. Her chamber was on the second floor, overlooking the Atlantic. On the way to her room, she stopped at the chamber her niece had been given.

Lauren's room overlooked the sunken gardens. Rose velvet drapes had been left open, allowing fog-tinted moonlight to flow into the room. A thick needlepoint carpet cushioned her footsteps as Julia crossed the room. She paused beside the big canopy bed where Lauren lay sleeping. Lauren's thick, light brown curls lay fanned across the pillow; her cheek was turned, her chin resting on a teddy bear named Kip that showed all the signs of being well loved—the light brown plush on his belly was worn away, one ear drooped, and if you looked closely, you could see the stitches where Julia had repaired his leg. Still, that teddy had been salvaged from the wreckage of Lauren's young life.

Lauren had kicked the covers off, as she always did. Julia covered the girl, drawing the sheet and blanket up over her small shoulders. Five years ago Julia hadn't had the slightest idea of how to mother a child. But a drunk driver had plunged her into a crash course on motherhood. Five years ago she had taken over guardianship of her brother's only daughter, who at the time was three years old.

Necessity was a wonderful teacher. Over the past five years, Julia had learned a great many things. How to cope with the loss of her parents, her brother Mike, and her sister-in-law Diane, a woman who had been her best friend since they'd met in Mrs. Horne's seventh-grade English class. How to handle—for all intents and purposes—being a single mother. How to face herself in the mirror every morning with the knowledge that she might have prevented that accident. She was still working on that last one. Some days were better than others. She brushed her lips against Lauren's brow and left the room.

By the time she reached her chamber, she was so tired she felt like crawling into bed without changing her clothes. Still, she forced herself to get ready for bed. After climbing between the cool linen sheets, she lay for a long time wide awake, her body exhausted, her mind a jumble of thoughts. The excitement of travel, of visiting this huge, ancient pile of stones, made sleep elusive. She closed her eyes, concentrating on her breathing, coaxing the rhythm into a slow, deep cadence until she finally hovered on the verge of sleep.

Still, something pricked at her consciousness. Her skin tingled. She had the distinct feeling she was being watched. She opened her eyes and tried to focus. Someone was standing by the foot of her bed. A man. The man she had met on the clifftop that evening.

Moonlight flowed through the windows, carving his image from the shadows. His dark hair fell in tousled waves around his face. He wore a pirate's shirt, black, close-fitting breeches, and a smile that tore at her heart. She had never seen such longing in a smile before, such need.

For a moment, her sleep-drenched mind could only take in the sheer male beauty of this man. Then it registered. *A man was standing in her bedchamber.* She jackknifed into a sitting position, breaking free of her drowsy state like a swimmer breaking the surface of a pool.

"What are . . ." Her words faded in a sudden gasp of breath. She stared at the spot where Gavin MacKinnon had been standing. That space was filled with moonlight. She leaned over the edge of the bed. He wasn't hiding on the floor.

She stood and glanced around the room. A pair of wing-back chairs stood in front of the porcelain-tiled fireplace. A tall rosewood armoire stood against the far wall. A vanity stood between a chest of drawers and the door leading to the bathroom. Even though rationally she knew he couldn't have made it across the room without her seeing him, she still rushed across the room, pulled open the door, and stared inside. Moonlight from the window poured over the porcelain bathtub, the brass handles glimmering in the soft light.

"I wasn't dreaming," she whispered, heading back for bed. "I wasn't asleep."

Still, Mr. MacKinnon had obviously been nothing more than a figment of her imagination. She had just manufactured his image, imagined him standing by the bed looking at her as though he wanted to take her in his arms and hold her until the end of time. She fell back against her pillow and stared up at the dark folds of the blue velvet canopy above her head.

She had just met the man and already she was spinning fantasies about him. She clenched her teeth and rolled over to her side. *Cautious and steady,* that was her motto. Still, she couldn't deny a very reckless urge when it came to one incredibly compelling Scottish pirate.

Julia squeezed the top plank in the paddock fence, her fingers sliding against the smooth white painted pine.

The tang of cedar chips drifted on the cool morning breeze. Sunlight filtered through the leaves of an oak growing beside the paddock, sprinkling gold medallions on the horse and rider as they passed Julia. Lauren looked so small sitting atop that horse. She waved to Julia, smiling as though she had just been given a wonderful present. There was no reason to worry, Julia assured herself. This was perfectly safe.

"Lauren will be fine," Helen said, resting her forearm on the fence beside Julia. "Annie is a true lady. She would never think of harming a little girl."

Julia studied the chestnut mare named Annie as Lauren rode the animal out of a gate on the far side of the large paddock. The animal seemed gentle enough, walking with a lazy sway of her hips, her long tail swishing slowly. The three other young girls who lived at the castle—Megan and Shannon, the housekeeper's daughters, and Nicole, the daughter of Helen's secretary—were also mounted. The muted sound of horse hooves thudding wood chips accompanied the parade of little girls and horses as they formed a chain and rode out of the paddock with a groom in the lead and one in the rear.

"I never had children of my own." Helen's gaze remained fixed on the girls as they rode across the wide expanse of lush green lawn, headed for one of the woodland paths. "It is my greatest regret."

Julia looked at the small woman standing beside her. Helen's bun was perched on the side of her head this morning; loose strands of gray and brown had fallen free of their pins to flutter in the breeze. Although the years had etched lines upon her face, the beauty that had been hers as a youth could still be seen.

Helen lifted her face to the breeze. "When I lost

Frederick, I couldn't imagine ever giving my heart to another man. Frederick was my one and only love."

Her one and only love. What would it be like to meet him, that man who made your heart soar, only to lose him after an all too brief span of time? Was it worse than never meeting him at all?

"I keep telling Julia that she needs to settle down and have babies of her own." Angela nibbled a cinnamon pastry, crumbs falling on the lavender flowers embroidered along the front edges of her white cardigan. She brushed them away as she continued. "She hasn't allowed any man to get close to her, not since that horrible debacle five years ago. She is gun-shy."

"I prefer to say cautious." Unbidden, an image of Gavin MacKinnon rose in her mind. Julia had only just met the man. It was ridiculous to think of him in the context of happily ever after. Yet she couldn't get him out of her mind or her dreams. Last night he had invaded her sleep, holding her, kissing her, loving her. Never in her life had a man made her feel this way. It was foolish, reckless, and far too exciting. "I have hopes. One day the right man will sweep me off my feet."

"I understand how you feel, as though there is only one man out there for you." Helen tucked a wayward strand of hair behind her right ear. "After I lost Frederick, I shut myself off from the idea of ever marrying anyone. I admit, sometimes I wonder if it was a mistake. Perhaps it is better to live with affection and companionship, the love of family, even if you can't give your heart completely. Of course, you are too young to think of those things."

Julia had nearly settled for something less. She wasn't ready to give up looking for that one special man, the one destiny meant for her. *Her one and only love.* Inwardly she cringed at the fatally romantic notion, but she couldn't change who she was—a hopeful romantic right down to her bones. At the moment her hopes were pinned on a stranger with eyes as dark and mysterious as the Atlantic in a storm.

"Come back here!" A masculine shout shot from the stables. A moment later a huge black horse charged through the open stable doors. Hoofbeats pounded the ground as the beast dashed across the paddock, kicking up cedar chips in his wake. Two grooms chased the horse, legs pumping with all their might. Julia watched their progress, expecting the chase to end when the horse reached the fence. Instead the animal jumped, soaring over the white-painted planks in a glorious arc of power and grace.

"I see Emerson is at it again," Helen said, her voice low and unconcerned.

"This has happened before?" Julia stared, following the horse's progress as he dashed across the lawn and plunged into the woods.

"Yes," Helen said. "Nearly every morning Emerson decides to take a solitary run. No one is quite certain how he gets out of his stall."

"You never have any trouble finding him?" Julia asked.

"He comes back on his own." Helen lifted her brows. "I suppose he knows where his oats are."

"On his own. That is strange," Angela said. "Still, you could probably put his runs to an end if you made him a gelding."

"He is a wonderful stud. And as long as he doesn't hurt himself, I don't mind. Besides, if it is the Ghost of Dunmore, I like to think he enjoys his morning rides."

"The Ghost of Dunmore?" Julia asked.

"Yes." Helen smiled, a glint of humor filling her eyes. "Dunmore is haunted by at least one spirit. Perhaps more."

"You mean you have your very own ghost and you never told me about him?" Angela asked.

"I've never actually met him. Although I have heard the piano playing in the music room when there has been no one in there."

"You actually heard the piano?" Julia asked.

"On occasion I was nearly certain I did. Of course it was always at night and I was always half asleep." Helen turned her gaze toward the castle. "Every old castle and country home in Great Britain boasts a ghost or two. I suppose any time a structure is witness to the passage of centuries, there will be tragedies and legends that arise from them."

Julia had never really taken ghost stories seriously. Still, she supposed there were more things to this world than what could be seen and touched. "Who is the ghost supposed to be?"

"No one is really certain. Through the years several people have reported catching a glimpse of a young man wandering the unfinished tower. Since the last MacKinnon earl died so tragically, many feel it must be he."

"Well, I would prefer not to see a ghost, if there are any." Angela rubbed her arms. "The whole idea gives me shivers."

"I have lived here a long time, and I have yet to see one. If we have ghosts, they are a solitary lot." Helen linked her left arm through Julia's and her right through Angela's. "Shall we take a look at the library? I want to show you the MacKinnon journals."

Although Julia wanted very much to see the journals and explore the rest of the library and Dunmore, she found herself anxious for a long walk along the clifftops. And she didn't try fooling herself as to the reason she wanted to prowl the grounds of Dunmore—Gavin MacKinnon. He liked to walk the grounds of Dunmore. Well, she liked taking long walks. Perhaps, if she walked long enough, she might just bump into him again. She drew in her breath. *Don't get your hopes up.* She had learned a long time ago that it wasn't safe to pin any hopes on a man, especially one like Gavin MacKinnon.

The mellow scent of leather drifted from the sofas and chairs, wrapping around Julia as she followed her grandmother and Helen into the large library. In spite of the sunlight filtering into the room, Helen switched on the overhead lights, chandeliers of brass and crystal that cast golden light upon the hundreds of books lining the mahogany and brass bookcases. Cut velvet drapes in a green and burgundy floral pattern framed the long windows and a pair of French doors at the far end of the room. A thick wool carpet of burgundy and ivory medallions, a replica of the one Adams had designed for the room, cushioned their footsteps. The gallery wrapped around three walls of the room. It was reached by a wooden spiral staircase. Julia glanced at the leather-clad volumes, wondering what treasures she would find hidden between the covers.

"I keep most of the family journals on these shelves." Helen pulled a book from the bookcase to the left of the large fireplace. "I think you'll find this one particularly interesting."

Julia paused in front of the fireplace, her attention snagged by the portrait hanging above the polished mahogany mantel. From the confines of an ornately carved frame, a man gazed down at her.

Unlike most of the portraits she had seen at Dunmore, this was not a formal pose. This man looked as though he had just dismounted from the glossy black stallion that stood beside him. He didn't wear a coat. His white shirt was open at the neck. It was loose fitting, with full sleeves, a shirt any Hollywood pirate would be proud to wear. Black breeches hugged his narrow hips and the strong lines of his legs before plunging into knee-high black boots. Dark, tousled waves framed a face carved with strong lines and angles, a face designed to test the limits of a woman's heart. Her own heart thumped wildly against her ribs. It was the face of . . ."Gavin MacKinnon. That's him."

Helen moved to her side, holding a large brown leather-bound book in her hand. "Yes. That's Gavin MacKinnon. The seventh earl of Dunmore."

Although the words registered in Julia's brain, they didn't make sense. "The seventh earl of Dunmore?"

Helen looked up at her, light reflecting on the wide lenses of her glasses. "Yes. Why do you sound so surprised?"

Julia's mind wrestled with the facts Helen presented her. "This is the man I met last night on the cliff path."

Helen frowned. "You couldn't have met this man."

Julia looked up at the portrait. He seemed to be smiling right at her, and the smile conjured a disturbing sense of familiarity. "But I did. I know it's him."

"Julia, this man died in 1818."

Chapter Three

Coincidence is God's way of performing a miracle anonymously.

—Anonymous

Beneath the soft white cotton of her sweater, chills scattered across Julia's arms. "The man I met last night looks exactly like the man in this portrait."

Helen looked surprised, her blue eyes growing wide behind her lenses. "Exactly?"

Julia rubbed her arms, trying to quell the goose bumps rising there. "Yes."

Angela joined them in front of the portrait. Since she insisted she only needed glasses for reading, she wore her gold-rimmed glasses on a chain around her neck. She slipped them on to take a look at the portrait, then let them drop once more, where they settled against the lavender silk blouse peeking out from her white cardigan. "And he called himself Gavin MacKinnon?"

"Yes."

Angela squinted up at the portrait. "He must be a descendant."

Julia drew in a breath with difficulty. Could genes combine to produce two identical men who lived nearly two hundred years apart? Yet what other answer could there be? "I suppose he must be."

"According to the history I've been able to piece together about the family, Gavin was the last of the MacKinnon earls. His younger brother Patrick was killed in an accident in London a couple of months before Gavin died. Gavin's son died from a fall from the cliffs a few days after Gavin's death. His mother died from a fall down a flight of stairs several months after Gavin's accident. His sister Alison, inherited Dunmore upon her mother's death. By Scottish tradition she was able to give the title and Dunmore to her husband, an Englishman by the name of . . ." Helen hesitated a moment, tapping her lower lip with the pad of her forefinger. "Talbot. Yes, I believe the name was Talbot. The sister died soon after her marriage; a fever I believe. She didn't have children. The entire family died out within a few years."

"The entire family?" Julia asked.

"Yes. Within a span of two years." Helen looked up at the portrait. "It's very sad. The bloodline died with this man."

"At least the legitimate line of the family." Angela fiddled with the chain of her glasses. "I suspect Gavin MacKinnon was quite popular with the ladies."

Julia thought of how the man she had met could set

her pulse racing with a glance. The man looking down at her from his perch above the mantel had that same devilish glint in his dark eyes. "He would be."

"The Gavin MacKinnon you met is more than likely a descendant from one of this man's liaisons," Angela said, warming to her solution of the mystery. "One of his mistresses must have decided to use the MacKinnon name."

Julia didn't appreciate coincidences. And she wasn't at all certain she trusted this handsome stranger who called himself Gavin MacKinnon. "I wonder why this man is lurking about Dunmore."

"You sound as though you think he has some nefarious reason for being here," Helen said.

Julia shifted on her feet, uncomfortable with her own suspicions. "I don't suppose there is any way he could lay claim to Dunmore?"

Helen shook her head. "My great-grandfather won Dunmore in a card game back in 1861 from one of Talbot's grandchildren. I'm certain all of the proper papers were transferred at the time."

"Perhaps it's curiosity that's brought him here," Angela said. "If he is a descendant, he probably knows about the earl."

"I hope he is a descendant." Helen studied the portrait for several moments before she continued. "I've always thought of this man as the 'tragic earl.' I have never been able to look at this portrait without thinking it a shame for such a man to die so young. It would be nice to think one of his direct descendants lives today."

"He was a fine figure of a man." Angela smiled at Julia, a glint of speculation in her blue eyes. "I can see why the young man you met last night made an impression."

An impression that had her anxious to hike around

the countryside, searching for him. "I suspect he makes an impression on most women he meets."

Helen kept her gaze on the portrait as she spoke. "So much promise, and it all came to an end before he ever saw his thirtieth birthday."

Julia glanced up at the portrait, wondering about the man who had lived and died so many years ago. She couldn't prevent a pang of regret for a life lost so young. "How did he die?"

"An accident. It happened here, at Dunmore."

"This is the Ghost of Dunmore?" Angela asked.

Helen nodded. "Yes. The last MacKinnon. He is the one most people believe to be haunting the castle."

"Well, if you must have a ghost haunting your home, at least he is very easy on the eyes." Angela titled her head, and grinned up at the portrait. "I might not mind meeting him after all."

"The whole idea of a ghost is so very sad," Julia said. "A spirit roaming about the earth, lost, lonely."

"Yes. Tragic." Helen handed Julia the book she had been holding. "This is one of his mother's journals, the last one she kept. Her journals have helped me enormously in piecing together the history of the castle and the MacKinnon family. I thought she might give you an idea for a novel."

Julia smoothed her fingertip over the gold lettering tooled on brown leather. "M. J. MacKinnon."

"Mary Josephine."

A chance to touch the life of a woman who had lived nearly two hundred years ago. The prospect excited her as it could only excite someone who found history fascinating. "Are you certain you don't mind my reading this? It's very old."

"It's in very good condition. And I trust you will handle it with care. I also have bundles of letters you can read, Mary's and her daughter's. The correspondence really helps reveal their lives." Helen patted Julia's arm. "I'm certain you will find inspiration here."

Julia glanced up at the portrait of the "tragic earl." There was no doubt she could find inspiration at Dunmore. Could she also find the living image of this man? She was more than a little curious about the Gavin MacKinnon she had met last night. She only hoped she would have a chance to delve a little deeper into his story. Still, she wasn't going to conduct a search for the man. He knew where she was staying. If he wanted to see her, he would come to her.

I wonder if Gavin shall ever find true happiness, the happiness I knew with his father, my beloved Duncan. Lavinia changed my son. How could she not have changed him? Her beauty and charm fooled us all. If I could not see her plans, how could a boy of one-and-twenty know she intended to use his tender heart, his sense of honor against him? Marriage to her left wounds deeply cut. He is bitter toward members of my sex, cynical in his views of the female heart. And why shouldn't he be?

No one knew the depths of Lavinia's treachery until a fortnight ago. If not for a chance observance of the boy by Henrietta Clemenson, we might never have discovered his existence. Lavinia hid my grandson for more than six years. Not out of any devotion to the boy. No, Lavinia hid his existence to keep my son from returning from India. When I think of how that child has been treated by his mother and her parents, I want to weep. At last he is safe with us.

I know there are those who still believe Gavin murdered Lavinia. They see the motives, understand his rage. Still I know he is innocent of that crime. His annulment would soon have been granted. He had nothing to gain by her death.

Julia closed Mary MacKinnon's journal, her chest heavy with a certain sadness. What kind of monster hid her son from his father so that she could maintain an unencumbered lifestyle? She had spent the morning with Mary's journal, stopping only long enough for lunch before delving back into the past. The journal had shed light on Gavin's unhappy marriage and the woman who had married him for wealth and a title.

She looked at the portrait hanging above the mantel. Gavin gazed at her, a devilish glint in his eyes, as though he dared her to flirt with him. He should have been wearing a sign: LADIES, PROCEED AT YOUR OWN RISK. The portrait had been painted the year he died.

Once again a wave of familiarity swept over her. She was alone in the room, alone with Mary's words and Gavin's portrait. She left Mary's journal on the polished top of the claw-footed mahogany desk and crossed the room, drawn to the portrait of the seventh earl. The artist had captured a spark of vitality in oils. Gavin looked confident, the type of man who would accept any challenge life threw at him.

"You died too young," she whispered. She knew the pain of losing loved ones. She understood the terrible sorrow Mary must have felt when she lost her sons.

"You look sad, lass."

Julia sucked in her breath. For one fleeting moment she thought the portrait had spoken to her. Then she saw someone out of the corner of her eye. She pivoted and found Gavin MacKinnon standing near the desk. Excitement slammed through her, shaking her limbs.

Images swirled inside her, like leaves caught in a silent whirlwind. She could almost feel his arms around her, his lips pressed against her neck, his breath a warm caress, his hands sliding upward over her. . . . She trembled and tried to block the images. This was not good for her composure. Not good at all. "What are you doing here?"

He smiled, not just with his lips, but with his incredible eyes. "I came to see you. I didn't mean to startle you."

Her heart stopped, then surged into a headlong rush. "I didn't hear you come in." She glanced at the door leading to the hall. It was closed. It was also on the opposite side of the room. "You didn't come in that way."

"No. I was walking through the gardens when I saw you in here."

"You just came in? Without even knocking?"

"The door was open."

"Do you often just barge into homes?"

"I didn't barge. I walked through the open French door." He sat on the edge of the desk, as though he owned the place.

Had he also found his way into her bedchamber last night? Even as the thought formed, she dismissed it. He couldn't possibly have disappeared into the moonlight. She had fabricated his presence. She glanced up at the portrait, then at the man sitting a few feet away. She hadn't imagined the resemblance. The two men were cast from an identical mold. "And you just decided to stop by this afternoon. To see me?"

He lifted his brows, his expression revealing his surprise at the suspicion she hadn't kept from her voice. "Aye. I had to see you again."

He wanted to see her again. She felt light-headed, as though she had been plucked from sea level and deposited on the peak of Everest. She drew in her breath, trying to quell her all too feminine response to this gorgeous male. As much as she would like to believe he was here because of her, she couldn't dismiss her suspicions concerning this particular coincidence. "I wonder if you might not have another reason for coming to Dunmore."

He was dressed much as he had been the day before, although today he wore a dark green riding coat over a white shirt that he had left open at the neck. Buff-colored breeches molded his long legs and were tucked into close-fitting shiny black boots just below his knees. Once again she was struck with the restrained power this man exuded. "And why do you suppose I'm here?"

"I'm not sure." She looked up at the portrait, then back at the man sitting on the edge of the desk. They were identical, right down to the glint of mischief in their dark eyes. Even the clothes were of a similar style. "Did you know the first owners of Dunmore were named MacKinnon?"

"Aye. I'm aware of the history of Dunmore Castle." He lowered his gaze to the journal on the desk. A muscle flickered in his cheek as he ran his fingertip over the gold lettering on the journal. "Are you reading Mary MacKinnon's journals?"

"Yes." For some reason she suddenly felt like an intruder, with no right at all to read the thoughts of a woman who had died nearly two hundred years ago. She felt a strange need to justify the intrusion into Mary MacKinnon's privacy. "Helen thought I would enjoy them. I'm something of a history buff."

He looked up from the journal, his face an unreadable mask. "And so you're taking a look into her life."

"Yes. I am." She frowned, a thought striking her. "How did you know that was one of Mary MacKinnon's journals?"

He shrugged, dark green wool stretching over the breadth of his shoulders. "It looks like a journal and it has her name on it."

"It has initials on it. You knew the *M* stood for Mary." Julia suspected he had done a great deal of research into the MacKinnon family. It made her all the more suspicious of this handsome stranger. She cast a pointed look at the portrait. He followed her gaze, glancing up at the portrait of the seventh earl. Still, he refrained from commenting on his resemblance to the man in the painting. She glared at him, daring him to deny the obvious. "Do you have any connection with the family?"

He smiled, a slow curving of sensual lips that made her feel as though he was sliding his arms around her. Her skin warmed and tingled. "I'm a direct descendant of the first MacKinnon."

She had thought as much. "And you had no other reason for coming here, except to see me?"

"You're very suspicious." He stood and moved toward her with the lithe grace of a born athlete.

"I prefer to say cautious." She resisted the urge to step back as he drew near. It wasn't for fear of bodily harm. Physical injury would be mild compared to the havoc this man wreaked on her senses.

Gavin paused, so close she could catch the scent of leather and sandalwood drifting from his skin. Memory stirred within her, a memory that seemed to come from a great distance. She felt as though they had stood this way before, in this place, in another time.

His hair was tousled into rich, glossy waves that framed his face. The moonlight the night before had not done this man justice. The afternoon light revealed the subtle nuances of his face. Faint lines flared from the corners of his dark eyes, lines forged by his easy smile. Dark pinpoints of beard lay beneath the surface of his skin, tempting her to test the texture of his freshly shaven jaw. In her dreams she had kissed that finely chiseled jaw, tasted the heat of his skin beneath her tongue. With her gaze, she traced the full curve of his smile.

"Tell me, who was the man who destroyed your trust in members of my sex?" he asked, his dark voice tinged with that intriguing burr.

She had to swallow hard before she could use her voice. "I think it's reasonable to be suspicious."

He studied her face, as though he was making notes for a portrait he would paint. "I understand how difficult it can be to trust when you have been betrayed."

She wanted to lick her dry lips, but all the moisture had evaporated from her mouth. "Are you speaking from experience?"

"Aye. Unfortunately, I am." He lifted his hand as if to touch her face. Her skin warmed in anticipation; her pulse quickened. She held her breath, waiting for a touch that didn't come. Instead, he closed his fingers into the palm of his hand. Emotion flickered in his eyes, a glimmer of surprise, as if he had been caught off guard suddenly. He frowned and stepped back from her.

Julia hid her turmoil behind a smile. She wanted this stranger to touch her, and more. She caught herself wanting to feel his arms around her, the brush of his breath against her cheek, the slide of his lips upon hers. All of this was more than unusual for a woman who had been in only one serious relationship her entire life. She really had to sort through these sensations later, when she had a clear head.

She stepped back, hoping some distance would cool the heat flaming in her blood. Who was this man? And what was he doing here, besides turning her world upside down? "I don't mean to be insulting, but you look exactly like the tragic earl. And you share the same name. At least you say you share the same name. It just seems too much of a coincidence to think you happened upon Dunmore by accident."

He met her gaze, his black brows lifting over his incredible eyes. "The tragic earl?"

"That's what Helen—Mrs. Bainbridge—calls the last MacKinnon earl. And it just seems to fit. He died before he was thirty."

He nodded. "Aye, I know."

She studied him for a moment, hoping her worst thoughts about this man were unfounded. She could find nothing of the villain in his eyes, nothing to suggest he had come to Dunmore for any nefarious reason. Instead she found a dark sadness in his gaze, a reflection of the emotion she felt when she thought of the man looking down at them from the portrait. "You've done research about the family. Is that why you're here? To do more research?"

He smiled at her. "I told you, I came to see you."

She ignored the sudden surge in her pulse. "And you have no interest at all in Dunmore?"

"I'm not here to steal the family silver, if that's what you think."

"Why *are* you here?"

He studied her for a moment and she had the impression he was weighing his words carefully. "I've been waiting a very long time for you to come to Dunmore."

She stared at him. "You have?"

"Aye. I need to speak with you, on a matter of grave importance."

Grave importance? "You do?"

"Aye. I do."

What could he possibly want to discuss with her? Her mind got sucked into the same whirlwind that had gripped her heart the moment he stepped into the room. "What is it you want to discuss?"

"Julia!"

He frowned. "Someone is looking for you."

"My grandmother." Still, she couldn't look away from his eyes; she was trapped in the connection between them. It seemed almost tangible, as though someone had wrapped thick bands of silk around them, binding one to the other.

"Julia!" A rattling of the door punctuated Angela's words.

"She seems to want you for something."

"Yes. She does." Julia dragged her gaze from his and turned her head toward the door. "I'm in here, Gram."

"I know, dear." The brass doorknob jiggled. "But the door is locked."

"Locked?" She turned away from Gavin and crossed the room. She gripped the brass handle. It turned in her hand. The heavy door opened on well-oiled hinges, revealing Angela standing in the hall.

"I came to see if you wanted to play cards." Angela smiled. "Why did you lock the door?"

"I didn't. In fact it wasn't locked."

"It wasn't?" Angela jiggled the handle on the hall side of the door. "That's odd. Are you sure it wasn't locked?"

"It needs a key to lock it," Julia said, smoothing her fingertip over the empty keyhole. "I suppose it just stuck."

"I suppose." Angela stepped into the library and glanced around the room, fiddling with the chain of her glasses. "I thought I heard you talking to someone in here."

"I was." Julia smiled in anticipation of introducing Gavin to her grandmother. "I want you to meet some-one."

Angela frowned. "Who?"

Gram really needed to wear those glasses all the time. "Mr. MacKinnon."

"Mr. MacKinnon?" Angela looked around her. "Where is he?"

Julia turned, her gaze raking the space where she had left Gavin. He had vanished.

Angela lifted her glasses and peered through the lenses. "I don't see him, dear."

"He left." Julia hurried across the library and out the open French doors. The doors opened onto a stone ter-race and a sunken garden beyond. A cool breeze swept across the garden, stirring the silvery green leaves of the white birch growing near the terrace. The soft breeze brushed her face with the scent of flowers from the many colorful beds planted in a geometrical pattern around a lily pond. Woodlands stood on the far edge of the garden. Gavin was nowhere in sight.

Angela joined her at the stone balustrade of the terrace. "I wonder why he ran off so quickly. You didn't make him feel unwelcome, did you?"

"No, I didn't."

Angela didn't look convinced. "You were very suspicious of him. Are you sure you didn't chase him away?"

Julia tapped her fingers on the stone balustrade, thinking of the way she had questioned him. "I just asked him a few questions."

"Still suspicious about him, I see." Angela slipped on her glasses and glanced around. "After seeing him again, do you still think he looks like the earl?"

Julia leaned back against the thick stone balustrade. "They could be identical twins."

"I would love to meet him. It isn't every day that a man catches your interest. And you are interested; I can tell."

"I just met him."

"Sometimes all it takes is a glance. I married your grandfather two weeks after I met him."

"That's different. There was a war going on. People did things on impulse. I don't intend to do anything on impulse."

"Impulse?" Angela released her breath in a sigh. "Julia dear, it usually takes you twenty minutes to decide which side of the bread to butter in the morning."

Julia crinkled her nose. "Are you saying I'm indecisive?"

"Not indecisive. Cautious." Angela removed her

glasses and let them fall against her blouse. "You usually like to take a few weeks to investigate anything before committing yourself. As I recall, it took you two months to decide on the precise car you wanted."

It was true. Julia liked to explore all possibilities before deciding on a course of action. "And your point would be?"

"My point is, sometimes you just have to follow your heart and not your head." Angela hesitated for a moment before she continued. "You have to put the past behind you."

Julia knew precisely what part of her past Gram meant. "I have."

Angela twisted the chain of her glasses, setting them spinning. "Not all men are as manipulative and untrustworthy as Nathan Riley."

Julia rubbed her arms. "I know. I don't judge all men by Nathan. Not really."

Angela lifted her brows. "I think you do. I think that is the reason you won't allow any man into your life."

"I know absolutely nothing about this man, except that he is a direct descendant of the tragic earl." And that he could make her skin tingle, her heart race, her imagination soar.

"So, the earl did have a mistress or two." Angela tapped the corner of her glasses against her chin. "It doesn't surprise me, not after seeing his portrait. I would suspect that man had a way of putting all manner of naughty thoughts in a woman's head."

The Gavin MacKinnon she knew had the same ability, Julia thought. She stared past the woodlands. The fields she had hiked the night before gradually slid into hills that rolled into the rugged slopes of Ben Cuimhne. Where had Gavin gone?

"Do you want to play cards?" Angela asked.

Julia wanted to remain in the library and read Mary MacKinnon's journals, all of them. Still, she had locked herself away most of the day. "Sure."

Julia followed Angela back into the library. Her grandmother stopped in front of the portrait of the tragic earl and slipped on her glasses. "My goodness, he was a handsome man. Do you think he might inspire your writing?"

"I hope so."

Julia stared up at the devilish-looking earl, but another man filled her thoughts. There was something about Gavin MacKinnon, something more intriguing than a handsome face and a splendid body. For some reason he seemed so familiar to her . . . The sound of his voice, the way he smiled. As much as she wanted to draw him into her arms, she couldn't shake the feeling that he was hiding something. And what did he want of her? How could he possibly have been waiting for her to come to Dunmore? Each time she thought of him—and she thought of him more than she should—she had more questions.

Who are you, Gavin MacKinnon? And what do you want from me?

Gavin stood on the cliff walk staring at the rolling expanse of the Atlantic. The last rays of the sun stretched out across the water, setting flame to the dark waves. Never in his life had he been attracted to a woman the way he was attracted to Julia Fairfield. He wanted her in every way a man craves a woman. He wanted to hold her in his arms, touch the smooth skin hidden beneath the thick luster of her honey-colored hair. He wanted to see himself reflected in her dark blue eyes. He wanted to kiss her, taste her skin, explore every hidden valley, every secret of her body.

He felt connected to her, as though she had once been a part of him, a precious piece that he had lost somewhere in time, and searched for all of his life. Romantic notions for a man who had lost his belief in romance a very long time ago. Still, there was something about her and the feelings she evoked in him that he just couldn't ignore. Why did she seem so familiar to him? He suspected it had something to do with the reason she had been chosen for this mission.

The dark gray-green of the Atlantic crashed against the jagged rocks far below. Gulls swooped over the rolling water, cawing, diving, searching for sustenance. The sounds echoed through him, touching all the empty places deep within him. It seemed he had been in this place an eternity, waiting. One woman alone could help him. *Julia.*

He had a mission here. Nothing would stand in his way. He would do everything possible to make that mission a success. Once it was completed, he would leave. He could not become involved with Julia Fairfield. There was no future in these feelings Julia stirred inside him, only the bitterness of what might have been.

He needed Julia's help or all would be lost. He only prayed he could rely on the most unreliable of all the beings in creation: a woman.

Chapter Four

Fool! All that is, at all,
Lasts ever, past recall;
Earth changes, but thy soul and God stand sure;
What entered into thee,
That was, is, and shall be:
Time's wheel runs back or stops; Potter and clay endure.

—Robert Browning

Although we came to London to present Alison to Society, it has become my mission to see Gavin properly settled with a woman who will love him, a woman who will find a way to his shuttered heart. I hope and pray he may meet a special woman who will heal the wounds Lavinia left carved across his soul. Still, I doubt he shall find her in London this Season.

I have seen too many silly females throw themselves in his path, using every feminine trick imaginable. One can be certain to see at least three young women swoon against him at any party we attend. In the last week two females have stepped out in front of his curricle while he was driving me around Hyde Park. Both were uninjured. Their ploy was obvious to me as well as to my son. Gavin grows weary of the games.

Although he has sworn never again to marry, I have hope for him. My hope lies with a certain young lady, the daughter of my dearest friend, Rebecca Fitzgerald. When Alison and I visited the Fitzgeralds in Philadelphia last year, I discovered Emma had not only blossomed into a great beauty, but I am pleased to say she is of a practical nature, much like my Alison.

It is little wonder the girls share a close friendship in spite of the separation of the vast Atlantic. Like Alison, Emma has yet to find a man who can touch her heart. Perhaps Gavin is the man she has been waiting for without knowing it. I look forward with great hope and anticipation to the Fitzgeralds' visit to Dunmore this summer.

Julia frowned at the journal. Mary's words were filled with such hope, a mother's wish for happiness for the son she adored. She had been so unsuspecting. So certain Gavin would live a long and happy life. But then, tragedy usually hit hard and fast, like a drunken driver crossing the median.

Julia stood and rolled her shoulders back, easing out the stiffness of hours spent reading. She glanced at the portrait of Gavin. Had he met that one special woman before he died? Had he fallen in love with her? Had she chased away all the ugliness of his marriage? Had they lost it all just as they were discovering love? Was Emma that woman? The journals were triggering all manner of questions, the kind she needed to answer in the book she intended to write.

"Julia, it's time to set aside your book and come take a walk," Angela called from the doorway. "Helen promises to show us something special this morning."

"I'll grab a jacket."

After donning a blue windbreaker, Julia joined Helen and Angela in a walk through the gardens. She pulled the collar of her jacket close around her neck. The sun had hidden behind gray clouds this morning, and it looked as though it might not make an appearance the entire day. A damp wind swept in from the ocean, chilling her through the navy blue nylon of her jacket and her red cotton sweater beneath. She followed Helen and Angela through the gardens, walking a gravel path that led to an unfinished wing of the castle.

They passed through an arched gate set in a stone wall and entered a large walled garden. The scent of roses infused the salty air, brushing her face. Julia froze, memories crashing through her. She glanced around. Ivy clung to the stone walls that shielded the garden from the fierce ocean winds. Hundreds of old-fashioned roses grew in a star-shaped pattern around a central fountain.

She brushed her fingertips over the damp petals of a garnet-colored rose. Memory stirred within her, bringing with it a dull ache. *I'm too late,* she thought. Too late for what? The memory eluded her. Only the pain remained, the horrible longing that came with terrible loss. Her heart pounded. Her skin tingled. She had been here before. Yet she knew she had never set foot in this garden until now.

"Julia." Angela touched her arm. "Are you all right? You're very pale suddenly."

Julia looked into her grandmother's concerned blue eyes. "I just had the oddest feeling."

Angela frowned. "What was it?"

"I felt as though I had been here before." Julia swallowed hard, trying to understand the poignant longing streaming through her. "It's uncanny."

"Is something wrong?" Helen asked.

"No. I'm fine. I just . . ." Julia forced her lips into a smile. "I have the strangest feeling about this garden. A sadness that I can't explain. It's as though I was here before, and something dreadful happened. Isn't it strange?"

Helen frowned. "There are those who would say déjà vu is simply a product of chemicals in the brain. Of course, there are others who believe the feeling comes when we have crossed a path we have walked once before. Perhaps even in a different life."

"A different life?" Julia rubbed her hands over her arms, trying to warm her suddenly chilled skin. "I suppose I created the garden in my mind out of pieces of research I've done in the past. My imagination gets the better of me at times."

Helen nodded. "It would be a logical explanation."

"But not nearly as romantic." Angela fiddled with the chain of her glasses. "If you use it in your book, use the past life version. I like that better."

Julia smiled. "I will give it consideration."

Past lives? Julia drew in a deep breath as she followed Helen and Angela along the garden walk. Was it possible? She wasn't at all comfortable with that question. Still, there was something about Dunmore, something that had crept into her imagination, twisting fantasy and reality until she had trouble telling one from the other. It must be the book she intended to write. The characters were already coming to life in her mind; that must be the reason for these odd sensations.

The path led to a stone terrace that stretched in a wide arc from the base of a tall stone tower. It was a magical-looking place, designed by someone with romance in his heart.

Helen paused on the terrace. "The tragic earl had a passion for building. He was the inspiration behind the west wing of the castle. The long, sweeping East wing, which culminates in this glorious tower was his last project. You can really see an Italian influence in the design."

Julia shivered at the words. "Gavin MacKinnon designed this wing?"

"Yes. Isn't it wonderful?" Helen turned her gaze toward the double doors leading into the tower. At least they would have opened to the tower, if they had not been filled in with brick. "It has a fairy tale quality."

As far as Julia could see, there was no longer any way to enter the tower from the garden, unless you broke a window. She peered through one of the long diamond-paned windows, a chill creeping up her spine. A scaffold stood along one side of the huge circular room. Wall panels lay stacked on the floor. Buckets and brushes were scattered about. It looked as though the workmen had walked away from the room last night and planned to return this morning. "It's eerie," she whispered, her breath condensing on the glass.

"It's where Gavin MacKinnon died," Helen said softly. "Afterwards Mary had all the doors leading to this wing bricked closed. It's as it was the last day he lived. Mary meant it to stand as a monument to Gavin."

"I understand how she must have felt," Angela said, her voice barely rising above the distant sound of waves crashing against rocks on the shore below. "We aren't meant to live longer than our children."

Julia could see the pain Gram normally kept hidden, the open wounds that would never truly heal. And once again she felt the sting of guilt. If only she could change the past, alter the decisions that had led to so much tragedy. Yet that wasn't possible. One could only learn to live with what had come to pass.

The tall case clock in the entry hall stirred, then sounded the last hour of the day. Julia closed Mary MacKinnon's journal and glanced at the laptop sitting open on the emerald desk pad atop the big claw-footed desk in the library.

Find a different ending for the tragic earl. The MacKinnon should meet the love of his life. Then they should live the rest of their lives together. That's the way it should have been.

At least in books, she could make things work out the way they ought. Her chest felt tight. She had spent the day reading personal letters of the MacKinnon ladies, and all of Mary MacKinnon's journals. Although the rest of the entries were interesting, Julia had consumed every word about Gavin. The man fascinated her.

Mary's words had painted a portrait of the man more vibrant than the one in oils hanging above the mantel. Julia felt as though she knew Gavin, knew his triumphs, his struggles, his joys, and his sorrows. He had lived a bold life that had ended far too soon. A man who had died before ever claiming his one and only love. Had that woman been Emma Fitzgerald?

According to Mary's journal, Emma was to have come to Dunmore the month Gavin died. Because of illness in the family, her trip was delayed. She arrived several months after Gavin's death. All the hope Mary had held for her son had long since been buried. Julia couldn't help wondering what might have happened if Emma had arrived earlier. The decisions we make every day sway the course of our lives. She knew that fact far too well.

The entries in the last journal had been sporadic, particularly the last year, the year of so many tragedies. First her youngest son had died in a carriage accident in London, then Gavin in the tower, her grandson in a fall from the cliffs and finally her own death from a fall down the grand staircase of Dunmore. At least Mary never knew about her daughter's death a year after her own.

Thanks to this woman's words, Julia had met a man from another time. A fascinating, all too tragic man. Julia had hoped to find inspiration for a novel at Dunmore; she had found it in Gavin MacKinnon. Perhaps this time she would even be happy with the result.

"You're smiling as if you have a secret to tell."

Julia jumped, startled at the sound of that deep Scottish burr. She swiveled the big leather chair and found the present-day Gavin MacKinnon standing a few feet away, smiling at her. Her heart crashed into the wall of her chest. "What are you doing here?"

"I wanted to see you."

Julia stood a little unsteadily. She had hoped to see him again. She had just never expected to see him here, at this time of night. "You wanted to see me, so you just decided to break into the house? At midnight?"

"I didn't break into the house, Julia." He approached her, his stride slow and sure, filled with the athletic grace and assurance that radiated from him along with sheer masculine power. He sat on the edge of the desk, at an angle, so that his left foot dangled just above the carpet. He was so close, she could catch a subtle fragrance of sandalwood and the salty scent of the mist clinging to his clothes. "I saw the light in the library and came to see you."

She should be angry, or frightened by the boldness of this man. Yet she couldn't dredge either of those emotions from the turmoil washing through her. It seemed so natural for him to stroll into this room and sit here. "How did you know I was in here? It could have been Helen or anyone."

"I had a feeling it was you." He rested his hand on his thigh, drawing her attention there. It was a large hand, well formed, his fingers long and tapered, his sun-darkened skin a sharp contrast to the buff-colored riding breeches he wore. She tried not to think of that hand stroking her skin, as he had in her dreams, but she couldn't quite manage to pry the image from her mind.

"And what's this?"

She frowned, confused suddenly. "What?"

"This strange little box, with the blue light coming from it."

Strange little box? "It's my laptop."

His black brows lifted. "Laptop?"

"My personal computer." He looked confused. "Haven't you ever seen one before?"

"No. I can't say I have." He studied the small computer for a moment. "It captures the words you put into it?"

How could he manage to live in today's world and not ever have seen a laptop computer? "Yes."

"You're making notes." He turned his head and grinned at her. "Is it for a book you're writing?"

She stared at him, feeling exposed suddenly, as though he had discovered all of her darkest secrets. "How did you know?"

"A good guess." He glanced down at the screen. "You're going to write about the last MacKinnon earl?"

"Perhaps. He led an interesting life." She only hoped she could do the tragic earl justice. Too many times she felt inadequate in putting her thoughts on paper. Perhaps her lack of confidence came from teaching the great works of literature to the freshman at Chamberlain. "Of course, the ending would have to be changed. No one wants to read a romance where the hero is killed in the prime of his life."

"Aye. The ending should be changed."

He lowered his gaze as he spoke, hiding his expression. She caught a note of sadness in his voice, a sorrow in him that couldn't be explained by a distant connection to a man who had died almost two hundred years ago. It only added to the mystery of this man. "Well, it's pretty clear you don't work in an office. Not if you have never seen a laptop computer."

"No." He looked up and smiled at her. Yet a trace of sadness remained in the dark depths of his eyes. "I was never expected to do anything, except take care of my family's estates. But I did go to India for a few years. I got involved in several enterprises that proved to be very profitable."

Add wealthy to the list of his charms. The man was

just too good to be true. "Drugs?" she asked, taking a stab at what she hoped was humor.

Gavin frowned, as though he wasn't certain what she was talking about. "Tea."

The skin at the base of her neck prickled. What had she read about the tragic earl? Hadn't he gone to India? Yes, he had; she was certain of it. He had left soon after his marriage, driven to put as much distance between himself and his wife as possible. Mary MacKinnon had mentioned her son's involvement with the East India Company. Shipping tea. "You were involved in shipping tea from India?"

"For a few years. Still, it wasn't what I wanted to do."

Her heart hammered against her ribs. It could be a coincidence. Couldn't it? Just one of a hundred. "And what was that?"

"I would have liked to have designed buildings and seen them take shape. But my family thought it was beneath me to go into such an enterprise. So I kept myself amused by making improvements to my family's estate."

Julia clenched her teeth. That was one too many in a long line of coincidences. "What game are you playing?"

His black brows lifted in surprise. "Game?"

"Don't play innocent with me; you don't have the face for it." She snatched Mary MacKinnon's journal from the desk and held it against her chest, like a shield. "I may be gullible enough to believe a few coincidences, but you have gone a step too far. What do you hope to gain by coming here and pretending to have the same name, the same background, as the last MacKinnon earl?"

He held her gaze a long moment before he spoke. "I'm not playing a game, Julia."

The soft burr of his dark voice rippled through her. She stared straight into his eyes, expecting to see some sign of his lies, hoping against logic to see only the truth. "You can't really expect me to believe you could have so many things in common with a man who died nearly two hundred years ago."

He curved his hand into a fist on his thigh. "There is a reason for it. Still, I wonder if you are ready to hear it."

Julia squeezed the journal against her chest, a tendril of fear curling upward along her spine. Not the fear that came from a threat to her person, but the kind that came with disillusion. In two days this man had managed to find his way into a secret little place deep inside of her, where she hid her hopes and dreams. "Tell me what you are doing here, and why you have so much in common with a dead man."

He glanced down at the tip of his boot for a long moment before he spoke. "I think you should sit down, Julia."

Her stomach tightened at his words. They were the type of words that preceded something awful. She remained standing, clenching the book in a desperate hope of retaining her composure. "Tell me."

He looked up at her, his gaze as solemn as a judge about to pass judgment. "I am Gavin Duncan Campbell MacKinnon, seventh earl of Dunmore."

She stared at him, his words tapping at her brain, the sense of them utterly lost. "You are the seventh earl of Dunmore?"

He nodded. "Aye."

She wasn't certain what she had expected to hear, but she knew it wasn't this. "You are saying you are a man who died in 1818?"

A muscle at the corner of his mouth twitched. "Aye."

She stared at him, thoughts swirling through her brain. "Do you honestly think I will believe you are a dead man?"

"It's the truth. I came back to Dunmore because I've been given the chance for a miracle, but I can't make it happen without you."

She shook her head, trying to clear away the fog. "I don't know what kind of game you're playing, but I am not about to . . ."

"It isn't a game. I wish it were."

It figured. For the first time in her life she had actually thought she had met the man of her dreams and he was either a con man or a certifiable lunatic. What luck.

He leaned forward, reaching out as though he intended to take her hand. Instead he clenched his fingers against his palm and lowered his fist to his thigh. "I know this is difficult to believe, but I am the earl of Dunmore."

She stared into his eyes, seeing the conviction of his words burning in the dark depths. "You really believe you are a dead man."

"I realize this isn't easy to understand or accept. But it is the truth."

She closed her eyes, shutting out the compelling image he made sitting before her. "You need help."

"Aye. I need your help."

"No." She looked at him. "I mean you need therapy. You aren't well. It isn't healthy to go running around pretending to be dead."

"I'm not ill. And I'm not insane. I'm—for lack of a better term—a ghost."

"There, you see. You're just proving my point." She sank into the chair, burgundy leather sighing beneath her weight. Her luck with men hadn't changed. Would she always come up empty?

"Julia, I can prove to you who and what I am."

She smiled at him, feeling sad and somehow cheated. Would therapy help him? Was she insane to even think of starting a romantic relationship with a man who thought he was dead? She suddenly had a horrible image of herself sitting with this gorgeous lunatic in a room where the wall coverings were done in early mattress. "Unfortunately, you already have."

"You're still up," Angela said.

Julia jumped at the sound of her grandmother's voice, her gaze flying to the door. "Gram. You startled me."

"You're certainly jumpy tonight." Angela walked toward her, the blue satin of her robe flapping around her legs. She held a plate full of cookies in one hand and a glass of milk in the other. She glanced around the room, squinting. "I thought I heard you talking to someone."

Julia looked at Gavin, who remained sitting on the desk, then looked back at her grandmother. She wasn't wearing her glasses. "Mr. MacKinnon stopped by to see me."

Angela paused beside Julia's chair. "At this time of night?"

Julia smiled at Gavin, her chest so constricted that it hurt to breathe. "Midnight is his favorite time of day."

Gavin smiled, a glint of mischief entering his eyes. It made her wonder what outrageous thing he would say next.

Angela glanced at the desk, then back at Julia, a curious expression on her face. "He seems to have a habit of disappearing before I get a chance to meet him."

Julia frowned at Gavin. He was smiling at her in a way that released a trickle of fear into her blood. He was sitting no more than a foot away from Angela.

Even without her glasses, she should have seen him. "Gram, can you see my laptop?"

Angela turned and glanced down at the small computer. "It's right here. Did you forget where you put it?"

"No." Julia's throat tightened. "You don't notice anything strange about the desk?"

Angela turned and examined the desk, staring straight through Gavin. She frowned when she looked at Julia. "Nothing that I can see. What is it?"

Julia stared at Angela. Why couldn't Gram see MacKinnon? Yet the answer was there, sitting right before her. There were simply too many coincidences, too much that made sense, if she was only willing to accept a completely irrational explanation. *A ghost.* The man of her dreams was a ghost.

Chapter Five

No, no, I'm sure,
My restless spirit never could endure
To brood so long upon one luxury,
Unless it did though fearfully, espy
A hope beyond the shadow of a dream.
—John Keats

"Julia?" Angela squinted at her. "All the color has drained from your face. Are you ill?"

Julia swallowed hard. "No."

"Are you sure?"

"Yes. I'm fine. Perfectly fine." Except she was seeing things, such as the gorgeous ghost sitting behind her grandmother. She was the one who needed therapy. "I'm just a little tired."

Angela nodded. "You should go to bed. All of this will still be here when you get up in the morning."

Would Gavin still be here in the morning? "Yes. Rest. I need some rest. I just need to put a few things away before I go to bed."

"Do you want some cookies?" Angela asked, offering Julia the plate of chocolate wafer cookies.

"No. Thank you."

Angela kissed Julia's brow, surrounding her with the mingled scents of floral perfume and chocolate. "Good night, dear."

Julia forced her lips into a smile. "Good night, Gram."

She stared at Gavin as Angela left the room. She listened to Gram's slippered footsteps growing fainter, until she was certain her grandmother was out of hearing range. She closed her eyes, took a deep breath, then looked straight at Gavin. "She couldn't see you."

"I thought it best if she didn't see me."

"I can still see you."

Gavin smiled. "That's because I'm still here."

"You can't be here. You don't exist."

He laughed softly, a deep rumble in the quiet room. "My mother was fond of saying that there was a great deal more to the world than what we could see and touch. I don't think I ever really appreciated those sentiments until after I died."

She leaned forward and poked his shoulder with her finger. A warm, tingling sensation shot through her arm. She could feel something, but definitely not the bulk of solid flesh. "Oh, my goodness."

"Julia, you aren't going to faint, are you?"

"I never faint. I will not faint."

"I'm glad to hear it."

"This can't really be happening. I've made you up; that's what I've done. I've always had an overactive imagination." She stared straight into his eyes and willed her words to be true. "You are a figment of my imagination."

He leaned forward and smiled. "Do you really believe that?"

She closed her eyes, wondering which was worse. Either she was having a conversation with a man who didn't exist, or she was talking to a ghost. A ghost! "Oh, my goodness."

"Take a deep breath, lass."

Julia tried, but her throat was too tight.

"Julia, you have to breathe. You're going to faint."

She would not faint. She never fainted. Still, she couldn't quite convince her paralyzed muscles to draw a breath. Blood pounded in her temples. Pinpoints of light danced against her closed eyelids. Something touched her face, a warm tingling brush against her skin. The warmth slipped beneath her skin and spilled into her blood, spreading through her limbs like a soothing balm. Fear and panic melted under that warmth. The tightness in her muscles relaxed. She dragged air into her lungs like a swimmer who has spent too long below water.

"Julia, open your eyes. Look at me. There is no need to be frightened. I'm not here to harm anyone."

That was a matter of opinion. She looked at him, stared at his handsome face, and saw in his eyes all that she had wanted to find in a man. "How did you do that . . . warmth thing?"

He laughed softly. "If you exist for nearly two hundred years, you learn a few things."

"You're really a ghost?"

He smiled, a slow curving of his lips. Longing filled the dark depths of his eyes and wrapped around her. "You know the truth, lass," he said, his dark voice colored by a trace of sadness. "Don't be frightened of me. I'll not hurt you."

He was wrong. With a single confession, he had managed to destroy all the delicate little hopes she had planted in his name. Of course, that confession was the most remarkable she had ever heard. Julia rubbed her damp palm against her knee; the blue denim of her jeans felt rough against her skin. "Are you sure I'm not dreaming?"

"Julia, I wish it was a dream." He lowered his eyes, his gaze touching her neck, where the soft cotton of her sweater fell away from her skin. "I wish I could face a brand-new day with all the hope and promise of a mortal man. But any hope I had for my future died a long time ago."

Only now did she realize how much hope she had placed in him. She laid Mary's journal on the desk beside him. *Dead.* She stood and walked to the fireplace. She stared into the lifeless hearth, where streaks of black etched the stones. The man of her dreams was dead. She had heard of star-crossed lovers before, but this was just a little ridiculous.

"Julia, I know this is all difficult to accept."

She laughed, the sound hollow and far too close to hysterics to suit her. "You have a flair for understatement."

He moved to her side, bringing with him a scent of sandalwood and mist. "There is something that needs to be done, and I can't do it. Not without . . ."

She glanced up at him when he didn't continue. "Without what?"

A muscle bunched in his cheek. "I need your . . . help."

The words seemed forced. He was obviously not accustomed to asking for help from anyone. "You need my help? How in the world could I possibly help you?"

"It's difficult to explain."

"Why doesn't that surprise me?" She rubbed her arms, wanting nothing more than to curl up into a tight little ball. "Let's see. . . . You're a ghost who needs my help. If I can manage to grasp that concept, I can take on nuclear physics."

His expression betrayed his puzzlement. "Nuclear physics?"

She waved her hand. "Never mind. What is it you need from me?"

He rested his arm along the mantel and studied her for a moment, his dark eyes filled with emotion. "I need you to save my son."

"Save your son?" She stared at him. Could a ghost father a child? No, she wouldn't even imagine that as a possibility. "What do you mean? I thought your son died a few days after you did."

"Aye. But he shouldn't have died that day." He curled his hand into a fist against the smooth mahogany of the mantel. "Neither should I have died as I did. It wasn't my time."

Regrets crowded her chest, hurting her. She thought of her parents, of Mike and Diane. She would always mourn them. She looked up into Gavin's beautiful eyes and wondered how long she would mourn what might have been. "Many people die before their time, Gavin. It's a sad fact of life."

"Aye, it's true. But there are times when mistakes are made. I was granted one chance to alter the past, to make things right. But I can't do it unless I can convince you to . . ." He glanced away from her. "I can't do it unless you help me."

"Me? You mean me specifically, or do you mean any woman?"

"You." He looked down at her, and she could see a glimmer of frustration in his eyes. "You are the only woman who can help me. I've been waiting for you for nearly two hundred years."

His words swam in her head. "You've been waiting for me?"

"Aye. For an eternity, it seems."

The words were there; she understood their meaning, but they made absolutely no sense. "I don't understand how you could possibly have been waiting for me."

"I can't explain it." He gazed at her for a long time, his expression revealing his confusion. "I don't know the reason for it. But we must be connected, you and I. Our lives intertwined in some way."

She felt the truth of what he said, knew it for fact, even though it tested everything she thought logical. "How can I help you?"

"You can go back, and save my son."

She stared at him, not quite believing what he had said. "Do you mean you actually want me to travel back in time and prevent your son's death?"

"Exactly."

"You can't be serious. Isn't it against the laws of physics to change the past?"

Gavin grinned. "I think this chance to change history comes from a higher authority than the laws of physics."

Her breath lodged in her throat. She supposed if ghosts could exist, time travel with a ghost might be possible. "You can actually take me back to your time?"

"We can leave as soon as you're ready."

She felt as though she were on an elevator and all the

cables had snapped. "You're serious. You want me to go back in time."

"I've been waiting a long time for you to come to me, Julia. I can't be any more serious. You are my chance to make things right. My only chance for a miracle."

She looked up into his eyes. The hope shining in the dark depths mocked her every inadequacy. "I can't be your miracle, Gavin. There must have been some mistake."

He shook his head. "There hasn't been a mistake, Julia. You are my only chance for a miracle."

"I can't be anyone's chance for a miracle. I can't go flying back in time. I have responsibilities. Lauren. My grandmother."

"Julia, you are the only one who can do this."

She shook her head. "I can't do this. I'm sorry; I can't."

He leaned toward her, his expression fierce with determination. "Julia, you have to save my son."

She stepped back from him, a sudden fear gripping her. "You stay away from me."

A muscle in his cheek flickered with the clenching of his jaw. "You have nothing to fear from me."

She wasn't at all certain she believed him. She could see the flare of temper in his dark eyes. He was a man accustomed to giving commands, a man who faced any challenge head-on, a man who went to any lengths to get what he wanted. She would not be bullied or manipulated into doing anything. Not ever again. "I'm sorry, I really am, but I am certain there has been a mistake. You must be looking for someone else. Not me."

"You're the one, Julia. You are my only chance."

"Please. Please, just stay away from me." She turned and ran from the room.

"Julia, come back. We need to talk."

She clenched her teeth and kept running away from him. She couldn't help him. She couldn't. And just looking at him hurt her so much that she wanted to cry. She didn't stop running until she was in her bedchamber. The door closed with a soft thud behind her. She turned the key in the lock, then realized it was foolish. A locked door couldn't keep a ghost out of her room.

"A ghost." Tears blurred her eyes as she stumbled across the room and sank to the edge of the bed. He was a ghost. She hugged her arms around herself. As insane as it sounded, she couldn't deny the truth. And he needed her help. "This has to be a mistake. I'm hardly the heroic type."

Now, if she were a heroine in one of her books, she would take the challenge. She would fly back in time, rescue Gavin and his son, and win her happy ending. But she wasn't a heroine in a book. She was an English professor with a little girl who needed her. But Gavin had a little boy who needed her, too. It was just too fantastic to believe. Except she did believe it. "I can't think about Gavin. I can't think of the boy. They both died a long time ago."

Gavin stood in the library, fighting the urge to go to her. There was no point in continuing the discussion. At least not tonight. Still, it was difficult to wait. He had existed in this form for nearly two hundred years. A creature caught between two worlds, cursed with all of his mortal failings. Patience had never been one of his virtues. Hope had been his sustenance all these years. The hope of one day setting things right.

His miracle depended on a woman. He shuddered at that thought. Aside from a few of his female relations, he had a poor opinion of women. Honesty and loyalty were foreign to their nature. Any man who allowed one of them close to his heart would one day pay the price. His own bitterness had been bought at a high cost. He had gone to his grave without changing his views on the fairer sex.

Still, he had a feeling about Julia Fairfield. Without understanding the reasons, he realized he would have chosen her of all women to work his miracle.

Julia, he whispered, the sound of her name doing odd things to his sense of balance.

He had only just met her. Yet he felt he had known her all of his life and beyond. He was connected to her. He sensed it, a connection that defied his experience. The soul lived on long after the body was no more. He had lived before, loved before. Had he loved Julia? Was it possible? Had he known Julia before, in another place, another time? When he looked into her huge blue eyes, he caught himself believing in that most ethereal of emotions—love.

Was this part of the Almighty's plan? Was he to find love now? Love, when there was nothing he could do about it, except look at her and contemplate what might have been.

No. He could not have fallen in love. His heart had turned to stone a very long time before his body had turned to dust. It was no doubt another emotion, one that had blinded him in the past. Apparently lust was still an ailment that could plague him, even in his present state.

He had no doubt he lusted after Julia. He wanted her as much as a mortal man desired his next breath. Still, he had no intention of allowing lust to get in his way. He had a mission to accomplish. He would find some way to convince her to help him. And he would use any means available to him.

Gavin clenched his jaw. Right now it took all of his will to remain where he was. He wanted nothing more than to go to her, to do anything he could to convince her to help him. Lord help him, he had to find a way to gain her trust. He only hoped he had more luck with women in death than he had had in life.

Chapter Six

Cold in the dust this perished heart may lie,
But that which warmed it once shall never die!
That spark unburied in its mortal frame,
With living light, eternal, and the same.
—Thomas Campbell

The next morning, Julia stood at the open French doors of the green drawing room, watching as Lauren presided over a very proper tea party. A table had been placed in the garden beyond the wide stone terrace. White linen ruffled in the breeze, the tablecloth spilling over the edges of the low table. Lauren and the three other girls who lived at the castle had become close friends in a space of a few days. They all sat at the child-sized table in the shade of a tall chestnut tree, wearing oversized straw hats that Helen had dragged from storage, sipping imaginary tea from floral porcelain teacups.

Julia would fight anyone who threatened to take her away from Lauren, even a ghost with a noble cause. Still, she knew he wouldn't give up easily. That type of man never did.

She stiffened, sensing the moment Gavin entered the room. Her heart pounded as she felt him drawing near. Without looking, she recognized the instant he paused behind her. As irrational as it might be, she could feel the energy emanating from him; it bathed her back in comforting warmth. She stared at the children, gathering her courage for the encounter to come.

What would the girls think if they knew a ghost resided in the castle? Though Julia wasn't frightened for them. She didn't imagine for a moment that Gavin was dangerous. At least not dangerous to anything except her heart.

"My son was seven when he died."

A hard hand squeezed her heart at the soft sound of Gavin's dark voice. She turned and faced him. Morning light flowed over his face, burnishing every detail. It was just her luck to run into a ghost who looked solid and real and so handsome her heart ached. "I'm sorry about your son, Gavin. I regret that you both died before your time. But there is nothing I can do to help you."

"You are mistaken, Julia." He smiled, but the smile did not reach his eyes. She saw a hard glint in those dark depths, the determination of a man who would face any challenge life or death presented to him. And she had just become his number-one target. "You are the only one who can set things right."

"You're wrong. I can't help you." Her chest ached,

as though his needs were a boulder pressing against her. "Please, just leave me alone."

"I can't, lass. I've been waiting too long for you to come to Dunmore."

"I keep telling you, I cannot possibly be the right woman to help you." She marched out of the drawing room, intending to ignore him. If she ignored him, he might eventually lose interest in tormenting her. She kept her chin up, her eyes focused straight ahead, but she could still see the ghost walking beside her down the hall.

She would work on her book, she thought, marching into the library. That was what she needed. She would just focus her thoughts on her book, concentrate, forget Gavin was even there. She flipped open her laptop and pressed the power button.

He sat on the edge of the desk, draping a finely muscled masculine thigh near her left hand. "I'm not going away, Julia."

She stared at the blue screen, trying in vain to ignore the infuriating male sitting so close. *He is a ghost,* she reminded herself. "It won't do any good, Gavin. I told you, I have responsibilities. I can't go anywhere with you."

"Once you save my son, I will bring you back to your niece and your grandmother."

It sounded so easy. She glanced up at him, straight into the cold determination in his eyes. "What if something were to go wrong? What if I can't save your son? What then?"

One corner of his mouth tightened. "You will save him."

She saw doubt flicker in his eyes. He wasn't as confident of her success as he pretended to be. And what would he do if she failed him? "How can I be sure you would bring me back to my own time?"

He rested his hand on the desk, close to the fist she held against the polished desktop. "I give you my word. I will bring you back safely."

"No matter what happens?"

"I promise you."

She stared at his hand. It was such a strong-looking hand. Still, she didn't trust him enough to place her entire future in his hands. "I can't do it, Gavin."

He released what sounded like a frustrated sigh. Neat trick for a man who was no longer breathing, she thought. "Are you always so stubborn?"

"Look who's talking." She glanced up at him and immediately wished she hadn't. He was smiling in a way that made her want to capture that smile beneath her lips. Which of course was impossible, because he was a ghost. A tight band cinched around her chest. It wasn't fair. It just wasn't fair.

"Julia," he said softly. "Save my son."

"I can't, I can't." It was too hard, being near him, knowing he was so very far out of reach. Too humbling, knowing she could not help him or his son. "Please, go away. Haunt someone else."

"Julia?" Angela asked from the doorway. "Is something wrong?"

"Wrong?" She glanced at Gavin, then at Angela. "Nothing is wrong. Do you see anything wrong?"

Angela moved toward her, a puzzled expression on her face. "You were carrying on a conversation with your computer. What did you mean, 'haunt someone else'?"

"I was just . . ." *Trying to exorcise a ghost.* Gavin winked at her. Julia balled her hands into fists on her lap. "I was just . . . going over some dialogue for my book."

Angela smiled, seemingly content with the explanation. "I've never known you to do that before."

Julia slanted a glance at the ghost, who sat grinning at her. "Gavin MacKinnon is inspiring me."

"You know, dear, I have a feeling this book could be the one that gets published. You know what they say: third time is the charm."

Gavin leaned toward her. "Julia, I need to talk to you."

Julia slanted him a glare. "Not now."

Angela smiled. "Well, of course not now. Not until after you finish the book."

Gavin stood, strolled to the fireplace, and rested his arm on the mantel. Julia glared at him. "I'm still not even certain there is a story in the life of Gavin MacKinnon."

Angela gestured with her hand, as if to toss away Julia's words. "Of course there is. Just look at the man."

Julia's heart stumbled. "You can see him?"

"Of course I can see him." Angela moved to where Gavin was standing. He sidestepped, avoiding a collision. Angela glanced around. "My goodness, there is a draft in here."

Julia stood, the blood pounding in her temples. "You can see Gavin MacKinnon?"

Angela frowned. "My eyes haven't gotten that bad."

Julia tried to swallow but couldn't manage to find enough moisture in her mouth. "You can really see him?"

"Julia, what has gotten into you this morning?" Angela glanced up at the portrait. "Of course, I can see him."

"Oh." Julia's legs weakened as hope deserted her. "The portrait."

"What did you think I meant?"

Julia clenched her teeth as Gavin walked toward her. "The portrait. Of course. What else could I mean?"

Gavin leaned toward her. "Julia, I will bring you back to your family."

"Go away," Julia whispered.

Angela stared at her. "Go away?"

Julia rubbed her throbbing temples. "Not you, Gram."

Angela glanced around, as though looking for someone else in the room. "Who do you mean?"

Julia shook her head. "No one."

"Are you feeling all right, dear?"

"Yes, I'm fine. Perfectly fine."

"I'm glad you are both here," Helen said as she entered the room. A tall, slender young man walked beside her. *That's all I need,* Julia thought. *More people.*

"Great," Julia muttered, drawing a horrified look from her grandmother. She forced a smile. "It's always great to see you, Helen."

"Why, thank you, dear." A momentary look of puzzlement crossed Helen's features before she turned and smiled up at the young man standing next to her. "I want you to meet someone."

Helen introduced the gentleman as her attorney, a Mr. Farley Bennett, who was also the eldest son of her only sister. Helen's words buzzed in Julia's ears, barely registering on her poor abused brain. Her attention was riveted on the ghost who stood a few feet away, observing everything, invisible to all except Julia. *Lucky me.*

Apparently Mr. Bennett had traveled all the way

from London to deliver a few papers for Helen to sign. Though, from the speculative gleam in Helen's eyes and Gram's satisfied grin, Julia wondered if Mr. Bennett had been invited with something else in mind. Matchmaking was not beyond the scope of either lady.

"Aunt Helen tells me you are a writer, Miss Fairfield."

Julia watched as Gavin strolled over to get a closer look at Farley Bennett. What was he up to?

"Miss Fairfield?"

Julia glanced up at Mr. Bennett. He had a quizzical look in his blue eyes. "Pardon me?"

Farley frowned, looking uncomfortable. "I understand you are an author."

"Oh. No. Not really. I write, but I've never had anything published. I actually teach English literature at a small college outside of Chicago."

Gavin stood beside Farley, tilting his head as he examined the unsuspecting mortal. Farley was nearly as tall as Gavin, yet his shoulders failed to fill out his brown tweed sport coat the way Gavin's would have. Still, he was an attractive man, with thick, light brown hair swept back from a wide brow, a slender nose, and a generous mouth. And he had one major advantage over Gavin—Farley was still breathing.

"I'm sure Dunmore can provide a great many ideas for books, especially if you like gothic romance," Farley said. "I remember all the stories about Dunmore from the days when my parents would bring me here as a boy."

Gavin grinned at her. "Pretty puppy, isn't he?"

Julia shot him a dark look. "Yes, the history of Dunmore is fascinating. Although I'm not sure I'm really interested in doing a story concerning the last MacKinnon. There is something about the man that irritates me."

"Really?" Farley looked surprised. "I have always thought he lived an interesting life."

Julia smiled. "Of course, there is the question of whether or not he murdered his wife."

Gavin looked at her from beneath his lashes. "I didn't. And that was a low blow."

Farley laughed softly. "I should think his possible homicidal tendencies would only make him a more dashing figure."

Gavin lifted his black brows in mock shock. "I would watch out for this one, Julia. He seems a little blood-thirsty to me."

Julia curled her fingers against her palms. She had tolerated all she intended to take from the infuriating ghost. "If you will excuse me, I feel a little chilly. I think I'll run upstairs and put on a sweater."

"But you're wearing a sweater," Angela said.

"Oh, so I am. But it's not the one I want." Julia walked from the room, wondering just how long it would be before someone decided to have her committed.

"I see they still play at matchmaking in this century," Gavin said as he strolled down the hall beside her. "What do you think of Mr. Bennett?"

She glared at him. "What I think of anyone or anything is none of your concern."

"Someone has to look out for you, Julia. I feel it's . . ."

"Go away. Leave me alone."

He grinned. "I can't do that."

She ducked into the drawing room and turned on him. "Stop following me. Stop bothering me. Go away."

"Julia, after you save my son, I promise to stop haunting you."

She crossed her arms over her chest, feeling defensive. "Why am I the only one who can see you?"

He shrugged, broad shoulders lifting the white cotton of his pirate's shirt. "I don't have any reason to allow anyone else to see me. They can't help me."

"Are you sure you don't enjoy driving me crazy?"

He smiled, a grin designed to add an extra beat to any female heart. Her own was already racing too hard to feel the full impact of that smile. "Julia, come back with me. Make things right."

She stared up into his eyes, hoping he couldn't see the pain he had inflicted upon her unsuspecting heart. "I keep telling you, there has been a mistake. I can't possibly help you."

"Julia?"

Julia jumped at the sound of her grandmother's voice. She turned and found Angela standing in the wide doorway. Helen and Farley stood a little behind her in the hall. They all were looking at her as though she had just announced her intention to take a flight to the moon, without benefit of a spacecraft. "I suppose you're all wondering what I was doing?"

"Well, yes, dear." Angela moistened her lips. "It did look a little . . . peculiar."

"There is a simple explanation, really." Julia rubbed her damp palms together, resisting the urge to look at the ghost standing next to her.

Angela smiled, her eyes remaining troubled. "Was it dialogue, dear?"

"Dialogue? Yes. Yes, it was." Julia snatched the idea like a hungry frog catching a fly. "Dialogue. I . . . ah . . . I had some ideas for dialogue. I just thought I would try them out."

"Oh, dialogue," Helen said, relief filling her voice. "For your book."

Julia nodded. "Yes. For my book. The book I'm writing about the last MacKinnon. That book."

Angela frowned. "Are you sure you're feeling all right, dear?"

"Yes. Fine. Perfectly fine. I just need to get my sweater. A different sweater." She hurried out of the room, trying not to notice the odd look Farley Bennett slanted at her as she rushed past him. The man must think she was a lunatic. She wasn't entirely certain she wasn't crazy. She rushed up the stairs and ran down the hall to her room. She closed the door behind her. If Gavin MacKinnon weren't already dead, she would strangle him.

Gavin paused in the hall outside Julia's room, frowning at the sound of the lock sliding into place. "Julia, we need to talk."

"I've said all I intend to say," Julia shouted from the other side of the door. "Now just go away."

He shook his head and walked straight through the solid oak panel. He shivered at the sensation of his energy passing through wood. It wasn't particularly pleasant, but she left him no choice.

Julia stood by the dresser, clutching a blue sweater in her hands, her eyes so wide that he could see the whites all around the dark blue irises. "You just walked through my door."

"Aye. It's one of the few advantages of being a ghost."

She closed her eyes and drew in a deep breath. "I really wish you wouldn't do that sort of thing."

"You locked the door."

"That's because I didn't want you to come in." She glared at him, her eyes narrow slits of blue. "I have no doubt at all that everyone downstairs thinks I've lost my mind. Thanks to you."

Gavin shrugged. "You're a writer. You're expected to be eccentric."

"Of all the ghosts in Scotland, you have to be the one haunting Dunmore."

He grinned at her. "You're lucky I'm here to give you advice."

She rolled her eyes toward heaven. "I wonder if I'll still think I'm lucky when I'm sitting in a padded cell."

"It's clear your grandmother and Mrs. Bainbridge are going to try making a match between you and that Englishman." He sat on the arm of a wing-back chair near the hearth. "He isn't the man for you."

"Oh?" She tossed the blue sweater on the bed and grabbed a pale yellow one from the drawer. "And what makes you an expert on the right man for me?"

The first time he had looked at her, he had thought her a pretty woman; not a remarkable beauty, but lovely. Now he realized he had underestimated her. With color high in her cheeks and her eyes wild with fury, she was extraordinary. And he was a blasted ghost. "If I were alive, I'd show you the kind of man you need."

"Arrogant? Domineering? Infuriating? Thank you, but I have had enough of your type in my life."

He rose and moved toward her. She took a step back, then froze and lifted her chin at a militant angle. He smiled down into her wary eyes. Lord, how he wanted to hold her, kiss the tight line of her lips until she opened them for him, until he could taste all the dark sweetness of her mouth. Yet he couldn't hold her. All he could do was look at her beauty, and think of what might have been. "He hurt you very deeply."

She frowned. "What do you mean?"

"The man who made you suspicious of all men. I don't know what he did, but he hurt you."

"My past is really none of your concern."

"I think it is. I think the man who hurt you is one of the reasons you won't trust me to bring you back here, safe and sound." He saw the truth of his words reflected in her eyes. "You can trust me, Julia. I'm a man who believes in honor."

She turned away from him, but not before he caught a glimpse of something in her eyes, a glimmer of sadness. She leaned her shoulder against the window frame and stared out at the ocean glittering beyond the cliffs. "You expect me to be some heroine out of a romance. I'm not. For heaven's sake, I don't have enough courage to send a manuscript to New York and you expect me to travel back to 1818."

He stared at her slender back, seeing her tension in the way she held her shoulders. His miracle depended on this woman. "You can do this, Julia."

She shook her head. "No. I can't. I would only disappoint you, Gavin. You have to find someone else, someone much more capable than I am."

Placing his faith in anyone wasn't easy for him. Placing his faith in a woman was nothing short of sheer desperation. He had always managed to fight his own battles. Yet, for some reason, he had a feeling Julia could do anything she set her mind to do. "There is some reason the Almighty chose you to be my miracle. I don't pretend to know why, but I do know you can do it."

"I wonder," she said softly.

"What do you wonder?"

She shook her head, denying him entrance to her thoughts. She turned to face him. "Let's say you could actually take me back in time—how do you expect me to change the past? Do I just stroll up to the front door of Dunmore and say, 'Hi. I'm from the future and I've come to make sure you and your son don't die.' "

"I have a plan."

Julia groaned. "I had a funny feeling you would."

"I've had a long time to think about this."

"Well, I need more time to think about it. You can't just pop into my life and expect me to drop everything and go flinging back nearly two hundred years." She shook her head. "When I heard myself say that just now, I had the terrible feeling I had lost my mind."

"I'm really here, lass." He hesitated, uncomfortable with the truth of his next words. "And I need your help."

She rubbed her fingertip against the skin between her brows. "I need time, Gavin. Time to sort through all of this. Just give me a few days."

He clamped down hard on the impatient voice screaming in his brain. He sensed that he would gain nothing by rushing her. "I've waited nearly two hundred years for you, Julia. I can wait a few more days."

That evening Julia sat at the long table in the family dining room and tried to focus on something other than Gavin MacKinnon. She glanced over her shoulder. She couldn't see him. Yet she sensed his presence, watching her. A sharp jab in her ribs brought her attention to her grandmother, who sat beside her. "What?"

Angela lifted her brows, a look of pure exasperation

on her features. She glanced at Farley Bennett, who sat directly across from Julia. "Farley was just wondering how you became interested in writing romance."

Farley cleared his throat. "I would have thought an English professor would have preferred to write something more substantial."

The back of Julia's neck prickled. "More substantial?"

Farley tugged on the lobe of his left ear. "You have to admit, there is something very formulaic about romances. Boy meets girl, boy loses girl, boy gets girl in the end."

Julia managed a smile in the face of his innocent insult. "I suppose you could break down any popular fiction into its basic parts. For example, in a mystery, a body is found, someone hunts for clues, and the murderer is caught."

"I seem to have tread on your toes. I apologize. I didn't mean to trivialize your interest. I just thought a woman of your intelligence . . ." He paused, frowning at his own slip. "I appear to be doing it again."

"It's obvious you have never read a romance," Helen said.

Farley dabbed at his lips with his linen napkin. "No, I haven't."

"And yet you will find elements of romance in nearly every type of fiction." Helen sipped her wine. "Look at the classics, Jane Austin for example."

Jane Austen had died a year before Gavin. She might actually go back to the time of the Regency, Julia thought. The opportunity for research would be incredible. It would be a nice place to visit, if she could be certain of a round-trip.

"And there is always a happy ending," Angela said.

"I find that very reassuring. You certainly can't find fault with a happy ending."

A happy ending. Julia swallowed hard, forcing down a bite of roast beef. Gavin and his son deserved a happy ending. But could she do it?

"I suppose it could make some people too aware of what they lack," Farley said, smiling at Julia. "Someone special to share their lives."

Julia forced her lips into a smile. He was an attractive man, but he couldn't compare to the ghost of Gavin MacKinnon. *Someone special to share her life.* There was no future with Gavin. No matter what she did, even if she managed to save his life in 1818, she could have no future with Gavin.

"I like to think of romances as hopeful," Helen said.

"And are you a hopeful romantic, Miss Fairfield?" Farley asked.

"I try to be. It isn't always easy." *I need you, Julia. Only you can set things right.* Was it possible to go back in time? To change things that went wrong the first time? A chance to change the past, to set things right. It was seductive.

Gavin stood beside Julia's chair, glaring at Farley Bennett across the dinner table. In his day he could have sent the young man scampering away like a pup with his tail between his legs. Only now things were different. The young man couldn't see him, which only added to Gavin's rising temper.

He didn't like the way Bennett looked at Julia, as though he were contemplating having her for dessert. A sense of possessiveness rose inside him, spreading like poison through his being. The emotion startled him. It felt too much like . . . jealousy. Jealousy? Impossible. He had only indulged in jealousy once in his life, for a woman he had later learned to despise. Jealousy was a useless emotion. Still, the feeling was there, like a stone in his shoe, irritating him with every step.

He looked down at Julia, his gaze caught on the curve of her neck, where her blue silk blouse spilled open, exposing pale skin. He leaned toward her, drawn to her. He wanted to press his lips against her skin, inhale her fragrance. He wanted . . . things beyond his reach.

He turned and marched from the room. It irritated him, infuriated him, watching that mortal male drool over her. His chest ached, in the place that had once held his mortal heart. Odd how he could still have sensation when his mortal body had long ago turned to dust. Yet he could feel pain as sharply as he could feel desire or love.

Love? He froze in the hall. Had he really fallen in love with Julia? He had vowed a very long time ago never to imagine himself infected with that disease again. Although he had imagined himself in love once, he had later recognized it as infatuation. An infatuation that had caused nothing but trouble. He had never truly loved a woman in his lifetime.

Still, Julia left him with an uneasy feeling. The Almighty had a purpose to everything. He didn't want to face the reason behind Julia's arrival at Dunmore. Still, he had no choice in this matter. He had been set along this path for a reason, one he had to figure out on his own.

His feeling for this woman would not obey his commands. It would not go away and leave him in peace.

The emotion had plunged too deeply into his soul. Perhaps she had always been there. Was that part of the lesson he must learn?

He closed his eyes and focused on the garden outside the tower. When he opened his eyes he was standing in the garden, facing the wing he had never had a chance to finish. He thought of his mission. There were things he hadn't told Julia about his last day on earth, things she should know. Still, he couldn't risk revealing his suspicions. Not yet. Not until she had agreed to go back to his time. Otherwise, she might be too frightened to help him.

"Julia," he whispered. "I need you."

He was only just beginning to realize all the many ways he needed her, wanted her. A woman beyond his reach. He stared at his hands and thought of how much he wanted to touch her. Caress her cheek, plunge his fingers into the silk of her hair, stroke the delicate skin of her wrist. Why had he never met her in his lifetime? He felt certain, without knowing why, that she would have altered his life. And now? What would happen if she came back to his time?

He looked into the wing where he had lost his mortal life. "Come back to me, Julia. Let me hold you, if only for a brief moment in time."

Chapter Seven

Our doubts are traitors, and make us lose the good we oft might win, by fearing to attempt.
—William Shakespeare

Julia sat on a stone bench in Gavin's private garden, staring at the blue screen of her laptop. The cursor blinked at her from a document with the heading CHAPTER ONE, each electronic pulse mocking her feeble attempt to find the first line of her book. Perhaps it was insane even to consider writing a book about Gavin. The man haunted her, even when he kept out of her sight.

Farley had left for London that morning, after spending the weekend. She had spent most of the past two days in his company. They had taken long walks along the cliff path, and she had thought of Gavin. On the picnic they had shared yesterday, she had tried to concentrate on the conversation, but her mind had drifted to Gavin. It was the same at every meal, each attempt she had made to play bridge or croquet on the lawn, or . . . everything. She couldn't keep her mind off Gavin.

Farley was interested in her. She could see it in his smile. He had such a nice, gentle smile. He was just the type of man she wanted in her life: quiet, sensitive, intelligent. So why did he fail to coax a single tingle, when a ghost could make her heart race?

The air shifted on her cheek. She stiffened, sensing the moment Gavin drew near. She glanced to her right and found him standing a few feet away, watching her. He smiled when she met his gaze, a smile that sent her pulse into a headlong gallop.

"I see Mr. Bennett has finally left," he said, strolling toward her.

"Yes." She tucked her hair behind her ear. "But he will be back. Next Friday."

He sat beside her on the bench and stared down at her empty screen. "He cares for you."

She stared at a dark wave of hair where it lay against his neck. "He is a very nice man."

Gavin turned his head and looked at her, a fierce expression in his eyes. "He isn't right for you."

"You're wrong." She glanced away from him, afraid he might see her doubts. "He is perfect for me. Just the type of man I want in my life."

"And does he make your blood race? Your heart pound? Your skin tingle?"

She slanted him a look meant to cut him off at the knees. "That is none of your business."

He brushed his fingers over her cheek, a phantom

caress that still managed to send tingles shooting along every nerve in her body. "If things were different, I would make it my business."

"We are not well suited." She drew away from him on the bench. "Even if you weren't a ghost. I have this problem with arrogance."

"Arrogant, am I?" He considered this for a moment. "Confident, I think."

She lifted her brows.

He laughed. "And perhaps a wee bit arrogant. But I can't imagine why a woman such as you would not take the challenge of a man such as I."

"I did once. And he very nearly destroyed me. Everything I did was not quite good enough. He wanted me to change my hair, my clothes, the books I read, the movies I saw." She shook her head, remembering how much she had tried to please Nathan. "I don't plan to get involved with that type of man again."

"And you think I'm that type of man?"

She glared at him. "You're the type of man who likes to have his orders obeyed."

"Aye. But something tells me you're woman enough to stand beside a strong man."

She knew better. "I'm not a fighter, Gavin. I hate conflict of any kind. A man like you would end up walking all over me. And I won't let it happen. Not again."

"I wouldn't try to change you. Why would I? I like everything about you." He studied her for a moment, his brows drawn together over the straight line of his nose. "And I can't imagine any man or woman breaking your spirit."

She looked into his darker-than-midnight eyes and

knew the danger lurking there. He was the type of man who could turn a woman into clay, easily molded into anything he wanted. Even as a ghost. "I can imagine it."

"I don't think you realize your own worth. Have you ever taken a good long look at yourself in a mirror?"

"I'm well aware of my faults."

One black brow lifted; a determined glint entered his eyes. "I don't know what you were like when you knew this man who hurt you, but I know you now. And I know you're a strong woman, Julia Fairfield. Too strong for the likes of Farley Bennett. You need a man to match your fire."

A choppy laugh escaped her, a nervous sound she couldn't prevent. "You have me mixed up with someone else."

He shook his head. "What we survive in this life makes us stronger. You don't even realize the strength you have within you. But I do. I believe in you, Julia."

Did he? He shouldn't. She wasn't strong. She was weak and needy and frightened. Yes, most of all she was frightened of failure.

He turned his head and stared toward the tower. "When I realized my miracle depended upon a woman, I was appalled. I had trouble trusting women when I was alive."

"After what Lavinia did, I can well imagine you would have some difficulty learning to trust again."

"Aye." He tilted his head and smiled at her. "You could have changed my mind, Julia. You could have made me see how much I would miss if I didn't learn to trust again."

"That's easy to say now, when we can hardly test your theory."

His black brows lifted. "And it would seem you have the same problem I did in my life. You don't trust the opposite sex very easily."

She shook her head. "I suppose I don't."

He studied her for a moment, a thoughtful expression on his face. "Then I suppose trust is a lesson we both need to learn."

Could she trust this man, this ghost? There was so much at stake.

"Tell me something, Julia."

She held her breath, hoping he wouldn't ask her for a decision concerning a certain flight back in time. She wasn't at all ready to give an answer. "What?"

"Have you made any progress on the book you're writing about me?"

She eased the breath from her tight lungs. "No. I've been too distracted. And I wouldn't hold your breath waiting for it to find its way into book stores. I'm not sure it will turn out to be very good."

"Is that the reason you've never sent anything to a publisher?"

She frowned at him. "How did you know that? No, never mind; you were eavesdropping."

He shrugged. "A ghost has so little company of his own. Tell me, have you never had a book published because you aren't a very good writer? Or is it because you think you aren't good enough?"

She pressed the sleep key on her laptop and closed the lid. Although she didn't look at him, she could see Gavin from the corner of her eye, sitting beside her, watching her, waiting for an answer to a question she had asked herself a hundred times. She knew the truth. She just didn't like to look it in the eye. "I have never sent anything to New York, because until I do, I can imagine my manuscripts are good enough to be published. If I submit them and they are rejected, then I will know I'm not any good. And somehow that is worse than not knowing."

"I suppose you can look at it that way." He stretched his legs out before him. "Still, if you never submit a manuscript, you will never have a chance. Sometimes we have to risk our pride for a chance to get what we really want. I know. I've only recently learned that lesson."

She imagined it had cost him dearly to ask for her help. Still, he had managed to do it. She would love to have the same type of courage.

He held her gaze for a long moment before he spoke. "You have all the courage you need, Julia," he said, as though reading her mind. "You can do anything you put your mind to. I know it. You have a great inner strength. All you have to do is believe in yourself."

Inner strength? She had never thought of herself as a particularly strong person. Still, being around Gavin made her feel more confident than she had in her entire life. He had a way of looking at her that made her feel . . . special. With a glance he could make her feel as though she were the most desirable woman on the face of the planet. He made her feel important. It was just her luck to feel this way with a man who no longer found it necessary to breathe.

"Julia!" Angela called from the far side of the stone fence.

"I'm in here, Gram." Julia glanced at Gavin. "Please go away. She is beginning to think I'm in need of therapy."

He winked at her and rose from the bench. She watched as he strolled across the garden and left by the arched entrance leading to the cliff walk. She stared long after he disappeared. She would have to give him an answer soon.

"Were you working, dear?" Angela asked, sitting down beside Julia.

Julia sighed and set her laptop on the bench beside her. "Trying."

Angela rubbed her palms together. "Pity Farley had to go back to London today."

Julia smiled at her grandmother's thinly veiled attempt at matchmaking. If she hadn't met Gavin, would she be so uninterested in Farley? "He has clients who expect him to be there."

"He is very attractive."

"Yes. He is."

"And I'm certain he likes you. Otherwise I doubt he would have made plans to come back next weekend."

Julia drew her fingertips over the petals of a garnet-colored rose growing beside the bench. It was an old-fashioned rose, one that opened wide to reveal its heart. "Farley is a very nice man."

Angela moaned. "The kiss of death."

The breeze caught Julia's hair, flinging a lock across her cheek. She smoothed it back and anchored the strands behind her ear as she spoke. "What do you mean?"

Angela folded her hands on her lap. "He is nice, but you have no interest in him."

"Not romantically." Instead, she was interested in a man who had died 154 years before she was born. Talk about women who fall for the wrong men.

"What about the young man you met on the path? Gavin MacKinnon? You haven't mentioned him in days."

Her chest hurt just at the mention of his name. "I don't think anything would work out with him."

Angela slipped on her glasses and studied Julia for a moment. "Is something bothering you, dear? You've been distracted for days."

Julia wanted to confide in her, but she wasn't certain how Gram would react to the truth. "It's the research I've been doing for my book. It's a sad story."

"Yes, it is. The entire MacKinnon family destroyed in a few years' time." Angela removed her glasses and let them drop to the front of her rose-colored sweater. "It must have been dreadful for Mary MacKinnon, to survive her sons. At least she never knew her daughter died so early in life."

Julia stared at the huge tower, her gaze narrowing against the reflection of sunlight on the hundreds of diamond-shaped windowpanes. "If someone gave you the chance to go back in time, to alter events, to make a tragedy like that one disappear, would you take it? Even if it wasn't to change a personal tragedy?"

Angela was quiet for a long moment. "We can't go back and change the past."

"But if we could? If someone came to you and told you that you could go back in time and prevent a tragedy such as the one that befell Gavin MacKinnon and his son, would you do it?"

"If it were possible, yes, I think I would. Who wouldn't go back and right a wrong?"

Julia drew in her breath, tasting the faint spice of the sea. "It would take a fool to turn her back on a miracle."

"Julia, has all of this research into the past got you thinking about the accident?"

Julia rubbed her palms against the knees of her navy blue cotton slacks. "I suppose it has."

"It wasn't your fault." Angela slipped her arm around Julia's waist. "You have to let go of the guilt."

"It's not guilt." Julia fought the sting of tears. After all this time, she still could not talk about it without feeling her throat tighten. "It's . . . regret. It's hard not to think of the decision that set things in motion. If I hadn't planned the wedding, Mike and Diane wouldn't have been in town that weekend. If I had never planned the wedding, the accident wouldn't have happened. Or, if I had gone through with the wedding, everyone would have been at the reception the night it happened. Either way, I could have prevented it."

"You weren't responsible for what happened."

"I understand." She smiled at her grandmother. "At times, it's just hard to make my heart believe what my head knows."

She felt a soft brush against her cheek, as though someone had stroked her with his fingertips, so gentle, so soothing. It was Gavin. He was beside her. She could sense him, even though she couldn't see him.

She stared at the tower. Could she do it? Could she change the past? She couldn't keep from thinking that a mistake had been made. She glanced up at the blue sky above her and wondered how on earth she could be anyone's chance for a miracle.

That night when she went to tuck Lauren in, Julia found her niece sitting on the side of the bed, holding the photograph she always kept on the bedside table. Lauren smiled when she saw Julia, but there was a lingering sadness in her brown eyes.

Julia sat on the bed beside her and looked down at the photograph. A smiling couple looked up at her. It was a portrait of a young couple sitting in front of a

Christmas tree, with their first and only child sitting on the floor between them. Mike, Diane, and Lauren. It had been taken the Christmas before Mike and Diane had died.

"I don't remember them," Lauren said softly.

Julia's chest tightened as she looked from the photograph of her brother and his wife to the young girl sitting next to her. "You were very young when they died."

Lauren nodded, her gaze riveted on the photograph she still held. "I just wish I could remember something from the time I had with them. But I don't. Sometimes I pretend I do, but I can't remember. Not really."

"Your mommy would read you stories every night, before you went to bed." Julia wrapped her arms around Lauren's small shoulders and held her close, tears burning her eyes. "And your daddy would hold you in his arms and dance with you to Johnny Mathis songs."

Lauren slipped her arms around Julia's waist and held her close. "I'll keep trying to remember, Aunt Julia."

Julia rested her cheek on Lauren's soft hair. "If you just remember how very much they loved you, it will be enough, Lauren."

"You won't ever go away, will you, Aunt Julia? You will always stay with me?"

The desperation in Lauren's soft voice tore at Julia's heart. "I'll always be here for you, Lauren."

Lauren squeezed her arms tighter around Julia. "Promise."

Julia smoothed her hand over Lauren's soft brown hair. "Promise."

Julia stayed with Lauren until the girl had fallen asleep. She kissed her cheek and left her alone with what she hoped would be pleasant dreams. When she reached her own room, she glanced around, looking for an elusive ghost. She couldn't see him and she couldn't sense his presence. It should be safe, she thought. She needed a nice, long, hot bath.

After filling the tub with hot water and lilac-scented bubbles, she glanced around the large bathroom adjoining her bedchamber. From the history of Dunmore, she knew that in the early nineteenth century, the larger bedchambers had been fitted with baths that boasted hot and cold running water, as well as Bramah water closets. Still, in Gavin's time this room would have been a dressing room. She wondered if Gavin had watched all the improvements take place at Dunmore. And she wondered if he was watching now.

He wasn't in sight and she still didn't have a sensation of being watched. She hesitated a moment before slipping out of her clothes and stepping into the big claw-footed bathtub. Warm water and silky bubbles wrapped around her as she sank into the tub. She leaned back against the smooth porcelain, the scented bubbles brushing the base of her neck. She closed her eyes, sighing as she allowed the warm water to melt away her tension.

All day long she had kept thinking of one thing: What if one of her parents or her brother or Diane had been given a chance to make things right? What if their chance depended on someone just like Julia? She would hope that person would help them. She wanted to help Gavin. She just wasn't certain she could trust him. There was so much at stake. Lauren needed her.

Could she trust Gavin to bring her back, no matter what? It was one thing to leave Lauren because of something beyond her control, an accident or fatal disease. It was another to go sailing back in time with a ghost she hardly knew. Did she have the right even to risk it?

"Now, isn't that a pretty sight."

Julia started at the sound of Gavin's dark voice. She opened her eyes and found him standing a few feet away, grinning at her. She crossed her arms over her breasts and sank lower in the tub, her knees popping out of the bubbles. "I'm taking a bath."

"I might be a ghost, but I can see perfectly."

"Out!"

"I'm a ghost. What harm could there be in my being here?"

It made her think of impossible things. "Voyeur."

He sat on the edge of the tub. "All I can do is look at you. Would you deny me that simple pleasure?"

"Yes." Still, she couldn't deny the pleasure she took in looking at him. He looked as though he had just come in from a walk along the cliffs, his hair tossed into wild dark waves around his face, his white shirt open halfway down his chest, his breeches so close fitting she could see every strong line of his legs. He was a ghost. There was no reason for her heart to race, but it did. "Leave."

He slid his gaze over her, looking at her as though he wanted to devour her. "Do you have any idea how much I would like to climb into that tub with you?"

Her imagination picked up the thread of his words and spun a lovely, erotic tapestry in her head. Heat skimmed across her belly and rose along her neck. "The tub isn't big enough for two people. Even if you were still a person. Which you are not."

He looked at her from beneath lowered lashes. "I'm still a man back in 1818, Julia. Come back to me. Let me hold you, the way I long to hold you."

A whole squadron of butterflies took flight in her

stomach when she thought of being held by this man. "You'll say anything to get what you want."

"Only the truth." He trailed his hand through the water. The bubbles parted as though a human hand slid through the water. Yet not a single bubble clung to his hand. "Why is it I never met you when I was alive?"

She corralled more bubbles with her arm, drawing the white froth over her breasts. "Because you died nearly two hundred years before I was born."

"I suppose that's a good enough reason. I have this feeling about you." He paused, looking at her as though he were trying to solve a puzzle that had been plaguing him. "Were you the woman I was meant to meet and never did?"

Soul mates. She looked up into his eyes and once again felt an odd sense of familiarity. They were connected in some way she didn't yet understand, in a way that was best not explored. "And I suppose you would have fallen madly in love with me had we met."

"After the disaster of my marriage, I vowed never to become entangled with a woman again." He rested his arm on his thigh and leaned toward her, so close she could have reached up just a bit and kissed his mouth. She couldn't, of course, because he didn't have solid lips to kiss. "Still, I don't think I could have resisted you."

He, on the other hand, was the type of man she had avoided since the disaster of Nathan. "It's easy to say, now. When there is no chance of ever making a commitment."

"No chance." He leaned back, his breath escaping on a soft sigh, the sad sound all too real. "Who were you in 1818, Julia? And why didn't I ever meet you?"

Past lives. Love that endured beyond forever. Was it possible? If it was true, then in this lifetime, her true love had never been born, because he was still wandering around Dunmore. She glared at him, suddenly angry at him for directing her down this twisting, depressing path. He was not her true love, she assured herself. She refused to believe this arrogant male was the missing half of her soul. Her one and only love would be a sensitive man who respected her feelings. He would be quiet. A little shy. Someone who would not try to dominate or manipulate her as Nathan had. Certainly not a man like Gavin MacKinnon. She was not at all equipped to deal with a man like Gavin. And if she told herself that often enough, she might actually start to believe it. It was far too hopeless to think of the alternative. "Wait for me in the bedroom."

"Hmmm. Sounds intriguing."

She shook her head, wishing it didn't sound so intriguing to her as well. "Were you always such an outrageous flirt?"

He ran his fingertip over the curve of her jaw, spreading a tingling warmth under the phantom touch. "I knew a great many women in my time. But none of them compares to you."

It was a line, of course. He was determined to get what he wanted from her, and he would say anything to get it. Still, she caught herself wanting to believe she meant something special to him, something besides a chance for a miracle. *Soul mates.* Was it possible? "Leave."

He leaned forward, and the bubbles stirred away from her breasts. "I could stay and help you dry off."

"Out!"

He raised his hands in surrender. "As you wish, milady."

She watched, expecting him to walk straight through the door. Instead he passed his hand over the shiny brass doorknob. The door opened, as though connected to an electric eye. He strolled out of the room, and the door closed softly behind him. "You stay around for nearly two hundred years, you learn a few things," she whispered.

She got out of the tub and dried off quickly. Instead of donning the nightgown and robe she had laid across the back of the vanity chair, she chose fresh clothes from the walk-in closet that opened to both the bath and the bedchamber. She chose black linen slacks and a pale blue silk blouse. As she slipped on a pair of black flats, she considered her choice of clothes. Lord help her, she was dressing for him as though he were a fully functioning male. Perhaps she did need therapy.

Gavin was sitting on the arm of one of the wing-back chairs when she entered the bedroom. He stood when he saw her, a smile curving his lips. "I thought you were going to wear that silky blue gown draped over the chair in the other room."

She frowned, wondering how many times he had slipped into her bedchamber undetected. "And encourage your outrageous attempts at seduction?"

"Seduction?" He moved toward her, each stride slow and filled with a predatory grace. He smiled when he reached her, a lazy smile that whispered of sensual pleasure. "My darling Julia, I only wish I could seduce you. I wish I could carry you to that bed and make love to you. I wish I could touch you, really touch you. You cannot imagine how much I want you."

She fought against the warmth flowing through her

veins. He was a ghost, for heaven's sake. They had a clinical name for women who lusted after dead men. "I'm afraid you won't be so interested in flirting with me when I tell you what I need to tell you."

He frowned. "From the look in your eyes, I can see I won't be pleased with what you have to say."

"No. You won't." She drew in her breath. "I can't help you, Gavin. I can't go back with you to your time."

He lifted one black brow. "You can. But you have decided not to."

"I want to." She turned away from him and walked to the fireplace. "If it weren't for Lauren, I actually think I would do it."

"I will bring you back to her. She will never even know you were gone."

"I assume it will take more than a few minutes. How will they never know I am gone?"

"The passage of time for you in the past will not be the same as for those you leave behind."

"I suppose that is possible." She closed her eyes. "Still, if you aren't telling me the truth, I would be trapped there, in 1818."

"I am telling the truth."

She wanted to believe him, but she couldn't take the risk. Not with Lauren's future. A tingle across her back told her that he had moved behind her. "I'm sorry, Gavin. I can't do it."

"Julia, I understand another man has destroyed your trust in men." He rested his hands on her shoulders, those ghostly hands that still managed to tingle the skin beneath their touch. "I have never in my life lied to a woman, not for any reason. I will bring you back. I swear it."

She wanted to trust him. Yet she couldn't. There was just too much at stake. "I'm sorry, Gavin."

"Julia, if you don't learn to trust again, you will never find happiness."

She knew it was true. But recognizing a fault and conquering it were two entirely different things. She shook her head.

The pressure on her shoulders increased, as though he were squeezing her. "You're my only hope, Julia."

A dark current in his voice prickled the back of her neck. She turned to face him. He was frowning, his eyes filled with a cold glint of determination. She didn't like that look, not one bit. "Gavin, if you're thinking what I think you're thinking . . . you'd just better not be thinking it."

"You want to help me. You just don't trust me. And I'm afraid there is really no way for me to convince you."

Panic started low in her chest and shot upward. "Gavin, you wouldn't."

"You leave me no choice." He slipped his arms around her. "I promise, Julia, I will bring you back."

"No!" She struggled against his embrace, but the energy binding her to him was far too strong. The room wobbled, everything around her blended together, like a watercolor in the rain. She felt as though the floor was dropping away from her. She gripped Gavin's shoulders, those phantom shoulders that suddenly felt more solid than anything in the world.

"Trust me, Julia."

His voice sang with the blood pounding in her ears. The world swirled in her vision, all the colors blending into black. She whipped her arms around Gavin's neck, held on for dear life. They were flying; she was certain of it. When they landed she would strangle him for this. And then she would force him to take her back to her own time.

"I promise, lass," Gavin whispered, his voice swirling through her brain. "I will bring you back. No matter what happens."

Chapter Eight

In time there is no present.
In eternity no future.
In eternity no past.
—Alfred, Lord Tennyson

The woman wanted more than a tumble in his bed. Beatrice MacQuarrie wanted marriage. It was for that reason that Gavin had left the widow's home without accepting the all too obvious invitation for much more than dinner. He urged Vulcan into a gallop. The horse responded in a heartbeat, stretching out beneath him. Hooves pounded the hard-packed dirt road. He leaned low over the horse's neck, Vulcan's black mane whipping against his shoulder. A cool wind tinged with the salt of the ocean brushed his face. Yet it wasn't enough to cool the lust smoldering in his blood.

Beatrice knew precisely how to heat a man's blood. Unfortunately, it was all she could warm. He could still feel the press of her soft, plump bosom against his chest, the wet slide of her tongue upon his neck, hear her soft words ringing in his ear: *It gets so lonely at night, Gavin.* Still, aside from the uncomfortable pinch of his breeches, he had had no trouble leaving her tonight. The lovely Beatrice was as cold and calculating as Napoleon when it came to acquiring something she wanted. At the moment, she wanted his title and everything that went with it. He had fallen for that particular trap once. He would never do it again.

He could control lust. A man was a fool if he allowed his emotions to rule him, even one as basic as lust. He took his pleasure on his terms, as he took everything else in life. Although he was a generous man with his mistresses, no woman had ever gone to his bed thinking she would find a permanent place in his life. He had pleasure and gifts to share. Nothing more. All the tenderness had been seared out of him at an early age. Disappointment awaited any woman who thought she could trick him into marriage.

Strands of mist drifted over the road. Moonlight shimmered on the vapor, spinning the mist into silver, like a fairy's touch. His mother would say it was a night for magic.

A short distance from the gates of Dunmore a figure materialized from the mist, directly in front of him. His heart surged at the sudden danger. He pulled back on the reins, trying to swerve Vulcan from his path. A woman's scream ripped through the mist.

Vulcan snorted at the sudden jerk on his bridle. The beast reared and pawed at the air. Gavin kept his seat, fighting to control the huge animal. Vulcan stamped his hooves, slowly calming until he stood docilely by the side of the road.

Gavin leapt from the saddle and ran back to where the woman had appeared. Mist swirled around his legs. Pale fingers of white curled around the dark shape of a woman crumpled in the middle of the road. He sank to his knees beside the horribly still figure, his heart pounding. She lay on her side, her blond hair thrown over her cheek.

Gently he turned her, lifting her head and shoulders, cradling her on his lap. He smoothed the hair away from her cheek, the silky strands sliding through his fingers. Moonlight poured over her face, painting the high crests of her cheeks, the dark fringe of her lashes, the slim line of her nose, the full, slightly parted lips. His mind registered her beauty even as his heart feared the worst. A dark trickle of blood stained her brow high on the right side, near her hairline.

He pressed his fingers to the pulse point in her neck and held his breath. Her skin warmed his fingers. A pulse throbbed beneath his touch, steady and sure. "Thank God."

He slipped his arm under her knees and lifted her in his arms. Her head lolled against his shoulder, her soft sigh brushing his neck. For a moment he froze on the road, struck with an intense sense of protectiveness and something more. Something he couldn't quite identify. Something surprising.

He frowned down at her. He had never in his life seen her before. Yet, for some reason, she seemed familiar and somehow . . . important. It was as though he had known her before, held her before. A clean scent drifted with the heat of her skin; an elusive floral scent, a fragrance that made him want to press his lips against her neck and breathe the essence deep into his lungs. "Who the devil are you?" he whispered.

A soft moan was her only reply. He turned toward the house and whistled for Vulcan. The horse trotted after him like a puppy as he carried the woman through the gates and down the long, tree-lined drive leading to Dunmore. What the devil was a woman doing walking alone out here in the middle of the night? That and a hundred other questions flitted through his brain as he carried her to his home. He climbed the three wide stone steps and gave one of the tall front doors a hearty kick.

Nothing happened. He kicked the solid oak once again. Since he had sent most of his staff to London with his mother, there was only a handful of servants at Dunmore. Apparently no one could hear him.

He clenched his teeth and shifted her in his arms. Her head fell back, spilling her hair over his arm, exposing the vulnerable curve of her neck. Heat swept over him, from his head down to his toes, a heat more fierce than any Beatrice had conjured this night. He dragged his gaze from her, shaken by the intense emotion gripping him. Although he had become cautious in his escapades with women, he was not a monk. He was accustomed to lust, knew it intimately, explored it as often as possible. Of course this must be lust, more virulent than most cases, but lust at any rate.

He bent, shifted her weight, and managed to open the door. He stepped inside the large entry hall and yelled, "Erskine!"

Gavin didn't wait for the butler. He carried her across the marble floor of the entrance hall and headed toward the wide staircase that rose in a graceful curve to the upper floors. "Erskine!"

When he reached the first step, his butler scampered from the hall leading to the kitchen. "Milord?"

"Send for Henderson, and tell Iona to come straight up to my room."

"Aye, milord." Erskine bobbed his head.

Gavin hurried up the stairs, careful not to jostle the woman in his arms. He went straight to his room and laid her down upon the dark blue silk counterpane. After lighting the lamp on the bedside table, he turned and stared down at the stranger.

Aside from the blood on her brow, she appeared to be uninjured. Her breathing was steady, though each breath was perhaps a little too shallow.

Her hair spilled across his pillow, the honey gold mane framing her pale face. He wondered what color eyes were hidden from his view, and he prayed she would open them soon.

Her clothing was of a strange fashion. She wore trousers, but like none he had ever seen before. Her tailor should be shot. Still, the black linen hugged her small waist before being gathered into two front pleats and falling loosely around her slender hips. The left side of the trousers was dusty from her collision with the road. The blue silk shirt had buttons running along the entire front, with embroidery of a floral pattern on the pointed collar. The material was costly, the workmanship exquisite. She was obviously not a servant.

"What were you doing here tonight?" he whispered.

She stirred, her lips moving with a soft sigh. "Please don't do this," she muttered. "Please don't!"

The terrified whisper tore through him. He sat on the

edge of the bed and cupped her cheek in his hand. "You're safe now."

"Gavin," she whispered.

She might have slapped him. He stared at this stranger who seemed so familiar. How the devil did she know his name? Suspicion gripped him, latching onto his vitals like a viper sinking its fangs. He had learned a long time ago that there was usually method behind most of the illogic of women. He suspected this woman had not been wandering about Dunmore to take in the evening breezes. He stood and studied her sleeping face. Was she another huntress?

Although there were many in London who believed him a murderer, it did not deter the huntresses in search of prey. This past year he had discovered that a title coupled with enormous wealth could cleanse the blackest of reputations. In January he had accompanied his mother, his sister, and his younger brother to London. At first he had been concerned that his reputation might prove poison for his sister. Yet the table in the hall of his house on Pall Mall had nearly bowed beneath the weight of the invitations they received.

At parties, the more coy of the ladies dropped handkerchiefs at his feet, so many he could have rigged a schooner with fresh sails. The bolder ladies fainted from the heat and conveniently fell against him. They dropped at such a rate, he feared half the female population had been afflicted with apoplexy. In the space of a week, five different women had stepped out in front of his carriage while he drove through Hyde Park. No accident had occurred. Each young lady had managed to step out of the way, fainting only after he climbed down to make certain there had been no injury. Then there were the women who found their way into his home via a connection to his mother or sister.

In March he had left his family in London and returned to the solitude of Dunmore. A week later, Beatrice MacQuarrie had shown up at his door. Claiming to be bored with Town life, she had also returned to the island. He knew what game she was playing.

Now a beautiful young woman just happened to be prowling the grounds of Dunmore in the middle of the evening. What was her game?

He stood as his housekeeper, Iona, bustled into the room. Dark gray wool fluttered around her plump hips as she hurried toward him. She halted beside him, breathing hard, her cheeks flushed, her blue eyes round and as alert as an osprey hunting fish. The little woman had been his mother's nurse when she was a child. Now she looked after everyone at Dunmore. "What's happened?"

"There has been an accident." At least it appeared to be an accident. "Make her comfortable. She appears to be close to my sister's size. See if Alison has left behind a nightgown this woman can wear."

Iona nodded. "Aye, milord."

Gavin left the room and went directly to the library. He opened a cabinet across from his desk and poured a generous portion of brandy from a decanter into a crystal glass. The stopper fell back into the decanter with a soft ping. He sipped the brandy, the pungent aroma filling his senses, the heat of the aged liquor spreading like balm through his tight chest. When the woman in his bed awakened, he would have some answers. He only hoped he could believe them.

He turned and noticed the small boy sitting in one of the leather armchairs near the lifeless hearth. Brandon's slim legs peeked out from beneath his big white nightshirt, his bare feet dangling above the carpet. He hugged a book against his chest, the look in his dark brown eyes haunted, as though he expected Gavin to slap him. Gavin's chest tightened when he thought of all the careless blows this child had received in his young life. And once again he wanted to strangle Octavia Harcourt.

Gavin had known his son for only five months of the entire seven years the boy had been on this green earth. He had learned of his existence nearly a year after Lavinia's death. Gavin had been stunned by the news that he had a son. He had questioned the child's paternity until the day he had first met the boy. The resemblance the boy had to his sire eliminated all of Gavin's doubts. Why the hell had Lavinia never told him about the boy? Yet he soon realized the answer to that riddle.

A child would have intruded on the life Lavinia had styled for herself after he had left for India. Lavinia had enjoyed her life as a married countess. She had lived in the house on Berkeley Square, given parties, taken lovers—in short, she had lived her life precisely as she had chosen.

Things would have changed with a child. Gavin would have returned for a child. He would have expected her to be a proper mother. Aye, he could well understand why Lavinia had never told him she had given birth to his child. And the Harcourts had never betrayed their only daughter. No, they had only betrayed the wee lad put into their care.

"Couldn't sleep?" Gavin asked, keeping his voice soft.

Brandon shook his head, a dark lock tumbling over his brow. "I thought I might read a little."

Gavin set his glass on the cabinet, crossed the distance, and hoisted his son in his arms. Brandon gripped his shoulder, a momentary fear crossing his features before he accepted his father's hug. Gavin turned and sank to the chair, cradling Brandon in his arms. "And what are you reading?"

Brandon grinned at him, just a smile, but that innocent grin pierced him, unfurling inside of him in a ribbon of warmth. "*Marmion* by Walter Scott."

"Ah, a good Scots writer."

Brandon rested his head on Gavin's shoulder and looked up at him. "Are there any barbarians living in the Highlands, Papa?"

Gavin lifted his brows, surprised by the candid question. "I think most of the barbarians died out a few years ago. And why would you be asking me such a question?"

Brandon glanced down at the book he held closed upon his lap. "Grandmother told me I had to be very careful or I would grow up to be a barbarian, like all the Highlanders. That's why she made me sit in the chapel for three hours every day. She said I had bad blood and I had to be especially pious or I would end up wearing animal skins and carrying a club."

Gavin tightened his arm around the boy's slender shoulders. "Your grandmother told you many things that weren't exactly true."

"I know. She said you hated me and never wanted to see me." Brandon tilted his head and smiled up at his father. "That's not true."

"No, lad. That's not true." Gavin smoothed the dark hair back from Brandon's brow. "You're very important to me."

Brandon's expression turned pensive, a question forming behind his clear brown eyes. "I don't understand why Grandmother tried to stop you when you came for me. She doesn't like me. She never did."

"Your grandmother thought keeping you from me would punish me for crimes she imagined I'd committed."

Brandon nodded. "Like murdering Lavinia."

"Aye." Gavin stroked the lad's hair, his chest tight with emotion. "I didn't murder your mother."

Brandon nodded, a lost look entering his large eyes. "I didn't know her well. But I did know that she didn't like me either."

Gavin hugged the boy close against his heart. "I love you, lad."

Brandon slipped his arms around Gavin's neck and hugged him. "I'm glad you found me, Papa."

Gavin closed his eyes against the sting of tears. "So am I, lad. I'm very glad I found you."

Gavin held the boy until Brandon's breathing slipped into a deep, even rhythm. He carried his son to his bedchamber and tucked him into bed. For a moment he stood beside the bed, smiling down at the boy's sleeping face. Seven years had been stolen from him through the treachery of a woman. He couldn't get those years back, but he could make certain they made the best of the years ahead of them.

His thoughts drifted to the woman lying in his bed. What was it about her? He didn't even know the color of her eyes; he had never heard her voice. Yet he felt he knew her. He ran his hand through his hair. He needed answers.

Two hours later, he stood in the hall outside his bedchamber, waiting for Henderson. The woman had not roused while Iona tended to her. Gavin was beginning to wonder if she was more seriously injured than he had first thought. It seemed an eternity before Dr. Henderson finally emerged from the room.

Short and stout, the surgeon had come to live on the island five years ago upon his mother's request. He was the only surgeon on the Isle of Mist. Fortunately, he was also very skilled. "How is she?"

Henderson removed his glasses and rubbed the bridge of his nose. "From what I can tell, aside from the bump on her head, she appears to be sound physically. The head injury might be nothing, and then again, it could be serious. We won't know until she awakens."

"When do you think that might be?"

"It's hard to tell. A few hours, perhaps." Henderson fitted the wire frames of his glasses back over his ears. "Right now, the best thing for her is sleep."

When the surgeon left, Gavin returned to his chamber. He found Iona standing at the foot of the bed, staring at an ivory strip of cloth. She frowned at Gavin when he drew near. "I don't know where this woman comes from, but they wear some odd garments there."

Gavin took the strip of material and held it up by what appeared to be straps. Ivory lace was fashioned into two cones, each connected to a wide band of stretchy lace. He had never seen this type of material before.

"I blush to tell you what that garment is for."

Gavin could only think of one possible use for such a garment. Blood pumped slow and heavy into his loins at the image rising in his mind.

"And these. I've never seen pantalettes like these." Iona shoved a filmy piece of ivory silk at him.

He refrained from taking it from her. His imagination didn't need any more stimulation. Instead he lifted the trousers from the bed. A pair of serrated metal strips lined the front placket where the buttons should have been.

"It took me a while to work out that little puzzle." Iona took the garment from him and pulled on a small metal tab. The placket closed as she drew the tab upward, the metal edges fitting together to form a seal.

Gavin ran his fingertip over the metal strip. "Remarkable."

"Where did she come from, milord?"

Gavin shook his head. "I have no idea."

"Would you like me to sit with her."

"No. I'll stay with her."

After Iona left, Gavin pulled an armchair beside the bed and took up his vigil. He didn't want to leave her alone. For some irrational reason, he sensed that she needed him, and that bothered him. He wanted to be here when she opened her eyes. He wanted to know exactly what had brought her to Dunmore.

Julia's head ached. Light pounded upon her lids, demanding that she open her eyes. Yet she hesitated. She didn't want to open her eyes. Somewhere in the back of her mind she knew she wasn't going to like what she saw. She couldn't remember what it was; she only knew she wanted to remain sleeping.

She turned her head. Pain burned high on her brow. A moan crawled up her throat and escaped in a pitiful little whimper. In spite of her best efforts, her body was succumbing to the pull of morning. She pried open her lids and blinked.

Sunlight poured through the windowpanes, assaulting her senses. What in the world had she done to deserve this blasted headache? Something moved to her right. She turned her head and tried to focus on the blurry image. A tall figure stood beside her bed, a man in a pool of sunlight.

"I see you're finally coming round."

His dark voice washed over her, the soft Scottish burr triggering a distant memory. "Gavin," she whispered.

He sat on a chair by the bed and leaned toward her. "You seem to have me at a disadvantage."

Sunlight touched his hair, shaping a halo around his head. But the expression on his handsome face was far from angelic. If this was an angel, he had fallen a long time ago. His black brows were tense, carving a slight line over his slim nose. Beneath those slanting black brows, he stared at her with eyes as black as polished ebony and every bit as hard. World-weary eyes. Wary eyes. Suspicious. Bitter.

"Who are you?" It wasn't merely a question; it was an accusation.

"That's an odd question." She rubbed her throbbing temples.

He lifted one black brow. "It seems appropriate under the circumstances."

What was it about Gavin? There was something she should remember. Something about last night. Memories shifted in her poor abused brain, gathering into images. "You want me to . . ." She stared at him, all the pieces clicking into place. "You! Don't you dare come near me."

Both brows lifted above puzzled eyes. "I assure you, I mean you no harm."

"Don't you touch me." She scrambled off the other

side of the bed. "I have no intention of going anywhere with you."

"I shall remember that if I ever take the notion to invite you to go somewhere with me. Did you have a place in mind?"

"Don't you play games with me." She pointed an accusing finger at him. "You know exactly what I mean."

He planted his elbows on his thighs and rested his chin on the back of his clasped hands. "Perhaps you could refresh my memory."

There was something different about him. Something she couldn't quite place. He seemed harder than before. It was then she began to notice her surroundings. The bed was a large four-poster, with thick, heavily carved mahogany posts holding a canopy of dark blue silk brocade. Gold lions pounced across the silk. The same lions attacked invisible prey on the thick counterpane. It wasn't the bed in her room at Dunmore.

She turned and stared at the rest of the furnishings. The room was huge, larger than her bedchamber. Mahogany wainscoting covered the walls. A tall armoire stood against the opposite wall across from a large chest of drawers. A dressing table stood next to a door that led to what she assumed would be a dressing room. Twin wing-back chairs upholstered in coffee-colored leather sat near the fireplace. "This isn't my room."

"No. This is my bedchamber."

She glanced down at the nightgown she was wearing. Soft cotton lawn fell to just above her ankles. Intricate embroidery in soft pastels formed flowers and leaves from the neckline to just above her breasts. Tiny loops of fabric secured small pearl buttons from her neck to her waist. It was lovely. Modest. And she had never in her life seen it before. "This isn't mine."

"It belongs to my sister."

She plucked at her long sleeve. "How did I get into this?"

He released what sounded like a bored sigh. "My housekeeper saw to your needs last night."

"Your housekeeper." Realization slammed into her, snatching the breath from her lungs. She stared at him for a full twelve beats of her frantic heart before she could find her voice. "You did it."

"Did what?"

Oh, she wasn't in the mood for clever ghosts. "You brought me here."

"It seemed the best thing to do at the time."

"Did it?"

"Aye. You needed assistance."

She did not need assistance in making up her mind. She had made her decision. It was based on the needs of her niece. Gavin simply had decided to ignore her wishes. She stalked him. When she came around the side of the bed, he stood, looking like a lion who thought an annoying mouse might try to bite him. "Nothing gives you the right to kidnap me. I don't care how noble your cause."

"Kidnap you?"

She paused a foot in front of him, so angry she could strangle him, if he weren't already dead. "What would you call it?"

His black eyes narrowed. "I see. That's how you intend to play it."

She frowned. There was something different about

him. Something that just didn't seem right. "The way I intend to play it? I had nothing at all to do with this."

He rolled his eyes toward heaven. "And what do you plan next? If you think I'll pay you to prevent some little manufactured scandal, think again. I've already murdered a woman. Kidnapping pales in comparison."

"Murdered?" She stared up at him, a pointed little suspicion poking her straight in the ribs. "You told me you didn't murder your wife."

He frowned. "And how did I do that when last night was the first time I ever laid eyes on you?"

"Last night? Are you saying you only met me last night?"

"Aye. When you came running out of the mist straight into the path of my horse. You're lucky I didn't run you down." He leaned forward until the tip of his nose nearly touched hers. "Now I'm thinking I should have left you in the dirt."

She stared at him, seeing the honest anger in his eyes. "You really don't know me?"

"No. Unfortunately, the situation seems to dictate I shall."

The look in his eyes left no doubt. The scent of sandalwood drifted to her senses with the heat of his body. It was then that she realized the differences in him. She could feel the heat of his body. And his cheeks . . . there was stubble on his cheeks, black and rough-looking.

His hair was tousled, his shirt open at the neck. Even though he looked as though he hadn't slept all night, he also looked incredibly handsome. And absolutely real. She tried to swallow, but her throat was too tight. She poked his shoulder with her fingertip. Instead of plunging into tingling energy, her finger slammed into solid muscle. "You're real."

He frowned. "And what were you expecting me to be?"

She stared up into his black eyes. "A ghost."

He blinked. "A ghost?"

"Yes. You are a ghost. At least you're a ghost in my time. But this isn't my time. This is your time. Isn't it?" She rubbed her throbbing temples. "What year is it?"

Gavin didn't reply. Instead he stared at her, as though he expected her to bite him.

"It's 1818, isn't it?"

He hesitated for a moment. "Aye. The tenth of April."

She turned away from him. The soft cotton of her gown brushed her bare legs as she paced to the windows. "Since it's 1818, you're alive. Which means your ghost isn't here. Or does it?"

She glanced around the room. Nothing. She couldn't see him. She couldn't sense anyone, except the tall man standing near the bed. If she couldn't find Gavin, she was literally stranded here. Stranded 181 years away from Lauren, away from Gram, away from everyone and everything she knew. Alone. Completely and utterly alone.

"Gavin, if you are here, show yourself. Please, show yourself." Her chest tightened. Tears burned her eyes. She squeezed her hands, fighting to maintain some semblance of control. "Gavin, please."

A warm hand settled upon her shoulder. She glanced at that strong-looking hand, his long, elegantly tapered fingers curled against the white cloth—so solid, so warm, far too real. He was the only person she knew in this entire world. And he had no idea who she was. She looked up at him, saw the wariness in his eyes, the suspicion that she understood. He didn't know what to make of her. For all he knew, she was either crazy or worse.

He could toss her out on her ear, abandon her in this place. She had no money, no friends, no chance of surviving without him. Gavin's voice whispered in her memory.

I promise, lass. I will bring you back. No matter what happens.

She had wondered if she could trust him. Now she had no choice. Gavin expected her to save his son. Nothing would happen until she had a chance to accomplish that mission. She knew that for the truth. If she had a prayer of making it back to her time, it rested squarely on Gavin MacKinnon's broad shoulders. This Gavin MacKinnon—the living, breathing man standing so close that she could feel his warmth radiating against her.

She swallowed hard, pushing back the panic lodged in her throat. "I need your help."

Chapter Nine

Three things a wise man will not trust,
The wind, the sunshine of an April day,
And a woman's plighted faith.
—Robert Southey

Gavin frowned, surprised at the sincerity in her voice. This woman could not be trusted, he reminded himself, just as the flames she had ignited in his blood, the smoldering heat coiling through his veins could not be trusted. Both would ruin a man. A moment ago she had threatened him with a scandal. No doubt she was a cunning little baggage on the hunt for money and possibly more.

She rested her hand on his sleeve, a light touch that betrayed the tension coiled within her. His chest tightened in response. "Please, Gavin. You're the only one who can help me."

She was looking at him as though he could move mountains in her name. And he caught himself wanting to ask where she wanted them. She was a good actress; he had to hand her that. So sincere. So utterly beguiling. A part of him knew he should get rid of her as quickly as possible. She would prove nothing but trouble. Still, perhaps it was best to wait until he knew precisely what game she was playing before he sent her packing.

He took her arm. As he led her toward the fireplace, she leaned against him as though she might draw some strength from him. Against all the sane dictates of his brain, his body responded. He felt a stirring inside of him, in a place he had kept guarded for a very long time, so long he had thought it decayed and empty. He crushed the insane urge to slide his arm around her and hold her close.

Only a fool would draw a viper close to his heart. Yet the desire was there, pumping strong and hard through his veins. Lust tempered with something new. Something he couldn't quite identify. Something that left him edgy. The woman was definitely dangerous.

She sat on the edge of the chair and folded her hands in her lap, squeezing them together so hard that her knuckles blanched and her fingers turned red. She looked for all the world like a woman who needed all of her will to keep from unraveling.

Don't trust her.

He reminded himself of the treachery of women. The art of deception was taught to most of them as babes and nurtured through the years, until they were released upon Society to deceive and manipulate the male of the species. Women could look you straight in the eye and lie about anything, including love and devotion. He had learned that truth at a high cost.

He glared at her bowed head. This woman looked like one of the more accomplished of her sex. The type that could easily make a fool of any poor, unsuspecting male who forgot to protect himself. He had proof of that as well: the uncomfortable coiling of tension in his nether regions. He strolled to the fireplace, putting some distance between them.

"I'm going to need your help in getting back home."

Back home. Away from him. "Tell me where you live, and I'll make certain you get there safely."

"Far away." She laughed, a high sound far too close to hysteria to suit him. "Much too far away."

Her accent betrayed her origin. "You're an American, I assume."

She nodded. "From just outside of Chicago."

"Chicago. I've never heard of that town."

"No. I expect you haven't."

She moistened her lips, a quick slide of her tongue that left an inviting sheen. Soft pink lips. And what would he taste if he kissed those lips? He curled his hands into tight fists at his sides. He would not fall prey to feminine wiles. Not even those as lovely and alluring as hers. "Since you are so free with my given name, could you trouble yourself to tell me who you are?"

"I'm Julia." She tucked her hair behind her ear. Such soft-looking hair. The tresses fell in a thick honey-gold cascade to her shoulder blades. "Julia Fairfield. I suppose I should call you Lord Dunmore, but it just sounds so formal."

"Informality is an American trait, I think."

She smiled, a shy little smile that left her eyes filled with uncertainty. "Yes, I suppose it is."

"Under the circumstances, I see no reason to stand on ceremony." What was her game? He rested his arm on the mahogany mantel. "How did you come to be at Dunmore, Miss Fairfield?"

She turned her hands and opened her palms. "You won't believe me."

She did it again—surprised him. "How do you know?"

She peeked at him from beneath her lashes, not a coy look, but a look filled with . . . fear? "Because if I were in your position, I would not believe what happened."

Sincerity. The woman was very good at what she did. "Tell me."

She drew in her breath, her slender shoulders lifting the cotton of her nightgown. The garment was so modest, he could scarcely see more than a suggestion of her shape. Yet that was enough to heat his blood several more degrees.

"It might sound insane," she said softly. "It might even sound impossible. And I'm not at all certain how to explain it."

She intrigued him. Just where was all this leading? "Were you on your way here to see me?"

"Yes and no." She glanced up at him. "I came to Dunmore to visit a dear friend of my grandmother, Mrs. Helen Bainbridge."

He frowned. "There is no one named Bainbridge living here."

"Not now. But there will be. At least I think there will be." She tilted her head and stared toward the windows. "That is, unless I change history. If I do, then I suppose it's possible Helen's great-grandfather might not win Dunmore in a card game. And if I don't change history, then I suppose I could be trapped here. Still, I have to believe you will keep your word. It's my only hope, really."

He stared at her. In his experience the logic employed by women had never been particularly direct. Still, he had never experienced anything or anyone quite like Miss Fairfield. He had the uneasy feeling that if he listened too closely, he might very well end up with his wits twisted into a knot. Still, much to his discomfort, he discovered he wanted to know everything about her. "So you came to visit this Mrs. Bainbridge, who does not yet live at Dunmore."

She nodded. "That's when I met you."

"I didn't think you were in any condition to remember meeting me last night."

"I don't mean last night. I mean at Dunmore."

"This is Dunmore."

"Yes. But this isn't the Dunmore I'm talking about."

"I didn't realize there was another."

She frowned. "There isn't."

He drew in a long, steady breath. "There isn't another Dunmore, but this isn't the Dunmore where you met me."

She smiled. "Exactly."

He knew it. He never should have tried to make sense of her. He could feel his brain twisting into a knot already. "Perhaps you should rest awhile, Miss Fairfield. You had a nasty jolt last night."

She laughed, the sound hollow and frayed. "You're telling me."

"I'm sure after a little rest you will be thinking much more clearly."

She looked at him, staring straight into his eyes as she spoke. "I'm not insane. Although what I have to tell you might seem insane. I could lie, of course, but I've never been very good at lying, and there is far too much at stake for me to try now."

Very convincing act. If it was an act. Sometime during the conversation he had decided upon another possibility—the woman might actually have addled her wits last night. "I've never cared much for lies."

"I know. You had enough lies with Lavinia."

He clenched his teeth at the mention of that woman's name. Apparently Miss Fairfield was well versed on his history. "I've had enough dishonesty to last a lifetime."

"I'm telling you the truth." She rubbed her arms, as though she were chilled. "The Dunmore I'm talking about, the Dunmore where I met you, is nearly two hundred years in the future."

He wasn't certain what he had expected her to say, but he was certain it definitely was not this. "The future?"

"Yes." She unclasped and clasped her hands. "You see, I'm from your future. I met you in 1999."

He studied her for a moment. A soft rose deepened her pale cheeks, emphasizing the color of her eyes. Her eyes, those eyes that rivaled a highland sky, held his gaze without wavering. She looked so lovely that his chest ached, and she also looked absolutely serious. "You met me in 1999. I had always hoped for a long life, but I never expected such incredible longevity."

"I'm afraid you aren't alive in 1999."

"And in spite of this unfortunate circumstance, you still managed to meet me?"

I . . . ah—" She frowned. "I met your ghost."

"My ghost."

She nodded. "I know it sounds incredible. But it is true."

He looked down into her beautiful, desperate eyes and wondered what sat before him. An innocent female—he acknowledged the existence of a few, his sister being one; or, a consummate actress—of which he knew far too many. "I think you should rest awhile."

"I don't need to rest. I need you to believe me." She stood and walked to him. "You came to me asking for help. Only now you don't know me because you are alive in this century. Which makes perfectly good sense to me now that I think of it. I couldn't expect your ghost to be here while you are still alive, could I?"

He had to admit some logic to her reasoning. "No, I don't suppose you could."

"Of course not." She fiddled with the top button of her nightgown, rolling it back and forth between her fingers.

His mind conjured images against his will, of those pearl buttons sliding open beneath his touch, of pale skin caressed by sunlight and his lips, touching her, kissing her, drinking in the softness, the sweetness. He clenched his teeth.

She looked up at him, her eyes holding a myriad of emotions—one of which he recognized as hope, the kind born from desperation. "You said you had been given one chance for a miracle. You brought me back in time to save your son. I need your help to save him."

"My son." His muscles stiffened when he thought of a threat to Brandon. "What are you talking about? Save my son from what?"

She clutched his shirtsleeve. "There is going to be an accident in June. Two, actually. You will die in the tower, and your son will die the next day, from a fall off the cliffs."

He had already thwarted two attempts by the Harcourts to kidnap his son. Kidnapping was one thing, but this woman was talking about murder. Still, he would not put it past Octavia Harcourt. She wanted to punish him for her daughter's death and would use any means possible. "Who sent you here?"

"You did."

He gripped her arms and lifted her until her toes barely touched the ground. "I warn you, Miss Fairfield, I don't tolerate treachery of any kind. If you are working for the Harcourts, you will soon find you have allied yourself with the wrong side."

She stared at him, her blue eyes wide. "The Harcourts? Do you mean Lavinia's parents?"

"You know exactly whom I mean."

"I am certainly not on their side. For heaven's sake, they stole your son. Treated him as though he was some serving boy. As far as I'm concerned, you should have sent them both to prison for what they did."

"You know a great deal about me."

She grimaced. "You're hurting me."

Gavin realized at that moment how hard he was gripping her arms. It suddenly occurred to him just how delicate she felt beneath his touch. A wave of self-loathing washed through him. He had never in his life raised his hand against a woman. Even when Lavinia had pushed him to his blackest rage, he had never harmed her. Only a coward employed strength against the defenseless. He released her so quickly that she stumbled back a step. "How do you know so much about my son?"

She rubbed her arms. "It's all part of the history of Dunmore. I learned about him while I was doing research for a book I'm writing about you."

"You are an authoress and you are writing a book about me?"

She nodded. "I have written two novels, although neither one of them has been published, so I'm not exactly an author. I'm an English professor at Chamberlain College."

He stared at her. "Are you saying that they have women professors in America these days?"

"No, I'm not. This is still the dark ages when it comes to women's rights. It will take another hundred years before women get the right to vote. Fortunately, I'm not from around here. Things are a little better in 1999."

Either she was one of the most creative huntresses he had every met, or that bump on her head had done more damage than he had imagined. "Miss Fairfield, if you actually believe everything you have been telling me, then you obviously need some rest."

"I don't need rest."

"You've had a nasty bump on the head, Miss Fairfield," he said, taking her arm. "I'm sure with a little rest you will . . ."

She pulled away from him. "I'm not insane and I don't need any rest. I do need to know why the heck you brought me back here so early. You said it's April."

"Aye. The tenth day."

"The accident doesn't happen until June. There must have been a reason for bringing me back so early." She rubbed her temples. "I do wish you had told me your plan. Now I'm going to have to figure it all out on my own."

His plan at the moment was to calm her down and coax her to rest, until he could figure out just what game she was playing. He took her arm. "Lie down. Rest awhile."

She looked up at him, a determined glint in her eyes. "I'm not insane."

"I never said you were," he said, leading her toward the bed. "Rest."

She sank to the edge of the bed. "You did bring me back here. You were granted a chance for a miracle, only I am the one who has to make it happen."

"We'll speak more later." He gripped her shoulders and gently eased her back upon the bed. Her hair spilled across his pillow. The golden strands caught the sunlight, weaving a halo about her head. She looked like an angel, an angel sent to earth just for him, a beautiful, muddled angel. Without conscious thought he touched her hair, lifted a handful of shimmering gold, and slid the silken strands through his fingers.

The expression on her lovely face shifted, sliding from determination into surprise. Her lips parted, drawing his gaze. He imagined those soft lips beneath his, parting, welcoming him. The subtle floral fragrance of her skin swirled through his senses, more intoxicating than the heady aroma of aged brandy. Heat seeped into his blood, drawing muscles taut and ready. He looked into the pure blue of her eyes and found his own longing reflected there. He felt connected to her, as though his life were a tapestry and this woman the golden thread weaving together the pieces.

He lowered his head until he felt her soft, startled sigh brush his lips. He wanted her, with a hunger that pierced his bones. He wanted to strip away that prim white cloth and explore every inch of her, discover all the hidden recesses, the mysterious feminine secrets with his hands, his lips, his tongue. Never in his life had lust sunk so quickly, so deeply. He closed his hand on her hair, fighting the attraction. There were a thousand reasons why he should not kiss her. And still it took every scrap of will to pull away from her.

He stood and stared down at her. She was eyeing him as though he were the first of his species that she had ever encountered. And it seemed she was both fascinated and frightened by what she saw. "If you are working for the Harcourts, I will have little mercy on you."

She released her breath in an agitated huff. "I am not working with those horrible people."

He frowned. "There is something else you should know, Miss Fairfield."

"What?"

"I won't be tricked into marriage ever again. If you have set your sights on becoming a countess, tread carefully." He smiled, knowing the smile was as cold as his heart. "You will get hurt. I will not be manipulated or blackmailed into anything."

Her eyes grew wide. "You think I came here to trick you into marriage?"

"You wouldn't be the first of your kind to attempt it."

"Of all the conceited . . ." She sat up, anger flashing in those heavenly blue eyes. She swung her long legs off the bed and stood, facing him like a cat with her back up. "Let's get this straight, buster. You're the one who kidnapped me."

"Kidnapped you?"

"All right; it wasn't you exactly, it was your blasted ghost."

If it was a story, it was inventive. "My ghost kidnapped you?"

"That's right. And let me tell you, death didn't do a thing for your attitude. You are every bit as arrogant in 1999 as you are now."

He grinned. "But not nearly as creative as you. I shall have to read one of your books some day."

"There is no need to make fun of me." She drew a sharp breath between her clenched teeth. "You're the one who needs my help."

"To save my son?"

"That's right. And if you think for one moment that I'm here because I'm interested in having anything to do with you, think again. I've had enough arrogance from the male of the species to last a lifetime." She poked his chest with one long finger. "I wouldn't marry you even if you hadn't died a hundred and fifty-four years before I was born."

He had thought her lovely before, but this fit of temper burned through any demure loveliness. She was a tigress, all fire and fight, the passion of her anger deepening the blue of her eyes, the rose of her cheeks. He tried but couldn't dismiss the images flashing through his brain—this woman with all of that anger turned to a much more enjoyable heat. Good lord, the woman was dangerous.

"We shall talk when you are willing to tell the truth, Miss Fairfield." He turned on his heel and left her.

When he was safely in the hall, Gavin released the breath he had been holding. He couldn't remember the last time a woman had scorched him this way. The answer was far more startling than he expected. *Never*. Never in his entire life had he reacted so intensely to a woman.

And she was either a scheming little witch or an innocent female who just happened to believe she came from his future. Where she had conversed with his ghost. Apparently his luck with women had not changed.

The wise thing to do was to get rid of her. Send her packing. Yet he needed to know the truth about her. If she was working for the Harcourts, it was better to keep her in sight. If she was a fortune-hunting wench, he would show her that he was immune to her charms. Either way, he would teach her a lesson she would not soon forget.

Julia released her pent-up breath. The nerve of the man. The utter conceit of the scoundrel. "Arrogant, pompous . . ." She grabbed a pillow and tossed it toward the closed door.

Did he really imagine every woman he met salivated at the idea of marrying him? Granted, he was the most devastating male she had ever met. And yes, she admitted a certain animal attraction to him. All right, the attraction was as virulent as ebola. And it could have just as deadly results.

Gavin hadn't touched her. He hadn't kissed her. He had only looked at her. That's all. A smoldering look, and she had been ready to tear off his clothes. Never had this happened to her before. Her skin was still tingling, her blood pounding through her veins as though she had run a marathon. Still, that didn't give him the right to be so . . . so . . . rude!

Although she had never in her life indulged in casual affairs, she was ready to jump into bed with the man. Still, she suspected there would be nothing casual about an affair with Gavin. No. He was the type of man who would brand his image across her soul. He was the type of man who . . . could destroy her.

"Wonderful."

Well, she would not succumb to this weakness.

Gavin might be alive in this century, but he was no closer to reality for her. She couldn't stay.

This was all his fault. Every bit of it. He had kidnapped her. He had demanded her help. And what was this business about bringing her here two months early? She paced the floor, slapping a heavy blue velvet drape when she reached the windows. Gavin should have prepared her for this.

She would just have to figure it out, that's all. She was going to save Brandon and get back home. Lauren and Gram were back in her century, waiting for her. They needed her. And she needed that pompous, arrogant, conceited ghost's help to find her way back home.

Julia stared out one of the long windows. The Atlantic Ocean stretched out from the cliffs, the dark, rolling waves glittering in the sunlight. It looked the same today as it would nearly two hundred years from now. She had to convince Gavin that she was telling the truth. She would need his help to save Brandon. And she had a feeling saving the boy was the only way she would ever find her way back to her family.

Soon after Gavin left, a short, plump woman came to the room with an armful of clothes. "I see you're up and about. I'm Iona MacPherson, the housekeeper here at Dunmore."

"I'm Julia Fairfield."

"Lord Dunmore said you're an American," Iona said, dropping the stack of clothes on the bed. She smoothed her hand over her hair, slicking back a wayward strand that had escaped her bun. "You're a long way from home, lass."

"Yes." Julia thought of her family. "A very long way from home."

Iona studied her, as though she were a specimen under a microscope. "And you're traveling alone?"

Julia realized that any lady of quality would not be traveling alone in 1818. "I didn't have a choice."

Iona tilted her head, her perceptive blue eyes alert and filled with curiosity. "Missing your family?"

"Yes." Did Gram and Lauren even know she was gone? "I miss them very much."

"Well, now, I don't mean to pry, but I can tell quality when I see it. And you're quality." Iona lifted a white muslin gown from the stack of clothes she had tossed on the bed. "Traveling alone, disguised as a boy, I would wager your family has no idea where you are."

Disguised as a boy? "No. I'm afraid they don't."

Iona patted her arm. "I thought as much. It's because of a man, isn't it?"

Julia released her breath in a sigh. "Yes."

"You didn't like the choice your mama and papa have made for your husband, did you?"

Julia frowned at Iona's deductions. "My parents didn't . . ."

"They didn't understand your feelings. I read something just like it last week, in a novel from the circulating library. The *Reluctant Bride*, it was called." Iona shook her head. "I can't say I blame you at all. I wouldn't be wanting to marry a man I didn't love. No, I wouldn't."

"Iona, I really . . ."

"Now, don't you worry, lass." Iona winked at Julia. "The laird will look after you. There isn't a better man on this green earth than Lord Dunmore. Once he realizes you're in need of protection, he'll see no harm comes to you."

"Iona, I'm afraid you have the wrong idea of what happened. My parents didn't have anything to do with my coming here. It wasn't because of an arranged marriage."

Iona nodded, a knowing look in her eyes. "It's all right, lass. No one here will be trying to send you back."

"But I . . ."

Iona pressed her fingertip to her lips. "We'll say no more about it. I know it must be painful. Now, I've brought you some of Lady Alison's clothes. Though I'm afraid they will be a bit too short. You're a wee bit taller than she is. Still, I'll set Bridgett on to the task of altering them. A flounce of lace here and there and you'll have something to wear. It'll have to do until we can have some clothes made for you. Here you go. Try this one on."

Julia accepted the white muslin gown from Iona. Twin bands of black embroidery bordered the center seam from the high empire waist to the hem. The stitches holding together the seams were small, and carefully made. Yet they did not have the regimented precision only a machine could make. For her writing, she had perused dozens of research books on costume and fashion. And now she was holding a gown from 1818. "You don't think Lady Alison would mind if I borrowed some of her clothes?"

Iona waved her hand. "Lady Alison is as generous as her dear mother. You needn't worry."

Julia lifted a pair of lace-trimmed drawers from the pile of clothes on the bed. "I thought these didn't become popular for a few more years."

"You Americans have an odd way of putting things

sometimes. But then, I've never seen such strange pantalettes as what you were wearing last night. And that little harness for the bosom." Iona raised her brows. "Not like any improver I've ever seen. Sure now, the styles are different where you come from."

"Yes. They are." Julia stared at the pantalettes, an idea taking shape in her mind. "I think it will be a few years before the styles make it here."

Iona waved her hand. "Americans. Always trying something new. Come now, let's get you dressed. I'm not much for dressing the hair, but I'll give it a try. Moira is in London with milady, so I'm the best there is for now."

As Iona fussed over her, Julia thought of what she would say the next time she saw Gavin. She would prove to the man just exactly where she had come from. It wouldn't be easy, but she would do it. No matter what.

When Iona was done, Julia studied the results in the cheval mirror that stood in one corner of the room. The fashions of the day did not allow for a bra. She felt a little bare without it, especially in this gown.

The gown was cut low over her bosom, revealing far more flesh than she felt comfortable displaying. Even though she had never been bosomy, the dress managed to make the most of her modest assets. A petticoat and pantalettes were all she wore beneath the flimsy white muslin. Iona had swept her hair into a topknot, allowing her own natural curls to frame her face. She looked as though she had just stepped off the pages of *Sense and Sensibility*.

"Oh, now, don't you look bonny." Iona peeked out behind her and smiled at her in the mirror. "The laird will be pleased."

Excitement coiled through her, igniting a fire low in her belly when she thought of seeing Gavin again. Julia frowned at her image in the mirror. He was an arrogant male. The kind of man who expected people to jump at his command. The type she avoided out of self-preservation. She had gotten too close to his type before and nearly found herself crushed beneath his domineering fist. Still, she wasn't frightened of Gavin. And if she were very honest with herself, she would have to say she was looking forward to the next confrontation. Confrontation? She had always run from confrontation.

But it wasn't precisely the confrontation that she looked forward to with Gavin. No, it was the excitement. A delicious, tingling, steal-your-breath, heat-your-blood kind of excitement. That was what she was looking forward to. It was intoxicating. Dangerous. And more than a little foolish.

She frowned at the woman staring back at her. Even if she were the type of woman who could tame a man like Gavin MacKinnon—which she was not—the situation was hopeless. Gavin MacKinnon had died before she was born. There was no future for her here.

She drew in her breath and prepared for battle. She had to beard the lion in his den. She had no one to rely upon except herself. She would have to be strong, or risk losing everything.

"Now, you'll be needing something to eat. You'll have a nice cup of chocolate and some of Cook's cinnamon pastries while I have Cook prepare something for you."

No sense in going to battle on an empty stomach. "That sounds wonderful."

Chapter Ten

What is life when wanting love?
Night without a morning!
Love's the cloudless summer sun,
Nature gay adorning.
—Robert Burns

Gavin sat in a leather armchair near the hearth in his library. He hadn't invited the man who sat in the matching chair across from him. Yet he had known Russell Lampkin would come. The bastard had no choice.

Lampkin crossed his legs in an attempt to appear calm, but the vein throbbing at his temple betrayed him. Tall and slender, he wore his dark blond hair in carefully disheveled waves to give him the poetic look so popular these days in London.

His bottle-green coat and buff-colored pantaloons were the latest fashion, tailored by Schweitzer and

Davidson. Gavin knew, because he had made it his business to know all about the fashionable young man sitting before him. A wise man gathered intelligence before entering battle. He thought of the woman in his bedchamber and wondered what battles lay ahead for them. Strange, but he was actually looking forward to the next confrontation. The woman had a way of igniting his blood. She might be dangerous, but she was definitely not a bore.

Lampkin picked an imaginary piece of lint from his sleeve. "I was surprised to hear that you had acquired all of my vowels."

Gavin rested his chin on his folded hands. It had taken less than three days to acquire all of Lampkin's gaming debts. He suspected that since that time, the man had acquired more. "Twelve thousand pounds."

Lampkin smiled, a cultivated curving of his lips that served him well with members of the fairer sex. Too well, as far as Gavin was concerned.

"I don't have the money at the moment to pay them, but I shall soon come into a fortune. After June I shall pay them in full."

"Aye, your fiancée is very wealthy." Gavin fixed Lampkin with a cold stare. "I wonder if she knows about you and your penchant for ruining young girls who are not so well fixed."

Lampkin frowned. "What are you talking about?"

"Felicity Taverner. A girl of sixteen summers."

Twin patches of color rose on Lampkin's cheeks. "What do you have to do with Felicity Taverner?"

"Her father is a good friend of mine."

Lampkin slid his finger in his collar. "What did the girl tell you?"

"You are the father of her child. At least you would

have been, if the child had lived." Gavin sat back in his chair, resisting the urge to plant his fist in Lampkin's jaw. Although enjoyable, breaking the man physically would be far too simple. "Felicity ran off because she was ashamed of what she had done with you. Her father found her, but it was too late. She miscarried and later died of a fever. But not before she confessed everything to her father."

Lampkin shifted in his chair. "She lied. She must have used my name to protect her real lover."

"I don't think so. I think you ruined her and left her when you found a female with a plumper purse."

Lampkin smiled, his lips stretching far too wide. "You can't prove it."

Gavin shrugged. "I don't need to prove it. I only need to collect twelve thousand pounds from you. Today."

"You know I can't pay you. Not today." Lampkin tugged on his starched collar. "I'll get you the money. Just give me a few more weeks."

"After your marriage to your wealthy Miss Barnaby." Gavin smiled. "I wonder if Miss Barnaby would still be interested in marrying you if she knew about Miss Taverner."

Lampkin licked his lips. "She wouldn't believe you. You're a murderer, for heaven's sake. She certainly wouldn't take your word for anything."

"You call me a murderer." Gavin rose from his chair. "And what should I call you?"

Lampkin scrambled to his feet. "I didn't mean to say . . ."

"Shall we say pistols at dawn?"

All the color drained from Lampkin's face. "I've heard you can drill a hole in a coin at twenty paces."

Gavin stared straight into Lampkin's terrified blue

eyes. "Shooting targets will not be nearly as enjoyable as putting a bullet between your eyes."

Lampkin took a step back. "I don't intend to duel with you."

"No. I wouldn't expect you to. It would take far more honor than you possess."

Lampkin's eyes narrowed with fury, but he made no reply to the insult.

Gavin pulled an envelope from his coat pocket. "Your ship sails from London a week from tomorrow."

Lampkin opened the envelope and stared at the papers inside. "New South Wales. You expect me to travel to New South Wales?"

"You have a choice. You can travel there as a free man, or I will have you thrown into prison as a debtor. Which will it be?"

Lampkin opened his mouth to speak, then closed it. His throat worked against his collar, his eyes speaking of murder. He pivoted and marched toward the door. At the threshold he hesitated, then turned to face Gavin. "Someday you shall get what you deserve, Dunmore."

Gavin lifted his brows. "Be glad I'm not giving you what you deserve today, Lampkin."

Lampkin lifted his chin, then stormed out of the room, colliding with someone in the hall. A sharp yelp sliced the air, a purely feminine sound of pain. Gavin could only see Lampkin's shoulder, but he had a fairly good guess who had stood in the man's way. He frowned, wondering how long Miss Fairfield had been standing in the hall.

Julia was eavesdropping, not one of her usual pastimes. Still, considering the circumstances, she thought it wise to learn everything she could about Gavin and the situation in which she found herself. She stood in the hall outside the library, squeezing the slacks and blouse she held, listening intently to every word of the conversation between Gavin and some man named Lampkin.

Her heart ached for poor young Felicity. She could imagine what that child had felt, pregnant, deserted, ashamed. Any man who would use a girl in that way deserved more than deportation. He deserved to be strung up by his thumbs and to have a particular part of his anatomy surgically removed.

"Someday you shall get what you deserve, Dunmore."

Julia stiffened at the threat in Lampkin's voice. The man was angry enough to kill.

"Be glad I'm not giving you what you deserve today, Lampkin."

A shiver rippled along her spine at the soft threat in Gavin's voice. She backed away from the door. Gavin was a man she never wanted as an enemy. Yet how in the world could she convince him that she was on his side? She had to . . .

Lampkin stormed through the doorway and rammed straight into her. She yelped as his booted foot came down on her toes. He grabbed her arm, mumbling an apology. She muttered something about no injury done. He inclined his head in a small bow, then continued down the hall.

She turned and watched him leave. He was elegant and handsome in a smooth, too pretty fashion. She could see why a young girl would fall for any line Lampkin might throw at her. He was the type of man who would rehearse his lines in front of a mirror, she thought. Practice his seduction techniques.

"I see Mr. Lampkin has captured your interest, Miss Fairfield."

Julia flinched at the sound of Gavin's voice. She

turned and found him standing a few feet away, one broad shoulder leaning against the doorjamb, his arms crossed over his chest, his face an unreadable mask. Unreadable except his eyes. Anger simmered in those black eyes.

"If you are interested in pursuing the man, I can arrange passage for you. I understand he will be taking a long sea voyage soon. It should give you several months to become acquainted."

Julia tried to ignore the delicious excitement coiling through her, tingling her skin, snatching her breath. The thrill of just looking at him made her feel restless and so very much alive, as though she had only been moving through life until she had met him. "No, thank you. I have never cared much for men who find it amusing to pull the wings off butterflies."

One black brow lifted. "I see you were listening long enough to hear about Miss Taverner."

Heat prickled her neck. "I didn't intend to eavesdrop. I came to see you."

"And stayed when you found the conversation interesting."

"I don't usually . . ." She lifted her chin. "Yes. I listened to the conversation. And I have to say, it was very gallant of you to champion Miss Taverner."

He smiled, if that cold curving of his lips could be called a smile. "You sound surprised."

"Given your misogynist views toward women, I am surprised you would lift a finger to help any of my sex."

"Misogynist?" He rubbed the tip of one long finger along his jaw, from his ear to his chin. "Miss Fairfield, I do not hate women. I assure you, I often find pleasure in the company of your sex."

She clutched the garments she had brought as evidence, trying not to imagine the pleasure this man found with other women. Yet the images were there, emblazoned across her mind, in full Technicolor. And with the images came a stab far too close to her heart, an emotion that could only be one thing: jealousy. Lord help her, she felt possessive of a man who had died 154 years before she was born. It was a sure route to disaster. "You enjoy a woman as long as she is in your bed, Lord Dunmore. When you have scratched your itch, you send her on her merry way."

He lowered his eyes, his gaze resting on her breasts. Heat simmered across her skin, tingling as though he had touched her with his hands and not just a look. "I have never taken a woman to my bed promising more than I intended to give, Miss Fairfield. If a woman wants more than pleasure, she is a fool to think she will find it with me. I make no promises. I break none."

"You have allowed what happened with one woman to color your view of all." The words struck a familiar chord within her. Had she done the same with men? She had no right to continue, but something spurred her on. Perhaps it was the sentiment expressed by his mother in her journal, or the bitterness she saw in his beautiful eyes, or something deep within her—something she didn't want to acknowledge. "I assure you, we are not all after a man's wealth and title. You do yourself a disservice to close off any possibility of finding true happiness, Lord Dunmore."

His eyes narrowed slightly, like a tiger considering his prey. "And who is to say I am not happy, Miss Fairfield?"

He wasn't happy. She could see it. What's more, she could sense it, the loneliness lurking behind the cynical mask. That loneliness resonated deep within her. For reasons she wasn't certain she wanted to understand, she was connected to this man, connected as she had never been to anyone else.

"A man living with bitterness can never be content. Until you get past what happened with Lavinia, you will never truly find happiness." The truth of her words rang like a bell inside her, a truth meant as much for her as for Gavin. She had to put what had happened with Nathan behind her. Now that she was here, she had to trust Gavin to take her back home. She had no choice.

He studied her, a hard glint in his eyes. "And have you come here to help me forget my unfortunate marriage, Miss Fairfield?"

It was a challenge tossed like a gauntlet at her feet. It required a courageous woman to take that challenge. A woman willing to butt heads with an arrogant male. A woman certain enough of her own strengths to match his. She had never been that kind of woman. She was not equipped to handle such a man. Yet she had a wild urge to step into the ring with him. When had she become so reckless?

Gavin frowned. "Miss Fairfield?"

She drew air into her tight lungs. "I'm afraid I won't be here long enough to alter your thinking, Lord Dunmore."

His brow lifted, a glimmer of surprise entering his eyes, surprise and something else. Disappointment? "Does this mean you are ready to tell me where you live?"

"I told you the truth," she said, moving toward him. She paused a foot in front of him and held out her blouse for his examination. "Now I am going to show you proof."

He glanced down at her blouse, then met her gaze. "Your shirt is proof you came from my future?"

Julia clenched her teeth at his sarcasm. "Take a good look at it. Have you ever seen stitches like these?"

He strolled into the library, carrying her blouse to the bay window. Sunlight flowed through the diamond-shaped panes, slipping gold into his dark hair. He examined the seams and the embroidery, then looked at her. "The stitching is uniform."

"That's because it was done by a machine. A machine that hasn't been invented yet."

A frown marred his brow as he handed the blouse to her. "This is your proof?"

He still didn't believe her. "Look at these," she said, shoving her slacks at him.

He took the black linen from her. "You are quite proud of your trousers. I must say, I don't care much for the cut of them."

She leaned forward and grabbed the front of the trousers. The scent of sandalwood swirled around her, teasing her nostrils, tempting her to lean closer. The attraction this man held for her was nothing short of suicidal. She glanced up at him, straight into his eyes. Those wonderful dark eyes. Heat flickered in the black depths, an intriguing look that set her heart racing until each beat pounded in her throat. She had to swallow hard to use her voice. "Have you ever seen one of these, Lord Dunmore?"

His gaze lowered to her neck. Heat spread beneath his gaze, sliding over her skin like warm fingers. "The fastener?"

"Yes. You've never seen this." She worked the zipper, appalled at the tremor gripping her hands. Slowly she slid the tab up, sealing the garment, and then slid it back down, opening it again.

He met her gaze, a smile curving his lips. "The fastener certainly makes it a great deal easier to undress."

The look in those eyes was far too seductive. She wondered how many women had tumbled into his bed all because of that dark, sultry look. He was the type of man who ate timid females for breakfast. She stepped back, hoping the distance might ease the tension coiling low in her belly. "The fastener is called a zipper. Have you ever seen anything like it?"

He shook his head. "No, I haven't."

She smiled, feeling more than a little triumphant. "That's because it won't be used on clothing for another hundred years."

His left brow rose, just a little. "And this zipper is supposed to prove your story?"

"You admitted you had never seen anything like it."

"That simply means someone somewhere has managed to devise an ingenious little fastener." He considered the zipper for a moment. "You're an American. They are always coming up with something new."

"Oh, for heaven's sake." She yanked the slacks from his hand. "How the heck am I going to make you believe me?"

He smiled, a man secure behind his armor. "I would give up if I were you."

She turned away from him and crossed the room. Stubborn oaf! What was she going to do if she couldn't make him believe her? She had to stay near him, at least until she could prevent the accident, almost two months from now. She would be in a real pickle if he decided to kick her out of Dunmore. And why the heck had Gavin brought her back so early?

She paused at the fireplace and looked up at the portrait hanging above the mantel. The portrait was of a handsome, dark-haired man dressed in a red tartan kilt, standing at the base of the grand staircase of Dunmore. Even though the man in the portrait had blue eyes, the resemblance to Gavin was unmistakable. "Your father?"

"Aye."

"I haven't seen this portrait before. I wonder what happened to it." She glanced back at him. "In my time, your portrait is hanging here."

He frowned, a certain wariness entering his eyes. "And what portrait might that be?"

The dark current in his voice drifted like frost across the base of her spine. "A portrait of you standing beside a large black horse."

His eyes narrowed. "Where did you see it?"

She didn't like that look in his eyes. It made her feel too much like a mouse confronting an angry lion. "I told you. It was hanging above the mantel at Dunmore."

"The portrait has only recently been completed. The last time I saw the one you described, it was sitting in a shop in London, where my mother was still deciding on the proper frame for it. It has never hung on any wall of Dunmore."

"Not in your time. But it does in mine."

He stalked her; long, slow, predatory strides designed to frighten her. It worked. "You obviously saw the portrait in London."

"No, I did not. I saw it here." She pointed up at his father's portrait. "It's in a thick, ornately carved cherry wood frame."

"That only proves you have been sniffing about in my affairs. What were you hoping to do, Miss Fairfield? Find something to blackmail me?"

She took two steps backward, then froze. She fought the urge to run. She would have turned and dashed out of the room, if she'd had somewhere to hide. She didn't. Instead she forced her chin up as he paused in front of her. "I'm not some stalker, Lord Dunmore. And I'm not a blackmailer. I wouldn't be here at all if you hadn't needed my help."

He leaned toward her, so close his nose nearly brushed the tip of hers. "I don't like people prying into my affairs."

He was too close, so close he pushed her into dangerous territory. She kept wondering things she shouldn't. What would it be like to . . . kiss him? Foolish, idiotic female. That kind of thinking would lead to disaster. "There is a great deal about this entire situation I don't like. Unfortunately, I have no choice but to stay here until I can save you and Brandon."

"You do have another choice, Miss Fairfield. You can tell me where you live so I can send you back home."

Home. The word twisted in her heart. Home, to Lauren and Gram. Home, where she would be safe from the desire this man ignited within her. "I wish it was that simple, Lord Dunmore. I wish you could just send me back to my family. But it isn't that easy."

"I'm not a man you want to play games with, Miss Fairfield."

She stared up into his dark eyes, where bitterness burned as brightly as anger. Experience had carved wounds across his soul. He was like a soldier who had survived a long, bloody war. All the softness in him had been pounded into steel. All of his trust ground into dust. He needed someone to teach him to trust again, to love again. And as much as she wanted to deny it, she wished she could be that woman. "I don't play games, Lord Dunmore."

One black brow lifted. "You won't win at this."

She glared at him. In another time, another place, she might have cowered beneath that ferocious glare. But circumstances did not allow her the luxury of cowardice. "If you're trying to frighten me, you're wasting your time. I intend to . . ."

He wrapped his large hands around her waist and hauled her off the floor, lifting her straight up until her nose was level with his. She dropped her slacks and blouse and gripped his shoulders. A gasp tore from her lips. He clamped his hard mouth over hers, shutting off any chance she might have had to protest.

Julia's heart stopped, then plunged into a dizzying race. She pushed against his shoulders, stunned by the fury in his kiss. It was bold, brazen, a kiss designed to overwhelm, to dominate, to subjugate. She was an enemy, and the enemy would burn in the face of his heated assault.

She curled her hands into fists against his shoulders, determined to resist him. Yet a traitor dwelled deep within her. She had dreamed of being held by this man, of tasting his kisses, and more. She had wept for the loss of this man. And now he was here, living, breathing, more vital than any man she had ever met.

He slanted his mouth over hers, opening his lips, daring her to respond. Emotion flooded her, streaming through her, as bright and crackling as current through a wire. He might imagine she was his enemy, but she knew the truth. He meant to cow her. Well, she would not be cowed by any man. Not ever again. She slid her arms around his neck and returned his kiss, parting her lips beneath his, meeting his challenge head-on.

She tasted his surprise, felt it in the shudder that ran through his powerful frame, and that response made *her* feel powerful. She plunged her fingers into his hair, the silky strands sliding against her skin, cool near the tips, warm near his scalp. She kissed him with all the pent-up desire she had only suspected dwelled deep within her. Kissed him without reason or restraint, surrendering to the heat and promise of passion.

He shifted her in his grasp, sliding one arm around her, clutching her against his chest as though he were drowning and she his only chance at life. She recognized the instant his kiss altered, the moment anger withered beneath the hotter flame of desire. She sensed the need simmering just beneath the blatant heat of his hunger, knew it dwelled in a place closely guarded. She wanted to find her way to that secret place, drag him from the darkness, dissolve all of that bitterness in the heat of her hope.

A low growl issued from deep in his chest, a primal sound that whispered to a secret place deep within her. Heat unfurled inside her, like a scarf caught in the rippling currents of a stream.

Without warning, he dropped her on her feet and backed away from her. He stared at her, as though she had just dropped at his feet from the far side of the moon. She had some satisfaction in knowing that he was not completely unscathed by the encounter. His breathing mirrored her own, short and choppy. She bet his heart was also working like a sledgehammer. Her own felt as though it might break one of her ribs. "Was that meant to teach me a lesson?"

He glared at her, and she could almost see him drawing his armor close around him. "If you play with a lion, you're going to get mauled, Miss Fairfield."

She didn't know how she managed it, but she stood unflinching beneath that ferocious look. "Lions can be tamed, Lord Dunmore."

A muscle flashed beneath his cheek with the clenching of his jaw. "Are you feeling brave enough to try, Miss Fairfield?"

Chapter Eleven

Alas; the love of women! it is known
To be a lovely and a fearful thing.
—George Gordon, Lord Byron

It was a mistake. A miscalculation. A tactical error that could cost him dearly. Gavin recognized it, acknowledged the possible consequences of the challenge he had thrown at Miss Fairfield's feet. A hard glint had entered her beautiful eyes. She had drawn her saber and was ready for battle. If he had been thinking clearly, he never would have kissed her. The trouble was, he hadn't been thinking clearly then. Worse yet, he wasn't thinking very clearly at present.

Miss Fairfield had an annoying way of shutting down his intellect. It was lust. The lust he had prided himself on controlling since he had once mistaken it for a far deeper emotion. Lavinia had cured him of allowing lust to blind him. Yet here he was with the blood pounding through his veins, his fingers itching, heat scalding his loins. He wanted her. He wanted to rip off her clothes and take her, right here, right now. He wanted to kiss her, to explore her, to lick every luscious inch of her, from her delicately arched brows to her toes. And that was only the beginning of what he wanted from her.

She had felt like heaven in his arms, slender, delicately curved, as though she had been fashioned for him, only him. She had kissed him with an ardor he had never before tasted in a woman, kissed him as though she had been waiting her entire life for his kiss. She had looked at him as though he was the most fascinating man on the face of the earth, the only man who mattered. It was foolish to imagine such romantic nonsense. Yet he couldn't quite shove it out of his brain.

He tried to convince himself that it was all a masquerade. A man was a fool to trust any member of her sex. They all wanted one thing from a man—everything he owned. Miss Fairfield might be one of the most intriguing females he had ever met, and he had to admit she was creative in her methods. Still, she was a female, which meant she could not be trusted.

"You don't frighten me, Lord Dunmore."

He could see that truth glinting in her eyes. He might not frighten her, but she made him more than a little uneasy. "In that case, Miss Fairfield, you are a hen wit."

"I won't be bullied by you or any man." She closed the distance between them, standing so close that the skirt of her gown brushed his legs. "You've taken refuge on a mountaintop, sequestered yourself safely away from any chance at finding true happiness with a woman. You think to make all women pay for one woman's treachery."

He didn't feel very safe, not at the moment, not looking into those gorgeous, furious blue eyes. "I have learned true happiness for a woman means total enslavement for a man."

Julia shook her head. "What you need is a woman who will drag you off your mountaintop. Show you just what it means to love and be loved."

She had been right earlier: he wasn't happy. He wanted something more from life than a solitary existence. Something he had given up hope of ever finding. Until this strange female had careened into his life. This strange, beautiful, utterly dangerous creature before him. This woman could shatter his defenses. He sensed it the way any wild beast senses the approach of a predator. "In my experience, women equate love with the coin in a man's purse."

"I can't imagine that's true."

"Unfortunately, I know it is."

"I cannot believe most women look at you and only see a bag of coins."

He suddenly had an insane urge to ask her what she saw when she looked at him. It wouldn't matter what she said, of course. He would scarcely believe anything she had to say, even if it was flattering, which he doubted. "Women are born and bred to see opportunities and seize them. I suppose I cannot really fault your sex. There is little else to occupy you except the acquisition of a wealthy husband. Still, I choose not to participate in the farce."

"Not all women want a man for money alone."

"True; there are a fair number who want a title as well."

She planted her hands on her hips, her chin tipping to a militant angle. "More than a few women are forced into marriages with overbearing brutes. The brute has decided the girl would make an appropriate ornament, something pretty to hang on his arm. She isn't strong enough to resist because she knows she is supposed to get married and have children, and even though he isn't the man of her dreams, he is handsome and charming and successful and so very good at twisting her around his finger."

He saw a flash of something more than anger in those beautiful eyes. A glimmer of bitterness? "You speak from experience, Miss Fairfield?"

She glanced away from him, but not before he caught a glimpse of pain in her eyes. "I don't need to speak from experience. I know many women in this time are forced into marriages because it is the only option they have."

Gavin sensed her retreat, that she was falling back into the fairy tale she had been weaving since she had awakened this morning. Only now he wondered exactly what lay beneath the tale. Somehow she had managed to insinuate herself past his defenses. He didn't know precisely what game she was playing, but he had a feeling she was truly in some kind of trouble. "Do you want to tell me the real reason you are here?"

Julia released her breath in a slow stream of air. "I have told you, but you refuse to believe me." She snatched her clothes from the floor. "Even when I show you proof."

The garments were extraordinary. Was it possible? He had been born and bred on the Isle of Mist. He had been fed tales of fairies and magic from the time he was a lad. He had an aunt who often had glimpses of things to come. Still, to believe this woman had traveled through time, brought to him by his own ghost . . . that would take a great deal of faith.

"My present is your future, Lord Dunmore," she said, as though she could read his mind. "I was born in 1972. I came to Dunmore in the summer of 1999, where I had the misfortune to run into your ghost."

Apparently she intended to keep hiding behind her fairy tale. Only now he wondered exactly what she was hiding, and why she was here. She intrigued him in more ways than he cared to admit. Intrigued and infuriated him as no other woman ever had. And he intended to strip away every shield she thrust between them. He would have the truth. If it killed him.

"I see you have a guest," Beatrice MacQuarrie said as she entered the room.

Gavin dragged his gaze from Julia to the small, dark-haired woman sauntering toward him. She was swishing her hips the way a cat might swish her tail. And there was a feral gleam in her eyes, the look of a feline who has caught another cat prowling in her territory. Beatrice walked directly to Gavin, slipped her arm through his, then looked at Julia. That look was a clear sign, shouting NO TRESPASSING.

Irritation churned in his gut. Apparently he had been too subtle with Beatrice last night. She thought she had her mark on him.

As he introduced the women, he noticed the tension coiling between them. He recognized the jealousy in Beatrice; she wore it like a blazing red cape. But Miss Fairfield's reaction was by far more interesting. She was staring at Beatrice as though she wanted to break all her fingers.

"Miss Fairfield is visiting from Chicago."

Beatrice smiled, her dark eyes remaining as cold as a December wind off the highest peak of Ben Cuimhne. She rested her hand on his chest and smiled up in a blatantly intimate way. "Chicago? It must be one of those rustic little provincial villages so common in America."

Julia's smile looked so brittle that he thought it could actually shatter. "It has great promise."

He knew enough about women to recognize jealousy when he saw it, and Miss Fairfield burned with it. He quelled the unexpected surge of satisfaction swelling inside him.

Beatrice looked down her slim nose, raking Julia from her head to the tips of her black shoes. "Apparently the fashion is for short skirts these days. I really should warn you, Miss Fairfield, it's quite out of fashion here."

Color rose along Julia's neck. Gavin followed the progress of her blush, crushing an insane urge to brush his fingertips over the rosy expanse of skin. "My luggage didn't make the trip. Lord Dunmore has allowed me to borrow some of his sister's things."

"That was so very kind of Gavin."

Beatrice leaned closer, pressing her plump breasts against his arm. Her ample bosom nearly overflowed the bodice of her apple-green gown. Compared to Beatrice, Miss Fairfield's charms were hardly noticeable. Yet Gavin noticed them. She was tall and elegantly fashioned. He preferred her delicate proportions to Beatrice's more obvious endowments.

Much to his annoyance, Julia excused herself, leaving him alone with Beatrice. What was it about the Fairfield woman? How the devil had she managed to get into his blood so quickly? So completely? It was as if he had known her before, loved her in some distant dream. *Loved her?* The romantic notion appalled him nearly as much as it took him by surprise.

Beatrice squeezed his arm. "It's such a beautiful

morning. I hoped we could take a ride to the lake." She trailed her fingers over his jaw. "It's so warm today, I thought we might even take a little swim."

The predatory look in her eyes prickled the skin at the nape of his neck. He pried her fingers from his arm. "I have other plans this afternoon."

"Yes. You have company." She crossed her arms over her chest and tapped her toe on the carpet. "Is Miss Fairfield the reason you left so early last night?"

"Miss Fairfield arrived unexpectedly last night."

Beatrice's delicate nostrils flared. "Who is she?"

Gavin lifted one brow, a silent warning of his rising irritation. "An acquaintance."

One corner of her mouth twitched. "I'm surprised you would allow her to stay here."

Not as surprised as he was. He should have tossed her out on her ear. She was up to something. She had done a great deal of research about him before coming here. He didn't know precisely what game she was playing, but he knew she was trouble. All women were trouble. "And why are you so surprised to discover that I have a guest?"

She tilted her chin. "I've never known you to bring a mistress to Dunmore before."

He had met Beatrice eight years earlier, when he had made his first trip to London for the Season. She had been straight out of the schoolroom then, determined, like all the young huntresses, to snag a wealthy husband that year. She had set her sights on him, but it was Lavinia Harcourt who had made the kill.

Beatrice had settled for his good friend, Carlin MacQuarrie, a man of wealth and property but no title. From what he had heard from Carlin in the years that followed, he had fared only somewhat better than Gavin that Season. Beatrice was as cold and calculating as Lavinia had been. It was ironic that Carlin had died in a riding accident the same year Lavinia departed this world. "Although it isn't any of your concern, Beatrice, Miss Fairfield is not my mistress."

"None of my concern?

He released his breath in a sigh. Subtlety was lost on this woman. "I thought we had things clear between us last night."

Temper flared in her dark eyes, but she kept her voice soft and inviting when she spoke. "I thought I might change your mind."

He shook his head. "You're wasting your time and talent on me, Beatrice. I have no intention of taking another bride."

She shaped her lips into a practiced pout. "That's because you made the mistake of marrying Lavinia instead of me all those years ago. I know I can make you happy."

For the second time today a woman had implied that he wasn't happy with his life. And for the first time in a long time he had to admit that there was an emptiness in his life, an emptiness Beatrice MacQuarrie could never fill. "I'm sure you will make someone happy. But I'm afraid it won't be me."

"You just need more time to realize that I am the right woman for you."

He shook his head. "You'd be wise to find a man who can appreciate your charms."

Her eyes narrowed. If she had been a cat, her tail would be twitching. He could almost hear her hiss as she spoke. "You'll regret this, Gavin MacKinnon."

Gavin sat on the arm of a wing-back chair as Beatrice stormed from the room. Although he had no desire to make an enemy of the woman, he hoped at last that this would convince her to give up the hunt. A few moments after Beatrice left, Iona entered the room.

"That one is trouble," Iona said as she walked toward him.

"All women are trouble, Iona."

She huffed softly. "You've just not met the proper woman, milord."

Gavin shook his head. "I shall leave it to my brother to try his hand at finding the proper woman."

Iona paused beside the fireplace, her blue eyes bright, as though she had secrets she wanted to share. "I've had Miss Fairfield's bedchamber prepared and I've started Bridgett on the task of altering some of Lady Alison's gowns."

He knew Iona well enough to realize that she had more on her mind than the obvious. "I'm sure Alison will be returning from London with so many new gowns, she will never miss a few."

"Lady Alison is a fortunate young lady. To have an understanding mama." Iona ran her fingertip over the mantel, then examined her fingertip, as though checking for dust. "I always think it's a pity when a young girl is forced into something against her will, such as poor Miss Fairfield."

Gavin stiffened at the mention of her name. "What about Miss Fairfield?"

Iona folded her hands at her waist. "I don't suppose she told you why she was running away, did she?"

He thought of the fairy tale she had told him. "Miss Fairfield's reasons remain a mystery to me. Did she tell you anything?"

Iona's face glowed with the secret she was anxious to share. "She's running away from an arranged marriage."

"She told you that?"

"Well, not in so many words, she didn't." She pressed her fingertip against her chin. "But I was able to piece it together from what she did tell me. That poor child has nowhere to go. I told her that she could depend upon you to protect her."

Gavin fixed her with a steady glare. "You did, did you?"

Iona lifted her chin. "Aye, and I know you won't be making me out to be a liar. You're a fine man, you are. And that poor dear lass needs someone to lean on right now."

It made sense. He recalled the bitterness in Julia's eyes when she had spoken of women being forced into marriage. If she was running away from an arranged marriage, she wouldn't want anyone to know the real story for fear they would send her back to her parents. Still, what the devil was she doing on the Isle of Mist? It wasn't exactly a place people bumped into on their way to London.

Had it only been an accident of fate that brought Julia to his door? Or was there some calculation on her part, some reason she had singled out his home? And there was another possibility, one he didn't like to consider. The woman might have been sent here by someone intent on destroying him.

"You won't be sending her back to her parents, will you, milord?

Gavin frowned. "At the moment, Iona, I don't even know who her parents might be."

Iona smiled. "And if you do find out, I'm trusting you will be doing the right thing."

Gavin's chest tightened when he thought of anyone being forced into an unhappy marriage. He knew far too well the hell that could be found in that type of union.

He had discovered the truth a few weeks after his marriage vows had been consummated.

The first night of the marriage, Gavin had not understood Lavinia's restraint. She had allowed him to make love to her before their marriage; in fact, she had seduced him one evening after a ball at her parents' town house. It was that incident that had led to their marriage three weeks later. Yet, on their wedding night, he had discovered the passionate woman who had all but torn off his clothes in her parents' garden had turned to ice. He had taken his time with his bride, plying all the gentle persuasion he had learned from his experience with genteel members of the demimonde. Yet, through it all, Lavinia had never melted. It had been like making love to a beautiful statue, as cold as carved white marble.

For several weeks he had tried to melt the ice. But the fiercely affectionate young woman he had married had disappeared. In her place was a cold, demanding stranger, a woman who shunned his every touch. One night, three weeks after their wedding ceremony, his wife told him precisely what she thought of him. *Beast* she had called him. *Scottish barbarian.* She wanted nothing to do with him. If it hadn't been for his title and wealth, she never would have allowed him to touch her. Aye, he knew far too well the hell of an unhappy union.

And now Miss Fairfield was here, with her mystery and her fairy tale about traveling through time. What the devil did she hope to gain by coming here with her story? He didn't like the feel of this. He didn't have many enemies, and fewer still who would want to see him destroyed. Lavinia's parents, Clarence and Octavia Harcourt, topped that list. They still believed he had murdered their daughter.

He needed answers.

Chapter Twelve

'Twas ever thus, when in life's storm
Hope's star to man grows dim,
An angel kneels, in woman's form,
And breathes a prayer for him.
—George Pope Morris

For the first time in her life Julia understood the meaning of the word jealousy. She knew precisely why it was called the green-eyed monster. It had claws and fangs that sank into soft tissue, tearing at your vitals until you wanted to toss back your head and howl. A short while ago she had actually wanted to pry that woman's hand off Gavin's arm and break all her fingers. Violent thoughts from a woman who carried spiders outside instead of killing them. That's what jealousy did to a person.

Julia marched through the gardens, muttering to herself. She had no business being jealous over Gavin MacKinnon. He was hardly available to her. The feelings he evoked in her were purely physical. She assured herself that this was only a temporary aberration, a reaction to the stress of being yanked back to this time and place. The jealousy and the lust she felt were simply caused by . . . tension.

And if she explained these facts to herself a few hundred times, she might actually start to believe them. At the moment, she merely wished the uncomfortable emotions warring inside her would just go away and leave her some peace.

"Lions can be tamed," she muttered. Good heavens, where in the world had she come up with that? She was not a lion tamer. She had never been a lion tamer. She was the type of woman lions devoured for breakfast. Still, there was something about Gavin MacKinnon that brought out an entirely different side of her.

Unfortunately, that side was far too reckless for her well being.

She would not allow this man to turn her inside out. She was not the type of woman to become embroiled in some catfight over a male. Calm, composed, in complete control; that was the type of woman she was. Lord help her, she had to get through the next two months without doing something utterly foolish, such as losing her heart to a man who had long ago turned to dust.

Julia didn't realize where she was headed until she entered the garden outside the unfinished wing. She paused on the gravel path and stared at the huge tower Gavin had designed but had never finished. It stood today much as it would in her time, except the doorway leading to the garden was not bricked closed.

A pair of French doors stood open to the terrace

overlooking the garden. Julia paused at those doors and glanced inside. No one was in sight. Apparently the workmen had left to take their noon meal. In two months Gavin would die in this room. The thought sent chills scattering across her skin.

She rubbed her arms as she stepped inside the room. The crisp fragrance of cut wood mingled with the scent of plaster. A huge scaffold stood in the center of the room for those craftsmen who were creating the ceiling roundels fifteen feet above her head. She stepped around a pail that looked as though it had been filled with plaster at one time.

Ladders were placed against each of the three doorways, where the moldings were being fitted against the walls. Through an open door she could see an oval staircase curving upward from a large circular hall. The balusters had not yet been put in place; they lay in three stacks of brass at the base of the stairs. Wood was piled in stacks around the room, creating a maze of lumber and buckets and tools. Hammers and chisels lay with other tools dropped by the workmen and craftsmen who were employed to create Gavin's tower and the adjoining wing. Somewhere in this room, Gavin would die. How would it happen? She had to be here on that day. She had to prevent it.

Even though it was far from complete, this room held the promise of great beauty. She turned in a circle, taking in the details. Pouncing lions alternated with laurel wreaths in a frieze running in a circular pattern around the top of the room; the pattern ended three quarters of the way around. In her day the frieze was complete, the walls partially painted. In two months something in this room would prove fatal. She just had to figure out . . .

"What the devil are you doing in here?"

Julia jumped at the sound of Gavin's voice. She pivoted and tripped over a piece of lumber. She pitched forward, straight into the scaffolding. She hit the scaffold hard with her shoulder. Wood groaned. Metal clanged. She glanced up in time to see a bucket falling from the scaffold right above her. Before the message to run could connect with her feet, Gavin tackled her.

He wrapped his arms around her waist, taking her with him in his plunge to the floor. He pivoted at the last moment, hitting the oak planks first, cradling her against his chest. Her teeth snapped together as she hit his chest. Her head rammed his chin. His low groan sliced through her a heartbeat before the bucket slammed into the floor behind them. The explosion of metal hitting wood ripped through her, a sharp reminder of how close she had come to getting killed.

For several moments she lay stiff in Gavin's arms, her nerves taut from the near disaster. He drew in his breath. She rode the soft swell of his chest, lifting with the inhalation, falling with the soft exhalation that brushed damp heat against her cheek. The heat of his body wrapped around her with the mellow scent of sandalwood. As her panic subsided, she became aware of every place their bodies touched.

She lay snuggled between his thighs, his long legs embracing hers, his strong arms still wrapped tightly around her waist. His chest pressed against her breasts. Through the thin layers of her clothes she felt the hard thrust of his hips and tried her best not to think of the intimate male flesh centered there.

She lifted herself away from him, pressing her forearms against his chest. He was blinking, as though trying to clear stars from his eyes. She cupped his cheek in her hand. "Are you all right?"

He frowned, his dark eyes focusing on her face. "I think I'm lying on a hammer."

She cringed. "That must hurt."

"Aye. It does."

He stared up at her, as though he was expecting something from her. Something important. Yet for the life of her she couldn't manage to focus her thoughts well enough to decipher what it might be. He had a way of doing that—stealing her reason, turning her into a creature focused on sensation and emotion. At the moment she was trying very hard not to think of how right it felt to lie with him.

He swallowed hard, his Adam's apple sliding up and down beneath the smooth skin of his neck. "Miss Fairfield, I wonder if you might get off my chest."

Realization careened into her. "Oh. Yes. Of course."

She was making a complete fool of herself. She scrambled to relieve him of her weight. She brought up her knee, and connected with a far too vulnerable part of his anatomy. He sucked in his breath. Oh, dear; this wasn't going well.

In her rush to stand, she pushed down on his chest to gain leverage. The air whooshed from his lungs. She sat back on her heels with a giggle of nervous laughter. She clapped her hand over her twitching lips. "I'm sorry."

His thick black brows drew together, carving twin lines above his nose. "Are you?"

She coughed, trying to quell the giggles. "Of course."

"Yes, of course." He raised himself up on his forearms. "I can't imagine what made me think you found this amusing."

It seemed so intimate, sitting here like this, as though they were lovers clowning about on a Sunday afternoon. She bit her lower lip as she carefully rose to her feet. Once she gained her balance, she offered him her hand. He looked at her outstretched hand for a moment, as though judging the wisdom of touching her, before he took it and rose to his feet.

"Are you all right?"

He worked his shoulders, rolling them up and back before he spoke. "As much as I hate to spoil your merriment, aye, I seem to be fine."

She stared down at the bucket that had fallen. It had crashed right into the spot where she had been standing. It had once held plaster, the thick, dried remains of which could still be seen in the dented metal bucket. Beneath it, fresh cracks radiated in both directions along the thick oak plank of the floor where it had crashed. She didn't want to think of what that bucket would have done to her head. She had no doubt at all that Gavin had saved her life.

"Why are you in here, Miss Fairfield?"

She flinched at the sharp tone of his voice. "I wanted to get some idea of what might have caused the accident."

"The accident?"

"Yes. The accident that will kill you in June."

He stared at her a moment, and she could see he was trying to decide whether she was crazy or just pretending to be crazy. "*You* could have been killed today, Miss Fairfield."

"I would have been fine if you hadn't startled me."

His lips drew into a tight line. "You have no business being in here. It's too dangerous."

He was right. Still, she didn't care for his tone of voice. "I am not a child, Lord Dunmore. You don't need to speak to me as though I were."

He leaned toward her. "If you didn't run about acting

like a child, I wouldn't need to be scolding you like one."

She would not stand for any more of his arrogance. She turned, took a step, and tripped over a hammer. She pitched forward, straight toward a stack of lumber. Gavin whipped his arm around her waist and dragged her back. Her back collided with his chest. For one heart-stopping moment he held her close, as though they were lovers watching a sunset. It felt . . . familiar, as though they had stood this way a thousand times before. It was impossible, but more than a little compelling.

"Are you unharmed?" he asked, his chest rumbling against her back.

No. She was not all right. She was frightened and edgy and completely ill equipped to handle this situation. "Yes. I'm fine."

When he slipped his arm from around her waist, she hesitated for a moment before she turned to face him. She only hoped he wouldn't notice the blush of embarrassment she could feel heating her cheeks. "I suppose you think I'm a clumsy . . ."

Her words ended in a sharp intake of breath as he swept her into his arms. She lashed her arms around his neck, momentarily frightened that he might drop her to teach her a lesson. He seemed fond of teaching her lessons. Yet he made no move to drop her. Instead he held her close against his chest, one powerful arm beneath her knees, the other wrapped around her back. "What are you doing?"

He grinned at her wariness. "I'm making sure we both make it out of here without another mishap."

He carried her as though she were as light as a child. The thick muscles in his chest shifted rhythmically against her as he strode through the maze of lumber and buckets and tools. Yet she didn't pay attention to her surroundings. He could have carried her through Eden and she wouldn't have noticed a single flower. The man carrying her held her attention far too closely for her to notice anything else.

Although he had shaved the stubble she had seen on his cheeks this morning, dark pinpoints of beard slumbered beneath the smooth surface of his lean cheeks. She quelled the insane urge to touch his cheek, to slide her fingers over that lean expanse of sun-darkened skin. This close, she could see every line time had carved on his face, the faint traces of lines at the corners of his dark eyes, between his brows, at the corners of his mouth. She wondered if smiles had carved those lines or frowns, and somehow she felt certain this man had known more frowns than smiles. That certainty touched a melancholy chord within her.

Someone needed to teach him to trust again, to smile again, to love again. It would take a woman strong enough to meet him toe to toe. A woman willing to risk everything for him. She was not that woman. No, certainly not. Even if she lived in this time and place, she was hardly the type of female who could tame this man.

Sunlight greeted them as they left the room. Still, he didn't set her on her feet. He carried her across the terrace and into the garden, pausing only when he reached a stone bench. He smiled, a devilish grin she hadn't seen since she had awakened in this time and place. A smile she had found irresistible when he was a ghost. But only now did she realize the true potency of that smile. If she had been standing, her legs would have given out beneath her.

"If I set you down, do you think you can manage to keep out of trouble?"

"Will you keep holding me if I tell you no?" As soon as the words escaped, she wished she could take them back. What was she thinking, flirting with this man? He already thought she was some fortune hunter on the prowl.

His expression revealed a flicker of surprise before wariness entered his eyes.

"I mean, yes, of course. I can stay out of trouble." She lowered her eyes, afraid of what they might betray. "You can put me down now."

He hesitated a moment before slipping his arm from beneath her knees. She slid down the powerful length of his body. By the time her feet touched the gravel, her legs were trembling so fiercely that she had to grip his shoulders to steady herself. She looked up into his eyes, certain suspicion would stare back at her. What she saw stole the breath from her lungs.

Hunger simmered in those black eyes. A hunger so stark and raw that it glowed like fires on a moonless night. A hunger she recognized, because it hummed through her own veins. The depth of it startled her. The raw need sank deep into her bones. Never in her life had she felt this powerful pull, as though her very existence were tied to this man. Her body felt tense, like a bowstring drawn too far. The tension quivered through her body.

She watched his eyes, amazed by the emotion she saw there, the same longing and need that coiled deep inside her. She felt entranced, as though he had cast some powerful spell over her, altered her from the conventional, responsible, dull female she was into a temptress. She leaned into him, allowing her body to mold to the hard planes of his powerful frame.

He slid his hand down her back, his palm warming her through the layers of her clothes. He lowered his head. His breath touched her cheek, warm and scented with a trace of cinnamon. It felt so right, being in his arms, as though she had been born for this moment, this man. A man who only existed in this time and place. The irony of the situation spilled into her blood. The impossibility of it sank like a blade into her heart. This was wrong. She shouldn't be within a hundred years of this man. Yet she couldn't pull away from him.

He kissed her, his lips sliding slowly upon hers, taking complete possession. Warm and firm and heartbreakingly gentle. It was a kiss straight out of the most hopeful corner of her imagination. A groan started low in her chest and rose, escaping against his lips in a soft whimper of pleasure. She had kissed other men before, but never had she truly felt this kind of pleasure. It shimmered within her, rising and spreading, until its heat and light rivaled the sunlight shimmering around them.

He pressed soft kisses against her cheek, forging a tingling path to the curve of her jaw. Shivers skittered over her skin as he nuzzled the sensitive skin beneath her ear. "Who are you?"

The question fluttered through the haze in her mind. "You know me. You've always known me," she whispered, her own words surprising her with the truth they held. She felt she had known this man since the beginning of time and beyond.

He slid his tongue down her neck. She quivered in response, her entire body coming alive beneath his touch. "What are you doing here, Julia?"

"Holding you," she whispered, sliding her fingers

through his thick hair. She hadn't realized just how much she had longed to have her arms around him until this moment. "I can't believe I'm really holding you."

He tightened his arms around her, holding her close against the solid strength of his body. A sigh fluttered past her lips as he opened his mouth against the curve of her neck and shoulder. "What brought you here?"

"A miracle," she whispered.

He slid his hands over her back, warming her through the layers of her clothes, all the while pressing soft kisses against her neck. "Who sent you here?"

The question pierced the fog he had generated in her brain. She pulled back and looked up at him. Sunlight shaped a golden halo around his head. He looked like some dark avenging angel, beautiful, dangerous, tossed from heaven to wreak havoc with any mortal female who crossed his path. The hard glint of determination in his black eyes triggered a warning bell inside her head. "What a lousy trick."

His black brows lifted. "Trick?"

She pulled away from him so quickly that she stumbled and nearly tripped over her own feet. When she regained her balance she glared at him. Anger pounded through her veins, swallowing all the warmth he had conjured with his treacherous touch. "What did you think, Gavin? Did you think you could seduce the truth out of me?"

He shrugged, apparently completely unscathed by an encounter that still had her trembling. "It was a possibility."

She curled her hands into tight fists at her sides. "I did tell you the truth."

He sighed, a bored expression crossing his features. "The fairy tale about traveling through time."

She swallowed past the knot in her throat. She would not fall apart now. "It's not a fairy tale. I only wish it were. I wish I were back home with Lauren and Gram. I wish I had never in my life set eyes on you."

He regarded her for a moment, his expression an unreadable mask. "What's wrong, Miss Fairfield? Not feeling up to taming the lion?"

"No, I'm not. I've never been up to taming a lion. I'm not up to changing the past. But I'm here." She swiped at her cheek, wiping away the single tear that escaped her control. "And I am going to do what I have to do to save you and Brandon. Even if you are the most despicable man I've ever had the displeasure to meet."

Chapter Thirteen

O Woman! in our hours of ease
Uncertain, coy, and hard to please,
And variable as the shade
By the light quivering aspen made;
When pain and anguish wring the brow,
A ministering angel thou!
—*Sir Walter Scott*

Gavin watched her until she ran through the arched entrance and disappeared from sight. He would not chase after her, even though every instinct within him screamed for him to follow her. He had been justified in his actions, he assured himself. A man under attack had every right to defend himself. So why did he feel as though he had just kicked a kitten?

He hated the weakness she found inside him, the treacherous emotions he couldn't seem to crush when she was near. He had learned long ago to control his emotions, all of them. Yet this woman, with her huge blue eyes and her outrageous stories, burned all of his control to ashes. He drew in a breath, clenched his hands into fists at his sides, and gathered his composure.

He had never met anyone quite like Miss Fairfield. One moment she was a temptress in his arms, luring him, heating his blood as no woman had ever done. The next she turned into a vulnerable creature who awakened all his softer instincts.

It must be part of some feminine strategy. Yet it was one he had not before encountered. He supposed he might think more clearly when his blood cooled. He knew his thought processes were muddled at the moment. It was not easy to dissemble when the blood was pumping hard and fast into his loins. It had taken all his will to keep from taking her, right here, in the middle of the garden, where anyone could have interrupted them. Still, he was master of himself, and thus master of the situation. He could deal with Miss Fairfield.

The woman clutched her fairy tale the way a miser guarded his pennies. And it *was* a fairy tale, he assured himself. Perhaps it was easier fabricating this outrageous story than facing the truth. If she was running away from an arranged marriage, she would be reluctant to trust him. If she was working for the Harcourts, she was certainly a skilled actress. Were the Harcourts, or more precisely Octavia Harcourt, clever enough to come up with such an outrageous ploy to penetrate Dunmore's defenses?

He rubbed the taut muscles at the back of his neck. As much as he wanted to deny it, he hoped she was not in league with the Harcourts. Yet what would that make her? A clever fortune hunter? A clever lady in trouble?

Or a Bedlamite who believed she had traveled through time to save him? It galled him to realize how much he hoped she was innocent. He could tolerate and accept insanity. Treachery was another matter.

He turned and left by the gate opposite the one she had taken, deciding a long walk along the cliffs might take the edge off the sharp blade of lust twisting in his loins. He had learned all about the treachery of women eight years ago. He had learned from an expert, and he had learned his lesson well. He would never again trust another woman with anything as vulnerable as his heart. He would get the truth out of Miss Fairfield, one way or another. And lord help her if she was out to betray him. He would make the little witch regret the day she was born.

Julia didn't stop running until she reached the sunken gardens on the far side of Dunmore. She would have kept running, only she had nowhere to go. She sank to a stone bench under a chestnut tree standing near the stone wall enclosing the garden from the woodlands. She stared across the wide expanse of sculpted flower-beds, over the lily pond to the terrace and the library beyond it. A few days ago she had stood on that terrace beside her grandmother. Of course, that wouldn't be for nearly two hundred years.

Did they know she was gone? Were they worried about her? Or, since this was the past, had it all happened before the day she had left? Did that mean that no one would even know she had vanished back into the past? She abandoned that train of thought. If she pursued it, she was certain her brain would end up with a cramp.

She closed her eyes, fighting against the burn of tears. Gavin was the most infuriating creature ever put on the face of the earth. How had he managed to be granted a chance for a miracle? Of course, his miracle did depend on her. Apparently God had a wonderful sense of humor. Still, it was lost on her. She couldn't understand what horrible sin she had committed to be put through this hell. Oh, how she wished the man had never been born.

"Are you all right, miss?"

The soft question pulled her out of her private misery. She opened her eyes and looked straight into a pair of inquisitive brown eyes. A child stood before her, a boy who couldn't be much more than seven years old. A handsome child, with large black eyes and thick, dark brown hair. A boy who looked far too much like his father to be mistaken for anyone but Gavin's son. "You must be Brandon."

He smiled, a shy little grin. "Yes. Are you the lady my father brought home last night?"

He made her sound like a stray cat. But then, under the circumstances, she felt a little like a stray, friendless and a long way from home. "Yes. I'm Julia Fairfield. I'm afraid I got in your father's way last night on the road."

He considered this for a moment, his expression far too mature for one of his years. From what she knew of Brandon MacKinnon, he hadn't had much opportunity to be a child. "It was an accident, wasn't it, miss? You didn't walk out in front of my papa on purpose?"

"I can't imagine why I would step out in front of a galloping horse on purpose. Can you?"

"Yes, Miss Fairfield, I can." Brandon sat beside her

on the bench. It was then Julia noticed the man standing a short distance from them. Tall and broad, he was a bearlike figure with thinning dark brown hair and brown eyes, who regarded Julia with a glimmer of suspicion. A bodyguard?

"I saw a woman step out in front of my father's carriage when we were driving through the park one day in London," Brandon said, drawing her attention back to him. "She jumped back before we hit her. When my papa got down to make certain she was all right, she fainted. Only I saw her eyes open when Papa lifted her. She was just pretending to be asleep. Grandmama said it happened when she was out with Papa one day, too."

Julia frowned. "Why would a woman do that?"

"Uncle Patrick told me it was because my papa is a very wealthy earl. Lots of ladies want to marry him. And they will try any trick they can to catch him."

She thought of everything Gavin had endured at the hands of her gender. "I suppose I can understand why your father doesn't trust women very much."

Brandon studied her for a long moment. "You don't seem like those women, Miss Fairfield. You're much too pretty to be throwing yourself in front of a horse. You could get my papa's attention without doing that."

For the first time since she had awakened this morning, Julia was beginning to feel better about the entire situation. "Thank you, Brandon. That's very kind of you to say."

He glanced down at his black boots, then up at her. "You looked very sad when I saw you sitting here."

"I was thinking of home, and how much I miss my grandmother and my niece." The breeze ruffled his hair, flinging a thick dark wave over his brow. She smoothed the soft strands back from his brow as she continued. "My niece is a little older than you are."

He frowned. "Is there some reason you can't go home to see them?"

She thought of the reason that had brought her to this place and time. "I have something important I have to do before I can go home to them. Until then, I hope your papa will let me stay at Dunmore."

"He is very nice. I'm sure he will let you stay." He swung his feet back and forth, grazing the grass with the tips of his boots. "He is a fine gentleman."

She could argue that point, but not with this child. Brandon seemed very determined to see his father in a flattering light.

"And he isn't at all mean or cruel. And he wouldn't think of wearing animal skins and carrying a club. Ever."

For a moment she could do nothing but stare at him, caught off guard by this last statement. "No. I suppose he wouldn't."

He smiled up at her. "You know, I don't believe there are any barbarians left in the Highlands. I haven't seen one since I came to live at Dunmore."

The breeze rippled her skirts against her legs, the soft air filled with the scent of flowers. "Had you expected to find barbarians living here?"

He nodded. "Grandmother always said the Highlands were filled with barbarians. She said my father abandoned me and my mother because he was a horrible man who didn't have the ability to care for anyone but himself. She called him the Scot barbarian."

"Your father didn't know anything about you."

"I know."

Octavia Harcourt should be sent away for what she'd done to this child. "Your grandmother was not being very fair to you or your father when she said those things."

Brandon looked up at her with those soulful eyes that had seen far too much cruelty in his short life. "Sometimes Papa seems so sad. He really wishes I had been here when I was a baby. I think it would be nice if he married a nice lady, so he could have more children. And I could have brothers and sisters."

If she succeeded in saving Gavin, would he find his one and only love? An unexpected pain stabbed her far too close to her heart when she thought of Gavin with another woman. Yet she had no hold on him, no chance to ever be the woman in his life. "Perhaps all he needs to do is find the right lady."

Brandon smiled, seemingly satisfied with her response. "Would you like to go fishing with me, Miss Fairfield?"

"Fishing?"

"There is a stream not too far away from here. I was going there with Gordon when I saw you."

Julia glanced at the suspicious bear standing a few feet away, frowning at her. "I've never gone fishing before."

"It's all right." Brandon hopped off the bench. "I never went fishing until I came to live here with Papa. He taught me how to fish, and to tie flies and everything. I'll show you how."

She glanced down at the pretty muslin gown she was wearing. "Would it be all right if I just watched you fish?"

He grinned at her. "If you want to."

How could she resist that hopeful grin? She stood

and walked beside him along a path leading from the gardens into the woodlands. Gordon lumbered behind them. She glanced back at the big man, who hadn't uttered a word. "Does Gordon go everywhere with you?"

"Yes." Brandon glanced up at her, his eyes narrowing against the bright sunlight. "Papa is afraid Grandmother will try to take me back to Carthely Hall again."

Julia pulled her dress close around her as she passed a small clump of blackberry bushes growing near the path just outside of the garden. "Has your grandmother tried to kidnap you?"

"Twice." Brandon glanced down at the path as he continued. "I don't know why she wants me back at Carthely; she never liked me when I lived there."

A cool shade wrapped around them as they followed the path into the woodlands. Octavia Harcourt didn't want the boy, and apparently never had. Still, she was vindictive enough to keep him from his father.

Julia caught glimpses of the stream as they followed the path through the wooded area. Brandon led the way to a clearing, where the sunlight dipped and danced across the wide stream. The swiftly flowing water had carved a channel through rock-studded land. Water tumbled over mounds of rocks, splashing softly.

Brandon took off his coat and laid it under the shade of a tall birch so she wouldn't get her dress dirty. In spite of his brutal upbringing, the boy was every inch a gentleman. Julia spent the rest of the afternoon in Brandon's company, watching him proudly display the fly-fishing technique his father had taught him. As she watched him, she understood why Gavin had been granted this chance for a miracle. This child, with his shy smile and his quiet ways, this young boy deserved the chance to grow into the promise of his youth.

If she did things properly, this child would live a long and happy life. Suddenly, all of it, every infuriating moment with Gavin, seemed worthwhile. She realized the privilege she had been given, this chance to set things right. The privilege and terrifying responsibility. If she didn't handle this properly, all would be lost.

A soft groan drew her attention to Gordon. The big man had been standing beside a nearby chestnut tree. He was now slumped on the ground beneath that tree. Her heart crashed into the wall of her chest as Julia saw two men heading straight for Brandon.

She scrambled to her feet. "Brandon!"

The boy pivoted at her shrill scream. His eyes grew wide as he saw the two men advancing on him.

"Now come along, lad," one man said. "Your grandmother sent us to bring you home."

"No!" Brandon swung his long fishing rod, whipping it against the man who had spoken to him. It struck with a loud whack.

The man yelped and grabbed his arm. Brandon shot past him. "Grab him, Billy!"

The larger man lunged for Brandon, hurtling his big body toward the boy like a linebacker after a scrambling quarterback. He whipped one arm around Brandon's waist and hoisted the boy from the ground. Julia charged the big man, screaming at the top of her lungs. She lowered her shoulder and plowed into him. The big man groaned. He stumbled forward, releasing the boy. Julia's teeth snapped together. A stinging pain shot along her shoulder and arm. She stumbled back and snatched her breath.

"Brandon, run!" she shouted.

The boy dashed toward the path with Billy on his heels. She ran after them. The other man grabbed her arms from behind. She screamed and twisted, kicking back with her foot. She connected, hitting his shin with the heel of her shoe. He cried out, and his grip slackened. She twisted free and ran for the path where Brandon and Billy had disappeared.

She had gone no more than three feet when the man grabbed her arm. He cinched one arm around her waist and hoisted her off the ground. She clawed at his arm, screaming, hoping someone from Dunmore might hear her. He pivoted, trying to avoid her slashing feet.

"Bitch," he grunted as she scraped her nails across his hands. He squeezed so hard around her middle, the air jolted from her lungs. "I'm going to teach you . . ."

His words ended in a gasp. His arm disappeared from around her waist with a suddenness that sent her reeling. She staggered two steps, then tripped over her gown and sank to her hands and knees on the thick grass. She barely had time to draw a breath when a large hand settled on her shoulder.

"No!" she shouted, twisting away from his grasp. She lashed out at him, pouncing on him like a lioness attacking her prey. Her hands connected with his shoulders. Her momentum knocked him off his heels. He flew back, taking her with him. He whacked the ground. She whacked his chest, her head colliding with his chin. She had the satisfaction of hearing him groan before she sat up and swung with her right. She caught a glimpse of his face a heartbeat before her clenched fist connected with his chiseled jaw.

The impact shot upward along her arm, stinging every nerve, muscle, and bone in its path. She opened her hand and shook her fingers, sucking in air as she stared down into Gavin MacKinnon's face. He was staring at her, as though he were trying to clear stars from his eyes.

"Oh, my goodness," she whispered. Her heart quit, then started in a rush. Heat sluiced through her, like flame skipping over the surface of warm brandy. "What are you doing here?"

Gavin opened his mouth and shifted his jaw, as though he was testing to see if it still worked. "I thought I was coming to your rescue, Miss Fairfield."

It took a moment for her befuddled brain to process the information. He had a way of doing that to her, of stealing her wits. "Brandon—" She gripped his shoulder. "That man went after Brandon. We have to find him."

"I'm all right, Julia."

Julia looked up and found Brandon standing a few feet away, smiling at her. She struggled to her feet and ran to him. She threw her arms around him, dropping down on one knee to hold him close. He lashed his small arms around her neck and hugged her back so tightly that she could scarcely breathe. "They didn't hurt you, did they?" she asked, pulling back to look at his face.

Brandon grinned. "I'm all right."

She smoothed her hand over his cheek. "Are you sure?"

"I ran into Papa on the path." Brandon looked over Julia's shoulder, his expression filling with pride. "He knocked down that man with one punch."

Julia glanced up at Gavin. His dark hair fell in disheveled waves around his face, sunlight slipping gold into the luxuriant strands. He was rubbing his jaw, looking at her. The look in his eyes made it suddenly very difficult to breathe. He was looking at her as though he were seeing her for the first time, and he found the sight intriguing.

"I suspect Miss Fairfield might have dropped him if she could have caught up with him." Gavin shifted his jaw. "She has a prodigious right."

Julia stood and brushed the dirt from her gown. "I didn't realize it was you."

Gavin smiled, a glint of mischief filling his eyes. "That's comforting."

Was it? Funny, she found nothing comforting about the situation. She was irresistibly drawn to this man. A low groan drew Gavin's attention to the bodyguard lying under a nearby tree. She rested her hands on Brandon's shoulders as Gavin helped Gordon to his feet. How in the world could she keep from falling head over heels for the flesh-and-blood Gavin?

After leaving the Harcourts' two brigands in Gordon's care, Gavin walked back to Dunmore with Brandon and Julia. She kept her arm around the boy's small shoulders, as though the child meant something to her. Gavin rubbed his jaw, easing his fingers over the bruise she had left. She had defended the boy, risked her own safety to protect him. Did that solve part of the enigma of Julia? If she was working for the Harcourts, would she have defended Brandon? It wouldn't seem so, unless it was all designed to gain his trust.

Trust was not something he gave lightly. Still, he couldn't imagine the Harcourts were clever enough to concoct a story about traveling through time. In fact, if he was truthful with himself, he wanted to believe this woman had nothing at all to do with the Harcourts.

He glanced over Brandon at the woman walking beside his son. Julia had lost most of the pins from her hair during the excitement. The honey-colored tresses fell around her shoulders in a silky cascade. He flexed his fingers, itching to delve into those silken strands. Twice this day he had found himself flat on his back with this woman sprawled on top of him. And both times he had wondered what it might be like to find himself in that position under much more comfortable circumstances.

What cost would he pay if he took her in his arms? If he seduced the hell out of her? He wanted to unhook, unfasten, untie every feminine barrier. The memory of her lying between his thighs evoked images of this woman lying naked upon clean white sheets, and of him, holding her, smoothing his hands over her, kissing her, tasting her, drinking in the scent of her. Lust pounded through him. Aroused and heated, he fought the images and the desire they wrought.

He could handle Miss Fairfield. He would not fall prey to her wiles. He would not succumb to his own pounding hunger. He dragged his gaze from Julia and tried to crush the need sinking into his belly. But it remained, a serpent of fire slithering through his veins. He set his jaw. He would not relinquish his control. He would not tumble into her trap.

Chapter Fourteen

When love's delirium haunts the glowing mind,
Limping Decorum lingers far behind.
—George Gordon, Lord Byron

What would it take to get past Gavin's defenses? Julia stared at her image in the cheval mirror that stood in one corner of her bedchamber. Iona had once again swept her hair up into a topknot, transforming her profile into something that might have graced a Grecian urn. She had threaded a silk ribbon the same shade as the sea green crepe of her gown through the coil. She could use a touch of mascara. She could use a healthy dose of courage.

She drew in a deep breath. She had hoped this morning might have proved to Gavin that she was on his side. Yet, if anything, he had seemed more suspicious of her afterword. He had scarcely spoken a word to her since the incident.

Several times since then she had caught him watching her with a heated, predatory look in his eyes. She was hardly a child. She recognized lust in a man when she saw it, and Gavin MacKinnon burned with it. He wanted her, on a primitive level at least. She only wished she could claim indifference. It would be easier, so much easier. Unfortunately, the man merely had to glance at her and she was ready to rip off his clothes.

She could not become involved with him. In two months' time she would save him and Brandon, then return home. She would pick up the threads of her life and continue, without Gavin. She would think of him, of course, remember him and this time they had had together, but he would not be part of her future. It had to be that way. Gavin would never be part of her life. Once she accepted that fact, she could manage to press forward.

Unfortunately, Gavin had some twisted idea of who she was and what she wanted. It was war. The man would use any weapon at his disposal. She suspected seduction was just one of the weapons in his arsenal. And she had to admit, Gavin was heavily armed.

All he had to do was look at her and a hot tingling current rippled through her. Still, if he wanted a war, war it would be. She would not fall beneath his arrogant fist. He would not destroy her. She would not lose herself to him, body and soul. She was made of stronger stuff. He would see. She would make certain he . . .

She flinched at a knock on her door. That would be Iona, reminding her about dinner. Julia glanced at the crystal and gold clock on the mantel. She should have gone down to dinner five minutes ago. She was stalling. She knew it. She supposed there wasn't any point delaying further. She couldn't hide from him for the next two months. Could she?

"Courage," she whispered to the woman in the mirror.

She forced starch into her spine, marched across the room, and pulled open the door. "I'm sorry, I . . ." The apology she meant for Iona faded on her lips.

The sconce on the wall outside of her room cast a flickering light on the man standing in the hall. The soft glow touched his shiny dark hair and illuminated the devilish glint in Gavin's dark eyes. He was dressed entirely in black, except for the snowy bit of linen showing in the vee above his waistcoat. Tall, dark, and dangerous. He ought to wear a sign: LADIES BEWARE, APPROACH AT YOUR OWN RISK. Excitement swirled through her, heating everything in its path.

"And what is it you wish to apologize for, Miss Fairfield?" he asked, that deep Scottish burr doing something altogether wicked to her insides.

She clutched at her retreating courage. "Nothing. At least not to you. I thought you were Iona. And I was sorry about making her come back upstairs to fetch me for dinner."

"And I have come instead of Iona. Brandon is waiting for his dinner."

She frowned. "I didn't realize he would be joining us."

Gavin's eyes narrowed. "My son spent too many years away from his family, eating with the servants."

"I didn't mean . . ." Why was she always saying the wrong thing around this man? "I'm glad Brandon is joining us. I enjoy his company."

He studied her for a moment, in that way he had of

peering straight through her. "And you wouldn't be using the son to get into the father's good graces, would you?"

She glared at him. "You may be accustomed to women dropping at your feet, Lord Dunmore, but we aren't all interested in snagging you as a husband."

"I'm still trying to decide exactly what it is you are after here at Dunmore, Miss Fairfield."

"I told you. But you aren't interested in the truth."

"I'm not interested in fairy tales. I'll leave those to Brandon."

She released a frustrated sigh. "Fine. Don't believe me. I'll just have to make certain the two of you survive without your help."

Gavin offered her his arm. "Shall we?"

She hesitated for a moment before taking his arm. The scent of sandalwood swirled through her senses as he led her down the hall. The warmth of his body bathed her side. The subtle play of muscles beneath her hand plucked at her insides. Two months, she reminded herself. She could manage to resist this man for two months.

He smiled down at her, mischief glinting in his dark eyes. "I'm not sure I thanked you for trying to protect Brandon this afternoon."

She touched a small bruise on his jaw, her fingertip sliding against smooth, freshly shaven skin. "Did I do that?"

"Aye." He grinned at her, and for once there was no darkness in his smile. She forgot to breathe. "The two men the Harcourts sent didn't manage to lay a hand on me."

He paused at the top of the stairs and took her hand. She wasn't wearing gloves. Neither was he. The contact

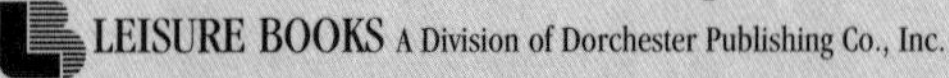

of his fingers sliding against her palm should not have sent a spurt of heat shooting through her. But it was there, smoldering, coiling, collecting in a molten pool low in her belly.

"You bruised your knuckles," he said, sliding his fingertips over the discoloration above the first and second knuckles of her right hand.

"It's fine." She jerked her hand out of his grasp. He frowned, a question glimmering in his eyes. She had no intention of giving him the answer to that question. "We're keeping Brandon from his dinner."

He studied her for a moment before he took her arm and started down the stairs. What did he see with those midnight eyes? Too much, she thought. Far too much.

"I don't understand why the Harcourts keep trying to kidnap Brandon," she said, hoping to turn the conversation to safe ground. "From what I have gathered, they have no real affection for him. Is it just for spite?"

"Hatred is a powerful emotion, Miss Fairfield, perhaps even more powerful than love. They would like to see me pay for Lavinia's death. And they don't care who gets hurt in the process."

A suspicion entered her mind, an ugly thought that just wouldn't go away. "You don't think they would hurt Brandon to get back at you, do you?"

He glanced down at her, an icy glitter in his eyes. "Miss Fairfield, I don't intend to allow anyone to hurt my son."

"I'm not here to hurt your son."

He took the last step before she did, then turned to face her, trapping her on the bottom stair. From her elevated position, she was eye-to-eye with him, and so close she could just lean forward and kiss him. She leaned back, resisting the temptation.

"Why did you come here?"

"I told you."

He studied her, curiosity and a glimmer of something far more heated in the dark depths of his eyes. "The fairy tale."

She released her breath, but it did nothing to ease the tension coiling inside her. "It's the truth. I know it sounds fantastic, and now that I think about it, I probably should have lied. But I have never been a person who tolerated lies, and so I am not experienced in constructing them."

He frowned, and she could see he was once again judging her, taking her measure with those incredible dark eyes. She could also see that she had managed to plant a small seed of doubt. He might not believe her, but he wasn't certain she was a villain. His doubt about her was the only thing keeping the beast at bay.

He covered her hand with his, the warmth of his palm bathing hers. "Shall we dine, Miss Fairfield?"

She felt as though she had been dropped into the deep end of a swimming pool, with her feet chained. If she didn't fight with all her might, she would drown.

Gavin contributed little to the conversation at dinner. He watched Miss Fairfield and his son. She seemed so unguarded with Brandon, warm and caring. Could it possibly be counterfeit? After dinner Brandon played the pianoforte, while Julia turned the pages of his music, and Gavin sat and listened and watched. Candlelight from the branched candlestick on the instrument flickered gold upon her cheek. She was smiling at Brandon, and Gavin caught himself regretting that smile. It made him think of things he had long ago given up.

It was so intimate, sitting in the music room, watching his son and this woman. She fit into Gavin's life, like a piece of a puzzle that had finally been found after years of searching. He sipped his brandy and tried to quell the uncomfortable emotion stirring within him. It was lust, he was certain of it. Still, it felt different than any bout he had ever suffered in the past. It sank deeper and burned hotter. He didn't know what game she was playing, but he knew she played it well.

When he tucked Brandon into bed, he discovered he was not the only MacKinnon male infatuated with the mysterious Miss Fairfield.

"Julia is very pretty. Don't you think so, Papa?"

Gavin smoothed the dark waves back from his son's brow. "The world is full of pretty ladies, Brandon."

"But she is different from the ladies in London." Brandon grinned up at him. "I think she was amazingly brave this morning."

"Aye, she was." Gavin frowned when he thought of Julia and her efforts to rescue his son. What was she after at Dunmore? Why had she concocted such an elaborate story? He had to find the solution, the answer to the enigma named Julia.

"I told her that you would let her stay here for as long as she liked." Brandon stared at him, his wide eyes betraying a measure of uncertainty. "You aren't going to make her leave, are you, Papa?"

He should send her packing. But he couldn't find the will to get rid of her. "I cannot very well send her home when I don't know where she lives, can I?"

Brandon smiled. "I think she is very, very nice. And I

don't think she would ever walk out in front of your carriage to catch your attention. I don't think she is like that at all."

What type of female was she? He would have the answer to that question. One way or another, he would get to the bottom of the mystery surrounding Miss Julia Fairfield.

After he tucked Brandon into bed, he returned to the music room, where he had left Miss Fairfield, only to find that she was not waiting for him. He stood in the doorway and clenched his jaw. He told himself the emotion roiling through him was not disappointment. He certainly did not care if the woman did not seek his company. She was a woman, like any, more intriguing than some, perhaps. Beautiful, certainly. Definitely clever. The clever ones were far more dangerous. His interest in her was certainly not of a personal nature. And if he told himself that a few hundred times, he might actually believe it.

Erskine paused in the hall behind him. "I noticed Miss Fairfield enter the conservatory a few minutes ago, milord."

Gavin turned and met the old retainer's perceptive gaze. "I won't be requiring you for the rest of the evening."

Erskine smiled. "Aye, milord."

Gavin waited exactly twelve seconds before making his way to the conservatory. In that short space of time, he armed himself for the battle to come.

The scent of orange blossoms brushed his face as he entered the large room. It was fashioned of glass and iron, a high dome encasing a wide variety of exotic plants and trees. His footsteps tapped softly against smooth stone squares as he searched for Julia. Moonlight poured through the glass panes high overhead, spilling silver upon the trees and flowers. Palm fronds brushed his shoulder as he drew near the large fountain that stood in the center of the huge room. Neptune rose from the center of the stone basin, his hand outstretched, a stream of water falling from his fingertips into the basin at his waist.

Gavin found her standing there, near the fountain. She was holding one of the orchids that dripped in a three-foot-long pendant from a banana tree. She stood in the moonlight, unaware of him. He felt as though he had crept upon a fairy in a magical realm. Moonlight flowed through the windowpanes high above, falling softly upon her hair, her face, her bare shoulders. Funny, he had never noticed how alluring that gown had looked on Alison.

As though she sensed his presence, she turned and faced him. As his gaze met hers, an odd sensation gripped him. He felt disconnected suddenly, as though he were looking at everything from a distance. His heart seemed to slow and grow heavy, each beat a thud in his ears. Images coalesced in his brain—Julia standing in a garden, a lacy white gown clinging to her slender frame. And she was smiling up at him, a sheen of tears in her eyes. As he tried to capture the images, they faded, leaving behind a vague sense of discontent.

Had it only been last night that this woman had careened into his life? Somehow, it seemed he had known her forever. Such a strange sensation to experience with a woman he had only just met. It left him edgy and restless and far too aware of every move she made.

"What are you doing here?" she asked, her voice a husky whisper.

He was beginning to wonder that himself. Something told him it had been a blunder, following her in here. It had seemed a good idea at the time, an excellent place to put Miss Fairfield off guard. He hadn't considered the scent of orange blossoms and orchids surrounding them. He hadn't anticipated the way moonlight would play across the porcelain perfection of her skin. "I didn't realize I needed your permission, Miss Fairfield."

A troubled look entered her eyes. "Did you follow me?"

He had a strange feeling that he would follow this woman if she ever tried to leave him. Follow her to the ends of the earth if need be. Track her down and haul her back here. The thoughts startled him as much as the emotions attached to them. "A good host does not abandon his guest," he said, certain his tone betrayed nothing of the turmoil inside him.

She didn't look convinced. "Lord Dunmore, I did not come here to be seduced."

Her direct attack caught him off guard. "Seduced?"

She nodded. "In case you have that in mind."

"I assure you, Miss Fairfield, I have never in my life forced a woman into anything."

"Perhaps not, Lord Dunmore, but you are not above plying your charm to coax her into something foolish."

"Plying my charm?" He studied her, understanding sparking inside him. "So, you think I'll talk you into something foolish, do you?"

She frowned. "I have no intention of getting involved with you, Lord Dunmore. So there is no point in attempting anything. If you had anything in mind."

He advanced. She retreated, straight into a palm tree. She jumped as the palm fronds flopped over her shoulders. He looked down into her wide eyes and wondered if the lady realized how much she betrayed to her enemy. "If you are immune to my charms, you have nothing at all to worry about, Miss Fairfield."

"Since I am immune, you are wasting your efforts."

"Miss Fairfield, I have never yet tried to seduce you."

She moistened her lips. "Let's keep it that way."

He turned and watched her as she put six feet of moonlight between them. She was afraid he might seduce her, which meant she was not as immune to him as she claimed. Did she feel it, too? The attraction. The connection. The spark that ignited each time he held her in his arms. She was safe. He had no intention of seducing her. He would not entangle himself with her. Still, it was tempting. So very tempting.

She glanced up at the glass panels high above them. "I wonder why the conservatory no longer exists."

Her words caught him off guard, like a right to the jaw. "Pardon me?"

"This room." She glanced at him, and he had the impression that she was deliberately trying to knock him off balance with her strange conversation. "This room no longer exists in my time. It must have been lost in one of the renovations the various owners have made to Dunmore. I wonder why. It's very beautiful."

He had designed this room two years ago. He had watched it take shape, planted the flowers himself, and presented the conservatory to his mother as a gift on her last birthday. To think it had been destroyed by a careless hand . . . It was just a story, he reminded himself. A story fabricated out of desperation or careful calculation. Which? "My mother will not be happy to hear that one of her descendants has gotten rid of her conservatory."

She looked at him, uneasiness filling her expression. "I suppose, if I'm successful, the conservatory might survive the wrecking ball."

"You mean if you change the past, and save me from the accident?"

She nodded, her expression growing thoughtful. "Yes. If I'm successful, I suppose Helen will never come to live here. Of course, she does only use Dunmore as a summer home. Still, she is very fond of the place."

He ran his fingers over the soft petals of an orchid. Her eyes lowered, her gaze following the play of his fingertips over the white petals. "If you change history, and she never comes to live here, she will never have the opportunity to miss it."

She lifted her eyes and met his gaze. "You don't believe a word I'm saying."

He didn't, but he did enjoy the sound of her voice. It was more than the unusual accent. It was the quality of tone. It made him want to hear her speak his name in a whisper. "Tell me about your home in Chicago."

She hesitated, studying him as though she were trying to decide if he was seriously interested. "It's a huge, old Victorian set on two acres of land. With a big white gazebo in the middle of a rose garden. My mother would work for hours in that garden. It was her pride."

There was a softness in her voice as she spoke of her home, a sadness lingering just beneath the surface of her words. "A Victorian? That's an American style of architecture?"

She smiled. "It's a style named in honor of Britain's Queen Victoria."

It was all a game, he reminded himself. A contest of strategy, like a chess match. Only a fool became distracted by an opponent's smile. Still, for the life of him, he couldn't prevent the acceleration of his pulse, the current of heat swirling low in his belly. "Queen, Victoria?"

"Let's see how well I remember British history." She flicked at a lacy palm frond with her fingertip. "The Duke of Kent will sire a daughter, who will be born next year. That daughter will be named Victoria. She will inherit the title from William in 1837 and rule until . . . right around the turn of the century."

She spoke with such ease of future events, which made her either very quick witted or very well rehearsed. "This Victoria shall inherit from William. What of Prinny?"

"He will rule as king after George the Third dies in a couple of years. He'll sit on the throne for about ten years before his death."

He acknowledged an uncomfortable sensation in the pit of his stomach. He was a Highlander, which meant he had grown up on tales of fairies and magic, things beyond the ken of mortal man. Still, he did not believe her tale. This woman had not dropped into his life from the future. It wasn't possible. Was it? "And so you live in America, in a home named for a future Queen of Britain."

"Queen Victoria had a large influence over the entire civilized world. The house I live in was built by my great-grandfather in 1892." She glanced past him, staring at the windows behind him, as though she were looking at something a long way from this place. "It was my parents' home. I inherited it after they died five years ago."

At last something of the truth. "Your parents could not be the ones trying to force you into marriage."

"No one is trying to force me into marriage."

"And how is it you aren't married, Miss Fairfield?"

She laughed, a soft, nervous sound mingling with the splash of water from the fountain. "In this time, a woman my age is called an ape leader, isn't she? On the shelf. I suppose you think I'm a dried-up old spinster."

"I think you're a beautiful woman. Uncommonly so." Hers was a beauty that grew each time he looked at her. A beauty that multiplied with each smile. A beauty that could steal a man's wits and everything else he owned.

She blinked, as though he had struck her. "Flattery. Since you think we are in some war, I suppose it's one of your tactics. The truth is, you think I am either insane or a fortune hunter."

"Or running away from something or someone."

"I'm not running away from anything. And I'm not married for the simple reason that I have never met the right man." She tilted her head. "Although I was engaged once. I ended the engagement three weeks before the wedding."

She had come close to marrying another man. It certainly shouldn't concern him. Yet the thought of another man touching her made his palms itch. "What made you cry off?"

She shrugged. "I realized I didn't love him and I never would."

He shouldn't have felt relieved by her confession. Yet he did.

"I don't think he ever loved me either. I met certain

criteria he had in mind for a wife, but he didn't love me." She cupped the flowers of a Jasminum and breathed in the fragrance. "If he had loved me, he never would have tried to manipulate me the way he did."

He knew all about manipulation. "In what way?"

"In every way. He was very good at twisting me around his finger." She allowed the blossoms to fall from her hand. "I only wish I had never become involved with him."

He sensed the sadness within her and wondered how deeply this man had hurt her. From somewhere deep within came a longing, a need that caught him off guard. He wanted to comfort her, to hold her, to protect her all of her days. "And now you are waiting for a knight in shining armor?"

"I was never looking for a knight in shining armor, Lord Dunmore." She glanced at him, then lowered her gaze. He caught a glimpse of sadness in that look, a wistful longing that whispered of hopes and dreams that were carefully tucked away. "I suppose I've always thought there was one special man for me. My soul mate."

"Soul mate?"

"Yes. The one man destiny meant for me to find in my lifetime. Someone I loved before, in a hundred lifetimes."

He had spent enough time in India to understand the concept of rebirth of the soul. Still, to believe each person was destined for one special person in this world was foolish. Nonetheless, the idea was more compelling than he cared to admit.

"I always thought one day we would meet, and both of us would know instantly how very right we were for one another. It would be as though we had met before, in a half-remembered dream."

He tried to scoff at the sentiment, but he couldn't muster the cynicism needed to dismiss her romantic notions. They touched him deep inside, in a place he hadn't realized existed, until this mysterious young woman plowed into his life. The first moment he had looked at her face, he had felt he knew her. "What is he like, this man of your dreams? Your soul mate."

"I always thought he would be quiet, sensitive, intelligent. A gentle man, who never raised his voice, never lost his temper."

No resemblance to him at all. It shouldn't bother him, but it did. "A paragon."

"I suppose." She strolled to the fountain and stared into the wide stone basin at her feet. "But now I wonder if he isn't very different from that image. I have this terrible feeling he isn't at all the way I imagined him to be."

Her words stirred inside him, lifting hope from the pile of ashes where he had buried all his boyhood dreams. "Why is it so terrible?"

She looked at him. She seemed to see straight into his soul with that look, as though he were as transparent as a crystal glass. "Because I have this terrible feeling he may be beyond my reach."

He held her gaze, unable to look away, even though the voice of sanity demanded that he break the connection between them. It was so strong, an invisible tether binding one to the other, a magnetic current coiling around them, tingling his skin, as though he stood naked in a summer storm.

She felt it too. He could see the reflection of his own desire in her eyes. It was the look of a woman drawn to a man in spite of her better judgment.

"It's getting late." She turned and marched toward the door.

He should let her go, and leave him in peace. Only he discovered he was not at all capable of sound reasoning. His blood was pounding so hard, it sang in his ears. He was heated and restless and angry, so angry that she could turn him into a creature consumed by emotion.

"Julia."

She pivoted at the sound of her name, her eyes wide as she watched him stalk her. "Don't," she whispered as he drew near.

The feeble protest bounced off him like a butterfly striking a bear. He gripped her arms and yanked her against his chest. He saw the panic in her eyes before he slammed his mouth over hers. He wanted to punish her, to teach her to keep her distance.

This was what happened when a clever woman barged into his life and made him want as he had never in his life wanted anything before. This was what happened when a woman dared to venture too close to his shriveled heart, when she made him long for more than a furious ride between her thighs. He meant to warn her with this kiss, to frighten her into running away from him. For he knew he could not find the strength to toss her out of his life.

The scent of her swirled through his nostrils, filling his lungs, sinking into his blood. The clean fragrance of roses, the heated, musky aroma that was purely female. She struggled in his arms, pushing against his chest, turning her head to escape his kiss, all to no avail. He whipped his left arm around her waist and lifted the right, cupping the back of her head, holding her prisoner while he slanted his mouth over her soft lips. At that moment he felt her surrender.

Julia looped her arms around his neck and held him, returning his kiss with a surge of passion that knocked the wind out of him. He stumbled back and bumped into a lemon tree. His grip on her eased. Still, she didn't pull away from him. She held him as though she would still be holding him when the earth crumbled to dust and the last stars expired in the sky. She held him as though he were the one man of all men who could make her come alive.

Gavin touched her lips with the tip of his tongue and she parted for him, welcoming him into the dark warmth of her mouth. He plunged past her silken lips, and knew he had never tasted anything so sweet. It felt so right, as though he had been searching for her all his life.

He slid his hands down her slim back, gripped her slender waist, and drew her closer, so close he could feel her belly pressed against his hardened flesh. Yet it wasn't close enough, not nearly close enough. He slipped his hand between their bodies, cupped her softly rounded breast and slid his thumb over the taut peak. She whimpered low in her throat and pulled back to look up into his eyes.

She looked bemused, a woman awakening from a lovely dream. Her soft lips were parted, moist and red from his kiss. "We can't do this."

Dimly, he realized there would be consequences to taking her. But he didn't care. He would pay any price, no matter how high. He wanted her. He would have her. He swept her up into his arms and carried her toward the door.

Chapter Fifteen

O happy state! when souls each other draw,
When Love is liberty and Nature law.
—Alexander Pope

Consequences. A thousand consequences ripped through Julia's mind, each declaring reasons she should not allow this man to make love to her. He carried her into his bedchamber and kicked the door. It thudded shut, sounding a sharp warning of the bridges she was about to burn. Still, with his arms around her, and his scent surrounding her, and his warmth seeping into her pores, how in the world could she think clearly? She had to try.

"Gavin, I . . ."

He kissed her, sliding his lips over hers. Heat kindled low in her belly and radiated in all directions, threatening to melt her brain to mush. In spite of all the sane reasons she should not surrender to this man and the longing burning deep inside her, she locked her arms around his neck and returned his kiss. She slanted her mouth against his, matching his hunger, claiming as he claimed, plundering as he plundered, startling the staid woman inside with the passion he unleashed within her.

He slipped his arm from beneath her knees, allowing her to slide down the hard length of his body. By the time her feet touched the floor she had to cling to him to keep from dissolving in a puddle at his feet. He pressed kisses along her jaw, slid his tongue down her neck, all the while he moved his hands down her back, the hooks of her gown falling open beneath his deft touch.

This had to stop. Of course it had to stop. She had no business being in this man's arms. Then why did it feel so right? Why did she feel more alive than she had ever felt in her entire life? It struck her then, just as sharp and clear as a jagged edge of glass, a truth she could no longer deny. She understood precisely why she had never allowed another man to touch that secret place deep inside her. She had been waiting for this man all her life. Only now she knew her one and only love would never find his way into her life. He had died before she was even born.

The truth cut so deeply, she couldn't breathe. She pulled her arms from around his neck and stumbled back, bumping into one of the chairs near the fireplace. She leaned against the high back of the chair, her gown slipping from her shoulders. She shoved her gown back in place and stared at him, her breathing ragged, uneven, as though she had run a long way and finally found her destination. Only this was not her time or place. "We can't do this."

Moonlight flowed through the windows, filling the

room with a pale glow, carving his figure from the shadows. He stood staring at her, a fierce look in his eyes. He shrugged out of his black coat and tossed it to an armchair near the fireplace. "I think we can."

She shook her head. "I don't belong here."

"Don't you?" He tugged his white cravat from his collar and tossed it to the floor. The neck of his shirt spilled open, revealing a wedge of dark hair. "Then what the hell are you doing here?"

"Is that what this is all about?" She glanced at the bed. The counterpane and covers had been turned down, revealing white linen sheets. "Was this your plan all evening? Are you doing this to seduce me into telling you the truth?"

He flipped open the buttons of his black waistcoat, all the while glaring at her. He tossed the garment to the floor as he demanded, "What is the truth?"

"I won't be used or manipulated by you. That's the truth." She ran for the door. He got there first, blocking the way with six feet, two inches of solid male dominance. She edged back, glaring at him. "I thought you never in your life forced a woman into anything."

He smiled, his dark eyes glittering with emotion. She saw anger in those dark depths, anger and hunger and a fierce determination. He was a lion with an antelope in his sight, and nothing would sway him from devouring his prey. "I never have."

"And what do you call this?"

He grabbed her arm and swung her around, pressing her back against the door. "A mating dance."

"If you think for one moment I am going to allow you to seduce me to satisfy your misdirected suspicions, you had better think again."

"Think again? I'm not doing a great deal of thinking." He nuzzled the skin beneath her right ear. Shivers scattered across her nerves, like sparks from a fire. "I haven't been thinking clearly since you plowed into my life."

Dear lord, neither had she. She closed her eyes, blocking out his compelling image, but she couldn't escape the heat and power of his potent masculinity. Her anger had deserted her, fleeing in the face of the inferno building between them. No matter how much she wanted to resist him, she wanted this more. "You're the one who turned my entire life upside down and inside out."

"Me?" He slid his hands over her shoulders, the heat of his palms sinking into her skin. He slipped the gown from her shoulders. The soft crepe fell with a whisper. "I've always marveled at how a woman can manage to take her own actions and spin them around so they are the fault of any male who happens to be in the vicinity at the time."

She shivered as he plucked open the ties holding her petticoat. "You brought me back here. It's not my fault you can't remember doing it."

He nipped the skin at the joining of her neck and shoulder. "Still talking about ghosts?"

"Ghost. Your ghost." She grabbed the edges of his shirtfront and tugged. Stitches screamed, linen split, as she cleaved the garment to his waist. She stared at his bared chest, amazed at her own wanton behavior. Somewhere in the back of her mind she realized that this was not at all like her. Distantly she recognized the changes Gavin had wrought upon her. The staid, ever polite English teacher never would have behaved this recklessly. "Oh, my goodness, I think I should . . ."

"Confound you." He slipped his hands around her neck and forced her chin up with the tips of his thumbs. "You are a witch, Julia. A sorceress who has cast her spell over me."

The door pressed against her back, but she hardly noticed, she was so lost in the turmoil in his eyes. "I have?"

He leaned forward, until his nose brushed the tip of hers. "There is something about you, Miss Fairfield," he whispered, peeling off her petticoat. "Something that defies my every attempt to resist you."

She stared at him, stunned by his confession. "You can't resist me?"

He growled low in his throat as he plunged his hand into the hair at the back of her head. Pins pinged against the oak behind her as he worked his fingers through her hair, releasing the tresses. She caught a glimpse of the hunger in his eyes before he crushed her lips beneath his. He opened his mouth over hers, kissing her as though he drew his life from her.

Hunger thundered through her. She flung her arms around his neck, kissing him with the wild abandon of a woman who has finally found the only man she will ever love. His hands slid over her, stripping away the last of her clothes, stroking her, as he explored her with his lips and his tongue. She leaned her head back against the door as he spilled kisses down her body, lingering at her breasts. He drew one taut tip into his mouth, flicked his tongue over the peak, suckled her.

Soft, whimpering sounds filled the air. Distantly Julia realized they were coming from her mouth, commanded by the man who moved down her body, sliding lower, nipping at her belly, dipping his tongue into the cup of her navel, his hands sliding over her hips. He knelt before her and rested his cheek against her body, his hair brushing against her hip.

"Beautiful," he whispered, slowly drawing his fingers along the inside of her thigh.

She felt beautiful, transformed by his touch. He released his breath, the long exhalation stirring the curls at the joining of her thighs, the damp heat penetrating deep into her woman's flesh.

Her breath stopped, caught in her throat at the first touch of his lips against her. Nathan had been her only lover, and he had never touched her this way. Still, deep in her soul she knew no man would ever touch her this way again. It was more than the pleasure he conjured with his lips and his tongue, more than the heat he ignited, the delicious, simmering warmth flooding her blood. This connection they shared defied her experience and her every attempt to describe it.

She slipped her hands into his dark waves, the luxuriant strands coiling around her fingers. She held him close against her, her hips tipping to offer herself freely to this man. And he accepted the offering, loving her until the pleasure rose and shimmered inside her, until she called out his name and shuddered against him.

He stood and swept her up into his arms. She looped her arms around his neck, lifted her lips to meet his kiss. Cool sheets touched her bare back as he lowered her to the bed. The ragged edges of his shirt brushed her sides, his bare chest pressed against her breasts, warm skin, silken curls, teasing her sensitive nipples.

He took her hand and slipped it between their bodies, pressing her palm against the hard length of his arousal. "This is what you do to me, witch."

She squeezed him through the soft wool of his

trousers. He buried his face against her neck, a soft groan slipping past his lips. He moved his hips, sliding against her hand, teasing her with the solid length of him. The hunger surged inside her. She fumbled with the buttons of his trousers, wishing zippers had been invented. Finally the flap fell open. He pressed against her hand, sheathed in soft cloth. More buttons! She slipped both hands between them and ripped the barrier aside.

"Yes." He laughed, a soft rumble against her neck. "Touch me, witch. Touch me with your magic."

She slid her hands down the heated length of his aroused flesh, holding him between her palms, teasing the soft tip with her thumbs, rubbing him against her belly. He released his breath against her neck. She stroked and explored him, and all the while her body was melting, the hot liquid core oiling her inner thighs.

"Gavin," she whispered, tipping her hips, trying to capture him.

He raised himself above her, withdrawing until only the ragged edges of his shirt touched her breasts. There was a fierce look in his eyes, hunger and more, a need she recognized, for it burned inside her too. "Do you want me, Julia?"

"I've always wanted you." She tipped her hips and led him to her entrance, the flesh made hot and wet and aching by his touch. "Always and forever."

A low growl issued from deep in his throat as he plunged deep inside her. It had been more than five years since she had felt the first sting of a man's entrance into her body. She had known pain that night, pain and a horrible feeling that it was all a mistake. Each time with Nathan had left her feeling more empty than before. He had called her frigid. It was only one of many things he had wanted to change about her. Yet he never had.

This was different. This joining filled her with more than pleasure. Her body welcomed Gavin as her lover, the pain no more than a sharp pressure, the initial discomfort of tight flesh stretching to accommodate his length and breadth. This time she knew it was right, as though her body had been designed for this man, only this man.

He kissed her, slipping his tongue past her lips, dipping and retreating to the same heady rhythm as his hips pumping against hers. She lifted to meet him, rising and falling, each delicious thrust stoking the fire inside her, until it flamed out of control, until she shuddered and shattered beneath him. Distantly, through the haze of pleasure clouding her mind, she heard her name escape his lips as he spilled his seed inside her, hot and liquid, pumping life into her.

Powerful muscles tensed against her. He held her against him, as though he would never let her go. Then, slowly, the tension relaxed, and he eased into her arms. Moonlight touched a thick wave curling below his ear. She brushed her fingertip over the silky strands and breathed his scent deep into her lungs. If she lived a hundred lifetimes she would always love this man. As the thought formed, she wondered once again at the connection they shared. *Soul mates.* She no longer doubted the possibility; she embraced it, and the man she had loved since the beginning of time.

Gavin held her, pressing his face into the curve of her neck, breathing in her scent. He was not a poetic man. He did not believe in romance. If he had not seen love between a husband and wife, he would not have believed it possible. He had long ago given up hope of every finding the emotion his parents had shared. Yet now, with his body still joined to this strange female, he wondered if he had at last found it.

Even as the thought formed, he dismissed it. It couldn't be love. He had only just met her. He knew absolutely nothing about her. She could be insane, for all he knew. Or worse. She could be a clever schemer here for her own purposes. Still, he could not deny the emotion gripping him, the sentiment sinking deep into his pores. He wanted to stay right here, with this woman, until his last breath.

Startled by the stunning emotion, he pulled away and looked down at her. She was lying with her head turned on the sheet, her eyes closed, her lips tipped into a satisfied grin. If she had been a cat, she would have been purring. Satisfaction curled warmly in his chest when he saw that little grin.

He smoothed the damp waves back from her cheek. His heart turned over when she looked up at him. In the depths of her blue eyes, he saw all of the hopes and dreams he'd buried long ago. Did she feel it too, this connection, this depth of feeling? Could he believe what he saw in her eyes? Could he believe what he felt in her touch? Could he believe in love? "Who are you?" he whispered, the sound harsh to his own ears.

She flinched, a dreamer yanked from slumber by a careless hand. "I told you who I am and why I'm here."

"Julia, the witch who traveled through time to save me and my son." He kept his voice harsh, lashing her with the impossibility of her story. He wanted the truth from this woman. He wanted to look into her beautiful eyes and know she meant every word that came out of her luscious mouth. He wanted to be certain what she had just given him, the emotion she'd unearthed inside him, was real and honest and unshakable. He needed that honesty. He needed to know what he sensed with her was real.

Her lips pursed. She looked as though she might cry. He expected that. His chest tightened with the certainty of what would come next—the weeping, the declaration of her ruination at his hands. He had heard it all before, in a moonlit garden in London, the night Lavinia had made her kill.

"I am not a witch," she said softly. "I am a fool. A silly woman who has allowed her romantic imagination to get the better of her."

And what was he, if not a fool? He was still wearing his shirt, as well as his trousers, though at least the latter were bunched around his ankles. He had taken her without even removing his shoes. The hunger had overwhelmed him, consuming him with a need he had never before known in his life. Not with Lavinia. Not with any other woman. The power this woman held over him terrified him. "Tell me the truth. Why did you come here?"

She stared up at him with none of the anger he expected to find in her eyes. What he saw was far worse than anger. *Disappointment.* She was disappointed in him. That look cut him straight to the bone. "There is no sense in telling you the truth, because you won't believe it. So I won't even try."

He had wanted the truth from her since the moment he had lifted her into his arms that first night. Now, he wasn't certain the truth mattered as much as he had thought it might. Would knowing her intentions destroy the hold she held on him? The answer was there, lurking in the shadows of his besieged brain. An answer he didn't like or want to accept. "And what is the truth?

That you came here from the future, brought here by my ghost, to act as my champion?"

Julia released her breath in a sigh that brushed his cheek with damp heat. "The truth is, I'm in over my head. The truth is, I never should have allowed all that nonsense about soul mates and love enduring beyond time to cloud my judgment. I'm here to save you and Brandon. To imagine there could possibly be some mystical connection between us, some bond that has lasted for lifetimes, is purely delusional on my part."

It was nonsense. To imagine a love lasting beyond time, a love so powerful that it connected one to the other through the ages, was nothing short of absurdity. Still, there was an allure to the notion.

Perhaps it was his Highland blood, or some shred of romance remaining hidden deep within him, but he couldn't dismiss the emotion this woman evoked within him, the sensation that she was now and always had been important to him. It was a weakness, this hold she had over him; a pitiful, dangerous weakness. "What did you expect from me, Miss Fairfield? A declaration of undying love? Did you think coming to my bed would win you a proposal?"

Her eyes narrowed, anger replacing the disappointment he had glimpsed in those beautiful eyes. "I wasn't thinking of anything at the time. That's the problem. I allowed my emotions to get the better of me."

He lifted his brows, deliberately forcing his features into a mocking mask. "You came to my bed because you find me irresistible?"

"Not anymore I don't." She pushed against his shoulders. "Get off me."

He lifted away from her, stifling a groan. The air cooled flesh made warm and wet by her body. He stood and pulled up the tattered remains of his drawers and his trousers while she scrambled from the bed. "What comes next, Miss Fairfield? Will you demand that I pay for ruining you? Do you expect me to offer the protection of my name in marriage?"

"You honestly believe you are God's gift to women, don't you?" She glared at him, her eyes slits of blue fire. Her hair tumbled over her shoulders in a riot of pale waves. Moonlight gleamed upon smooth, pale skin, sliding over high, softly rounded breasts, slipping seductively over her slim belly, tangling in feminine curls. His blood stirred, his sex awakening once more, as if answering her siren's call.

"No, Miss Fairfield. I honestly believe members of your sex are taught to use any means available to them to secure a husband." He fastened the buttons of his trousers as he spoke. "But if you think giving yourself so freely to me will pry an offer from me, you are mistaken. Any woman who throws herself into my path will get exactly what she deserves."

"At least what you imagine she deserves." She grabbed a pillow from the bed and clutched it in front of her, covering her breasts and her belly, as if she only just realized her state of undress. "I didn't come here to pry some marriage proposal out of you, Lord Dunmore. I wouldn't marry you even if I could."

Her words cut him. What the devil was she doing to him? He could almost believe she was a witch. With a smile she released the beast inside him. With a touch she destroyed his intellect, smothering the control he had nurtured for so many years. "And do you make a practice of bedding men you have no intention of marrying?"

"No. Of course not. But that doesn't mean . . ." She

released an agitated breath. "I made a mistake. It won't happen again."

He blocked her way when she tried to storm past him. Only then did he realize how very much he wanted her to stay. "What do you want from me?"

She stared up at him, her chin at a defiant angle. "At the moment, I want you to leave me alone."

"You are free to leave," he said, shutting out a voice inside of him that screamed for her to stay.

Some of the bravado left her expression. "If I had somewhere to go, I would. But I don't. I have to stay here until I can prevent the accidents. It's the only way I'm going to be able to get back home."

Sincerity filled her eyes, her words. Did she honestly believe this tale? "If my ghost brought you back here to prevent accidents that will happen in June, why the devil did I bring you back here so early?"

"I don't know. Maybe you wanted to torture me. Maybe you . . ." She hesitated, her eyes growing wide. "Oh, my goodness. I've been concentrating so much on you and Brandon, I completely forgot about the other tragedies that befell your family."

He frowned. "Other tragedies?"

She clutched the pillow to her breasts, pale curves swelling above the white linen. "We have to go to London. We still have time to stop it."

She was doing it again, twisting his brain into a knot. "Stop what?"

"The accident."

"I thought the accident wasn't to happen for another two months."

"Not your accident." She gripped his arm. "Your brother. Patrick."

"What about Patrick?"

"He was killed, in London, on the 14th of April, 1818. I should have thought of it before. He was coming home from White's when he was struck by a coach and killed." She fluttered her hand as she spoke. "How long does it take to get to London?"

"What nonsense is this about Patrick?"

She stared up at him. "We have to get to London by the 14th. Can we do it?"

"Aye. If we leave tonight."

"Then we have to leave. Tonight."

He took her arms and yanked her against him. The pillow pressed against him, a shield against the brush of her breasts. Still, he wondered if a shield existed to protect him from this woman. "Who put you up to this?"

"You still imagine I'm some part of a conspiracy against you? Do you honestly believe I'm working for the Harcourts or someone out to destroy you?"

Gavin didn't know what to believe, or trust. He knew his own instincts were unreliable with this woman. "It makes more sense than your fairy tale of traveling through time."

"I don't care if it's more logical. I'm telling you the truth. For some reason I don't pretend to understand, I was chosen to come back here and save you and Brandon. And if we can get to him, we have a chance to save Patrick."

He squeezed her arms, a part of him wanting desperately to believe her. Yet there was another part of him, the battered and bloody part, that refused to believe anything she had to say. Still, he couldn't afford the luxury of ignoring her. Not when it came to his family.

"If you don't help me get to London on time, your brother is going to die."

He didn't know what to think of her. He only knew he had to get to London. If she was working for someone, if Patrick's life was at risk, he had to try to save him. He forced open his hands and released her. "We leave in twenty minutes."

Julia looked out the coach window, watching the first rays of the sun stretch out across a rolling meadow, fingers of gold brushing dark green grass. She hadn't realized how cold she could feel until she found herself in a nineteenth-century coach with Gavin MacKinnon. She supposed the conveyance would be considered spacious by the standards of the day. Still, it scarcely provided enough room to stretch her legs. And it certainly provided no room to escape the brooding presence of the man sitting across from her on the black velvet squabs.

Brandon lay curled on the seat beside her, his head nestled on her lap. Although the trip would be grueling, Gavin would not leave Brandon behind. Gavin had taken along four burly footmen as guards, just in case Julia's insistence that they leave for London was merely a trick, designed to get him away from his son. Did Gavin actually believe she was in league with those horrible Harcourts?

She stroked Brandon's hair, the luxurious dark strands sliding like silk against her fingers, reminding her of the soft slide of Gavin's hair against her skin. The boy looked so much like his father. Still, Julia wondered if Gavin had ever been this innocent, this open to possibilities. She realized he must have been, but that part of his soul was lost, buried beneath bitterness and past mistakes.

Her chest tightened when she thought of what Gavin thought of her. He hadn't spoken a word to her in hours, not on the boat that took them to the mainland, not since they had entered the coach. He had in fact, scarcely glanced at her. Where was the passionate man who had made her heart soar with his kisses? Did it all mean nothing to him?

It was better this way, she assured herself. It was better to see the folly of her wishful imagination rather than expire for want of a man who could not possibly be a part of her life.

All that nonsense of soul mates and love beyond forever. How easily she had come to believe that Gavin was the man of her dreams, her one and only love, the man destiny had meant for her. It was a lot of foolishness.

She stroked Brandon's hair, taking comfort in his soft, even breathing. Soon this pain would disappear, she assured herself. Soon she would accept the cold, hard facts, the reality of the arrogant, far too cruel man sitting across from her. Soon she would return to her time, get on with her life, and think of these hours as one would a bad dream. It was better this way. Better to remember Gavin as a cold, unyielding, arrogant bastard, rather than the lover who could make her heart soar. Soon, she reminded herself. This would all be over in a few weeks.

In his defense, she supposed it was difficult to believe her story of time travel. If the situation were reversed, she would demand three forms of ID and a demonstration of the time machine that had brought him to her. All right, it did sound impossible. She could forgive him his skepticism, especially after his experience with women. Still, she couldn't forgive his callousness. He had seduced her to get at the truth. Making love to her had meant nothing to him.

Her neck tingled. She glanced up and found Gavin watching her, his expression unguarded, emotion naked in his eyes. He met her gaze and in an instant his armor slid back into place, shielding his expression behind an iron mask. He looked out the window, pointedly dismissing her. Still, in that unguarded moment, she had caught a glimpse of the loneliness in his eyes, a glimmer of a need so stark and hungry that it stole the breath from her lungs. He needed her. She sensed that truth on a level far deeper than mere intellect. And she also knew he would continue to hold her at a distance.

She could not imagine that he did not feel the connection between them. It was too powerful, too deep, to be merely lust. Morning light streamed through the coach window, illuminating the sharp lines of his profile. He was staring out the window, frowning as though he disapproved of the sunshine. What had made him turn so cold? Was it just male pride, the survival instinct of a man who had been put through hell by a woman he had trusted with his heart?

As if he sensed her gaze on him, he glanced at her, a challenge in his dark eyes. *Try to reach me,* he seemed to say.

Words this man's ghost had once spoken to her echoed in her memory. *You could have changed my mind, Julia. You could have made me see how much I would miss if I didn't learn to trust again.*

She glanced away from that icy stare. Gavin had been wrong. She was not the woman who could teach him to trust again. She wasn't even certain she could manage to prevent the accidents to Gavin, Brandon, and Patrick. It would be close. Because of her stupidity, they might not reach Patrick in time to save him.

Chapter Sixteen

Miracles do not happen in contradiction to nature, but only in contradiction to that which is known to us of nature.

—Saint Augustine

"That blackguard didn't even stop." Patrick MacKinnon handed his brother a snifter of brandy. "If you hadn't come by when you did, he would have hit me."

Gavin looked into his brother's blue eyes and suppressed the shudder gripping his stomach. It had been close. Far too close. He and Julia had arrived in London nearly an hour ago. Thanks to Miss Fairfield, Gavin had reached his brother in time to push Patrick out of the way of a coach speeding down St. James's Street. Now Gavin stood in front of the white marble fireplace in the gold drawing room of his house on Pall Mall, wondering how Julia had known about the accident. "I suppose it's possible he didn't see you."

"Not bloody likely." Patrick threw himself into one of the gilt-trimmed armchairs near the hearth. He took a long drink of brandy, then released his breath in a slow exhalation. "It was almost as if the coachman was trying to hit me. It was lucky you came looking for me tonight."

Gavin sipped his brandy, the heady bouquet flooding his nostrils, the aged liquor warming his chest. Still, it didn't ease the tightness centered there. Unless he was willing to believe her story, he could think of only one way Julia could have known of the incident that had nearly taken his brother's life.

Cold, unrelenting reality stared him straight in the face, and he still wanted to find some way to acquit her of the crime. Lord help him, the woman had her claws into him, so deep he wasn't sure he could free himself. Even now he wanted her. Even now, when he knew she was a calculating little bitch. He still wanted her.

"What brought you back to London?"

Gavin looked at his brother. Three years his junior, Patrick had not suffered the same unfortunate fate as Gavin. Perhaps seeing the mess Gavin had made of his life had taught him, alerted Patrick to the treachery of women. Perhaps it was due to his own nature. Patrick liked women, or rather he enjoyed them: actresses, opera dancers, lovely young widows, and occasionally a married woman. Given his own history, the latter was a practice Gavin found distasteful and dangerous. But Patrick was master of his own life. "Miss Fairfield brought me back to London."

"She's beautiful." Patrick grinned at him, a devilish glint in his eyes. "I'm hoping she isn't your mistress."

Images rose from the shallow tomb where he had buried them, images of honey-colored hair spilling over his pillow, of silken thighs parting for him, of soft lips moving hungrily beneath his. His blood heated several degrees at the mere thought of her. "No. Miss Fairfield is an unexpected guest."

"Unexpected guest. At Dunmore?" Patrick shoved a dark wave of hair back from his brow. "No one just shows up at Dunmore."

"According to Miss Fairfield, she came looking for me."

Patrick looked surprised. "How long have you known her?"

"Four days." Had he only known her four days? It seemed a lifetime.

Patrick lifted his brows in surprise. "You've known her four days. Three of those must have been spent traveling to London."

"Aye." Gavin sank into a matching chair across from Patrick, the cushion hard beneath the smooth gold silk brocade. "Still, for some reason I feel as though I've always known her. It's the most damnable feeling."

Patrick rolled his glass between his palms, a speculative look entering his eyes. "Has it finally happened? Has a woman managed to get past that massive stone wall you have built to keep them all at a distance?"

Gavin frowned down into his brandy. Julia had not only managed to get past it, she had damaged it, crushed stones into dust, leaving him vulnerable to her attack. "I don't trust her."

"The way you feel about women, I'm surprised you trust our mother. You do trust Mama, don't you?"

Gavin cast his grinning brother a dark glance. "It was Miss Fairfield who warned me about the accident tonight. She is the reason I was looking for you."

Patrick sat up, his eyes growing wide. "She knew someone was going to try to run me down tonight?"

Gavin stared into his brandy, trying to ignore the truth staring back at him. "Aye."

"And how did she do it?"

"According to Miss Fairfield, the accident was all part of the history of Dunmore."

"The history of Dunmore?" Patrick contemplated this for all of three seconds. "You're saying what happened today is already history?"

"According to Miss Fairfield it is." His brother's expression grew from curiosity to outright astonishment as Gavin delivered the facts of Julia's appearance and her strange tale. He omitted the evening he had lost control and plunged into Julia's fire. There was no need for anyone to know of his weakness.

Patrick stood and raked his hand through his hair, plowing deep furrows in the thick dark waves. "And she told you I would be killed tonight, by that coach?"

Gavin nodded. "She said we had a chance to prevent the accident."

Patrick stared at Gavin. "You're telling me this woman has come here from the future?"

"I'm telling you what she claims."

"It sounds incredible, as impossible as those stories of fairies and selkies Mama loved to tell us when we were lads." Patrick looked at his brother, a curious look in his eyes. "Still, if she isn't who she claims, how could she have known about the accident?"

"That's something I intend to find out." Gavin had

his own theory, one he hoped beyond all logic was not true. "Are you still bedding Beaufort's wife?"

"The day before yesterday, I ended it. And you were right about her. Regina did not take it well." Patrick rubbed his cheek. "I'm lucky she merely slapped me. I think if she had been carrying a pistol, she would have shot me."

Gavin glared at his brother. "You'd be wise to stay clear of married women."

"Aye. I've learned my lesson. No matter how tempting they may be, it's best to stay clear of them." Patrick drained his glass and crossed the room, walking toward the cabinet standing against the far wall. "Are you thinking Regina might have hired someone to run me down?"

"Never underestimate a scorned woman. Or a cuckolded husband." Gavin could speak from experience on both counts.

"Aye. It would be in Beaufort's style to come at me out of the dark." Patrick filled his glass, then turned toward Gavin with the decanter in his hand. "Want more?"

"No." Gavin didn't want to go into battle with a muddled head. Julia had a way of blinding him without the aid of brandy.

Patrick returned to his chair and sat on the edge of the upholstered seat. "If Miss Fairfield was plotting with Beaufort or someone else to run me down tonight, why would she have prevented it? It doesn't make sense."

Gavin shook his head. "None of it makes sense."

Patrick rested his forearms on his thighs and dangled his glass between his knees. "Unless she is telling the truth."

Gavin stared at his brother. "Do you honestly imagine she was brought from the future? By my ghost?"

"I'll admit it is hard to believe. It's certainly incredible, but impossible?" Patrick shrugged. "Who is to say what is impossible? Don't all miracles defy logic?"

A miracle. Had a miracle brought Julia into his life? "When did you become so philosophical?"

"I suppose nearly being trampled to death can do that to a man."

Gavin fixed his brother in a steady gaze. "Do you honestly believe she could have come from the future?"

Patrick opened his lips to speak, then closed them again. He frowned into his glass, then looked at Gavin. "It is absurd, isn't it?"

"Outrageous." Gavin wanted to shun the possibility. He wanted to deny the doubts she had planted within him. Yet his Highland blood refused to completely dismiss the tale. Could she be telling the truth?

"Well, she certainly is a great deal more clever than the females who keep dropping at your feet. I suppose she is after an offer of marriage like the rest of them."

Gavin thought of the night he had taken her to his bed. She had never once mentioned marriage. It had been the perfect opportunity to try that tactic. Yet she had not. "I don't know what she is after."

"But you don't believe her story. You don't suppose it could be true?"

"No, I don't." In spite of the conviction of his words, he couldn't banish his uncertainty. Could her tale be true? "Not for a moment."

"It is just too hard to believe." Patrick rolled his glass between his palms, his own doubts plain upon his face. "It would be a miracle."

Gavin managed a harsh laugh. "She must imagine we are all idiots to come around spewing such nonsense."

"Aye, she must think we are true mutton heads. She would have to be an idiot to imagine we would believe her." Patrick sipped his brandy, an uneasy expression filling his eyes. "The devil of it is, Gavin, she doesn't seem addled or dull-witted at all. She seems quite genuine."

Gavin nodded, an uneasy feeling gripping his stomach. "She's very good at what she does."

"I suppose." Patrick released his breath, then lifted his glass in a salute. "I don't know where she came from, but I am certainly glad Miss Fairfield managed to save my life."

"Aye." Gavin sipped his brandy. He needed the truth. He realized he could forgive her nearly anything except a lie. Still, in spite of all the logical reasons why she could not have been truthful with him, he found himself wanting to believe in her fairy tale.

It was a simple thing, tucking Brandon into bed. Yet it made her think of Lauren and Gram and everything waiting for her at home. A tight knot formed in her chest, a pressure that would not go away even though she tried to draw breath deep into her lungs.

"You look sad," Brandon said softly.

A single lamp burned on the table beside the bed, casting a flickering light over his features. He looked so young, so vulnerable. She reminded herself that he was the reason she had come here, to give him a chance for a long and happy life. "I was just thinking of home. I have a little niece about your age. I tuck her into bed every night."

"And you miss her?"

"Yes." She smoothed a lock of hair from his brow. "I miss her very much."

"She is lucky." He smiled up at her, a wistful look entering his eyes. "I know you would rather be with her, but I am glad you are here, Julia."

The true extent of the miracle Gavin had been granted glowed more brightly than the lamplight in the shadows of the room. She still did not completely understand the reasons she had been chosen to come to this place and time, but the opportunity she had been given filled her with a sense of awe. As long as she lived she would always remember this young boy and the knowledge that she had been granted the chance to save his life. "I'm glad I'm here too, Brandon."

He smiled, a wide boyish grin. "I was wondering, about what happened tonight. You saved Uncle Patrick. How did you know about the accident?"

"It was a miracle, Brandon. And we should never question a miracle."

"A miracle." Brandon stared up at her, as though she were an angle sent to his bedside. "Really and truly?"

She kissed his brow. "Really and truly."

"Did you hear that, Papa?" Brandon asked, glancing past Julia. "A miracle allowed Julia to save Uncle Patrick."

"I heard."

Julia's heart stumbled at the sound of Gavin's dark voice. She glanced over her shoulder. Gavin was standing at the foot of the bed, a tall, broad-shouldered figure in the shadows, just beyond the reach of the golden light of the lamp. Still, she could see his eyes. He was watching her, making certain his son came to no harm at the hands of this intruder. She stood and faced him. "I was just tucking Brandon in for the evening."

"And telling him a fairy tale as well."

The pressure in her chest expanded, pressing against her lungs. Would this man ever believe her?

"No, Papa. Julia wasn't telling me a story. She was telling me about her niece and the miracle that allowed her to save Uncle Patrick."

Gavin looked at his son and smiled, a real smile, genuine in affection, a smile that defied the shadows with a shattering warmth and light. Julia's heart contracted at that smile. She would give everything she owned to have that smile shine upon her.

She stood aside as Gavin sat on the bed beside his son. In another time and place, if destiny had not been so cruel, Brandon might have been their child. She might have been granted the chance to stand like this each night, watching as Gavin bent to kiss his son's brow. Regrets swelled up inside her, until they burned in her eyes. She turned away and left them alone. No matter how much it hurt, she had to face the facts. She did not belong here. She would never have a future with Gavin.

She took sanctuary in her bedchamber, closing the door, wishing she could shut out the images carved across her heart. "Why?" she whispered, leaning back against the door. "Why did you bring me here, God? I know it's an honor to be chosen to work a miracle. My head keeps telling me I should be grateful for this wonderful opportunity. But my heart . . ."

Julia swiped at the tears she couldn't prevent. "Why did you allow me a glimpse of what I have always wanted when it is so far out of my reach? Why couldn't you have sent someone else, someone who wouldn't fall in love with Gavin and his son?"

She sank into one of the Sheraton armchairs in the sitting area near the fireplace. She forced long, slow breaths into her lungs and tried to focus her thoughts in another direction. Tears cooled upon her cheeks, drying against her skin. Work. Her writing. She could always lose herself in one of her stories.

She glanced around the room, looking for details she could take back with her when she left. Mint green silk flowed down from the thick white molding at the high ceiling to white panels of oak trimmed in gold, the wainscoting rising three feet from the floor. Mint green silk damask covered the Sheraton chairs near the fireplace and the delicately turned settee at the foot of the large four-poster bed. The same mint green silk flowed in lush swags from each corner of the canopy above the bed, and covered the high mattress. It was a lovely room, not at all what she had expected. She had thought Gavin would toss her in the servants' quarters and feed her bread and water until she changed her wicked ways.

So much for prying Gavin from her thoughts. She had hoped rescuing Patrick might gain Gavin's trust. Unfortunately, saving his brother had only seemed to make Gavin more certain she was his enemy.

She heard the door open and turned to find Gavin standing on the threshold, looking at her as though she had just strangled his brother rather than prevented Patrick's death. He didn't wait for an invitation before he strode into the room. The door closed with a soft thud behind him.

A now all too familiar heat coiled through her, excitement sizzling along her every nerve as he moved toward her. In spite of his barely restrained anger, he was utterly devastating. His hair tumbled around his face and brushed the back of his collar in wild, disheveled waves. He had removed his neckcloth. His shirt had fallen open, revealing warm-looking skin and starkly masculine black curls. Just her luck to fall in love with a stubborn male who had allowed bitterness to shrivel his heart a long time ago.

Julia folded her hands in her lap, trying her best to appear calm, while inwardly her nerves knitted her stomach into a tight knot. He paused in front of her chair and glared down at her. The scent of rose potpourri drifted in the air. A soft, genteel fragrance completely at odds with the dark, sulfurous glare of this man. She dipped into her meager supply of courage and waited for the explosion she sensed coming. Still, he just stood and stared at her, as though he could bore a hole in her skull to read her mind if he just stared long and hard enough.

Finally, she could take the silence no more. "Did you want to speak with me about something?"

Gavin drew in his breath, his broad shoulders lifting the smooth black wool of his coat. "I would prefer you didn't fill my son's head with nonsense."

"I didn't."

"You were talking to him about miracles."

She held his gaze. "You might not believe in miracles, Gavin, but that doesn't mean they don't exist."

A muscle flickered with the clenching of his lean jaw. "I keep asking myself how you could possibly have known about that coach this evening."

She squeezed her hands together. "I told you: It is part of the history of your family. I read about it when I was doing research for the book I am writing about you."

"Did you?" He kept her pinned in a glacial glare. "Or did you know about it because you were in league with the blackguard who tried to run my brother down."

"You think I . . ." She closed her eyes and slowly counted to ten. It did nothing to cool her rising anger. "I did not have anything to do with what happened tonight."

"It's strange, isn't it? My brother's carriage breaks down and he has to walk home from White's. Then, just as we come upon him, a coach nearly runs him down. It's all very convenient."

"Convenient?" She stared at him. "How in the world is any of that convenient?"

He planted his hands on the arms of her chair and leaned forward, pinning her back against the chair with his glare. His legs pressed against hers, reminding her sharply of another time when those long legs brushed hers. "What is your plan, Julia? Is all of this some elaborate scheme to gain my trust?"

"My plan?" How could he imagine that she was still out to hurt him? She had made love to this man, given herself to him with all too reckless abandon. And this was how he treated her. "You are the most stubborn man I have ever met in my life."

"I'll give you one chance, Julia, one chance to tell me the truth."

The heat of his big body washed over her, reminding her of the few moments she had spent locked in this man's arms. She tried to push the images out of her mind, struggled to resist the need stirring inside her, and failed. She searched his eyes, knowing the man who had held her was hiding somewhere behind his anger.

She understood his anger, recognized the fear that spawned it. Since Nathan, she had held men at a safe distance, fearing that all men would be the same as one man. All men would look at her and see her as a work in progress, a project that needed tending, flaws and mistakes to be mended and altered. And this man, with his battered heart and his shattered faith, this man was the one man she wanted to draw near. "I did tell you the truth."

"You told me a fairy tale."

"Would you have preferred a lie, Gavin? A nice, conventional lie? Perhaps I should have lied from the beginning, told you something you could easily swallow as the truth. But I'm not made that way. I've never preferred a lie over the truth."

He lowered his eyes, his gaze resting on her lips. His hands flexed on the arms of her chair. He seemed to be struggling with some inner demon. Did he feel it too? The current coiling around them, stronger than anger or wounded pride. A need so deep and painful, she nearly screamed at the frustration of it.

He lifted his eyes and met her gaze. Flames flickered in those ebony eyes, turmoil and need. The same desire pounded through her veins. She needed this man. If only for a few precious moments, she needed to know what it was like to truly love and be loved. She needed to believe in what they shared. She needed him, if only for a brief moment in time. *Kiss me, Gavin. Please, kiss me.*

He drew in his breath, as though he had just surfaced from the bottom of a deep pool. "Tell me the truth."

She released her pent-up breath. It was all slipping away from her, this chance to share a few precious moments. All of it wasted because of his lack of faith in her. "After what we shared, you can still look at me and think I'm some deceitful little witch?"

He smiled. "You're not the first woman who thought she could bend me to her will by playing the strumpet in bed."

She fought back the tears rising in her eyes. "You are a real bastard."

His eyes narrowed. "I should toss you out on your ear."

"You want me to go. Fine, I'll go." She pushed against the hard width of his shoulders. "Let me up."

He hesitated a moment before he straightened. "I thought you had nowhere to go."

"I don't." She stood and tried to ignore the trembling in her limbs. He was an arrogant, stubborn brute, and she would not tolerate his insults one moment longer. Not when she needed so much more. "I'm only going to be in this hell for another two months. I should be able to find some way to support myself."

One black brow winged upward. "Support yourself?"

"That's right. I can find work as a teacher. Or a governess. Or something."

"Something?" He smiled, a cold curving of his lips that matched the ice glinting in his eyes. "I could talk to Madame Vachel about you. I'm sure she could find a position that would suit you."

"Vachel? What does she run? A dress shop?"

"She runs the most exclusive brothel in all of London."

He might have slapped her, hard, with the open palm of his hand. She stared at him, tears burning her eyes. She would not cry. Tears would not take away this pain; it was far too deep and ragged for tears to heal. She forced her chin up, when all she wanted to do was curl up into a tight ball and cry. "I have no way to prove to you what I have said is the truth. You either trust me, or you don't. And it's obvious you don't."

"You expect me to believe my ghost brought you here from the future to work a miracle." He released his breath in a frustrated sigh. "How the devil do you expect me to believe that?"

"On faith."

"Faith?"

"You can believe I am here as some horribly deceitful person, out to destroy you, or trick you into marriage, or for some other nefarious reason. Or you can believe in the possibility of a miracle."

"It would be a miracle to hear the truth from a woman." He leaned toward her, so close his breath brushed her cheek as he spoke, spilling the scent of brandy. "Tell me the truth, Miss Fairfield, or get out of my house."

She lifted her chin, meeting his angry glare with all the courage she could muster. "I have told you the truth. Is it really so hard to believe in a miracle, Gavin? Is it really so hard to believe in me?"

His dark eyes narrowed into hard, implacable slits. There was no mercy in those eyes, only bitterness and a certainty that she was the enemy. "As I recall, I gave you a choice. It seems you have made it."

"You are tossing me out?"

He shook his head. "You are the one who made the choice."

"Fine." She turned and marched toward the door, praying he would call to her or come for her. She pulled open the door and started down the hall. He couldn't just let her leave. Could he? Her footsteps slowed as she descended the stairs and made her way to the front door. Still, he did not stop her. She opened the door and stepped out into the London night. "Infuriating, stubborn oaf."

She marched down the walkway and paused at the street. Gas jets burned behind grimy globes atop the wrought-iron posts of the street lamps, creating yellow spheres in both directions. The street was deserted. Yet somewhere in the distance she heard the sound of horse hooves clopping along the paving stones.

She started to her left, went ten paces, then turned around, only to stop again a short distance from Gavin's house. It struck her then, like an open hand across the face: She had nowhere to go.

For the first time in her life she truly understood what it meant to be completely alone. Two months. If events worked out the way they had originally, she would be stuck here for two months. And if they had already been altered, who knew how long she would be trapped here? How could she survive? Was there an agency that placed governesses?

She could go back to Gavin, make up a story—she was, after all, a writer. And what would he do if she did lie to him? He would imagine she had been lying all the time and he would never give her his trust. Oh, this was a pickle. A fine pickle. And it was all because of one infuriating man.

She glanced up at the dark sky. All the stars were hiding tonight, lost behind thick, dark clouds. Silently she made a plea to the powers that be. Since she wasn't going to be any use here, it seemed a good time to whisk her back to her time. *Please, take me back home.*

She closed her eyes and waited. When she opened her eyes she was right where she had been, standing on the sidewalk outside Gavin's huge mansion. A fat drop of rain plopped on her cheek.

"Wonderful," she whispered.

Chapter Seventeen

For nothing worthe proving can be proven
Nor yet disproven: wherefore thou be wise,
Cleave ever to the sunnier side of Doubt.
—Alfred, Lord Tennyson

Gavin watched Julia march from the room. He balled his fists at his sides, fighting the treacherous impulse screaming inside him. He would not follow her like a lovesick puppy. He would not run to her and beg her to stay. His chest ached with the effort to control his emotions. "Infuriating thorn in my side," he muttered, crossing the room.

He stormed out of the room and down the hall. He reached the top of the stairs in time to hear the thud of the front door echo up the staircase. He hadn't invited her into his life; he certainly didn't need her to stay. She was a woman, like any woman. More alluring, perhaps.

Certainly more clever than most, because she actually had him on the verge of believing in fairy tales.

He squeezed the banister until his fingers ached. Each time he saw her with Brandon, he thought of how right she looked with his child. Each smile she gave the boy was warm and genuine, each touch gentle and caring. Each time he felt as though he were glimpsing the way things should have been. Damn her. Curse her treachery. Blast her for making him want her this way.

It was better if she left, he assured himself. He didn't need or want her in his life. She was trouble in every sense of the word. Far better to be rid of her. Even as he assured himself of how much better his life would be without her, he was running down the stairs. He reached the front door and froze.

This was nonsense. Utter nonsense. He gripped the handle, imagining he could feel the heat of her hand upon the polished brass. He craved that warmth.

Is it really so hard to believe in a miracle, Gavin?

A miracle. Was Julia his miracle?

Nonsense. He would not be sucked into this fantasy. He would not go after her. He had given her a choice. She had made it. He was not the unreasonable one, he assured himself. Then why did he feel like an oaf and a brute? Why did he want to run after her and beg her to come back into his home?

Because he was an idiot. Because she had insinuated herself past his defenses, found his every weakness, made him want and ache and shiver with need. He pulled open the door, marched outside, and nearly tripped over Julia.

She was sitting on one of the stone lions guarding the front entrance of the house, staring up at the sky as though she were waiting for an answer from heaven. And that answer had come in the form of rain.

Plump, heavy drops fell in sheets from the black sky. Rain tapped the slate roof of the arch over their heads. It plopped on the brick walkway beyond the arch protecting the entrance to the house. It poured across the front lawn, striking the leaves of the chestnut growing beside the sidewalk. He realized at that moment that he had never been so happy to see rain.

Julia tilted her head and looked up at him. Light from the lamps that flanked the front door fell upon her face, sprinkling gold on the tips of her long, dark lashes. She studied him, her features drawn into a sulky expression. "Did you come to chase me off your front porch? Afraid I might sully the lions?"

Gavin stared down into her defiant eyes and sought some means to extricate himself from the unfortunate trap he had laid. He never should have challenged her. He could see that now. Yet, how did he manage to drag her back into his house without revealing the hold she had over him? "It's raining."

She lifted her brows. "I noticed."

He clenched his teeth. She would not make this easy. "I may be a real bastard, Miss Fairfield, but I do not force women to wander about the streets in the rain. You are welcome to come in."

She glared at him with mutiny in her eyes. He stared into those beautiful, angry eyes and wondered what penance he would have to pay to coax her back into his life. The fact that he wanted her back in his life appalled him almost as much as the fact that he would pay any price to hold her once again.

Lord help him, he wanted to hold her in his arms. As much as he wanted to deny it, he craved the sensations she evoked within him, the excitement coiling through his veins, the heat and light she conjured within him.

For the first time in a lifetime he felt alive, and it was all because of this strange and beautiful woman sitting before him.

She sat staring up at him, a look of expectancy in her eyes. She wanted something from him. An apology? A declaration of his faith and trust in a story that belonged in the pages of a novel?

Still, she stared, silently demanding.

Come back to me, Julia. The words peeled like a bell in his brain, pitiful, supplicating words.

I need you. He nearly choked on the words crawling up his throat.

"Miss Fairfield, I won't be responsible for your catching a lung fever."

Still, she made no move toward him. The little she-cat intended to sit there and look at him until he fell to his knees and begged for her forgiveness. The sky would rain diamonds before that happened.

Lightning arced across the sky, a jagged streak of silver slicing through the darkness. Thunder rumbled, a low command to action. He took her arm and hauled her to her feet.

She tripped and pressed her hand to his chest to steady herself. Out of instinct, he brought his arm around her and held her close. Her soft curves molded to his hard frame. The lush scent of woman flooded his senses. She smelled of flowers and rain and a spice he would always know as *Julia.* His muscles tightened, like the string of a bow drawn by a hunter's hand.

Panic flickered in her eyes, followed by a quick flood of desire—the look of a woman drawn to a man against her will. His blood heated instantly. She was flame cast against brandy and he was wood, dry and brittle beneath the hungry flames. Blood pumped hard and fast, flooding his loins, humiliating his every attempt to deny the power this woman wielded over his senses.

He spread his hand against her slender back, remembering the feel of her skin beneath his touch. Memories rose and assaulted his self-control—her skin sliding against his, her hands stroking him, her mouth opening beneath his. Soft and supple, pliant and yielding. The memory of her need, of her desire for him was more potent than anything in his life.

He knew every curve and angle of her body. He had caressed her, kissed her, tasted her. But it wasn't enough. He wanted her now. In a dark, secret place inside him, he feared he would want her always. She stared up at him, her eyes reflecting the need thundering through him.

Her lips parted, her soft sigh brushing his chin with heat. With that soft touch, he abandoned any hope of resisting her. He lowered his head, brushed his lips against hers, and felt the demise of his defenses. He tasted her soft sigh, felt the tremor ripple through her before she pulled back.

She stared up at him, her cheeks flushed, her eyes wide and haunted, like a small wild creature trapped in a hunter's net. "I will not go down this path with you again, Gavin."

He held her when she tried to break free. He could crush her resistance. He felt her uncertainty. "You want me; I can feel it."

She looked him straight in the eye, a glint of steel entering her stunning blue gaze. "I might desire you, Gavin. I can't seem to help it. But I will not be some easy conquest for you. And I certainly will not allow you to seduce me again so you can try to drag a confession out of me."

He slid his hands over her shoulders and spread his fingers on her arms, pressing his palms against the smooth skin beneath her short sleeves and her drooping shawl. "What do you want from me?"

She held his gaze for a lifetime before she spoke. "I want you to know I'm here to help you, not to hurt you in any way. I want you to trust me, Gavin."

His chest ached with the weight of past mistakes. "Trust isn't something I give easily, Julia."

"I know." She rested her fingertips on his chin. "And I also know there is nothing I can do to prove to you that I'm telling the truth. But it is true, Gavin. Every word I've said."

He wanted to believe her. No matter how illogical and impossible her tale might be, he wanted desperately to believe it, and to believe in this angel who had fallen into his arms. Because if he could believe in her fairy tale, he could believe what he saw in her eyes, the emotion burning there—something hotter than desire, more lasting than lust, something that reached deep inside him and breathed life into the ashes of his hopes.

"Believe in me, Gavin."

The breeze swept over the lawn, throwing a fine mist beneath the arch where they stood. She shivered in the damp chill. Lightning flooded the night. Thunder rumbled over the arch where they stood, as though even the elements were pressing him, demanding from him a response to this woman. He dropped his hands from her arms.

He could not give her what she wanted. He was not capable of the trust she required. He had lost his faith a long time ago. Still, he could not find the will to turn his back on her. He opened the door to his house. "Come inside."

She hesitated for a moment before she accepted the invitation. He followed her into the hall, a single question pounding over and over in his brain: Could he trust her?

Julia stood beside one of the windows in her bedchamber, staring out at the storm-swept night. Heaven was giving earth a show tonight. A light show accompanied by the symphony of thunder, the rolling notes of the timpani, followed by great, booming crescendos.

If she closed her eyes, she could almost believe she was back home, listening to a great midwestern thunderstorm. Yet she was a long way from home. So far away from Lauren and Gram. Were they worried about her? She only prayed Gavin had told her the truth when he said they would never know she was gone. She hoped they would be spared any agony over her disappearance.

She looked up at the great, shifting mass of dark clouds and wondered what purpose had brought her here. Was there more than the obvious?

She had come to this place and time to save a young boy and his father from death. Was there more? Was her purpose to turn the tide of tragedy that had befallen all of the MacKinnons? If so, then why had she been chosen? What tie did she have to this place and time, to these people?

The answer seemed at once clear and clouded: Gavin. He was her tie to this place. He was her connection, her reason for coming back through time. Why Gavin? Why this man out of all men?

For so many years she had lain awake at night and prayed for someone to come into her life, someone with whom she could share her life, someone who would love her as much as she loved him. For so many years she had wondered if those prayers would ever be answered, if the loneliness would ever end. Was this the answer?

Was she to have two months with the man of her dreams? Two months to sustain her all the days of her life? If so, it didn't seem fair. Not fair at all. Especially when that man planned to waste the few precious moments they would have treating her as though she were his enemy.

She looked up at the sky and whispered a prayer: *Please let him believe me. Please let us share this time together.*

Believe in me, Gavin.

Julia's voice whispered in his head. Gavin lay in his bed, listening to the rattle of rain against the window-panes, the distant roll of thunder thinking of Julia. Was she thinking of him?

She found emotion in him, dredged it from places he had long ago forgotten existed. She had awakened a passion so powerful that he burned for her. And something else, something too soft and ethereal to define.

For the first time in a very long time he realized how lonely he felt. She did that to him. She made him imagine life with someone by his side. He smoothed his hand over the sheet beside him, feeling cool linen in a place where he wanted the warmth of Julia.

He closed his eyes, willed his body to release the hunger digging into his belly. He could have her. He could hold her in his arms. He could lose himself in her fire. Only if he was willing to believe in a fairy tale.

Every logical bone in his body told him that she must

not be telling him the truth. Still, he could not deny the pull, the attraction, the connection that made him want to believe in her fairy tale. He wanted to believe her. He wanted to believe in the fairy tale. Perhaps it was his Highland blood, but some part of him did believe in everything she had told him. Was she his miracle?

For so many years he had thought the Almighty had somehow lost track of him. His prayers went ignored, until he had stopped praying, stopped asking for an end to the loneliness, the bitterness that pumped like poison through his veins.

After Lavinia's betrayal, he had gone on, living each day alone, abandoning the hope that cut him like a blade. He had gone on, growing harder with each passing day, until all the softness within him had solidified into steel. He had thought there was no softness left until Brandon came into his life. Yet with the joy of his son had come the reaffirmation that women were the enemy.

And now there was Julia, and her story of miracles. Was it possible? Had God granted him a miracle? Had he sent this angel to him? Thunder rumbled over the house, rattling the windowpanes. It was as if heaven itself was angry with him this night.

Believe in me, Gavin.

Lord help him, he wanted to believe in the fairy tale. He needed to believe. Yet he couldn't push aside his doubts. He couldn't place his heart in her delicate hands. He would not make the mistake of trusting a woman again.

Despite his experience and his conviction, he did not have the strength to purge her from his thoughts. In spite of everything, one question burned like a smoldering coal in his brain: *Can I trust you Julia?*

The same question was still torturing him the next morning. He sat on a sofa beside his mother, in the sitting room adjoining her bedchamber. He was relating to his mother the circumstances behind his unexpected appearance in London and the strange young woman who had invaded his home with a mystical tale of time travel and miracles. When he had finished the story, his mother simply stared at him.

"She said she came here from the future?"

When he heard the words, Gavin cringed inside. He rubbed the smooth neck of his mother's Italian greyhound, Tina. The sleek little dog lay with her head on his lap, her legs stretched, her back paws pressed against Mary. "Aye, that's what she claims."

One corner of Mary's mouth tightened. "Do you think it's the clever equivalent of one of those silly women who keep throwing themselves in your path?"

He shook his head. "There is something more to it. She knew someone was going to try to run down Patrick last night."

Mary closed her eyes, a delicate shiver gripping her. "Thank goodness you could prevent that."

He drew his hand over Tina's back, against the grain of her hair, ruffling the soft, fawn-colored fur. "I keep asking myself, how could she have known about it?"

Mary studied him for a moment, reminding him of the way she had always known when he was up to mischief. There were times when she seemed able to read his mind. "She could be telling the truth."

Gavin managed a harsh laugh, when inside he felt like screaming. "You believe such things as this are possible?"

"There is far more to this world than what we can see

and touch, Gavin. If I believe in the Almighty, I must believe in miracles. At times, when there is no proof to hold and examine, we must rely on faith."

Faith. He had imagined his faith lost a long time ago. Still, since meeting Julia, it had stirred once more inside of him, taunting him to believe in miracles and a mysterious young woman.

"At times it is much easier to believe in the darkness rather than the light."

Gavin nodded. "Because we often see more treachery than miracles."

"Do we?" Mary smoothed her fingers over the polished rosewood arm of the sofa. "How do we know what miracles occur every day all around us? Last night, Patrick might have died. It was a miracle that you found him in time."

"Or it was carefully planned."

"To what end?"

Gavin frowned. "To gain my trust."

"You think she is trying to become your wife? Or do you think she is working with the Harcourts to destroy you?"

Gavin tried to draw a breath, but there wasn't any room in his chest. It was filled with too many questions, too many doubts, too much hope. "I don't know. Miss Fairfield defies my every attempt to label her. Is she an angel sent here to rescue me? Or is she one of the more clever of her kind, a woman who can blind a man to her every foul intention?"

"If Miss Fairfield is involved in some plot to destroy you, she must be truly venomous. What do your instincts tell you, Gavin?"

Gavin glanced at his mother. "I'm not sure I can trust my instincts when it comes to her."

Mary's brows lifted. "You are falling in love with her."

Gavin clenched his jaw. "She muddles my mind."

Mary smiled, a knowing look filling her eyes. "I think it is time I met Miss Fairfield."

Gavin sent Mary's maid in search of the lady in question. He stood by the fireplace in the sitting room, waiting, his heart picking up speed at the thought of seeing her again. A few minutes later, Julia entered the room. She looked at him, her gaze meeting his. Time itself seemed to cease moving. Sunlight flowed through the windows, striking the large oval mirror above the mantel, raining light upon Julia. The golden light limned her body, as though it were lending shape and substance, giving breath to a creature not of this world, a fairy delivered to this mortal realm.

Images flickered in his mind, strange glimpses of memories he had never made, and in each this woman stood before him. He saw her in a shifting array of costumes, a blur of color and shape denoting the passage of history on this earth. And somehow he understood that he had known this woman since the beginning of time.

"Gavin."

His mother's voice buzzed in his ears. Still, he could not drag his gaze from Julia.

"Gavin." Mary tugged his sleeve.

He started, like someone shaken from deep slumber. He glanced down and found his mother looking at him, a trace of surprise in her dark eyes.

Mary smiled. "Gavin, do you suppose you might introduce us?"

Gavin drew in his breath, trying to shake the odd sensations gripping him. His voice was far too husky as he presented Julia to his mother. His mother offered the younger woman a gentle, welcoming smile as she gestured for Julia to take a seat in the Sheraton armchair near the sofa. And then the two women sat staring at each other, as though in a mirror, with matching quizzical looks upon their faces.

Tina hopped down from the sofa and investigated the newcomer, sniffing at Julia's shoes. Julia bent and stroked the dog's sleek head, the movement drawing Mary from her contemplation of the younger woman. "I apologize for staring, Miss Fairfield, but you look a great deal like someone I know."

Gavin frowned. "Whom do you mean?"

Mary glanced up at him. "A young lady you have yet to meet. Rebecca Fitzgerald's daughter."

"Emma Fitzgerald?" Julia asked.

The startled look on Julia's face did not escape him. "Do you know her?" Gavin asked.

Julia shook her head. "No. I only know of her."

Tina trotted back to the sofa and jumped to the cushion beside Mary. Mary stroked the small dog's back, her gaze fixed on Julia. "The resemblance is uncanny."

That knowledge seemed to make Julia uneasy. She glanced up at Gavin, then back down to her tightly clenched hands. What had he glimpsed in that glance? Uncertainty, fear, a sudden understanding. Of what?

He watched as his mother served tea from the silver service on the tea cart beside the settee, elegantly filling an ivory porcelain cup, stirring in the sugar and cream Julia requested. He noticed the way Julia's hands trembled as she accepted the cup and saucer. She rested the dish against her thigh, as though she were afraid she might spill the tea should she try to drink it.

He caught himself wanting to sit beside her, slip his arm around her slender shoulders, and shield her from anything that might trouble her. He rubbed his chin, wondering if there existed a cure for this malady called Julia.

"Gavin, there is a great deal of correspondence for you in the study." Mary smiled up at him. "You may wish to tend to it this morning."

Gavin glanced at Julia, then back at his mother. The hint was obvious. For some reason his mother wished to speak with Julia privately. And for some reason, he was reluctant to leave Miss Fairfield. Still, he would not remain like a puppy salivating at her feet. With a few words he took his leave of the ladies. His neck prickled as he walked away from the room. Unless he missed his guess, he would no doubt become a topic of conversation. What opinions would Julia share about him?

It didn't matter, he assured himself. He was master of his house and his life. What one female might think of him, good or bad, certainly did not deserve a second thought. Yet he caught himself thinking about it, as well as the strange female who had invaded his life and his heart.

Chapter Eighteen

I seem'd to move among a world of ghosts,
And feel myself the shadow of a dream.
—Alfred, Lord Tennyson

Julia watched Gavin leave, hoping the pounding of her heart would ease now that he was not so near. Last night he had invaded her dreams, taking her into his arms, kissing her, holding her, loving her as though she were the only woman he ever wanted in his life. Treacherous things, dreams. They betrayed your every hope and left you hungry and needy in the morning.

Mary sat on an Empire sofa near the fireplace, her pale yellow gown spilling over the burgundy silk upholstery. With dark hair and dark eyes, she was a lovely woman, still slender and youthful at the age of four and fifty. "I thought you might be more comfortable if Gavin were in another part of the house. He appears to make you a little nervous."

Julia forced her wooden lips into a smile. "You are very perceptive."

Mary stroked the slender dog lying by her side. The dog curled onto her side and dropped one paw over Mary's hand. "If it is any consolation, you ruffle his composure as well."

Julia squeezed the handle of her cup. "I do?"

Mary smiled. "You would have to know him well to see it. He always wears such thick armor, it is difficult to tell when anything has pierced it. But I do know him well. You have made an impression on him."

"He thinks I'm in league with people out to destroy him. An impression, but hardly favorable."

"I'm afraid he seldom looks kindly upon members of our sex." Mary glanced down at her little greyhound. "I cannot shake the feeling that I have met you before. I suppose it must be your resemblance to Emma. It is more than simply the physical resemblance; it is the way you move, the way you hold your head. I actually thought you were Emma when I first saw you."

Julia held the delicate porcelain cup and saucer and tried to prevent her hands from shaking. She resembled Emma. Was it merely a coincidence? Her mind whirled with the possibilities. She could not stay in this time and place, but Emma belonged here. Emma, a woman who resembled Julia in more than simply appearance. The words of Gavin's ghost haunted her: *Who were you in 1818, Julia? And why didn't I ever meet you?*

Past lives. Love that endured beyond forever.

Had she returned to this place and time to save Gavin for the love of his life? The idea appealed to her sense of romance and more. When she left, Gavin would find the love of his life. He would live a long and happy life, while she returned home to live with . . . memories. Gavin's counterpart did not exist in her time. Something had gone wrong. "You seem familiar to me as well. It's very odd. So often since I have come back to this time, I feel I'm looking back at memories I made a very long time ago."

"Memories." Mary lifted her cup from the tea cart and took a sip, a thoughtful expression filling her eyes. "My mother would have said it is because we knew each other in another time and place. She had the gift of second sight and a great many novel ideas. One of my sisters inherited her abilities."

Julia stared at her tea, wanting to ease the dryness in her mouth but too unsure of her hand to try to take a sip. Past lives. Soul mates. Things that had once seemed far-fetched now seemed more than a little possible. *Who were you in 1818, Julia?* Did she finally know that answer?

"My son has told me that you claim to have come here from the future."

Julia met Mary's steady gaze. "I *have* come from the future."

Mary's brows lifted slightly. "It is quite a remarkable tale."

Julia knew this woman's most private thoughts, had read them in the pages of her journals. And now she wondered if those thoughts might prove a point. "Lady Mary, do you allow anyone to read your journals?"

"My journals?" Mary set her cup on her saucer. A slight frown marred her expression, just the faintest indentation of flesh above her finely arched dark brows. "No. I do not."

"When you came to London this Season, you made an entry in your journal that expressed your concern for Gavin's future. You said that even though you had come here for Alison, you thought it your mission to find Gavin a suitable bride. Still, you didn't think you would find her among the silly women here. You had another woman in mind for him."

"How did you know I wrote that?"

Julia took a deep breath, then proceeded with a big gamble. "I have read your journals. All of them."

"You come here and tell me you have somehow managed to violate my privacy?" Although her voice remained soft, the tone of it disturbed the dog sitting beside her. The greyhound lifted her head and gazed up at her mistress.

Julia set her cup and saucer on the small pedestal table beside her chair. "I come from a time when your journals are not private, but part of the history of Dunmore."

Color rose high on Mary's cheeks. "My journals are on display?"

"Yes. They are kept in the library of Dunmore, with other books on the history of the castle and of your family."

Her eyes narrowed. "I keep my journals locked in a cabinet in my chamber at Dunmore, all except for the most recent one, that is. And that journal is locked in the top drawer of the cabinet beside my bed."

"It is now. But in my time, in 1999, your journals are not locked away."

Mary considered this, eyeing Julia, taking her measure with perceptive dark eyes. "How do I know you haven't merely broken into my chamber and read my journal?"

"I didn't." Julia frowned, trying to think of some way

to prove she was not a burglar as well as a liar. "You haven't made this entry yet. But you will. Soon. You will write about Alison's engagement to Neville Talbot. You will say you are somewhat disappointed in her choice. You feel quite strongly that the man for her is Philip Montgomerie. Unfortunately Philip is out of the country and Talbot is here."

All the color drained from Mary's face. "I was about to write that this morning. You couldn't possibly have known. I have not shared my thoughts with anyone."

"I am sorry to have used your private thoughts as a means to prove to you that what I am saying is the truth. But I need very much for you to believe me."

Mary eased her cup and saucer to the tea cart. She folded her hands in her lap and drew in a long, steadying breath. "It is true. I had a feeling it might be. Although I don't claim to have the powerful sight my mother had, I can usually rely upon my instincts."

Julia held her breath. "You believe me?"

Mary nodded, her eyes wide with the realization. "I do. I believe you."

Relief flooded her, so unexpected it made her dizzy. Julia closed her eyes and said a silent prayer. Finally someone believed her. "Thank you," she whispered.

"I think we must thank *you.* You rescued my son last night."

Julia smiled. "I almost didn't fit together the pieces quickly enough. At first I couldn't understand why I had arrived two months before the accidents."

Mary looked down at her hands, then back at Julia. "You have come back in time to save my son and my grandson from accidents that will occur at Dunmore?"

"Yes. They were both killed in June of this year.

When I have managed to set things right, I will return to my own time."

Mary studied her. "You intend to leave?"

Her chest tightened when she thought of leaving Gavin, but she had no choice. "I am guardian of my brother's daughter. I have to return to her."

"I see." Mary smoothed her fingers over the wooden arm of the sofa, lost in thought.

Julia glanced around the room, for the first time taking notice of her surroundings. Her trip back to this time and place would provide marvelous research material, if she could ever concentrate on anything other than Gavin. A pair of porcelain greyhounds graced the mantel, one standing, the other sitting on either side of a crystal and gold clock. Everything seemed light, delicate, the chairs with their lyre-shaped backs, the small burgundy and gold flowers entwining with green leaves on the ivory silk wall covering.

It was a gracious room, elegant, as was this time in history. It made Julia wonder what it might be like to live this way for the rest of her life. Live here in this house, with Gavin. As soon as the thought formed, she crushed it. She had Lauren to think of back home. Back home where she belonged. The thought of leaving filled her with a horrible sense of loss. Yet it had to be this way. Even if Gavin asked her to stay—which she doubted he would—she could not.

"Since you come from the future, you know what is to transpire in the lives of my children."

Julia squeezed her hands in her lap, fearing the turn of this conversation. "I have read the history."

"I have been concerned for Alison." Mary glanced at her, a look of uncertainty in her eyes. "Talbot is a handsome young man, charming, from an excellent family. He inherited a respectable fortune upon his father's death. The family home in Hampshire is lovely. I keep telling myself he is an excellent choice."

"But you don't believe he is right for Alison?"

"Alison is a quiet young woman, who is more comfortable with a book than she is a dance card. That is why I waited until she was one and twenty to bring her to London. Talbot loves to entertain. He is a social butterfly, flitting from one event to the next. I am certain he will expect the same of his wife."

Julia knew the type of man too well. She had been overwhelmed by Nathan's social whirl.

"I'm afraid Talbot has swept her off her feet. I know he values her beauty and her intelligence. Still, I was surprised when he took an interest in her. From what I have heard about him, he showed no interest in marriage until this Season. Before my daughter, he shared the same proclivity for women of the world as does my younger son. Patrick has a penchant for quantity over quality. Widows, opera dancers, and . . ." Mary lifted her brows. "Other, equally inappropriate females."

"Talbot must have taken one look at Alison and decided she was the woman he wanted as his wife."

"True. Even the worst libertines tend to choose lovely debutantes when they decide to marry. And Neville Talbot is hardly a hardened libertine." Mary frowned down at the greyhound. "Still, I fear he plans to make Alison over into his image of the ideal wife. I can see it happening, and I fear my daughter will one day regret her choice."

Julia thought of the future looming ahead for Alison. "And you want to know how it turns out?"

Mary nodded. "Can you tell me? Will she be happy with him?"

Meddling with the past was one thing. Telling a mother her daughter would die a year after her marriage was another.

Mary raised her hand as if to keep Julia from speaking. "Perhaps it is better if you do not tell me the future."

"I am not sure I know it."

Mary frowned. "I thought you had read the history."

"Yes. But my coming here has already set things moving along a different path. Last night Patrick was to have died in an accident."

Mary sucked in her breath at Julia's words. "I'm sorry, but the thought sent a chill up my spine."

Julia nodded. "Fortunately we were able to prevent it. I can't be certain of other changes that might transpire. For all I know, the history I have read of your family may already be shifting. Nothing may occur as it once did."

Mary considered this, her dark brows lifting. "Even without knowing the original outcome, I shall choose to think of this as an opportunity for things to improve. Why else would heaven have granted us this chance for a miracle?"

A chance for a miracle. More and more Julia was beginning to think she, herself, had been given a chance for a miracle, a chance to meet the man of her destiny, a chance to spend a few precious weeks with him. If only the infuriating, stubborn brute would see past his bitterness and doubt.

"Do you have any idea why you were chosen to come back in time to save my son?"

"I'm not sure."

"I wonder." Mary glanced down at her hands. She wore only one ring, a large oval-shaped ruby surrounded by diamonds on the third finger of her left hand. She twisted it in the sunlight as she spoke, sending sparks of color scattering over her hand. "You are connected to my son, in a way that defies time itself."

Soul mates. A love that survives beyond forever. If it was true, why couldn't Gavin feel the pull of it as she did? "The first time I saw Gavin, I felt I had known him all my life."

Mary smiled. "That's the feeling I had the first time I met my husband. I felt I had known him since before the day I took my first breath."

Julia sensed the truth. Pity Gavin didn't feel the same for her.

"Your heart is in your eyes when you look at Gavin." Mary ran her hand over the greyhound's back. The dog lowered her chin to Mary's lap. "And although he would deny it, you have managed to get past that armor of his. You have definitely captured his interest."

"He doesn't believe a word I say. He thinks I'm a scheming little witch who has come here to somehow destroy him."

Mary sighed. "My son does not trust women. Still, I have a feeling you might change his mind. I wonder if you weren't brought back here for more than one purpose. Perhaps you were meant to meet Gavin, to be with him, to heal him."

The words Gavin's ghost had spoken to her echoed in her memory: *You could have changed my mind, Julia. You could have made me see how much I would miss if I didn't learn to trust again.* "I am not going to be here long enough to teach him to trust again. I must return to my own time." Julia glanced at the lilies rising from a crystal vase on a table against the wall. "After I'm gone, I hope Gavin has a chance to meet a woman who can make him happy. Perhaps you are right about Emma Fitzgerald. Perhaps she is the woman who can make Gavin happy."

Mary gasped softly, drawing Julia's attention back to her. "How did you know . . . No, never mind. You read about Emma in my journals."

"Yes. I know you have great hopes for Emma and Gavin. She won't be able to make it to Dunmore this June, because of an illness in the family. But she will come a few months later. The first time around, Gavin wasn't there to meet her. Perhaps this time they will have a chance to see if it was meant to be."

Mary regarded her for a moment, frowning slightly. "Perhaps. Still, I keep thinking you and Gavin are meant to be together."

Julia smothered the despair rising inside her. "I think in our case, something went wrong. Gavin's soul is still wandering around my time, as a ghost. We never had a chance at a future together."

Mary nodded. "Perhaps that is why you were sent back here. Gavin is very much alive now."

"I can't stay in this time. Even if Gavin somehow manages to stop thinking of me as his enemy, I have to get back to my family." Julia's chest tightened when she thought of Lauren. "My niece needs me. Nothing else really matters, not my feelings for Gavin or destiny or fate. I have to go back to Lauren. As soon as I manage to set things right, I'll be headed back to my time."

Mary twisted her ring, staring at the arm of Julia's chair. "Perhaps you were meant to live a lifetime in the few weeks you will have together. Sometimes that's all we have—a few precious moments to cherish for a lifetime."

The man of her dreams looked at her as some demon sent to destroy his life. Her few precious moments with Gavin might be limited to the heart-stopping passion she had found in his bed. And that wasn't enough. No matter how satisfying it might be for the moment, she would not give herself to him knowing she was making love while he was just having sex.

Her own happiness was beyond her reach, but she could save Gavin. She could do everything in her power to make certain he had a long and happy life.

Gavin sat on the edge of the large claw-footed desk in his study, staring at his mother. She had strolled into the room a few moments ago and described her conversation with Miss Julia Fairfield. "You honestly believe her?"

"Your grandmother had the gift of second sight, Gavin. She could always trust her instincts, and so can I. I suppose your tendency is to see all women in the same light as Lavinia has clouded your vision a bit. I thought you would have seen the truth."

"And what truth might that be?"

Mary stared straight into his eyes as she spoke. "Tell me something: When you first met Miss Fairfield, did she seem familiar to you, as though you had known her before?"

A bubble of apprehension rose inside him, filling his chest, pressing against his heart until each beat was a painful thing, as painful as listening to the words he could not ignore. "Aye. I felt I had always known her. As though she were somehow . . ."

Mary waited for him to finish. When he didn't, she looked at him, and he could tell she already knew what he had felt and what he was feeling now. "You felt as though she was important to you."

What was it, this connection they shared? Had it truly extended beyond time? "Is there any way she might have read your journals?" he asked.

Mary shook her head. "She knew my thoughts, entries I haven't made yet, but intend to. How can you explain that?"

"I can't." Gavin tried to draw air into his constricted lungs. "There is a great deal about Miss Fairfield that I cannot explain."

"Perhaps instead of trying to understand her with your head, you need to listen to your heart."

Gavin laughed, the sound bitter to his own ears. "My heart has led me astray in the past."

"Has it? Did you feel the same way about Lavinia as you do Julia?"

"No." He answered quickly. He didn't need to think about his response. He knew it. Deep in his bones, he knew he had never in his life felt this way about another woman. And he never would again.

"You were a lad when Lavinia played her nasty little game. In a very real sense she destroyed your innocence, your faith." Mary lifted a paperweight from the desk and held the round crystal to the sunlight flowing through the windows behind the desk. Light reflected through the crystal, casting a shimmering rainbow around the room. "Perhaps that is one of the reasons Julia was sent here, to you. She can help you reclaim your innocence, Gavin. She can help you believe in miracles again."

"I'm not sure I want to believe her. Because if I do, then I know one day soon she will vanish from my life."

Mary held the paperweight against her chest and looked at him. "You love her."

"Love?" Gavin curled his hands into fists against his thighs. "What is love? Is it lust in disguise as some deeper, noble emotion? Is it this horrible realization that your life will never be the same again because a certain woman dropped into your path? Is it waking up in the morning hungry for the sight of her? Is it the reason you can't sleep for thinking about her, wanting her? Is that what this is, this connection?"

"Aye." Sunlight reflected on the tears glittering in her eyes. "Love is all that and more. It is hope and despair. It is an emotion that grabs hold of you and won't let go, not even with the passage of time. Not even with death."

Gavin released his breath in a shaky sigh. "I'm not sure I like it. I don't think I want it."

Mary laughed softly. "I'm not sure you have a choice. My mother believed there is a mate for each of us, one soul chosen by the Almighty, one soul that completes us. In each life we live a brief moment on earth, but our souls survive."

Mary's words echoed those Julia had spoken to him the night he had taken her into his arms and into his bed. The memory of that night remained with him always, as did the bitterness of the words he had used to keep her at a distance.

Mary set the crystal on the desktop. "The essence of each life we live remains with us, locked in memories hidden deep in our souls. At times we have glimpses of these memories. And in each lifetime we have a chance to meet our mate, that one soul we are destined to love through a thousand lifetimes."

Mary paused, a wistful expression on her face as she stared down into the ruby on her left hand. Gavin wondered if she was thinking of his father, the man who had placed that ring on her finger. Was Julia the woman destiny had meant him to meet?

Mary looked up at him and smiled, her eyes filled with certainty. "Miss Fairfield is the one, Gavin. The one destiny meant for you."

The truth of his mother's words pounded against the stone surrounding his heart, threatening to shatter the protective shell. Since he had met Julia, he had tried to get her out of his mind. Yet she lingered there, like the haunting melody of a concerto he had known long ago.

"While you ponder the truth right before your eyes, I'm going to take Julia to Franchot's. She needs a proper wardrobe, if we are to take her about in Society."

Gavin frowned. "You mean to drag her about from party to party?"

"You make it sound as though I am going to torture her. Did you expect we would keep her hidden away in the house?"

Gavin crossed his arms over his chest. "I'm going to take her back to Dunmore."

Mary shook her head. "Oh, no. Not until she has had a chance to see London. She is an authoress, you know. She wants to do some research."

"Did she tell you she was writing a book about me?"

Mary nodded. "She is looking forward to seeing London."

He imagined Julia flitting from party to party, leaving a trail of besotted males in her wake. With that thought came a host of images—the earl of Dunmore trailing after the alluring Miss Fairfield, growling at any man who came within reach of his strange angel. "If she is writing a novel about me, she should be doing her research at Dunmore."

"She will." Mary patted his chest. "After I have had a chance to show her London."

"But I . . ."

"And besides, she and Alison took to one another from first sight. It was as if they had known each other for years." Mary glanced down into the crystal. "I have a feeling Alison needs someone like Julia now, someone besides her mama with whom she can discuss her plans, her concerns. Give them a few days to enjoy each other's company."

He had never been able to deny his sister or his mother anything. "I suppose we could stay a while in London. A few days."

"I knew you would be reasonable." Mary gave him an approving smile. "Meeting Julia has me wondering if we don't just go from life to life, meeting the same people over and over again."

Past lives? Love that endures beyond time? He was not a romantic man. Still, the notions were difficult to ignore. Especially with a blue-eyed angel in the house.

"Now, I need to see if my modiste can work a small miracle. The Sedgewick ball is in a few days. We shall need a suitable gown and a great many other things in a short time."

Gavin stared down at the crystal paperweight as his mother left the room. He had to deal with Julia Fairfield and this hold she had on him. And in spite of his better judgment, he knew exactly what he intended to do with her.

Chapter Nineteen

And love is loveliest when embalm'd in tears.
—Sir Walter Scott

Julia had always enjoyed family dinners at home, before the accident. Conversation would flow around the Fairfield table like a sparkling stream under a warm summer sun. Sitting here with the MacKinnons brought back those warm memories. When not entertaining, the family shared dinner in the dining room, seated at a large rosewood table where every night dinner was served by candlelight.

Mary sat at one end of the table, Gavin at the other. Conversation flowed around the table, involving everyone, except Gavin. Every attempt anyone made to draw him into the warm circle of company failed. He preferred to remain apart from it all, as though he were far away, lost in thoughts he did not care to share.

Candlelight from the branched candlestick in the center of the table flickered gold upon his features. Twin furrows marred the skin between his black brows. Julia tried not to notice the frown or the way he scarcely touched his food. Yet she was too aware of his every move to succeed in ignoring him. What was bothering him tonight? She had hoped they had come to a truce. Now she wondered if the hostilities had somehow escalated.

This afternoon, while they shopped, Mary had implied that Gavin might be ready to believe her. Yet he had scarcely said a handful of words to her all evening. He glanced in her direction and caught her staring.

Excitement sizzled along her nerve endings, turning her blood to fire and her brain to mush. One corner of his mouth tightened before he glanced away, focusing on his wineglass. She swallowed the tidbit of succulent duck in orange sauce, silently apologizing to Mary MacKinnon's French chef. The meal might have been sawdust for all she had noticed or cared.

Julia dragged her gaze from Gavin and tried to pay attention to what Patrick was saying about Westminster. Patrick had accepted her, actually liked her. He was warm and charming and witty, and he enjoyed her company. Yes, she should definitely concentrate on Patrick. Still, in spite of the fact that she focused on Patrick's stunning blue eyes, she couldn't purge Gavin from her thoughts. What latest atrocity had Gavin placed at her feet?

"They would have you believe the Stone of Destiny was stolen by Edward the First in 1296 from Scone." Patrick winked at her. "But is it the real stone that sits beneath the coronation throne in Westminster?"

Julia managed a smile. "Is it?"

Patrick grinned at her, a devilish glint in his blue eyes. "Not if you ask a Highlander. The truth is, the stone was hidden by Robert the Bruce before Edward could get his hands on it. The true Stone of Destiny is hidden in Scotland. Tomorrow I'll show you the lump of Scone sandstone Edward hauled back to London."

"How fascinating." Her gaze drifted back to Gavin, only to find he was glaring at her, a fierce look in his eyes. Goodness, the man looked as though he wanted to strangle her.

"The stone is to be kept safe until the day Scotland is once again free." Patrick sipped his wine. "And in your time, is Scotland finally under free rule?"

Julia frowned, wondering how much history she should share with anyone. "Scotland is a valued part of Great Britain in my time."

Patrick grimaced. "And so much for a poor Highlander's hopes."

So much for her own hopes. The hope that had surged within her at Mary's quiet assurance was shriveling now, withered by Gavin's brooding silence. Apparently he would never believe her. Instead of making the most of the few weeks they would have together, Gavin intended to allow the fire that burned between them to fade to ashes. Fine; if he wanted it that way, he would have it. She only wished she could quell the attraction she felt for this man, the insanity that made her want to grab him by those broad shoulders and shake him until he kissed her again.

"We were amazingly lucky this afternoon," Alison said. "One of Madame Franchot's patrons had ordered a gown and then changed her mind. It fit Julia as though it were made for her."

Julia sipped her claret, trying to dredge up a measure of the excitement she had felt when she had put on that gorgeous gown this afternoon. White gauze over gold silk. Gold rosebuds worked through the filmy gauze, making it shimmer like something out of a fairy tale. She had felt like Cinderella in that gown. Still, she couldn't find any pleasure in the memory. Maybe one tiny pleasure, she thought, grinning into her wine. The gown had cost Gavin a small fortune.

"It is a lovely gown made all the more beautiful by Julia." Mary held her wineglass between her fingers and looked at her elder son. "I am certain her dance card will be full within minutes."

Gavin frowned at his mother.

Julia shook her head. "I'm afraid it won't be."

Gavin's black brows rose, but he said nothing. It was Patrick who responded. "My dearest Julia, you are mistaken. I am so concerned I shall be cut out, I will ask you now to save me two dances. Both of them waltzes, if you should be so charitable."

Julia smiled, responding to Patrick's gallantry. "I'm afraid I can't do that."

The surprised look on Patrick's handsome face made Julia wonder if women ever refused this charming male. "I promise not to step on your toes."

Julia laughed. "I'm afraid I would be the one stepping on your toes. You see, I don't know how to dance—at least not any of the dances that are popular in 1818."

"Oh, my dear, I never even thought of that," Mary said. "I should have realized none of our dances survive in your day."

Julia smiled. "I am afraid I shall be a wallflower the entire ball."

"We can't have that. You would disappoint far too many gentlemen. Although, to tell the truth, I am only concerned with my own pleasure." Patrick took her hand and pressed his lips to her knuckles. "After dinner, I shall act as your dancing master."

"What a marvelous idea." Mary looked at Gavin. "I'm certain we can manage to prepare Julia for the ball."

Gavin looked down into his wine, as though the entire idea bored him.

Three hours later, in the white-and-gold-trimmed music room, Patrick led her through the steps of a Scottish reel while Mary played the piano. Alison sat beside her eldest brother on a gold brocade settee, watching, clapping, encouraging Julia through the lessons. Gavin had not said a word in three hours.

Patrick had patiently taught her the steps to lively country dances, the sedate quadrille, the lancers, and the mazurka. Writing about these dances would never be the same again. Still, if this were one of her books, it would not be Patrick teaching her how to dance. It would be Gavin.

"We have only the waltz left," Patrick said, drawing her into his arms. He gave her a wolfish grin, one designed to buckle the knees of unsuspecting females.

She couldn't deny that she appreciated that smile and his gallantry. Patrick MacKinnon was every inch as handsome as his brother. The sleek bottle green coat he wore molded shoulders as broad as Gavin's. His hair was the same shade of brown as his brother's, the thick dark waves gleaming in the candlelight that glowed from the many wall sconces. And, like Gavin, Patrick's face was carved with strong angles and curves, a face fashioned by the hand of God for the express purpose of pleasing the feminine eye. The black brows were similar, as were the slim nose and the sharply defined bones of his face. Yet the eyes were not at all the same.

Patrick's eyes were a startling blue, and the expression in them held none of the bitterness that always lurked in the depths of Gavin's beautiful dark gaze. This man enjoyed women. Julia suspected flirtation came as naturally to Patrick as breathing. She wondered why fate hadn't connected her to this brother, the more accessible of the two. But fate had linked her to the brooding man who sat across the room.

Now was the time he should claim her, she thought. Now, for the most romantic of all the dances. The rhythmic notes of the waltz floated across the large room. *Now, Gavin. Come to me now.*

She glanced in his direction as Patrick walked her through the steps. Gavin sat with his long legs stretched before him, arms crossed over his chest, looking . . . bored.

Infuriating brute!

She focused her attention on Patrick. And if her smile was a little too bright and her laugh a little too quick, she could not prevent it. It was better to smile and flirt than to allow everyone in the room to know how much her heart ached.

Patrick ignored her clumsiness, easing her over each rough spot with the practiced ease of a man comfortable with the female of the species. And all the while she smiled and wished it was Gavin's hand warming her skin through the blue muslin of her gown, Gavin's strong fingers curled around her hand. But most of all she wished it was Gavin who smiled at her in this way, a warm, generous smile that made her feel lovely and witty and valued. If the other MacKinnons could accept her for who and what she was, why couldn't Gavin?

She was still contemplating the strange twists of fate when she entered her bedchamber later that evening. She didn't realize she was being followed until she turned to close the door and found Gavin standing in the doorway. Her heart thumped against her ribs. Heat washed over her, like a summer rain, spilling over her bare skin.

The wall sconce in the hall outside her door flickered gold upon his face. Although his expression revealed nothing of his feelings, the emotion was there, simmering in the black depths of his eyes—anger so hot that she stepped back, afraid of being incinerated by that black gaze.

"What is it?"

He stepped inside and closed the door behind him. It shut with a soft click that seemed to whisper: *beware.* "Miss Fairfield, I would be remiss if I did not educate you in a few areas before you are thrust upon the ton."

"What areas?"

"While you are under my protection, I will not have you bringing scandal down upon this family."

"Scandal!"

"That's right, Miss Fairfield."

He stalked her. She backed away, lifting her hand to her neck. He wouldn't strangle her, would he?

Words swirled through her memory, words he had spoken the first day she had arrived in 1818: *I've already murdered a woman.* She had dismissed those words on that day, accepted the fact that he had been falsely accused. Now, staring up into the fury in those black eyes, she wondered if she had been too hasty in assuming his innocence. "And how do you imagine I would bring scandal raining down upon your family?"

A muscle flickered high on his left cheek. "If you flirt with a man as outrageously as you were flirting with my brother this evening, you will no doubt have every coxcomb in London making indecent proposals."

"I was not . . ." She bumped into one of the thickly carved bed posts at the foot of the bed.

"Is that what you want, Julia? Every man in London, panting and salivating over you?"

"Panting and salivating?" She stared at him, stunned by the accusation. "Over me?"

"Or are you just interested in snaring my brother in your net?"

"I am not trying to . . ."

"If you think I'll stand by and remain docile as you encourage other men, think again."

A thought wiggled its way through the anger and indignation blurring her mind. Was this jealousy staring at her from his dark eyes?

He stepped close to her, pressing her back against the bedpost. "While you are in this house, I won't have you flirting like some opera dancer looking for a new lover."

Hard mahogany pressed into her back. Still, with the heat and strength of Gavin pressing against her, she scarcely noticed the niggling discomfort in her back. "I was not flirting."

"I don't know what they call it in your time, but I can assure you that in this time and place you could not have been more obvious."

"In my time?" She stared up at him, her breath trapped in her throat. "Don't tell me you have finally decided I'm telling the truth?"

He closed his hands around her neck and tipped her chin up with the tips of his thumbs. "How the devil did you know what was in my mother's journals?"

The heat of his hands radiated against her skin. "I read the journals. All of them. Including the ones she hasn't written yet."

Turmoil coiled in his eyes. He slid the pad of his thumb over her chin. "You expect me to believe in a miracle."

"Yes. Because I'm telling you the truth."

Without thought, her body leaned into his, too steeped in the memory of pleasure to resist the magnetic pull he held for her. Her breasts snuggled against his hard chest, sending heat whirling through her. His jaw clenched. He wasn't immune to this fire, she thought. He burned with the same flames that flared inside her. "Believe in me, Gavin."

Chapter Twenty

Love's very pain is sweet,
But its reward is in the world divine,
Which if not here, it builds beyond the grave.
—Percy Bysshe Shelley

Gavin stared into her eyes and tried to resist, tried to find the doubts that would hold her at arm's length. Yet his defenses lay scattered. Any hope he had of protecting himself from this woman had crumbled a long time ago.

From the first moment he had looked at her face, he had been snagged within her silken net. She had chipped away at his doubts, assaulted his logic and reason, plying him instead with intriguing possibilities.

Magic.

Miracles.

He wasn't certain of all the reasons that had brought

her into his life. He only knew she was here, and he was hopelessly lost in her spell.

"You can believe in me, Gavin." She rested her hand on his chest, over the place where his heart beat hard and fast with the knowledge of his own surrender. "I have never lied to you. And I never will."

Need swelled inside him, filling him. "Julia, I . . ." His throat closed against the words. Yet they were there, swirling in his head, spinning round and round.

I need you.

I want you.

I love you.

He loved her. The truth sang through him, inescapable and frightening in its power. He hadn't really faced that reality until this moment, until he stood here before her like some wild creature who had been beaten and hunted, forced to wander the earth alone. Until now he hadn't realized the true extent of his need for her.

She tilted her head, the perplexed look in her eyes alerting him. She was waiting for his response, an affirmation of the sentiment he could no longer deny. "What is it? What did you want to say?"

He had said the words once, when he was a foolish, reckless young man, before life had taught him all the cruel lessons he had learned so well. But now he knew that the words spoken by that young man had never been true.

Love had been an illusion then. Still, he could not find the courage to utter those fateful words. He could not risk her throwing the words back at him. For if she did, the delicate infant of hope she had planted within him would die, leaving him more empty than he had been before he met her.

Instead of the shattering words that proclaimed his heart, he settled for . . ."I believe you."

She stared at him, her eyes wide. "You aren't just saying that, are you? You aren't just trying to trick me the way you did at Dunmore?"

He rested his hands on her slender shoulders. "I have never tried to trick you, Julia."

"But at Dunmore you seduced me to get at the truth."

He shook his head. "No, I didn't."

Realization kindled in her eyes. He wasn't certain how long they stood like this, without words, with only emotion swirling around them, delicate threads binding one to the other. Finally she spoke, the soft words barely rising above the pounding of blood in his ears. "I love you."

The power in those words staggered him, knocking him off balance. He gripped her shoulders and swallowed hard. And still his voice was raw as he spoke. "You love me?"

"I tried to deny the truth." She touched his face, brushing her fingers over his cheek, his lips, his chin, as though she were blind and this was the only way she might see him. "I tried so hard to believe that it was just an infatuation."

Infatuation. Aye, he had tried to slip these emotions under a safe label: lust, infatuation, insanity. Yet he knew the truth.

"I had hoped it wasn't true, but it is. And I can't hide or deny it any longer. I don't want to. I want you to know how I feel. I don't want to waste another moment on wounded pride." She smiled up at him. "I love you, Gavin."

He stared into her eyes and searched for something

that might betray her, some flicker of deceit. Yet what he saw defied his every attempt to dismiss her words. Her eyes reflected the truth of those simple words.

"I've been looking for you all my life." She rested the fingertips of her right hand upon his chin. "I truly believe I was brought here to be with you, if only for a brief time."

He felt it too, the inescapable truth. His love for her sank deep into his soul, as though it were part of him, more important than his limbs, essential for life itself. He hooked his fingers around the delicate bones of her wrists, afraid suddenly that she might disappear if he didn't hold on to her. And he knew he wanted to hold her for the rest of his life. He tipped back her hand, pressed his lips against her palm. Her fingers curled against his cheek, the soft, velvety pads smooth against his skin. He traced the ridges of her palm with the tip of his tongue.

She released her breath, a long, slow sigh that brushed his cheek with warmth. A soft, drowsy look entered her eyes as he slid his tongue over her wrist, tasting the petal-soft skin, feeling the race of her pulse beneath his lips. His pulse accelerated, and it took all of his will to keep from ripping off her clothes and taking her here, against the bedpost.

He wanted to take his time; he wanted to savor and relish every bit of her and this gift she had given him, this love he felt radiating from her into him. He lifted her small pale hand and rested it against his shoulder, then slid both arms around her and drew her close against him. His muscles tightened, his blood surged, his need for her pounded like a fist in his groin, and still he resisted the hunger.

He kissed her face, learning the curve of her cheek with his lips, flicking the tip of his tongue over the corner of her lips. She smiled, and he tasted that lovely little grin, brushing his lips over hers. Yet there was more to savor, more to taste and touch and impress upon his memory.

He needed to remember every detail of this moment. When he was old and gray he would take out this memory, and hold it, and remind her of the way she looked this night—an angel sent to this sinner. He would remember the way the rose scent of her filled his nostrils. He would remember every detail, and remind her of this night, the night he had realized how much he loved her.

He unhooked, untied, unfastened every tricky little feminine barrier, peeling away her clothes until she stood naked before him. Light from the lamp beside the bed slid over her body, gleaming on the pale satin of her skin. She smiled for him, unafraid, open and giving like his dreams of heaven.

"You're wearing far too many clothes," she whispered, peeling the coat from his shoulders. It fell to the carpet at his feet with a soft whoosh of wool.

Together they stripped away his clothes, until all the barriers lay scattered at their feet, until he stood as bare and vulnerable as she in the candlelight. She curled her arms around his neck, her breasts searing his chest as he lifted her up and laid her down upon the soft white linen sheet. Her hair spilled around her head, the silky strands capturing the candlelight, spinning a golden nimbus about her head.

He climbed into bed, knelt at her side, savoring the joy of just looking at her. Her breasts rose with each soft breath, lifting to him, softly rounded, rosy tips drawn into tight little buds, waiting for his kisses. She shifted against the sheet, sleek muscles sliding beneath soft, creamy skin, drawing his gaze along her belly to the dusky curls at the joining of her thighs, down the long length of her legs.

She brushed her fingers over his thighs, sending shivers across his skin. "When you look at me that way, you make me feel all hot and bubbly inside, like a pot of pudding come to the boil."

"Pudding." He leaned over her and brushed his lips against the curls at the joining of her thighs. He breathed in the lush, musky scent of her response to him. Her startled gasp sang through him. "Hmmm, you taste sweeter than any pudding I've ever tasted."

She laughed, a soft, delicious trill of sound that vibrated through him, drawing his lips into a smile. She drew her fingertips upward, over his arousal, from root to tip, dragging a moan from low in his chest. His organ bobbed at her touch, reaching for her in silent need. "I can't believe I'm really here with you. It seems I have been dreaming of this moment all my life."

And so had he. He shifted and knelt between her thighs, her smooth skin warm against his hips. He leaned forward, until his chest brushed her breasts, the contact sending sensation chasing sensation. He kissed her lips, dipping his tongue inside, teasing her tongue until he forced himself to move on, to explore and taste and savor every inch of her.

He brushed his lips over her breasts, the softly rounded mounds rising and falling with her soft, quick breaths. He suckled her, flicking his tongue over her nipple, exulting in her tiny moans of pleasure. He lavished attention on the other breast, and she responded to him, arching up, into his kiss, sliding her hands over his shoulders as he slid his tongue down, over her belly.

She moved restlessly now, shifting beneath him, soft whimpers escaping her lips. His need for her pounded with his blood, his loins heavy and aching. And still he held back, wanting to give her more, knowing it would never be as much as she had already given him.

"You're beautiful," he whispered against the smooth skin beneath her navel.

She sighed in response, her skin quivering delicately beneath his touch. "Funny, I was thinking the same thing of you."

He grinned against her belly as he trailed his fingers through damp feminine curls. She trembled beneath his touch. He lowered his mouth. The spicy musk of feminine arousal filled his senses. Soft curls brushed his lips. Her body tightened in response. She dragged her fingers through his hair, holding him, rising to meet him as he celebrated this moment with his lips and his tongue. He worshipped her, giving her pleasure instead of the words he longed to say. He pleasured her until she quivered beneath him, until she shuddered and whimpered his name.

He rose and thrust deep inside her, the pulsing contractions of her climax tugging on his aroused flesh. He kissed her, drinking the soft sounds of pleasure from her lips as he moved inside her. She lifted to meet him, kissing him, dragging her hands over his shoulders, his back, meeting each thrust with a hunger that matched his own. He felt the pleasure rise inside her, sensed the moment it crested and followed her there, plunging off the edge of the world, soaring with her, two souls freed from the bounds of this earth, safely locked one to the other.

When the last shudder eased from her body, he collapsed against her. He smiled against her shoulder, content for the first time in an eternity. The scent of rose water drifted from her skin, mingling with the earthy fragrance of their lovemaking. He slid his hand down her arm, wanting to touch her everywhere, to wrap himself around her and stay this way forever. And then he heard the soft sobs, felt the trembling in her, the sharp staccato breaths.

He raised himself above her and looked down into her face. Her eyes were closed. Yet the barrier did not prevent the tears from leaking at the corners of her eyes. His heart constricted. He cupped her cheek, afraid to discover the reason for the tears. "What is it? Have I hurt you?"

She shook her head. He saw her throat work, heard her attempts to swallow back her tears, before she opened her eyes and looked up at him. Devastating. The sadness in her eyes pierced him, filling him with a horrible sense of impending disaster.

"You didn't hurt me, Gavin."

He smoothed his thumb over her cheek, brushing away the warm tears. "What's wrong?"

"It's just so . . . perfect." She slid her fingers through his hair. "You. This moment. This is how it feels, when it's right."

"Aye." This is how it feels when it's right, he thought. When love binds man to woman. This is what he had been looking for all his life.

"It's like a dream, and I never want to wake up from it." She sniffed and drew in a shaky breath. "I want to stay this way forever, stay right here in your arms."

Forever. The word pealed in his mind, as pure as a bell on Sunday morning. He had loved her forever and beyond. He knew that in some secret place locked deep in his soul. He knew this woman was the missing half of him, his mate. "And the tears? Are they for joy?"

"I was just thinking how unfair life can be." She smoothed her hands over his shoulders. "Why did I have to meet you like this? When it is all so impossible."

"Impossible?" With one hand she delivered hope, with the other she snatched it out of his grasp. "And what is so impossible about you and me?"

"Everything." She pressed her lips against his arm, her soft exhalation warming his skin. "How am I ever going to live without you?"

Without him? The finality of her words plunged into his chest, as sharp and steely as a saber. "You aren't going to live without me. Tomorrow I shall obtain a special license. We can be married right away."

She stared at him, a look of wonder in her eyes. "You want to marry me?"

"Aye." If his declaration startled her, it surprised him far more. He had never thought he would marry again. But he had never expected to meet Julia. "We shall be married tomorrow."

"Tomorrow." She whispered the word as though it were a rare gift.

"Aye." He looked into her eyes, his breath tangled in his throat, while he waited for her acceptance. And still the words fought for life within him, the words that would only have meaning once they knew their freedom.

"I love you, Gavin." She drew in her breath. "Never doubt my love for you. No matter what happens."

The fatal tone in her voice aggravated the anxiety brewing in his belly. She was going to deny him. He could see it in her eyes. "I love you."

"Gavin," she whispered, his name a hushed prayer.

Strange, now that he had released the words, the constriction in his chest lessened. It felt right, speaking those words to this woman. "I had given up hope of ever feeling this way." He smoothed his fingertip over the arch of her brow. "Until you came into my life. Marry me, Julia."

Julia smoothed her fingertips over his jaw, fighting the tears that welled within her. She realized what it had taken for this man to offer her marriage, a man who had sworn never to marry again after the treachery he had endured. Yet she could not avoid the truth. Neither of them could ignore the limitations of this miracle they had been granted. "I love you. I love you so much I can't even begin to tell you with words. Yet, as much as I love you, I can't marry you."

He frowned, and she could feel the stiffening in his muscles. "And why is that?"

"I can only stay a short while. I came to set things right. When I do, I will return to my time."

"You say you love me in one breath and that you intend to leave me in the next. If you love me, you'll stay with me."

"It has nothing to do with my feelings for you. A little girl is depending on me to be the mother she lost."

"A little girl? You have a daughter?"

"No. My brother and his wife were killed in a car accident five years ago. My niece, Lauren, is eight years old, and I'm the only mother she remembers ever having. I am her guardian. I have to return to her."

He considered this for a moment. "We'll bring her here. I shall raise her with Brandon at Dunmore. I'll take care of her."

It all sounded so right, raising Brandon and Lauren

with this man beside her. Someone to share the weight of the world. Someone to hold and love. Someone to love her, as she had always dreamed of being loved. "It's not possible. I don't have the power to bring her back to this time, Gavin. I'm not sure I would have the right to bring her here, even if I could. I have to return to her."

He closed his fingers in her hair. "When?"

"I don't know. I thought in two months, when the accidents were supposed to occur, but now I'm not sure. My coming here has already set things moving along a different path. I'm not sure what it is, but I know there must be some reason why I am still here."

"Aye." He smoothed his fingers over her cheek. "You were brought here to be with me."

"Everything inside me knows this is right. We were meant to be together. But something went wrong." She smoothed her hands over his shoulders, the warm satin of his skin stretched tautly over solid oak. "You are a ghost in my lifetime. And I wasn't born in yours."

"I'm still having trouble believing all this." Gavin closed his eyes, a frustrated sigh slipping from his lips. When he opened his eyes there was a fierce look in their dark depths. "If you were really brought here to work a miracle, then why would you be ripped from my arms? Is the Almighty that cruel?"

She managed a smile. "Perhaps this is part of the miracle, Gavin. These few precious moments we can share. Others have a lifetime and never find happiness. We may only have a few weeks, but we have this gift, this amazing connection, this love. These few moments are a gift in themselves, a miracle."

He kissed her, slanting his lips over hers, as though he would devour her. She tasted frustration in that kiss, possession, and fear. The same feelings churned inside her. It was an impossible situation, with only one possible solution. She must leave this man behind. Pain splintered through her at that dreadful certainty.

She clutched him to her, wrapping her arms around his shoulders, kissing him as though this might be the last time she would ever hold him. *Would* it be the last time? She couldn't be certain when she would be ripped from his arms. She could only be certain of one thing: her love for this man. Her love would endure until the last day of her life, and beyond.

He moved inside her, his member growing hard and hungry deep within her. She answered his hunger, lifting her hips, meeting each possessive thrust of his body. For now he was here, in her arms. She gave herself up to the moment, to this blinding pleasure. Tomorrow might dawn a century from here. Tonight she would live a lifetime.

Chapter Twenty-one

God be thanked, the meanest of his creatures
Boasts two soul-sides, one to face the world with,
One to show a woman when he loves her.
—Robert Browning

Music flowed from the orchestra hidden behind potted palms at the far end of the Sedgewicks' ballroom, providing the tempo for couples waltzing around the dance floor. Other people stood around the fringes of the dancing area, conversing in little groups. The combined din of the voices nearly drowned out the music.

Gavin did not care for balls. At the balls he had attended earlier in the Season, he had seldom danced. Of those dances, none had been waltzes. In fact, he could not remember the last time he had waltzed. Yet here he was in the middle of the dance floor, moving through the sweeping steps of the waltz, hoping he could avoid stepping on his partner's toes. He glanced down at Julia, and his heart sped up.

She wore a gown of white gauze over gold silk. The hem was van dyked with gold beads edging each vee. Embroidered lace edged the rounded neckline and the short sleeves. Tiny rosebuds in gilt thread were worked into the gauze, making the gown shimmer with each move she made. She looked like a princess, the kind who lived in towers and inspired grand quests, noble deeds, and enduring passion. Romantic notions for a man who had abandoned romance a long time ago. Still, they would not be denied, any more than the feelings she awakened in him would be denied. How long would he have to hold her?

For the past few days he had escorted her around London. While he showed her the city, he had made a discovery of his own. What was tired and old and boring through his eyes was lively and new and exciting to Julia. And so he toured London like a schoolboy, and enjoyed every minute of it. Yet not as much as he had enjoyed the nights. At night she was his alone.

Gavin squeezed her hand, tighter than he should. He pressed his hand against her back more firmly than was necessary. Yet he couldn't help himself. He wanted to hold her so tightly, no one could ever yank her from his embrace.

Her skirt brushed his legs, and he realized he had drawn her closer than the twelve inches of space propriety allowed. Propriety be damned. When she smiled up at him the way she was smiling now, as though he was the only man she had ever wanted, the entire world disappeared. There was only Julia and the warmth and light she conjured within him.

"Are you enjoying your first ball?" he asked, leading her into a wide, sweeping turn.

She squeezed his shoulder. "It's really quite incredible. I've read about balls, for research. I've seen them depicted in movies. But I never really understood what it was like to be in a ballroom like this. With all the jewels and the beautiful gowns. And so many people. Movies really can't give you the true experience."

He frowned. "Movies?"

She laughed softly. "In my time, images can be captured by machines called cameras. And later they are shown on a screen to audiences. They are very life-like—the movement, color and sound. It would be like sitting on one of the settees that are against the walls and watching all of this."

Her words settled against his heart, each a lead ball reminding him of the sands drifting through the hourglass of time. Was it true? Had she come into his life to give him only a taste of what might have been? The thought of losing her made him want to whisk her away to Dunmore, to keep her hidden there, locked in his chamber, where he would not have to share a moment of what little time he had with her. Yet she took such joy in seeing London. Soon enough he would take her back to Dunmore, far away from the rest of the world.

As the last strains of the waltz faded, Patrick appeared to claim her for the next dance. Gavin watched as his brother took his place by her side. Jealousy sank its fangs into his belly. It was not that he feared Patrick might take her away from him, or that Julia might give her affection to his brother. Gavin knew he had her heart.

No, this jealousy did not spring from the normal

sources of that ugly emotion. It came from the simple but inescapable fact that she was here for but a brief space of time. For that reason alone, he regretted every second she did not spend in his company.

He left the dance floor as couples formed the figures for a country dance, and made his way toward one of the doors leading to the terrace. It was a squeeze, as most London parties were. The room was crammed with people, the air thick with the mingled aromas of sweet waters, cologne, and the underlying musk of overly warm humans. He would not have come here tonight if it hadn't been for Julia. Yet he could not resist bringing her. She had seemed so excited about attending a "real Regency ball." In spite of his dislike for the social whirl, he wanted Julia to enjoy the party.

He had wended his way a short distance through the crowd when someone bumped into him, splashing champagne against his arm. He turned as the man was making his apology.

"Terribly sorry, I . . ." The words died as Russell Lampkin came face to face with Gavin. His blue eyes grew wide, fear flooding his expression, draining the color from his cheeks. "You! What are you doing in London?"

Gavin suppressed the anger surging within him, the instantaneous urge to strangle the man. He pulled a handkerchief from his pocket and dabbed at the drops of wine seeping into the black wool of his sleeve. "I wasn't aware of a need to report my whereabouts to you, Mr. Lampkin."

"No. Of course not." Color returned in patches, splotching Lampkin's fair cheeks with red. "I didn't mean to imply you did."

Gavin pinned Lampkin in a cold stare. "Are you enjoying your last few nights in London, Mr. Lampkin?"

Lampkin swallowed. "Yes. I am. Now, if you will excuse me, please." He turned and scurried away, pushing his way through the crowd.

Gavin suspected the young man had no intention of leaving London. Still, he allowed Lampkin to make his escape. There would be time enough to deal with him. Tonight he had no intention of allowing Lampkin or anyone else to spoil the evening. He slipped out of the room by one of the doors leading to the terrace.

A cool breeze brushed his face as he stepped from the crowded ballroom. Yet even here the air was not sweet. The air in London was always tinged with a trace of smoke, even in the gardens of the most elegant neighborhoods. It made him long for the clean, misty air of Dunmore.

A few guests had ventured onto the terrace. Most of them hovered in the light spilling from the open doors leading into the ballroom, heeding propriety. Gavin made his way to the far end of the terrace, away from the light and noise. He leaned his hip against the stone balustrade and stared into the gardens. Nothing wild or expansive about this or most gardens in London. A brick wall enclosed the area, shutting out the unwanted masses.

Gaslights atop wrought-iron poles splashed light upon the gravel walkway that wended through the shrubs and bushes shaping the various carefully cultivated areas of the gardens. Roses planted in dark mounds spread out from the terrace. Beyond the roses, tall yew created dark green walls surrounding a perennial bed. He knew the gardens well, had taken refuge in the green depths on several occasions, escaping into them to avoid the crush within the house.

The quick tap of heels brought his attention to the woman marching toward him. Gavin drew in his breath and prepared for battle.

Beatrice MacQuarrie halted in front of him, moonlight catching the glint of fury in her eyes. "I see you brought that woman to London."

Gavin lifted one brow, a silent warning any sane woman would not ignore. Although he suspected Beatrice would prove immune to good sense, as well as good breeding. "Miss Fairfield is visiting with my mother and sister."

Beatrice's eyes narrowed. "I've heard a rumor you intend to marry her."

Gavin was amazed at how quickly rumors traveled though the ton. "London loves to gossip, Beatrice."

She planted her hands on her plump hips. "I thought you never intended to marry again."

"The right woman can often change a man's mind."

Beatrice released her breath in a huff. "I could have married Chasen last year, but no, I decided to wait for you. And now look at you, making a fool out of me."

The back of his neck prickled as he held her furious stare. "It would seem you are doing a fine job without my help, Beatrice."

She lashed out with her hand. He caught her wrist before she could slap his face.

She twisted in his grasp, issuing curses under her breath. "Let go of me."

He released her. Yet he remained tense, ready for another attack. She didn't strike again, but stood glaring at him, her eyes narrow, her nostrils flaring with each quick breath.

"I never intended to give you the wrong impression, Beatrice," Gavin said, pitching his voice low to keep from being overheard by the people standing on the terrace. Beatrice had already managed to catch the attention of a group of three gentlemen, standing with their drinks a few yards away. They glanced the other way when Gavin sent them a chilling look.

Beatrice did not seem to notice or care about the show she was giving them. "You implied it. You allowed me to dangle after you like a fool."

Gavin shook his head. "I never made any promises or offered any encouragement."

"I hope you burn in hell." With that she turned and marched away, disappearing into the shadows at the far end of the terrace.

Gavin rubbed the taut muscles at the back of his neck. His luck had never been good with women. Until Julia. And even now, his happiness was a tenuous thing, built on shifting sand. One day she would be taken from him. And he suspected there was nothing he could do to prevent it. He was a man who believed in taking control of his life. Yet now he felt as helpless as a babe.

Julia had read about London balls; she had seen glimpses of them depicted in films. Still, she had not truly been prepared for the heat of the room, or the glitter of the jewels, or the speculative glances cast in her direction. Lady Mary had introduced her as a dear friend who was visiting them from America. She had gone from plain Julia Fairfield, to one of the "Philadelphia Fairfields."

Still, as much as she was enjoying the spectacle of the ball, she wanted the company of one man. Earlier she had noticed Gavin slipping out onto the terrace. Soon after her dance with Patrick, she went in search of the love of her life. She stepped out onto the terrace, welcoming the cool brush of air against her warm cheek.

"Miss Fairfield."

Julia turned to find a short woman dressed in a purple gown standing in the doorway. Purple ostrich feathers bobbed in her dark hair as she approached Julia. Although the woman looked almost sixty, not a trace of gray touched her hair, just a glimmer of brass marking the art of a hairdresser.

The woman paused, her gaze dipping, as though she was taking in every aspect of Julia's appearance. When she once again met Julia's gaze, she was frowning. "I heard a rather disturbing rumor this evening."

Julia frowned. "Excuse me, but I don't believe we have met."

The woman folded her hands at her ample waist. Instead of introducing herself, she continued. "I wanted to warn you about Gavin MacKinnon."

"Warn me?"

"If you are planning to marry the man, you should know, he is a murderer. A cold-blooded murderer."

Julia stared at the woman, stunned by the venom in her voice. "Who are you?"

"A woman who knows." She rested her hand over her heart in a theatrical fashion. "He murdered my daughter."

"You're Octavia Harcourt."

"Yes. And I am also your savior." Octavia gripped Julia's arm. "If you care at all for your life, you will run from that demon."

"You have a great deal of nerve." Julia twisted her arm free of Octavia's hold. "As I see it, you are the demon here, Mrs. Harcourt. You kept Brandon away from his father."

Octavia lifted her chin. "For his own good."

"You treated him worse than a servant." Julia pinned the woman in a cold glare. "Tell me, why do you keep trying to kidnap him? You don't want him."

Octavia wrung her hands at her waist, the loose skin beneath her neck wobbling. "I want to keep him out of the hands of that monster."

"Gavin MacKinnon is one of the finest men I have ever met. I would be proud to be his wife."

"The man should be hanged." Octavia leaned toward her, the ostrich feathers in her hair poking Julia's chin. "You are a fool."

"And you, Mrs. Harcourt, are a nasty woman who should be put behind bars for what you did to that child."

Octavia huffed and turned. She strutted back into the ballroom like a hen with her feathers ruffled. Julia drew in her breath, trying to clear the scent of Octavia's heavy perfume from her nostrils. She turned, intending to continue her search for Gavin, only to discover he had found her.

Gavin stood a few feet away in the shadows near the balustrade. Although his face was in shadow, she could tell he was staring at her. Unfortunately, she couldn't decipher his expression. With his propensity to believe the worst of women, and the fact that she had just been seen conversing with one of his greatest enemies, Julia wondered if she would once again fall under suspicion. "How long have you been standing there?"

"Long enough."

Julia curled her hands into fists at her sides, silently praying he would trust her. "I just met Octavia Harcourt."

He moved out of the shadows and entered the wedge

of light spilling from the ballroom. The look on his face chased away all her fears. That look kindled warmth inside her, a sudden heat that licked through her veins like flames over dry wood.

"It seems you are my champion in many ways. I heard you defend me." Gavin took her arm and smiled down at her. Julia wished she had a camera to capture this moment and the look in his eyes. Instead she impressed his image on her memory. "I headed this way when I saw you come out."

"Then you heard her."

"Aye." He started walking toward the gardens, leading her away from the group of gentlemen standing a few feet away, casting curious glances in their direction. "But it's nothing I haven't heard before."

Julia shuddered. "What a horrible woman."

Gavin smiled down at her. "She believes I murdered her daughter. So I suppose her hatred of me is understandable."

Gravel crunched beneath their feet as they walked along the garden path. "How did Lavinia die?"

Chapter Twenty-two

For life, with all it yields of joy and woe . . .
Is just a chance o' the prize of learning love.
—Robert Browning

The question rattled through Gavin, like the bones of skeletons shifting in shallow graves. He glanced down at Julia, searching for a trace of suspicion in her eyes. "Are you beginning to wonder if I murdered her?"

"No. I'm just curious."

Gavin searched for a trace of doubt in her eyes, the suspicion he had seen in countless faces, the judgment. Yet he found nothing to make him question her belief in his innocence. Nothing but curiosity. He released the breath he hadn't realized he had been holding until this instant.

He led her past a row of yew and turned into one of the perennial gardens. Moonlight poured over a fountain in the middle of the garden. A plump stone cherub rose from a shallow pond to spill water from an urn back into the water at his feet. The soft splashing sound reminded him of that night in the conservatory at Dunmore, the night he had first plunged into Julia's fire. Memories of that night tingled over his skin, tempting him to toss her over his shoulder and carry her back to his lair.

"I suppose it's a subject you don't care to discuss," she said, a flicker of disappointment filling her eyes.

"No, I don't." He brought her to one of the three wooden benches arranged around the pond. After she took a seat, he sat beside her. "But I want you to know what happened. The truth of that night."

Gavin stared at the pond, while in his mind images crawled from their tombs. "When I returned from India, I decided I wanted a fresh start in life. I sent Lavinia a letter, telling her that I had petitioned for an annulment. That night she came to my house. She was furious. I knew she didn't want me as a husband; she never had. Still, she enjoyed the life she had arranged for herself. As a married woman she could take her lovers and Society would look the other way. Lovers and mistresses are common enough in the ton. Too many marriages are contracted for the sake of power and bloodlines rather than sentiment."

"She was a fool." Julia rested her hand over the fist he held clenched against his thigh. "To have you as a husband and not realize how lucky she was."

Moonlight caressed her cheek, turning her skin to cool alabaster. He touched her, smoothing his fingers over the pale flesh, finding warmth beneath the moonlight. He wanted to chase away the shadows he saw in her eyes, the lingering pain of a destiny neither of them could escape.

Yet all he could do was give her his heart. "I was also a fool. I realize now I never loved her. And that night, when she came to my house ranting about how I would ruin her with my bloody annulment, I kept wondering what insanity had ever led me into this woman's trap."

Julia squeezed his hand. "You were young."

He laughed, a harsh bark of disdain. "Not all young men are quite so foolish."

"Not all women are as cunning as Lavinia."

Lavinia had been cunning, cold, and calculating. She had used her beauty like a weapon. "That night, when she came to me, I was determined to rid myself of her. She tried tears, and I laughed at her. And then the tears vanished and she started screaming at me. I took her arm and ushered her to the top of the stairs. I told her to get out of my house and out of my life. She swung her hand to slap me. I stepped back. The next thing I knew, she was falling, tumbling backward."

Gavin paused, staring at the water tumbling like liquid silver in the moonlight. Yet in his mind he could see Lavinia falling, the horror on her beautiful face. "It must have taken no more than a few seconds, yet it seemed an eternity. Standing there. Watching her."

The soft splashing sound melded with the music floating from the ballroom. Yet it was the sound of a woman's scream that echoed in his mind. The images in his brain were so stark, so ugly, Gavin had to swallow hard before he could continue. "She hit the bottom of the stairs with a horrible thud. I could see her neck was at an odd angle. When I reached her, I saw the blood at the corner of her mouth. Her eyes were wide open. She was dead."

The warmth of Julia's hand radiated against his fist. "It wasn't your fault."

"I didn't push her."

"I know."

He glanced down at the slender hand pressed so tightly over his. He felt her faith in him, more real than the heat of her skin. "There was an inquiry. Although I was not brought before Parliament on charges, I know there are many who believe I killed her. I received a note the day after she died. It said I would burn in hell for what I had done."

"Who sent it? The Harcourts?"

"No. It wasn't them. They were much more direct with their damnation of me." Gavin shook his head. "I don't know who sent it. It could have been her latest lover."

"Who was that?"

"Lavinia was discreet in her affairs. I suppose I could discover who he was, if I tried." He smiled at her. "But I didn't care to know."

"I don't understand." She rested her hand on his shoulder and leaned against him. "How could any woman want another man, if she had you?"

The delicate scent of roses drifted across his senses. He traced the curve of her smile with his fingertip, her breath spilling across his hand. "There is only one woman I want."

"Gavin," she whispered, kissing his fingertip. "There is only one man for me. Now and forever."

The soft words spread like a balm over the ragged wounds carved across his soul. "Marry me, Julia."

The smile slipped from her lips, a haunted expression entering her eyes. "I can't. You've already had to face the suspicion of your first wife's death. What would people say when your second wife suddenly disappeared? I can't possibly leave you in that kind of position."

He slid his arm around her shoulders and turned on the seat to bring her close against his chest. "A miracle brought you to me. I cannot believe . . ." He paused as his sister came rushing around the corner of the hedge.

Alison hesitated when she saw them. "Oh, I'm sorry. I saw Julia come out and I thought I might . . ." She waved her hands. "I'm sorry. I don't mean to interrupt."

"Alison, what is it?" Gavin asked, rising from the bench.

"Nothing," she said tearfully. "I just wanted to . . . You carry on." Alison hurried across the garden, plunging through the arched entrance, headed away from the main path.

Julia grabbed his arm when he started to follow his sister. He looked down at her, as perplexed as any man when faced with the mysteries of the feminine mind. "Someone should go to her."

Julia patted his chest. "I will. You wait here."

Gavin followed her as far as the pond. He paused there, wondering what had happened to send his quiet sister fleeing in tears. He watched Julia disappear through the arched yew, fighting the urge to follow her. Another perennial garden lay on the other side of the bushes. It was as far as Alison could go without climbing a ten-foot-high brick walk. She would be all right, he assured himself. Julia could handle the situation.

And still he paced, prowling to the main path, then pivoting and returning to the pond and the playful cherub. The soft sound of feminine voices drifted through the archway, the words indistinct above the splash of water in the fountain. He stood, wondering if there was something more productive he might do, aside from standing like a dolt, waiting for the women to return. Still, he could think of nothing, and so he stood and waited and assured himself that Julia would save the day.

Gravel crunched behind him. He started to turn toward the noise, sensing someone nearby. It was then that he felt the blow. Pain splintered through his skull. Blood surged before his eyes. He had one sharp impression of falling and then darkness closed around him.

Julia found Alison standing in the adjoining garden. She was staring at a bed of lilies of the valley that spread out in tender green shoots near her feet. The flowers were still encased in green sheaths, not yet ready to share their blossoms with the world.

Alison glanced up as Julia drew near. Moonlight revealed the tears damp upon her cheeks. "I didn't mean to interrupt you and Gavin. I saw you come out, and I just wanted to talk to you. Even though we have only just met, I feel close to you."

Since coming back to this place and time Julia had marveled at how familiar the MacKinnons were to her. It was as if she had known these people before. "What is it, Alison? What is troubling you?"

"Have you ever felt as though you were living someone else's life?" Alison said, her voice barely rising over the soft sound of a waltz drifting from the ballroom. "As though you didn't quite fit into the life you were leading?"

Julia thought of the weeks she had spent as Nathan Riley's fiancée. In that time she had ceased to be Julia, but had completely been absorbed into his life. "Yes, I have."

"Tonight, standing in that room, I just felt as though a weight was pressing down upon me. I kept thinking of how much Neville enjoys parties such as this. He expects me to become his hostess, to glitter and shine as a jewel on his arm." Alison rubbed the base of her throat, as if to ease the tension there. "I have never been comfortable at parties. I prefer to sit and watch rather than draw attention. I cannot imagine being a hostess at such an elaborate entertainment."

"Then you will not give balls. No one says you must."

Alison shook her head. "Neville expects it of me. When I told him it made me uncomfortable, he said I must be brought out of my shell."

Chills chased chills across Julia's skin. She had a sudden sense of herself as a twenty-two-year-old girl, locked on a course to disaster. "Do you want to be brought out of your shell?"

Alison shook her head. "I would much prefer a quiet life, in the country."

"Then perhaps you should reconsider the gentleman with whom you have chosen to share the rest of your life."

Alison looked as though she had swallowed a bug. "I couldn't cry off. Just think of how terrible that would be for Neville."

"I once felt the same way. I was engaged to a man who wanted to change me into his ideal woman."

Alison's blue eyes grew wide. "You were engaged?"

"Yes." When she had first met Neville Talbot, Julia had wondered what it was that made him seem so familiar. Now she realized it was his similarity to Nathan Riley. Both men were tall, with dark brown hair. Both were handsome in a fine-featured way. Like Nathan, Neville possessed an easy, almost too polished charm. "My mother had a conversation with me a few weeks before my wedding was to take place. She told me that if I had doubts, I should cancel the wedding. If I wasn't certain I loved Nathan, I was not doing him any favor by marrying him. I was only spoiling his chance to find the right woman."

Alison fiddled with the ribbon at the center of her high-waisted dress. "Yes, I see how that may be true."

"You really should think . . ." Julia hesitated, a chill gripping her.

"Is something wrong?"

Julia frowned. "Did you hear something?"

"No. What was it?"

"I'm not sure." Julia turned back toward the garden where she had left Gavin. "I thought I heard a groan."

"A groan?" Alison asked, following her.

Julia didn't respond. She hurried through the arched entrance and glanced around. Gavin wasn't waiting for her as she had expected. "He isn't here."

Alison paused beside Julia. "I suppose he went back to the party."

"Yes. I suppose he did." She smiled at Alison, in spite of the uneasy feeling churning in her belly. "Are you feeling well enough to go back?"

Alison linked her arm through Julia's and strolled toward the main path. "I can't keep hiding from . . ." Her words ended in a sharp intake of breath.

Julia followed the direction of Alison's frightened stare. Her heart seemed to stop. A man was in the pond, floating face down near the base of the cherub. "Gavin!"

Julia scrambled into the pond, the water rising to her knees, her sodden gown wrapping around her legs. She grabbed his upper arm and tugged while pushing on the opposite shoulder. Gavin turned, his arm flopping against her thigh.

"Alison, I've been . . . What the devil!" She heard Neville Talbot's voice behind her.

"Help her!" Alison said urgently.

Through the pounding of blood in her ears, Julia barely registered the voices swimming around her. Water splashed behind her. As she clasped her hands under Gavin's arms, a strong hand closed upon her arm.

"Stand aside," Neville Talbot ordered.

Julia released her hold, allowing Neville to take her place. He slipped his arms under Gavin's and hoisted him out of the water. Julia slogged through the knee-high water as Neville dragged Gavin out of the pool. He laid Gavin on the thick grass beside the pond and knelt beside him. Julia fought her sodden skirts as she staggered from the pool. She fell to her knees beside Gavin. He lay sprawled on his back, his eyes closed, his lips parted.

Alison knelt at Neville's side. "Is he alive?"

Julia's heart pounded so hard that she could scarcely hear Alison's voice. She leaned over Gavin as Neville spoke. "He isn't breathing."

Alison groaned. "Gavin," she whispered.

Julia's head swam. "He has to be all right." She pressed her fingers to Gavin's cold lips. She could not feel his breath. She pulled open his coat and pressed her hand to his chest, over his heart. She nearly collapsed when she felt a slow beat beneath her hand.

"It's no good," Neville said, touching her arm. "He's gone."

"No." If he still had a pulse, there was still a chance. Julia tipped Gavin's head back, pinched his nostrils, and blew air into his mouth.

Neville gripped her arm. "What are you doing?"

"Call 911." Julia shouted before forcing another breath past Gavin's cold lips.

Neville's fingers bit into her arm. "911?"

Julia shook her head, remembering the time and place. Her Red Cross training was the only emergency help they would have. She only prayed it would be enough to save Gavin. She forced air past Gavin's lips, then shot Neville a glance as he tugged on her arm.

"Miss Fairfield, there is no . . ."

"Take your hand off me."

"Miss Fairfield." Neville released her and sat back on his heels. "He is gone."

Julia refused to listen. Instead she poured breath after breath into Gavin's lungs, while a silent prayer rippled over and over through her brain. *Please let him live. Please.*

Chapter Twenty-three

Pillow'd upon my fair love's ripening breast,
To feel for ever its soft fall and swell;
Awake for ever in a sweet unrest;
Still, still to hear her tender-taken breath;
And so live ever—or else swoon to death.
—John Keats

Gavin regained consciousness with a start, a swimmer breaking the surface of the water after spending too much time below. Julia sat on her heels, holding his shoulders as a coughing spasm gripped him. When it passed, he slumped back into Julia's lap, staring up at her. Her hair had fallen from its pins, long strands of gold spilling around her shoulders.

In spite of her smile, tears glistened in her eyes. As he stared at her and tried to gather his scattered wits, she cupped his wet cheek in her warm palm and whispered, "Thank you, God."

"You're alive," Neville gasped.

Gavin dragged his gaze from Julia to the man kneeling beside her. Neville stared at Gavin as though he had just witnessed Lazarus rise from his grave. His gray eyes were wide with fear. "I swore you were dead."

Gavin sat up and ran his hand over the back of his head, gingerly testing the bump beneath his wet hair. "Apparently I only feel as though I have been dragged through Hades."

"What happened?" Julia asked.

"Yes, what happened?" Neville asked. "I came looking for Alison and found you and Miss Fairfield in the fountain."

Gavin looked from Julia to the stricken face of his sister. Alison sat hugging her arms to her waist, staring at him with tears running down her cheeks. He realized that it wasn't a good time to hit his sister with the truth. "I must have tripped. And bumped my head on that silly cherub."

Julia stared at him, and he could almost read her mind. She didn't believe a word he said.

"You could have died," Alison said, her voice choked by tears.

"There now. Everything is all right." Neville patted Alison's arm. "It was fortunate you and Miss Fairfield found your brother when you did. I must say, Miss Fairfield, I've never seen anything more extraordinary than what you did to revive him. How did you think to blow air into his mouth?"

Julia smiled. "It's a common practice where I live."

"Fortunate. Very fortunate." Neville rose and tugged

at the wet sleeve of his coat. "We'd better get some blankets, before we all catch lung fever."

Julia helped Gavin to his feet. He slipped his arm around her shoulders and held her close to his side as he followed Alison and Neville back to the house. He held her, not to maintain his balance, but because he wanted to feel her close against him.

She slowed their pace, lagging behind Alison and Neville. "Did you actually fall?" she asked, keeping her voice low.

He looked down into her perceptive eyes and realized that he could not lie to this woman, not for any reason. "No."

She released her breath slowly, as if she had been holding it for a long time. "Who did it?"

Gavin shook his head. "I don't know."

Julia refrained from questioning him further. Yet he knew she would not let go of the subject. Neither of them could deny it, any more than they could deny the clock ticking over their heads.

Someone had tried to murder him tonight. And whoever it was would have succeeded if not for his angel. Who wanted him dead? Was this what Julia had been sent to prevent? Would she soon disappear from his arms?

That question was still spinning round and round in his brain as he entered her room later that night. A single candle burned on the table beside her bed, casting a flickering light. He crossed the room and paused beside the bed. The covers were turned down, revealing white linen sheets and plump white pillows. She was gone. For one heart-pounding moment he stood there, staring at her empty bed, a sense of horrible loss spilling like acid through him.

"Gavin."

His name came like a prayer from the shadows. He turned and found her sitting by the lifeless hearth, her knees drawn up to her chest, her toes peeking out from beneath her white nightgown. The tension in his chest released when he saw her smile. "I was afraid you were gone."

She shook her head. "I came to set things right. Apparently you are still in danger."

In danger in more than one way. If this woman left him, she would take his heart with her.

"Do you have any idea who hit you tonight?"

"I have several ideas." Gavin rubbed his fingers over the lump at the back of his head. "Lampkin, Octavia Harcourt, Beatrice MacQuarrie. I think any one of them would have loved to see me floating in that pond tonight."

She rubbed her arms. "What can we do?"

"Not much. It's not as if we can set Bow Street sniffing after any of them. There is no proof any of them did anything wrong. I'll just have to be careful."

She glanced down at her toes. Light from the lamp beside her bed reached into the shadows, touching her face with a soft illumination. "I've been wondering."

She looked so lovely, his heart ached just to look at her. "What?"

"The accidents that killed you and Brandon—were they really accidents?" She drew in her breath, the sound tight and forced in the quiet room. "Someone tried to murder you tonight, and would have succeeded if I hadn't been able to give you artificial respiration."

"Artificial respiration?"

"Yes. I put my lips over yours and blew breath into your lungs until you could breathe for yourself."

He wiggled his eyebrows at her. "I think I could use some of that now."

"Gavin, this is serious. Someone might have killed you the first time around. That same person is trying to kill you now."

"There is nothing I can do about it tonight. Tomorrow I'm going to escort Mr. Lampkin to a ship bound for New South Wales. That should take care of him."

"And what of Beatrice and Octavia?"

"The more I think of it, the more I think it was probably a man. I doubt Beatrice or Octavia could have struck me the way I was hit tonight."

She looked hopeful. "So you think it was Lampkin."

Gavin nodded. "Aye. He is coward enough to come at my back. Tomorrow I'll take care of him." He untied the sash of his dressing gown.

She moistened her lips. "I thought you were supposed to be in bed."

"Aye. I think I should be in bed."

"Are you certain you are feeling well enough for what I think you have in mind?"

"It was a bump on the head. Fortunately, I have a hard head." He pulled off his dressing gown and tossed it over the settee at the foot of her bed.

Her lips parted with a sharp intake of breath. The soft light of the candle fell upon his rising member.

She rose, as if drawn by strings. "You do look healthy. Very healthy."

He laughed, a dark rumble that started deep in his chest and vibrated upward. "Strange now, I feel very *healthy* whenever I think about you."

"Funny, I get this warm tingling sensation when I think about you." She slid her hand over her belly as she moved toward him. "I feel hot, as though I have a fever. And as far as I can tell, there is only one cure for it."

He climbed into bed and patted the sheet beside him. "Come closer and I'll see what I can do to cure that fever."

She paused beside the bed, her gaze traveling over him. "How did I ever imagine I could resist you?"

"Sounds foolish to me." He lifted her hand and pressed his lips to the tips of her fingers, then drew her forefinger between his lips. Her eyes took on a soft, drunken look, as though she had imbibed too much brandy. "Come to me, Julia."

She unfastened her gown, slowly slipping cotton loops over small pearl buttons. She slipped the gown from her shoulders. The soft material dragged his gaze as it slithered down her body, spilling over the soft swell of her breasts, her belly, the long length of her legs. His breathing accelerated with the sudden surge of blood into his groin.

She climbed into bed and straddled his thighs. "You have managed to drive me absolutely insane since the first moment I saw you."

"It's only fair since you muddle my brain, too." He slid his hands down her arms, but she resisted as he tried to draw her against his chest.

She moved her hands over his hips, the soft touch whispering into his blood. He took a deep breath, trapping the scent of rosewater and woman in his lungs.

"Will you indulge me in something, Gavin?" she asked.

He brushed his fingers over the delicate hollow at the base of her neck. "Anything."

She smiled. "Anything?"

The feral look in her eyes put a hitch in his breath. "Anything."

"Can you lie still for me?"

He lifted his brows. "Lie still?"

"That's right." She took his right hand and kissed his palm. His breath hitched as she slid her tongue over the mound at the base of his thumb.

He had never in his life been with a woman who had made such a request. Yet he had learned that Julia defied his experience. "If that is what you want."

"I do." She placed his hand palm up on the pillow beside his head, then did the same with his left hand. "I want you to lie there and allow me to touch you. I want to memorize everything about you. The way you look, the touch of your skin. Everywhere you are smooth, and all the rough edges. I want to tuck the memory of you in a safe place, so I can savor this moment for the rest of my life."

Her soft voice drifted over him, husky with desire, colored with a sadness he did not want to acknowledge or accept. She believed they would have only a brief time together. "We shall have more than a few weeks together, Julia. I know it. I cannot believe the Almighty brought you into my life only to snatch you away from me."

"Hush, my darling." She leaned forward until the tips of her breasts brushed his chest. "Just lie back and close your mind to everything except this moment. Indulge me."

He looked up into those heavenly eyes and knew he would indulge any request she might make of him. "Do with me as you wish, my love."

She brushed her lips over his nipple, stabbed the

small nub with her tongue, sending whorls of sensation spinning through him. "You are so beautiful, my darling. So strong."

He didn't feel strong at that moment. It took all of his will to remain still beneath her touch. He clenched his jaw as she slid down his body, exploring him with her hands, her lips, her tongue. He felt like clay beneath her hands, and she was an artist, shaping him, infusing life into what was merely flesh and bone before her touch.

She trailed her fingers along the length of his arousal, released her breath against him, the hot stream of moist air making him shudder. He tipped back his head and fought the moan sliding up his throat, but it escaped him.

"I have never done anything like this before," she whispered, before she kissed the flesh made hard and aching for want of her.

This was new to him as well; he had never experienced this intimate kiss, this torture, this delight. He gripped the pillow with both hands, fighting his every instinct, the hunger, the need. He wanted to drag her down upon the soft white sheets and plunge so deep inside her, nothing could ever take her away from him.

Finally, when he feared he would shatter if she didn't end her wicked assault, she straddled his hips. Feminine curls, damp with her own desire, brushed his hardened sex.

"My only love," she whispered, inching downward, slowly immersing him in her fire. "Forever and always."

"Forever and always," he whispered, rising to meet her kiss.

He allowed her to find her rhythm, following her, as

she rocked her hips against him, holding back when his loins screamed in agony for the splendor, that one shattering moment of total release. And soon he felt her pleasure shimmer around him; the first delicate contractions of feminine release tugged on his flesh. She grasped his shoulders, his name escaping on a sob. She moved her hips, matching his need, meeting his every thrust, until she shattered and shuddered, until the pleasure rose in a sparkling wave, sweeping them both into a realm where time itself stood still to pay homage to the perfection of love.

Julia lay against Gavin's side, her hand resting on his chest, her palm above the solid throb of his heart. The warmth of his naked body soaked into her skin. This was how she wanted to sleep each night of her life, snuggled against this man. But she would not have a lifetime with him. As much as she wanted to deny the truth, it remained, staring her straight in the eye. And with that truth came a question. Why was she still here?

She stared at the moonlight slanting across the carpet, trying to unravel the puzzle in her mind. "Gavin," she whispered, "are you asleep?"

He slid his hand over her arm, warming her bare skin. "Are you thinking you want me to indulge you again?"

She tipped back her head and looked up into his grinning face. Her heart shivered at the sight of him. Lord help her, she never wanted to leave him. "I've been thinking."

"So have I." He smoothed back the hair from her shoulder. "I've been thinking about how much I want you to marry me."

The soft words tugged at her. "I wish I could."

"Then marry me, lass. Be my wife. Come live with me at Dunmore."

"I can't stay, Gavin."

He ran his fingertip down the length of her nose. "We belong to one another. I know it in my soul."

"I know." She pressed her lips against his shoulder, breathed in the spicy scent of his skin. "I have to believe our souls will find each other again, in another time and place."

He tightened his arm around her and cupped her cheek in his other hand. "I don't want to lose you."

She pressed her fingertips to his lips, a horrible sense of loss washing through her. "You'll never lose me. I shall love you forever. No matter where I am."

He frowned, his eyes betraying the pain she sensed inside him. "There must be something I can do."

He was a man accustomed to command, a man who took control of his life. But no one could sway the hand of destiny. "You can. You can remember me when I am gone. You can try to find happiness with another woman."

A muscle flared high on his left cheek. "I don't want another woman."

"In a few months, a young woman named Emma Fitzgerald will come to Dunmore." Julia's chest tightened when she thought of another woman in Gavin's arms. Yet something inside her knew Emma might be the key to Gavin's happiness. Although it remained no more than a suspicion on her part, she felt certain there was a reason she and Emma were similar in more than appearance. "Give Emma a chance, Gavin. When you meet her, open your heart. You might see a little of me in her eyes."

He drew in his breath, his chest expanding, brushing her breasts. "And if you are still here when Emma arrives?"

Julia looked into his beautiful eyes and accepted as certainty the feeling lurking deep inside her. "I don't think I will be. I'm not sure why I'm still here now."

He brushed his fingertips over the swell of her breasts. "Because you were meant to be with me."

"I think it's because I haven't managed to set things right."

"Things will never be right until you are my wife."

Julia shook her head. "If I told you I could take you back with me to my time, but you would have to leave Brandon behind, would you come?"

Gavin frowned. "Brandon has lived his entire life thinking no one cared for him. I couldn't leave him, lass."

Julia nodded. "And I have a little girl not much older than Brandon waiting for me at home."

He held her gaze, and she saw understanding fill his eyes. Understanding and a horrible sadness. "Then it is hopeless?"

"Yes." She managed the single word, then drew in her breath and swallowed hard to loosen the tight knot of emotion lodged there. "Gavin, would Lampkin have had access to Dunmore in June?"

Gavin frowned. "No, he'll be far away by then."

"Then how could he have caused the accident that killed you?"

Gavin shifted, twin furrows marring his brow. "It makes me a bit uneasy when you talk about my murder like that, lass."

She crinkled her nose. "Sorry. But it's something to consider. How would Lampkin have been able to cause your accident?"

Gavin thought of the puzzle for a moment. "It's not possible if he sails on that ship tomorrow."

"I suppose." She drew a pattern on his chest, drawing her fingertip through the silky black curls in a serpentine pattern. "Would he have had a reason to murder Brandon?"

"No. But we can't be sure Brandon didn't actually die of an accident. For that matter, we can't be sure I died of anything but an accident."

"I suppose." Julia frowned. "Still, if I have managed to prevent your deaths, why am I still here? I keep thinking there is something I'm missing."

"You're here because the Almighty intends to allow us some time together." He turned so they were chest to chest on their sides. "And I'm hoping it's forty or fifty years."

Would it be possible to live a lifetime here, and return to her own time? But wouldn't she return as an old woman? She couldn't puzzle it out. Not now. Not with the heat of his arousal smoldering against her belly. "I see you're feeling very healthy again."

He laughed, a dark sound that moved through Julia like the notes of a piano concerto. And then he kissed her and the piano melded into a symphony, more poignant than any she had ever heard before.

Chapter Twenty-four

Love is the emblem of eternity: it confounds all notion of time: effaces all memory of a beginning, all fear of an end.

—Madame De Staēl

Julia stared out one of the windows of the morning room of Gavin's house on Pall Mall. A story below, a curricle pulled by a pair of matched chestnuts drove by the house. It was not the right curricle. It was not the right driver. How long would it be before Gavin returned? He had left more than an hour earlier, intent on putting Russell Lampkin on a ship sailing this morning. Would that alter history just enough to send her back to her own time? Would she vanish without ever seeing him again?

"I know Alison must do this herself. Still, I wish I was in there with her." Mary moved to the window beside Julia. She stood frowning down at the street. "I do hope she doesn't lose her courage."

Julia manufactured a smile for Mary. "She was very determined this morning. I think she will tell Neville what must be said."

Mary frowned into the sunlight slanting through the square windowpanes. "Talbot is a strong man. Manipulative. I hope he does not twist her thoughts around. I really feel she must go forward as she has planned."

Julia's chest tightened with memories of a different time and place. Alison was facing Neville this morning with the same words that Julia had told Nathan a very long time ago. It would not be easy. Still, she hoped Alison had the courage to end what never should have begun.

The door opened, and both Julia and Mary turned to watch Alison enter the room. Her dark hair was swept high on her head, with soft curls framing her face. She looked lovely, a delicate flower who could not survive in the bright light Neville shone on her. Julia wondered if Alison had found the courage to go through with her intention, but she could tell nothing from looking at her expression.

"Did you tell him?" Mary asked, her voice tight with apprehension.

Alison's slender shoulders lifted, then fell as she sighed. "It is ended."

Mary pressed her hand to her heart. "And how did Neville react?"

"With great calm." Alison smiled. "It brought home to me just how little he truly cared for me."

"How do you feel?" Julia asked.

Alison flung her arms wide and executed a pirouette. "As though I have been rescued from a dark tower room."

Julia watched Mary hug her daughter, a strange blend of joy and apprehension coiling in her own heart. Another change to the MacKinnon family history. She prayed Alison would now live a long and happy life. Although she was happy for Alison, and pleased that she had been there to help her through this crossroads, Julia could not hold back the thoughts breaking in her mind like waves crashing against a rocky shore. Was this the last act in the miracle? Would she soon be taken back to her own time?

She glanced out the window and waited, hoping she would still be here when Gavin returned.

Eight days later, Julia stood on the cliff path near Dunmore, watching moonlight skip over the rolling waves of the ocean. She had stood in this spot before, near an oak tree. Only in her time this tall, youthful oak was gnarled and scarred, an ancient sentinel that had stood for more than two hundred years. The mist was rolling toward the shore, filmy strands curling over the waves, shimmering in the moonlight like a silver veil.

Gavin slipped his arms around her waist and drew her back against his hardened frame. Lush heat radiated against her back, chasing away the chill of the night. "You're the one, Julia."

The dark masculine whisper rippled through her, striking familiar chords. She tilted her head and glanced back at him. "What did you say?"

"You're the one, Julia." He smiled, his dark eyes filling with the warmth she had come to crave. "The one and only woman for me."

Shivers gripped her. He frowned and rubbed her arms. "Are you cold?"

"No. It isn't that." She turned in his embrace and

rested her hands on his chest. "I heard you say those words before. Right here. When I first met you."

"When I first met you?" His black brows lifted. "That was in my bedchamber, and I was too stunned by your story to realize what I had in my hands."

"No." She curled her hands into the lapels of his dark gray coat, holding on to him. "I mean the first night I met you in my time."

He held her gaze a long moment before he spoke. "My ghost?"

"Yes." Julia slid her arms around his waist and held him close, breathing in the warm, spicy scent of sandalwood. A terrible feeling swelled inside her, a sense of finality. Her time here was drawing to an end. She could sense it. "Gavin, when I'm gone, give Emma a chance."

Gavin's arms tightened around her. "What's wrong, my love? You sound frightened."

She spread her fingers wide against his back. She could not shake the feeling that she would soon be taken away from him. Suddenly she wished they had never taken this walk. She wished they were safe and close beneath the covers of his big bed. "Let's go back to the house, Gavin."

Gavin slipped his fingers beneath her chin and tilted back her head, until he could look into her eyes. He searched her eyes, and she knew she could not hide the fear lingering there. "You once asked me to believe in you, Julia. You told me there were some things one had to believe on faith alone."

She brushed her fingertips against his chin. "I was afraid you would never believe me."

"But I did. You helped me find my faith again, Julia." He kissed her brow. "And that's why I know we will be together."

"Well, now, isn't this a romantic sight."

Julia started at the sound of a man's voice. Gavin drew away from her, turning to face the tall man who stood about ten feet away. Moonlight fell upon his face, revealing the handsome features of Neville Talbot.

"What are you doing here?" Gavin asked.

Moonlight illuminated the chilling curve of Neville's smile. "I've come to send you to hell," he said, lifting his hand. Steel glinted on the barrel of the pistol he held.

Fear speared through Julia. Gavin stepped in front of her, shielding her from the weapon. "Why, Neville? Why do you come at me like this?"

"For murdering the woman I loved. The only woman I shall ever love."

"Lavinia," Gavin whispered.

"He didn't kill Lavinia." Julia scrambled from behind Gavin and plastered herself against his broad chest, her heart pounding so hard that her chest ached. She stared at Neville, seeing the raw rage in his eyes. She knew now why she had not been taken back to her time before this moment. The path of Gavin's destiny had been altered, but the danger still existed. It stared at them from Neville's icy gray eyes.

"He has you blinded." Neville wagged the pistol at her. "The same way he tricked my angel into marrying him."

Gavin gripped her shoulders. "Lavinia told you I tricked her into marriage?"

"That's right." Neville's eyes narrowed. "And then you abandoned her."

"If that's true, why did I petition for an annulment?" Gavin tried to force Julia out of the line of fire. Julia dug in her heels.

"That's a lie." Neville stepped forward. "She wanted an annulment, but you wouldn't agree."

"That's not true." Julia pressed back against Gavin.

"Get out of the way," Neville said, gesturing with the pistol.

"No." Julia twisted in Gavin's grip. "You don't really want to do this, Neville. You must listen. Lavinia was not the woman you thought she was."

"You never knew her." Neville staggered forward a few steps, a man drunk with rage. "Get out of the way."

"Julia." Gavin gripped her waist and lifted her. He pivoted and dropped her on her feet, out of the way of Neville's pistol. "Get the hell out of here," he muttered before turning back to Neville.

Julia stood beside the tree, watching, searching for some way to prevent the tragedy unfolding before her.

"What did she tell you, Neville?" Gavin asked, moving away from Julia. "Did she tell you she would marry you?"

"Lavinia was going to marry me." Neville turned as Gavin moved slowly to his left, keeping the pistol trained on Gavin's chest. "She told you that night. That's why you murdered her. You couldn't stand the humiliation of your wife leaving you for another man."

Julia glanced from Gavin to Neville and back again. Gavin kept moving, slowly, arcing away from her, drawing Neville with him.

"I sent her papers that day, Neville." Gavin took slow, steady strides, cutting the distance between him and Neville. "Annulment papers."

"Stand still!" Neville shouted.

"Have you ever killed a man, Neville?" Gavin asked, taking a step to his left.

"I will do it." Neville swiped at his upper lip with the back of his left hand.

"It was you," Gavin said. "That night in the Sedgewicks' garden."

Neville cocked the gun, the loud click ripping through the quiet night. "I intended to take your title, your home, your wealth. Everything that should have been Lavinia's. But your sister has had a change of heart. So I will have to settle for this: your death."

Julia stared at Neville's profile, and all the pieces of the puzzle clicked into place. All the horrible tragedies, all the accidents, all could be traced to one man. She glanced around, looking for a weapon to use against him. She eased down and gripped a rock the size of a softball.

Gavin stepped toward Neville and the pistol. "You can still walk away from this, Neville."

"I don't want to. I want to send you to hell."

Gavin launched himself at Neville. Gunfire cracked the air. Gavin slammed into Neville. The two men struggled near the edge of the cliff. Julia ran forward, lifting the stone as Gavin swung Neville toward the edge.

Neville stumbled back, windmilling his arms. His balance shifted. She caught a glimpse of the fear frozen on his face as he toppled over the edge. His scream rose on the mist as he plunged to the rocks below. Julia looked over the edge, shuddering at the sight of his body sprawled against the boulders far below. Mist swirled in from the sea, coiling around the rocks, embracing the body cast into its depths. She dropped the rock. It fell over the edge, arcing in the moonlight before disappearing in the gathering mist. The scent of gunpowder lingered in the air, acrid and stinging.

"It's over," she whispered.

Gavin rested his hands on her shoulders. "Come away from the edge."

Julia turned and threw her arms around his waist. Together they stumbled back from the treacherous precipice. She hugged him. "It was Neville," she whispered. "All the tragedies. It was Neville."

"Aye." He drew in his breath, the sound oddly strained. He gripped her shoulders, leaning against her as though he needed her strength to support him. "You've done it, Julia. You made the miracle happen."

Something was wrong. She pulled back in the circle of his embrace. He was smiling down at her, a sadness in his eyes that ripped through her, sadness and pain and a horrible look of resignation. He staggered and whispered her name.

"Gavin!" she shouted, trying to steady him. She tightened her arm around his waist, pressed her hand to his chest. That was when she felt it: the warm, sticky liquid covering his chest. She pulled her hand away and stared in horror at the blood on her fingers. Blood covered his chest, seeping from a ragged hole in his shirt. It was close to his heart. Much too close to his heart.

Gavin collapsed; she couldn't prevent it. He sank to the ground, as if all the strength was draining from his body. Julia sank beside him, grief raking her body. Gently, she lifted his head and shoulders and cradled him in her lap.

He opened his eyes and looked up at her. "It looks as though time has finally caught up with us, my love."

Julia pressed her hand over the wound, knowing deep in her heart that her first-aid training would not be enough this time. Blood flowed over her palm and ran down her wrist. "Gavin, please." Tears burned her eyes. "Please hold on."

He lifted his hand and touched her cheek. "Don't cry, lass."

Tears blurred her eyes. She blinked, fighting to keep him in focus. The scent of blood sliced through her senses. "You can't die now, Gavin. You can't."

He closed his eyes, his throat working as if he was swallowing a groan. "You were right, Julia. This time together was a gift, a precious gift. I'm grateful you came to me. If just for a little while."

She pressed the heel of her hand hard against his wound. "Gavin, you have to hold on."

"I love you," he whispered.

"I love you." Her words cracked on a sob. "I will always love you."

His hand trembled against her cheek, as though he was struggling to touch her; then it fell, thumping softly against his chest. "Live your life, Julia. Remember me, but don't mourn me. Don't lock yourself away from the world."

She stroked the hair back from his brow. "I don't want to live without you."

"You have to live, Julia." Pain flickered across his features. He moistened his lips. "You have to live for both of us."

"Gavin," she whispered, grief closing around her throat like a vise.

"You have to go on, Julia." He smiled up at her, emotion naked in his dark eyes, love and pain and hope. "Marry. Have children. And think of me with a smile. Not with tears. Promise me."

Tears spilled from her eyes, blurring her vision, until his image shimmered before her. The thought of him living his life after she was gone had sustained her through these past few days. Now, to know that his life would end this night . . . pain pierced her, so sharp and potent that she could not breathe.

"Promise me," he said, the soft Scottish burr washing over her. "Promise me you will live your life. Promise me you will open yourself to the possibility of love."

She swallowed hard and pulled together every ounce of her strength. She had to be strong for him. She blinked, brushing away the tears from her eyes, wanting to see him clearly. He was looking up at her, fierce determination in his eyes.

"Promise me," he whispered.

She nodded and managed a smile for him. "I promise."

He closed his eyes. "You'll be all right, my love."

"Gavin, please don't let go." She pressed harder against the wound. "Please."

"You gave me back my faith." He looked up at her and smiled. "Now, have faith in me. Someday I'll find you again. In another time and place. Someday."

Faith. They would find each other, in another lifetime. She had to believe in the power of the love they shared.

"Have faith," he whispered, his voice cracking on the words.

"I will, my love." She kissed his lips and slid her hand though his hair, the silky strands curling against her fingers. Pain racked her body, great sobs rising inside her, until she trembled with the fight to hold them in check. "I will."

He fought to draw breath, the air wheezing into his lungs. He looked up at her, a quiet desperation in his eyes. His face looked pale in the moonlight. "Remember me and smile."

She nodded, tears spilling down her cheeks and falling softly against his face. "Always."

His fingers twitched. He lifted his hand, as if to reach for her, yet he had no strength. His hand fell back against his chest. She closed her hand around his, held it close against her breaking heart.

"Julia," he whispered.

She felt the soft release of his breath, felt it upon her cheek. "Gavin," she whispered.

He lay lifeless in her arms. He was gone. She buried her face against the crook of his neck and whispered, "Good-bye, my love."

Filmy strands of mist wrapped around them. She held Gavin in her arms, rocking slowly back and forth, while grief welled up inside her and escaped in harsh, racking sobs. For an all too brief moment in time she had known this man, loved him, and felt the warmth of his love for her. It was a gift. One she would remember until the last day of her life.

"It's time, Julia."

Julia flinched at the sound of Gavin's dark voice. She stared down at the man who lay lifeless across her lap. "Gavin?"

"I'm here, lass."

She turned her head toward the sound of that beloved voice. Moonlight shimmered on the mist, a glimmering column piercing the filmy veil. She stared, transfixed, as the gossamer strands swirled and parted, and a man materialized from the mist. Through a blur of tears she stared at the ghost of her one and only love. "Gavin."

He smiled at her, all the love he had for her naked in his eyes. "It's time, Julia. Time to go home."

"Why?" she whispered, the word tearing at her tight throat. "Why did you have to die?"

"I promised I would take you home, lass. No matter what happened."

She stared at him, a horrible realization gripping her. "You died because of me?"

"No, lass," he said, his voice a soft caress. "I died because of Neville Talbot. My family lives, because of you."

She smoothed her hand over Gavin's hair. "You were supposed to meet Emma. You were supposed to have a long and happy life. That's how it should have been."

"It wasn't possible." He sat back on his heels beside her and brushed his fingers over the tears she could not stop. "Don't cry, lass."

A soft, tingling sensation moved through her, conjuring warmth. The warmth slipped beneath her skin, spilling into her blood, spreading through her limbs like a soothing balm. Pain and despair melted under that warmth. Hope and the pure light of love filled up all the empty spaces. "I was so certain you and Emma would have a future together. I thought . . . I had some crazy idea I was Emma in this lifetime."

Gavin wiggled his eyebrows at her. "It wasn't so crazy."

"Why couldn't you have married her?"

"If things had been different, I would have met Emma. I would have married her." Gavin glanced down at the shell that had once housed his soul. "But after I died, Emma married a young man from Boston. They had five children. And if those children had not been born, if they had not had children of their own, you would never have been born."

Julia sat back at the impact of his words. "Oh."

He stood and offered her his hand. "Come, Julia. It's time to go home."

She lowered her gaze to the face of the man she would always love. "I can't leave you like this."

"Someone will come soon."

"Brandon." She looked up at him. "I have to be with Brandon. I have to tell him."

Gavin shook his head, a deep sadness filling his eyes. "It's for someone else to do. And not to worry, lass. He is a strong lad."

"Will he be all right?"

"Aye. My family will take care of him, love him as I do. Brandon will live a long and happy life. He will complete the east wing of the castle. He will marry. Have children. Grow old at Dunmore." Gavin smiled down at her. "All because you found a way to make our miracle come true."

"The accident . . . was it Neville who killed Brandon?"

Gavin nodded. "A great hatred burned inside him. He wanted to destroy me and my family. Because of Lavinia."

"Why didn't you tell me before I came back here?"

"I didn't know. These things were only just revealed to me, lass."

"And do you know about Mary, and Alison? Patrick? Will they be all right?"

"Aye. Alison will marry Philip Montgomerie next year. And Patrick will meet his match three years hence. My mother will live to see Brandon and her other grandchildren marry and have children." Gavin glanced off toward Dunmore. In the distance, gray stones rose, shaping the rugged walls of the castle. Mist swirled in from the sea, curling around the base of the castle, transforming mere stone to something magical. "I'll be looking down at it all, watching them, waiting. For I know one day we shall all be together again."

Tears clutched at her chest and burned her eyes. "It isn't fair. You should be with them."

"It is the way it must be." Gavin looked down at her and smiled, a gentle smile that swirled through her like a warm drizzle of honey. "I was granted a miracle, Julia. You made that miracle come true. My family lives on, because of you."

"I'm going to miss them. Will they know I'm all right?"

"They will not know you were ever here."

She stared at him. "What do you mean?"

"No one you met will remember ever knowing you. It's the way of some miracles."

She looked back toward Dunmore, thinking of all the people who had come to mean so much to her in such a short time. "Will I remember them?"

"If you want to remember them, you will."

"I do." She swiped at the tears spilling down her cheeks. "And what of you? You won't be at Dunmore when I return. Will you?"

"No, lass. I'll be passing on. Fortunately a mistake has been made, and they are going to allow a sinner a place in heaven." He offered her his hand. "It's time for you to go home."

She glanced down at Gavin's body, memories flooding her, making her smile in spite of the pain. They had shared a few perfect moments. It was more than some people knew in a lifetime. She slid her fingers through the dark silk of his hair, kissed his lips one more time, then gently eased his head and shoulders to the ground. She stood and faced Gavin's ghost. "Will I ever see you again?"

"Have faith, my love. Miracles happen every day. All around us." Gavin smiled and slipped his phantom arms around her. "Remember this: I'll be smiling down at you. All the days of your life."

She wanted to tell him how much she would always love him. But her voice failed her. A warm tingling sensation moved through her. She didn't know if it was a trick of moonlight, or if the tears she saw glittering in his eyes were real. She only knew she had loved this man since time began. She would love him always. "Good-bye, my love."

Gavin brushed his lips against hers, those phantom lips that caused her skin to tingle. "Until we meet again."

Until we meet again. She held on to that thought, clutched it to her heart as the world faded into colors around her and the earth slipped away from beneath her. Someday they would find each other again. She would just have to find a way to live this lifetime without him.

Chapter Twenty-five

Somewhere there waiteth in this world of ours
For one lone soul another lonely soul,
Each choosing each through all the weary hours,
And meeting strangely at one sudden goal,
Then blend they, like green leaves with golden flowers,
Into one beautiful perfect whole;
And life's long night is ended, and the way
Lies open onward to eternal day.

—Edwin Arnold

"Julia, it's time."

Julia awoke slowly, as though she were rising up through layers of darkness, each growing lighter and lighter until sunlight pulsed against her lids. She opened her eyes. Someone was leaning over her. She blinked, bringing into focus a face she had not seen in five long years. Excitement ripped through her, chased by a hundred questions. "Mother?"

Rebecca Fairfield frowned, twin furrows marring the smooth skin between her brows. "Julia, are you feeling all right?"

Julia sat up and touched her mother's arm, frightened that her hand would pass right through her. Her fingers met the soft warmth of her mother's skin. "You're real," she whispered.

"Julia, you're acting a little . . ."

"Mom," Julia cried, throwing her arms around Rebecca's slender shoulders. She held her close, breathing in the delicate scent of Anais Anais perfume. "You're really here."

Rebecca hugged her close. "And where else would I be, darling?"

"I thought . . ." Julia closed her eyes, afraid to finish the thought. It was far too ugly, too heart-wrenching to think about. Still, the questions remained. How had this come to pass?

Rebecca pulled back and smiled, faint lines crinkling at the corners of her blue eyes. "What is it? You look as though you've seen a ghost."

"A ghost." Julia glanced around, her head spinning with fragments of memories, her thoughts jumbled as though they had been cast into a whirlwind. She was sitting on a bed, in her bedroom in her parents' home. And her mother was sitting on the edge of the bed, her dark blond hair swept up in the French twist Rebecca always wore on special occasions. She was wearing a teal-colored gown, the one she had chosen to wear for Julia's wedding. "What's going on?"

"You apparently decided you needed a little nap before the ceremony." Rebecca squeezed Julia's hand.

"Everyone is waiting for you." Angela stood at the foot of the bed, dressed in lavender silk. "Your handsome young man is beginning to wonder if you have changed your mind."

Julia slid her legs over the peach bedspread, her gown rustling softly. She sat on the edge of the bed and stared down at her clothes. She was wearing a white silk gown covered in Brussels lace and pearls, a wedding gown she had never seen before. Or had she? She searched through her memory, snatching at the images flickering in the shadows. She stared at her mother, panic squeezing through her in sharp little bursts. "What day is it?"

Rebecca frowned. "Julia, what's gotten into you?"

Julia grabbed her mother's arm. "What day is it? The date."

Rebecca stared at her, an uneasy expression crossing her face. "It's the fourth of June."

"The year?"

Rebecca blinked. "The year?"

"Julia, are you all right?" Angela asked.

"Yes. I'm fine. Perfectly fine." Julia squeezed her mother's arm, her gaze moving from her grandmother to her mother. "Please tell me. What year is it?"

Rebecca looked completely confused. Still she replied, "It's 1994."

"Oh, my God." Julia pressed her hands against her heart. Sunlight caught upon the three-carat round diamond in the ring on her left hand, spinning a rainbow of color. She stared into the brilliance of that stone, thinking of the true nature of miracles. Was this her chance for a miracle? Had she been granted a chance to correct the most horrible tragedy in her life?

Or had it all been a dream?

No, she could not imagine it was a dream. It had all

been too vivid for a dream. Too real. She had met Gavin. She had loved him. The memories of those days with him were still with her, locked deep in her soul. "It had to have been real."

"What, dear?" Rebecca asked.

Julia looked at her mother's lovely face. She knew in her heart that this moment was her chance for a miracle. If she went through with this wedding, her parents, Mike and Diane would all have a chance to live. All Julia had to do was marry Nathan. Her blood turned cold.

"Julia, you're worrying me," Rebecca said. "Are you all right?"

"You are dreadfully pale, dear."

Julia forced her lips into a smile. "I'm fine. Just some last-minute jitters."

The door opened. Diane stood in the doorway, dressed in a dusky mauve gown, her light brown hair piled in curls on top of her head, white rosebuds entwined in the glossy strands. "Hey, what's keeping the bride? We're all ready to go. Lauren keeps tossing rose petals at the ushers. If you don't hurry, there won't be any petals left for your walk down the aisle."

Julia looked at her friend and swallowed her tears. "I'll be right down."

Diane grinned at her. "Better hurry. I heard Maggie Rawlings trying to figure out how to talk your guy into running away with her."

Julia rose to her feet. Marriage to Nathan was a small price to pay for the lives of her family. What difference would it make, really? Her one and only love would never come to her, not in this lifetime. "I'm ready."

Her father was waiting for her at the base of the wide staircase. Tall, fair-haired, looking very handsome and elegant in his black tux, he looked up at her, a glimmer of tears in his green eyes as he watched her descend the stairs. She could do this, she thought, as her father took her arm. Anything to save them.

"You look beautiful, sweetheart," Matthew Fairfield said. "He is a very lucky young man."

Julia forced air into her lungs. She stared through her veil, watching as an usher escorted her mother from the living room into the backyard. Music from a string quartet drifted through the open French doors, beckoning each of the four bridesmaids from the living room out into the large yard. They passed through her field of vision in a blur of mauve. Julia was far too busy trying to numb the fear gripping her to notice much of anything. Finally she heard the strains of Mendelssohn, the wedding march from his *Midsummer Night's Dream.* Her father moved and she followed, like an automaton.

The Fairfield backyard had been transformed into a lush garden of roses and orange blossoms. The sweet scents assaulted her, threatening to empty her stomach. Through her veil she saw a swarm of faces, people gathered on white chairs along an aisle delineated by a white cloth draped over thick grass. They stood as she passed, murmuring their appreciation of the bride's loveliness. Sunlight shimmered through the oak trees, casting golden light over everything, like fairy dust sprinkled by a magical hand. The air was warm and sweet, a perfect day for a wedding. Still, she fought the panic crowding her chest.

The music of the string quartet thundered with the blood pounding in her ears. An arch of white roses and orange blossoms stood at the end of the aisle. Her groom stood there waiting for her. She closed her eyes and whispered a prayer for strength. And then her father was leaving her, backing away, giving her into the keeping of the man who would be her husband.

She opened her eyes, stared at the face of the minister, and fought her panic. She could do this. Marriages need not last forever, she assured herself, taking some comfort in that thought. She heard a deep voice beside her, a soft Scottish burr. Her heart stuttered. She glanced up at the man speaking the vows that would bind him to her. Through the white tulle of her veil she saw him, tall, broad-shouldered, his thick dark brown hair swept back from his handsome face. "Gavin," she whispered.

Gavin looked down at her and winked. The tight band squeezing her heart snapped, releasing its stranglehold. Memories spilled through her mind, as clear as celluloid images flickering in a darkened theater. And Gavin was there, in every scene. She had met Gavin in her second year of grad school. He had come to Chicago, looking for her. And when they met, the rest of the world had faded into gray. There was only the two of them, two souls once lost, now found. Gavin had been her first and only lover, and he would be her last.

She looked up into his dark eyes as she spoke the words that would forever bind them in this lifetime. He lifted her veil.

"I told you I would find you again," he whispered before his lips touched hers.

In this kiss she realized the true extent of the miracle they shared. Finally things were as they should have been.

Later, as she danced with her husband across the wooden floor of the huge tent that had been erected on the lawn, she glanced around her. Candles glowed in glass globes atop each round table. Hundreds of small white lights were strung in swags over their heads, raining a soft golden glow upon the guests. The mingled scents of roses and orange blossoms perfumed the air.

Her father and her mother danced nearby, as much in love now as they had been on their wedding day. A short distance from them, Diane and Mike smiled down at the little girl who hung on to their hands and danced along with them. Lauren giggled as Mike and Diane hoisted her by her hands, letting her swing for a few bars of the music. Angela stood on the fringe of the dance floor, beside Gavin's grandfather, Douglas MacKinnon. From the way the widow and widower were smiling at each other, Julia wondered if Gram had met her match.

And there were others touched by this miracle. Gavin's parents were here, Mary and Duncan MacKinnon. Mary was the same as Julia's memory of her, and Duncan was the man from the portrait she had seen at Dunmore. The sound of feminine laughter brought Julia's attention to Gavin's handsome best man and his pretty partner. Even in this life, Patrick MacKinnon had the type of charm that could weaken a woman's knees. His sister Alison, dressed in a sleek mauve gown like all the bridesmaids, danced nearby with her fiancé, Farley Bennett.

Julia glanced past Alison to the older couple dancing nearby. She had once worried whether Helen Bainbridge would mind losing Dunmore. Now she realized Helen had gained a great deal more in this miracle than a castle.

Helen Bainbridge Stapleton glanced at Julia, as though she sensed her gaze upon her. She smiled at the bride before her husband swept her into an elegant turn. Gavin's grandfather had saved Frederick Stapleton during the Second World War, sending him home to the arms of his waiting fiancée. Helen and Frederick's three children and eight grandchildren were here as well.

As she looked around her, a question glimmered in Julia's brain: Had she managed to weave all of the people she loved into a dream? "Did it really happen?"

Gavin smiled down at her. "Are you wondering if you really lived for a while in a time of carriages and balls, and bitter young Scottish earls?"

The breath paused in her throat as she looked up into his beautiful dark eyes. "It was true?"

"Aye, lass." He brushed his lips against hers. "As true as the memories that awakened in me when I was a lad. The memories that brought me to you."

She slid her hand over Gavin's shoulder and toyed with a dark wave just above his starched white collar. "They are all here. Everyone except Brandon."

Gavin pressed his lips against the back of her hand. "I'm thinking Brandon has yet to come."

Julia rested her cheek against his shoulder, breathed in the rich sandalwood scent of his cologne and knew at last that she was home. "I love you."

"And I love you." He kissed her hair. "I always have. And I always will."

"Forever," Julia whispered.

Gavin squeezed her hand, his chest shifting with a soft exhalation that brushed her cheek. "Beyond forever, my love."

Epilogue

True love's the gift which God has given
To man alone beneath the heaven: . . .
It is the secret sympathy,
The silver link, the silken tie,
Which heart to heart, and mind to mind,
in body and in soul can bind.
—Sir Walter Scott

Dunmore Castle, Present Day

The package arrived late in the afternoon. Julia stood in her study in the east wing of Dunmore, staring down at the long box that sat on her desk. She had been expecting this package. Every day she awoke certain it would arrive, and every evening she went to bed hoping tomorrow would be the day. She sliced the tape holding together the top edges, set the letter opener on the desk, and opened the plain cardboard box.

For a moment she did nothing but stare at the contents, excitement tingling through her. Inside, stacked cover to cover, rested twenty-five copies of her very first book.

"*Beyond Forever,*" she whispered. She ran her fingertip down the spine, smiling as she silently read her name above the title. The cover felt slick against her trembling fingers as she lifted one of the thick paperback books out of the box. Her heart swelled as she gazed at the cover.

It was real now.

For so very long it had only been a dream, then ideas scratched upon paper, and finally a manuscript. She remembered holding it in her hands, that thick stack of printed pages, breathless as she searched for the courage to send this child of her mind out into the world. If not for Gavin, this moment would never have come to pass. Gavin had given her faith in herself. He had encouraged her every step of the way.

She clutched the novel to her chest and hurried to her husband. He was sitting on the floor of the gold drawing room in the tower of the east wing. Gavin had designed this wing long ago, and now it was their private part of the castle. Sunlight poured through the long diamond-paned windows that overlooked the Atlantic. The golden light spilled over the gold and ivory carpet where her husband and their three-year-old daughter Catherine sat on the floor, playing with blocks. Their six-month-old son, Brandon, lay sleeping in a rosewood cradle nearby.

Julia paused in the doorway, making a memory, capturing this moment in her mind. Gavin glanced up and smiled at her. Excitement tingled through her, gathering in a shimmering pool of heat low in her belly. He could still set her pulse racing with a glance.

"Did it come?" Gavin asked.

Julia nodded and rushed across the room. She sat on the floor next to him and presented the book. He ran his fingertip over the raised gold letters of her name, then winked at her. "I knew you could do it, lass."

"Let me see," Catherine said, scrambling onto her father's lap.

Gavin slipped one arm around his daughter, the other around his wife. Catherine started leafing through the book.

Julia leaned against her husband. "When people read this, they will think it's a fairy tale."

Gavin laughed, a dark rumble from deep in his chest. "Funny thing, fairy tales. Every once in a while, they come true."

She rested her hand on his chest, above the solid throb of his heart. "I remember a time when you refused to believe in fairy tales."

Gavin grimaced. "And I remember a time when you did not have the courage to send a manuscript to a publisher."

Julia knew now you could only grab hold of a dream if you had the courage to reach for it. "It seems a different lifetime. A different woman."

"Aye. Yet some things never change." He kissed her brow. "If you live a thousand lifetimes, you'll still be crazy about me."

She laughed. "And you'll still be the most infuriating, arrogant . . . adorable man I've ever known."

"Ah, lass." He nuzzled the skin under her ear. "I always thought you were the most perceptive woman I've ever known. Is there any wonder I'm hopelessly under your spell?"

Julia looked into his dark eyes, saw the promise of what would come, and silently gave thanks for the miracle that had brought them together.

AUTHOR'S NOTE

The Isle of Mist doesn't exist except in the realm of imagination. Still, even though my little tale is a child of the mind, I believe miracles happen every day. Sometimes we notice them, sometimes we don't. We all need diversions from time to time, moments when we forget our cares. I hope the few moments you spent with Julia and Gavin were enjoyable. I hope *Beyond Forever* left you with a smile.

My next book is sprinkled with just a hint of magic. Jane Eveleigh was coerced into marriage by Dominic Stanbridge, the arrogant marquess of Lancaster. Jane knows Dominic will use any ploy to undermine her defenses, but is he really playing a game when he claims to have awakened the day after their wedding a different man? Has a sorceress actually meddled in their lives, placing the soul of a sixteenth century Scottish Highlander in the body of a nineteenth century English rogue? *MacKenzie's Magic* will be available in the fall of 2000.

For excerpts from my books, a glimpse at my current project, and a little about me, visit my web site at: www.tlt.com/authors/ddier.htm.

I love to hear from readers. Please enclose a self-addressed stamped envelope with your letter. You can reach me at:

P. O. Box 4147
Hazelwood, MO 63042-0747

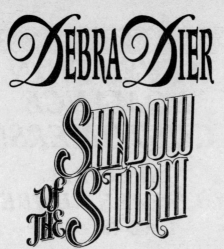